KT-104-165

THE
GOLDEN RULE

AMANDA CRAIG

In memory of Helen Dunmore (1952–2017),
champion and friend

ABACUS

First published in Great Britain in 2020 by Little, Brown
This paperback edition published in 2021 by Abacus

1 3 5 7 9 10 8 6 4 2

Copyright © Amanda Craig 2020

The moral right of the author has been asserted.

A CIP catalogue record for this book
is available from the British Library.

ISBN 978-0-349-14348-4

Typeset in Goudy by M Rules
Printed and bound in Great Britain by Clays Ltd, Elcograf S.p.A.

Papers used by Abacus are from well-managed forests
and other responsible sources.

Abacus
An imprint of
Little, Brown Book Group
Carmelite House
50 Victoria Embankment
London EC4Y 0DZ

An Hachette UK Company
www.hachette.co.uk

www.littlebrown.co.uk

One's real life is so often the life that one does not lead.

– Oscar Wilde

That which is hateful to you, do not do to your fellow.

– Rabbi Hillel, *The Talmud*

Treat others as you would treat yourself.

– *The Mahabharata*

Treat your inferior as you would wish your superior to treat you.

– Seneca, *Moral Epistles*

Therefore whatever you desire for men to do to you, you shall also do to them; for this is the law and the prophets.

– Matthew 7:12, *World English Bible*

Speaking of an institution such as marriage as natural is, of course, paying it a compliment, the compliment of saying that it meets a fairly central human need. The fact that it is found in some form in every human society is in a way enough to show this. But it might be thought that marriage became thus widespread only because it was, like adequate sanitation, a means to an end. This is pretty certainly what Hume thought, as evidenced by his very confused contrast of natural with artificial virtues. He regarded human sagacity simply as the power to calculate consequences, and counted chastity and fidelity, with justice, as artificial virtues, devices designed merely to produce safety and promote utility. In a species as emotionally interdependent as man this view of marriage is nonsense. Pair-formation could never have entered anybody's head as a device deliberately designated to promote utility.

– Mary Midgley, *Beast and Man: The Roots of Human Nature*

The golden rule is there are no golden rules.

– George Bernard Shaw, *Man and Superman*

Contents

1

Boiling Lava

By the time Hannah caught the train to Cornwall, she could have killed her husband.

It was one of those evenings in summer when everything seems to be suspended between frustration and release. The dash to Paddington Station in the rush hour, the airless tunnels, the fear of being too late to get to the platform in time had all made it feel like an endless nightmare that began even before her journey started.

'I can't take Maisy,' Jake announced, earlier that day. 'I'm busy.'

'You know it's your turn to look after her.'

'I can't change my plans now. Take her with you.'

'You know why this is an emergency. I sent you the booking reference for my train. I can't cancel, and I can't bring her.'

'Find someone else to look after her,' he said.

Hannah counted to five before answering. 'There's nobody I can ask.'

'Of course there is. You need to move on, Hannah.'

All the advice is to be calm and reasonable in a divorce. Only it is very hard to keep calm and reasonable while a marriage goes rancid. Lies, evasions, insults and bullying were bad enough. Getting the father of her child to pay for anything was worse. It was a common technique among husbands who wanted to move on themselves: it was called starving a woman out.

At almost thirty, Hannah was exhausted by debt, hopelessness, loneliness, anger and the knowledge that, despite having jumped through all the right hoops, the bigger life on which she had pinned her hopes was not going to happen. The sensation of failure was worse than hunger, and almost indistinguishable from it. They had lived apart for nearly two years, and he had recently applied to divorce her. He was also threatening to take Maisy away. She didn't know if he could do this. She had no money to fight it, if need be.

Fury was what kept her going, like sugar or strong liquor; it got her running along the platform at Paddington seconds before the whistle blew and her ticket became invalid. Afterwards, she wondered what would have been averted had she missed her train.

The carriage was crammed. Hannah, panting and sweating, couldn't even push her way to a seat. The air conditioning had broken down, as it so often did in a heatwave, and the stench made her head swim.

Meanwhile, Jake was with his mistress, on his third foreign holiday of the year.

'You'd like her if you knew her,' he'd said.

Hannah had never met Eve. She discovered her existence by accident when Jake left his iPad behind for their three-year-old daughter, to play on while he went out to the gym.

'Mummy, why does Daddy have a friend with no face?'

'What's that, sweetie?'

Hannah removed the tablet from her child's grasp and saw her husband's Facebook page. At first, she smiled at the pictures he had put up, mostly of himself and Maisy, but one or two of her, too, before the badger-stripe of dark hair grew back between the highlights. She herself did not use social media any more. What did she have to say about herself or her life that would be of any interest to anyone else? Then, she saw that he also had Facebook Messenger. In a few minutes, his nine-month relationship with a woman called Eve was revealed. Her rival's own marital status ('it's complicated') was there, and that she lived in London. Everything else – friends, family, education, profession, hobbies, photographs, email and surname – was a mystery. Eve's icon was a blank, the standard white silhouette of a head with bobbed hair, generically female. In many ways, this ignorance was the most terrible aspect of all, for it left Hannah to imagine someone who was her opposite: tall, confident, beautiful and rich. Scrolling back, it became clear that all the weekends when Jake was supposedly away working had been spent in five-star hotels in Paris, New York, Venice and Rome. While Hannah had budgeted and saved for the modest flat of their own that everyone under thirty dreamt of getting, Jake had been spending his money and time with another woman.

Confronted, he refused to tell her more.

'What's the point? Eve and I are together.'

'Why did you lie about our marriage being dead?'

'It is dead. It's been dead for years.'

'It isn't dead!' Hannah almost screamed. 'We still have sex, or do you not tell her that?'

This was true, although the last time had been several

months ago. She had been desperate, as usual, to sleep before Maisy woke again, and sighed with relief after it was over.

'We've never been right for each other. Face it, we're too different.'

Hannah thought she would die of grief and humiliation, but one kind of pain was followed by another, even more sordid. Divorce may start with the failure of love, but in the end, it is always about money.

'My card has just been declined in the supermarket,' she said, ringing him from the till.

'I cancelled it.'

'You *what?*' She could hardly breathe. 'Do you think that your child and I can suddenly live on nothing?'

'You're a grown-up; go back to work.'

'We both agreed that I should look after Maisy until she started school.'

'Think again.'

Back and forth he went, like a cat with a mouse, spending some nights with Eve and some with her. Hannah had pains in her chest, no resistance against infections, and almost no certainty that she even knew who she was. Jake, whose love had once made her feel like a goddess, now made her the lowest creature on the earth.

Why had it taken her so long to see him for what he was? He hadn't always been vile, was one answer. They had once been each other's best friend and support, just as they had once found each other irresistibly attractive and exciting. But while she had gone on adoring him, he had become increasingly critical and dismissive. 'Your face makes you look more intelligent than you are,' he had told her (as if anyone, least of all he, could quantify such a thing). They were from very different backgrounds, and although he had

4

claimed to admire hers, it was increasingly evident that he found her lack of connections irksome, especially after she gave up her job when Maisy was a year old to become a full-time mother. It had been a drip-drip-drip, and for years she had excused his remarks as being due to stress. Then it was her own fault for making him angry, and she would do anything to win back his affection, pleading with what he called her 'puppy eyes' and bursting into tears. He became brusque, no longer doing anything to help domestically, leaving her alone while he went out drinking with colleagues or away on what he claimed were training weekends. Once, he had been so furious with her for not being able to quieten Maisy that he had thrown a red-hot baked potato, straight out of the microwave, at her face. Her cheek was burnt, badly enough for her to spend the next three hours with half her face in a basin of cool water, trying to reduce the heat while awkwardly cradling their child. He had apologised after this, claiming it had been a second's loss of temper, a crazy impulse. She still had a small white scar from it.

Hannah had nobody to turn to. Being the first in her group of peers to have a child at just twenty-four isolated her even more effectively than his unpredictable temper. She was ashamed of her own family and intimidated by his; when pregnant, she had not bonded with anyone at the NCT classes, finding them patronising and much older than herself. (When she wheeled her daughter round in a buggy, she was always taken to be the nanny.) Almost none of her former friends had stayed in touch; why would they, when she was both desperately boring and boringly desperate? Her energies had been fully occupied by looking after their daughter and running the household on one person's income instead of two. One night when he was with Eve, she felt such despair that she considered jumping from the balcony of the flat to end her life. She came to her senses in time, and when Jake returned, she had all his things packed.

'Give me your keys,' she said, and in a moment of shame, he did.

Hannah then had to try to feed Maisy and herself on £20.70 a week, or £2.95 a day, this being child benefit, which took eight weeks to come in because by now Jake was earning well over the £50,000-a-year limit. He still wanted Maisy, as lovely as only a child with milk-teeth can be, but he did not understand that she was not a fridge-light. Feeding, clothing, washing, housing, entertaining, teaching and comforting a new person brought into this world continues even when you are not there to see it. Hannah could make meals out of vegetables, eggs, milk and bread, but they had no meat and very little cheese or fruit. She had to pay the council tax, the utilities and every other urgent yet incidental expense, and could do so only by first using up her savings and then getting into debt on her credit card.

At first her situation did not seem so unusual. Most graduates like herself had heaved furniture, waited tables, tutored tots and swallowed anger just to survive. They had grown up in the golden years of national optimism, when going to university was just the first step to a glorious new future in which every problem, from world hunger to global warming, would be solved; instead, they had come to adulthood with economic catastrophe, increasingly deranged world leaders and a sense of impending doom. The personal was political and the political personal, in an existence where the only certainty was debt for degrees that gave no obvious advantage. The older generations (who had experienced nothing but luck) mocked them for being anxious, depressed and vulnerable; those who could not or would not live with their parents rented flats where mould and mice were as commonplace as multiple occupancy.

When Jake and Hannah first rented their flat, they had been young graduate professionals with a starting salary of £21,000 a year each, which meant they could easily cover the cost. These days, she was terrified her landlord would discover that she now claimed benefits and throw her out.

Unlike the wives of rich men, she could not force her husband to give her alimony once they were divorced. A month after Jake left, Hannah had learnt to her horror that although it was possible that she might get some small settlement for Maisy, she herself would be left wholly exposed to poverty, otherwise known as benefits. It might help her case to consult a lawyer, but to do this even once cost £500, a sum that might as well have been ten times as much. *To those who have shall be given: but to those who have not shall be taken away.* In other words, *In order to get money in a divorce, you must already have some.*

Jake was adamant that he would not give her anything other than maintenance for Maisy.

'Stop leeching and get off your arse. You're bleeding me dry.'

'How can I be when you barely even pay the rent?'

It was as if two tectonic plates, his personality and hers, were pushing and grinding against each other. What seemed to be fixed for ever was suddenly heaved up or torn apart, a river of water turned to boiling lava. He began jabbing at her with his finger when he spoke to her, and the jabs turned to shakings and then to arm-twisting and pushing, though nothing frightened her as much as when he put his face an inch away from hers and shouted. She was terrified, and only her stubborn anger prevented her from collapsing into despair. She could not sleep or eat or read. The tiny amount of energy she had left over from keeping her child and herself alive went into loving her daughter, which she did with an intensity that was almost like religious zeal.

Leaning against the wall of the packed train Hannah thought about what it would be like to have a real holiday, somewhere hot but cooled by sea breezes or shaded by pine trees. Her journey down to Cornwall was not, however, for leisure. Her mother was dying. It had been happening over months, with stops and starts and hopes of remission because Holly was only sixty. Now there was no time left, according to her mother's sister, Loveday.

'If you want to say goodbye, come now, dear heart. She won't last another twenty-four hours.'

A hugely expensive ticket (£280) was bought immediately on her credit card. To bring Maisy too would only add to the cost and the strain. She had to remain in London. Hannah had wept and pleaded with Jake; he had been adamant. It was his weekend to look after her, but he was busy and he could not change his plans with Eve. She was even desperate enough to ask her mother-in-law for help, but Etta was away on holiday herself and couldn't step in. Hannah's one remaining friend from university, Naz, was too high-powered to even contemplate asking. In the end, she had turned to the single other person whom she might ask: her neighbour Lila. Lila's daughter Bella was Maisy's best friend at school, and the two mothers often collected each other's children.

'Course I'll take her, if she don't mind sleeping on the sofa,' Lila said. 'We'll spend most of the day in the park, it's so hot.'

'It's just that I must see my mum before . . . you know.'

'I understand.'

It wasn't free, though – it couldn't be, because Lila was also poor. Hannah gave her neighbour £10 to cover Maisy's food, and that was all she had spare. She had forgotten to refill her plastic bottle, and without the money to buy water, licked her parched lips. A man trod heavily on her foot, for which she apologised. The thought of standing like this for hour after hour, the stench of the toilets, sour breath and unwashed bodies brought a new level of misery.

I hate you, I hate you, I hate you, the train repeated. *I wish you were dead.*

The sliding glass door between carriages sprang open whenever anyone triggered the sensor. On the other side was First Class. There, every seat was as wide as an elephant, and the air conditioning worked perfectly.

Just one person sat inside: a woman, wearing a sleeveless green linen dress that framed her slim form as the dark hair did her pale face. A gauzy scarf was draped across her shoulders, rippling with every shade from emerald to malachite. From each ear hung a single large pear-shaped pearl and on one arm was a heavy platinum cuff whose rich gleam circled her wrist like a weapon. Before her were several small bottles of mineral water, and an iPad inside a green leather case. She was watching something on it.

The door snapped shut again, but Hannah went on gazing. Someone so elegant seemed to belong to a different species, not just a different class. What would it be like to have her life? All at once the woman in First looked up. Their eyes met, and after a moment, the woman smiled, her red lips curving, her dark eyes warm.

Hannah turned instinctively to see who was behind her,

but nobody else was facing in the same direction. Puzzled, she turned back; this time the woman beckoned.

Even then, she might not have dared to step forward, but the train gave a sudden jolt and she fell against the door.

It opened, and Hannah stumbled through.

2

The Black Tube

Chilled air washed around her. The relief was so delicious that she wanted to stand there, her flesh turning from liquid to solid.

'Hello,' the woman said. Her voice was soft and gentle.

'Do I know you?' Hannah asked.

'No, but I thought I'd invite you in.'

Hannah sighed. 'I don't have a first-class ticket.'

The woman smiled. 'That doesn't matter.'

'If I'm found here by a ticket inspector, it will.'

'I've got a spare. My companion couldn't come.'

One rectangle of orange and cream card appeared between long, white fingers like a conjuring trick.

'Take it,' the woman said. 'It'll only be wasted otherwise. I'm going as far as Fol. You?'

'St Piran.' Hannah looked around the empty carriage. 'I'll sit somewhere else?'

The woman shrugged. 'Be my guest. Water? It's free in First.'

'Oh yes, yes please.'

She drank a whole bottle, gasping.

'I'm Jinni.'

She looked as if she had materialised out of one of the bottles before her, and might turn back into green vapour.

'Hannah. Pleased to meet you.'

'Holiday?'

'No.'

She twisted her wedding ring on her finger, conscious of her uneven nails. Jinni held up her own manicured hand. There was a plain platinum band, also loose.

'Is *your* husband ... ?'

'A shit.' A concentration of venom changed Jinni's face like a convulsion. 'I'm travelling down to collect some stuff. You?'

Those in the grip of misery and fury long to unburden themselves: this is the secret of every organisation from the Church to social media. Hannah knew, however, that the woes of others are entertainment, especially where a marriage is concerned.

In the past few years, she had learnt that however sympathetic people seem, all the questions concerning a marital breakdown are about how you must be the author of your own misfortunes, especially if you were a woman. Even if she were to tell her mother's family, she knew the response would be the same: 'But surely you *must* have realised – suspected – understood ... ' Conversations with former friends and colleagues all went along the same lines. It was like having the nail that covered the soft, exquisitely tender part of a finger ripped off, again and again, until the nail itself will never grow back properly.

But someone else who is going through the same torment is another matter.

'Me too,' she said.

Jinni told her story first. Her husband, Con, was a violent bully and a miser. They had no children. Hannah mentioned hers.

'Clever of you to get a baby out of him.'

'I wasn't trying,' Hannah said. 'It just happened.'

'All the same, you'll get more money in the end because of her. I'll get practically nothing.'

'I don't think I'll get much either. He just wants rid of me.'

'Isn't it strange the way all women in our situation are alike?' Jinni said.

Like, yet unlike – because Jinni clearly still had money. She could afford both the First-Class ticket and, presumably, a lawyer.

'I suppose so,' Hannah said.

'Five hours! You could get to a real place in that time,' Jinni said. 'Luckily, I've brought wine.'

She opened her capacious leather bag, took out a bottle in a silver jacket and felt it.

'Still chilled.' She filled two of the plastic cups on their table. 'Go on, there's nothing else to do.'

Hannah hadn't drunk alcohol for years. The first sip was delicious and slightly fizzy.

'Nice, isn't it? Have some more.'

Being strangers in this cool bubble of space, moving rapidly through a familiar landscape without anyone else to see or hear them, encouraged a sense of recklessness.

They swapped stories of their husbands' unkindness, leaning towards each other across the table as if over a campfire, warmed by the wickedness of men. The more they exchanged, the more their anger swelled. Like Hannah, Jinni had been physically assaulted on several occasions – she did not go into details. Yet for Hannah, it was the financial worry that hurt most.

'Even running the washing machine is a problem,' she confessed. 'I have to do everything by hand, including sheets.'

'How appallingly tedious for you.'

It was worse than tedious, but Jinni would never have to grapple with drudgery. Hannah looked at her companion with a mixture of fascination, envy and sympathy. Jinni was, she guessed, a few years older than herself, although Hannah didn't want to pry.

'It's a long journey, isn't it?' she said. 'We don't have to talk if you'd rather not.'

'No, I always find it a drag.' Jinni gave another dazzling smile. 'I hate leaving London, but especially to see *him*.'

It became clear that she, or rather her husband, must have a second home in Fol, the town where the rich moored their yachts and the second-homeowners spent their summers. Hannah was well acquainted with it because ever since she was old enough to hold a Dyson, she'd earned money cleaning their houses. Fol was all that St Piran was not, wired up with the latest technology, 4×4 cars, pretty shops and Waitrose deliveries. In this Cornwall, everything was lovely apart from the Cornish. Hannah had grown up hearing her friends and family described as 'those ghastly people'.

The Cornish were used to being called odd and worse than odd. Stuck out into the Atlantic like the bunioned foot of Britain, cut off by the Tamar, with a language and superstitions of their own, they were halfway to Elfland even without the legends bowdlerised by tourism. To Hannah, it mostly came down to this: her mother couldn't afford to feed her all the protein that made Jake and his kind grow tall.

She sighed and leant back in the wide grey seat.

'If I could always travel like this, I don't think my marriage would matter. Or not so much.'

'Money does take the edge off some things, yes. But the rest is the same.'

Hannah nodded in sympathy. She couldn't imagine what kind of man would make a woman as charming as this suffer, but in suffering everyone becomes equal.

'It's such a dreadful feeling, isn't it? You feel ashamed, even if you're not the one committing adultery. I wonder how he can live with himself. Or how she can, for that matter.'

'Do you know her name?'

'Only that she's called Eve. Nothing else. Do you hate the other woman?'

'Yes,' said Jinni, almost absently. 'Though not as much as I hate Con.'

They slipped past small towns, a canal, field after field. Ox-eye daisies and cow parsley lined the track, billowing in the wind. The whole countryside was frothing, like milk coming to the boil. Not so long ago, it had taken a decision that filled city people with shock and horror; they were still travelling towards its consequences. Hannah dreaded seeing her relations, not just for the usual reasons, but because of this. She had never felt more alienated from them. It was yet another reason why she could not go back to live in Cornwall.

On, on, rattling away from London. Soon, the windows filled with wriggling rivers where white swans glided, and steep hills plunged, shaggy with woodland. They finished the wine. Hannah's head began to swim as the alcohol reached her empty stomach. Every beat of the train carried her closer to her mother, whom she both longed for and dreaded seeing one last time. She began to believe that if she could stay on this train, Holly would still be alive.

Her mind was always playing tricks like this on her, caught between hope and fear.

'I can't bear being with Con,' her companion said, staring out of the window. 'He's so controlling.'

Hannah dropped her gaze to Jinni's arms, toned and flawlessly smooth. Unlike her neighbour Lila, she had no scars or burns. But that didn't necessarily mean anything, because neither did Hannah, unless you saw her cheek.

'Why do men do that?'

'He treats me like trash because I can't give him kids. I had cancer, you see.'

Hannah was appalled. 'I'm so sorry. That's terrible – to blame you for something that's not your fault.'

'I hate him. My divorce is taking for ever. I wish he were dead. So much simpler, to be a widow.'

Hannah felt a violent lurch, as if the train had suddenly switched tracks.

'Yes. I think every woman in our situation feels that.'

'I'd kill mine if I thought I could get away with it. Wouldn't you?'

Hannah gave an ironic laugh.

'Yes. Probably.'

Jinni sighed. 'It's such a relief to say it, isn't it?'

'I've thought about it,' Hannah said. The words almost burst out of her. 'Over and over and over. It's almost the only thing I think about, some days.'

All at once, the train thundered into the first of the series of tunnels before Exeter. The air became brick, and the noise deafening. Their reflections shone dimly in the black glass, a parallel world of darkness and shadow.

Jinni leant forward, her eyes bright, and mouthed, 'Why don't we, then?'

Hannah grimaced. The noise and the wine made her feel reckless. She said, half-joking, 'Because as his wife, I'd be the first suspect.'

'Not if we swapped places.'

Hannah stared. 'They'd find out.'

Jinni's voice was barely audible over the noise of the train. 'You and I have just met, by chance, on this train.'

They shot out of the tunnel, and the turbulence ceased. Hannah said, uneasily, 'I think I know this story. It was a book, wasn't it? Or a film. It doesn't end well.'

'There are only seven stories in the world, don't they say?' Jinni said. Hannah suppressed a flash of irritation. People who didn't love reading always said this, in an attempt to reduce fiction to a formula. It was even stupider than thinking all life was just the genetic code. 'But the difference is that they were men. Nobody believes that women can do anything.'

'Isn't that a flaw too?'

'No. Nothing but this journey connects us.'

'But we're always being watched, somewhere, somehow.'

'Not on this train.'

Hannah found herself looking round, to check for the Recording Angel of modern life – and it was true, there was no CCTV. The commuters crowding the carriage had got off long before, and no ticket collector had been through. They were, as Jinni said, unobserved. All at once a sensation of vertiginous possibilities opened in her mind. To be free of Jake, his bullying, his meanness, his continual belittling of her ... All she'd ever had was her intelligence, and he'd been determined to deny even that.

Jinni's face was alight with passion, or possibly wine.

'We're getting off at different stops. You bought a ticket, Second Class, when?'

'Today.'

'I bought mine yesterday.'

By now, the train was rushing for the county border, the land disappearing into a river that became a wide estuary bobbing with boats. The sea at Exmouth flexed and reflexed. Hannah could hear her voice slurring slightly.

'A woman can't disable a man. They are always stronger than us. Physically.'

'You can if you have a Taser,' Jinni said.

Hannah gazed at her, round-eyed. 'Do you?'

'Of course.'

'Aren't they illegal?'

'So? What men do to women is illegal, and they get away with it. They know they can kill us, and we fear them because of it. This just makes us . . . a little more equal.'

Jinni opened her bag and took out a shocking-pink device. It looked like a ladies' electric razor. Hannah eyed it dubiously. A part of her wanted to giggle, and another part was impressed.

'Have you tried it out?'

'You just point and press. It delivers a kick that will knock out anyone, up to fifteen metres away.'

'How did you get it?'

Jinni smiled. 'You can buy anything on the Dark Web. Take it.'

The Taser was in her grasp before she had even thought about it. The sober part of Hannah's mind told her that she was being impulsive, even crazy, but it also told her that her companion was giving her something that might be useful.

'Write down my husband's address: Con Coad, Endpoint. I'll write down Jake's,' Jinni said.

Hannah flushed. 'I don't know it.'

'Really?'

'Yes. He moved out twenty months ago. We share Maisy, but he won't tell me where he lives now. He probably thinks I might stalk him.'

'You let your child go off to some unknown destination at the weekend?'

'I know where he works,' Hannah said defensively, 'and I have his email and mobile number.'

'He'll be on the electoral register. Even if he's ex-directory, you can find out where anyone lives if you pay.'

'I never had the money to do that.'

'Don't worry,' Jinni said. 'I do. For now. What does he look like?'

'I can show you his Facebook image.' She clicked on it, though it hurt her to see his smiling face. 'I deserve to be happy,' he had said to her. He looked it.

A part of Hannah knew this was happening far too quickly. Even if she had told a stranger more about herself during the four hours in which they had been travelling together than she had ever told anyone, why should she trust somebody whom she had only just met? Jinni could be a lunatic, trying to trick her into committing a crime. She could be a bored, rich woman amusing herself during a long train journey. Yet Hannah was intoxicated not just by drink but by a new sense of purpose.

She had dreamt of taking revenge on her husband many times. What did it matter whether she killed Con Coad, instead of Jake? She and Jinni were in the same situation, and their husbands deserved what was coming down the line. They so did. Hannah touched the small white scar on her cheekbone. It was one reason why she had just taken Jinni's Taser. Even if this was all a fantasy, or a wind-up, she had good reason to fear him.

The train was running alongside the sea now. The long bay at Dawlish curved ahead, its red rocks the colour of blood. Its thin railway line was the only one left into the furthest reaches of the West Country. Despite every winter storm and surge, it survived as a testament to what imagination and daring could achieve. The track seemed to defy gravity, floating above the waves whose swell rose periodically to smash like black glass.

'Let's do it,' Jinni urged, and Hannah answered, 'Yes.'

3

Crossing the Tamar

Once they crossed the Tamar, she could feel the change, a kind of sloughing off from ordinary life. In effect, they had entered another Britain: warmer, wilder, greener, stranger. Everyone felt it, she was sure, and especially if they were Cornish. The river was an ancient border, whose radioactive mass had once, millions of years ago, been part of Europe not England. Hannah longed to point this out to the Penrose clan, for it was something few who had voted to leave Europe seemed either to know or to care about. Like all poor places, it was proud, but unlike many, it had some reason to be so. Here was the land where, in the fabled Golden Age, King Arthur had once held court at Tintagel, the place from which the tragic Tristan had sailed to bring back the Irish princess Iseult for his uncle and king, a place that throughout its history had defied the power of London. It was entirely due to its tin mines that the Romans had considered Britain to be worth conquering. Warmed by the Gulf Stream, it did not feel like England, with its palm trees and exotic coastal flowers, and its people felt closer to the Irish than to the rest.

Even the train shifted from a high-speed Intercity express to one creaking and squeaking along narrow country cuttings whose beauty was matched only by their inconvenience. The sturdy cast-iron columns of urban stations changed to open platforms and white picket fences bobbing with blue hydrangeas that bulged in the twilight like staked heads.

Hannah let out a sigh. If anywhere was home, this was it. She had coped this far by compartmentalising her life, keeping her pain and anger separate from the practicalities of everyday survival. But now it seemed obvious what she should do. Murder was the solution to all her problems. She hated and feared her husband, and if she and Jinni were to swap places to help each other out, her suffering would stop. It was a beautifully simple solution, and one that might also solve her financial problems. She was to kill first, because Jinni told her that she was only staying this one night in Fol. Hannah could pick her moment any time after midday.

'So soon?'

'Yes. Better to do it now; nobody would think you are here for that. Con will be the only person there. Is yours in London?'

'Not this weekend. He's always jetting off somewhere,' said Hannah.

'Good. That'll make it easier to have him disappear. We want to do this, don't we?'

'Yes.' Hannah was excited, her head swimming pleasantly. She felt as if she were suddenly caught up in a new and marvellous story, one in which she was able to turn the tables on the person who had ground her down without conscience or charity. 'How will I get in?'

'It's a long drive, but the gate at Endpoint is always open.'

'Does he live alone?'

'There's a local yokel who looks after the property, but he won't be around.'

'Are you sure?'

'It's in the middle of nowhere, and a weekend. I don't have a photo, and he's not on Facebook or anything, but there'll only be him.'

'What does he look like?'

'Oh, you know – tall, dark, good-looking. Not many of those around in Cornwall. Tomorrow evening would be the perfect moment. I'll make sure he drives me back to the station, so people will see me leave.' Jinni leant forward and fixed Hannah with her intense gaze. 'You can't lose your nerve.'

'I won't. How will you . . . do mine?'

'Better you don't know, so you can look surprised when the police come. Make sure your mobile phone is turned off, or better still, leave it somewhere else.'

Hannah said, dreamily, 'Any ideas about what I should do after the Tasering?'

'Suffocation,' Jinni said. 'A plastic bag tied round his head.'

The image of a face sucking desperately for air rose in her imagination and was pushed down again.

'Someone could see me arrive.'

'They won't. Con likes his privacy.'

She nodded. Of course, an abusive man wouldn't like witnesses any more than a murderer.

'So I get him unconscious on the ground . . . how long would I have?'

Jinni stood up. A wave of perfume washed out from her,

musky and sweet. Her feet were shod in silver sandals, twined into complicated knots of leather.

'I think five minutes would do it. Here's my station.'

With a magnificent motion, Jinni swept up all the bottles and rubbish into a plastic bag, then went out through the exit door. Hannah, watching her glide along the platform at Fol, could see a big saloon car waiting with its headlights on.

Her own arrival at the next station was less luxurious. She would be walking two miles in the dark from the station to her mother's empty bungalow on the edge of the ugliest small town in Cornwall.

St Piran was the kind of place people drove through on their way to the pretty coastal places like Fol and Fowey or Truro. The oldest part, which consisted of a fine Methodist chapel, a town hall and the sixth-form college, was Georgian, as were a small number of cottages near the harbour, but from the railway station on there was nothing but red-brick segueing into pebbledash bungalows and large discount stores. The verges were lined with litter, and during daylight, the few people who walked around wore tracksuits and trainers, not because they were taking exercise but because they were unemployed and had no other clothes. It stank of old chip oil, stale lager and piss.

Past midnight, it was deserted. Hannah dragged her small wheeled suitcase along the gritty road, a dreary, intermittent sound as if someone were trying to clear their throat. The same angry humiliation she always felt at being in her home-town rose up in her. It could have been as charming as Fol, but somehow one had all the luck and the other all its oppo-site. It was a place to which those on benefits were exported from cities all over Britain, out of sight and out of mind.

Further away from the main road, she could smell the sea.

The ugliness of the bungalows was softened by the semi-tropical growth of spiky yucca, blue echium, pink valerian and ferns. Her mother's patch would probably be a jungle. Tomorrow, she could drive to the hospice, but she was too tired and too drunk to do so now. There'd be so much to sort out later, with Maisy. Her weary mind kept turning over these plans, while another part fizzed and crackled with the thought that she now had a Taser in her bag and was planning to kill a total stranger. The longer she walked, the odder it seemed. Had she dreamt it? She had intended to bury herself in *Persuasion* but instead had found herself in quite a different story, a vulgar and brutal thriller of the kind she avoided when she had any time to read at all.

By the time her mother's lane came into sight, she had lost all consciousness of where she was, her body putting one foot in front of the other with the dull obedience of an animal.

A few fat flies began to batter against the glass as soon as the lights were on. The air was stale. There was a note on the Formica table, Holly's handwriting still legible if no longer firm.

Dear Han
   Have a good summer here. Rent paid to end August.
   Mum x

Hannah looked around the bungalow, which she had spent at least half her life hating and feeling ashamed of but which she now realised was the only place she thought of as home, because her mother lived there. Not that Holly owned it: she, too, rented – but from the council. It was ugly and shoddy, from its carpet-tiled floors to its avocado-green bathroom suite. It had a concrete gnome with a fishing rod in the garden, and nothing on its shelves but pot plants and knick-knacks. Her bedroom, pale pink with fairy lights looped around a small single bed, was the same as it had been fifteen years ago. A poster of Burne-Jones's *King Cophetua and the Beggar Maid* hung opposite. Hannah had been fascinated by it as a teenager, chiefly because its pale, pensive girl, with her long brown hair and drab dress, slightly resembled herself. There was something romantic about the beggar maid's elevated discomfort in the etiolated golden room, though the kneeling, bearded king gazing up at her was not to Hannah's taste.

Mostly, her walls were full of books. They were the only books in the house and ascended from floor to ceiling like choirs of angels in a medieval painting. Most were second- or third-hand because ever since she was eight, she'd spent all her earnings on them, having exhausted the small stock of children's literature in the now-defunct town library. The majority came from Mum's friend Mr Kenward. He had been the librarian at Knotshead, a progressive public school where Holly had been the resident nurse. Soon after Mum returned to St Piran with Hannah, he retired to Fol, setting up a bookshop. He was eccentric but kind, and a man of some scholarship, but not, as far as anyone knew, Cornish. When asked why he'd come, he said, in a way that did not invite further questions, 'I felt like it.'

His bookshop had not exactly flourished, though it was the first choice for the better sort of greetings card and wrapping paper. The local schools tended to give out book vouchers from it as end-of-year prizes, and like every other shop it did most of its business with tourists in the summer holidays and before Christmas. Hannah haunted Fol whenever she could get away from St Piran, and its bookshop was where she felt most at home because from the time she had read *The Cat in the Hat*, all she had wanted to do was read.

There are people who read out of necessity, and people who read out of love. Hannah was one of the latter, and when she found a book she liked she sank into it as if into another world. Voices, music, pneumatic drills all became inaudible; she was the kind of child who would go off in break times not to play or talk but to read. It was the annoyance of her life that it was impossible to walk while reading, and that she needed to sleep or eat. She could remember her third birthday, but not a time when she did not want to read more than anything else in the world. It did not feel like reading, more like a waking dream of a richer and more wonderful life in which Mowgli, Mary Poppins, the Hundred and One Dalmatians, Bilbo Baggins and Pippi Longstocking were herself. In time, she learnt to be aware of how this was created, and of the precise combinations of words that summoned their effect, but the magic never faded. To sink into a story, old or new, was to enter another world of beauty, emotion, intrigue and danger, a better world in which people talked to each other about what mattered, and things happened.

The Fol Bookshop was the antechamber to wonders. There, among its second-hand Everymans and nearly new paperbacks, she had found many treasured copies of poetry, plays and, above all, fiction, much of it long since fallen out of fashion but almost all of it of interest and delight. Anything that old Mr Kenward gave shelf space to was good, and he also stocked new books and the latest issues of the *TLS* and the *Literary Review*, alongside comfortable chairs in which to read beneath good lights. There was even a wood-burning stove for days in which the rain lashed down and the damp felt never-ending. It was a glorious shop, with a bottle-green bay window that displayed its latest treasures on fishing nets, like treasure dragged up from the deep. She almost dreaded going there, knowing she would spend all her earnings, and yet it was the joy of her childhood.

'I don't know why you bother,' her mother said to her once she became a teenager. 'They only take up space.'

'Mr Kenward says that a book makes you king of infinite space, though it might also give you bad dreams.'

'Such nonsense! Why don't you learn hairdressing, like your cousin Mor?'

'Because I'm more interested in what's *inside* people's heads than outside them.'

Apart from Mr Kenward, she had nobody else to discuss books with. Her schoolfellows were the usual mixture of kindness and unkindness, but their lives revolved around games, sport, dancing, falling in and out of love and jumping off the quayside into the harbour for fun. Hannah learnt to aspire to more. The stories she read all seemed to be about the desirability of doing so, whether this was by the granting of wishes or by harsh endeavour. She longed to escape the small, mean tedium of the life into which she had been born.

She had another, more private, reason for this. Not knowing the identity of her father caused her to dream of being the secret daughter of somebody interesting. Knotshead had been full of the children of celebrities, aristocrats, multi-millionaires and artists: it was entirely possible that one of these had impregnated her mother. Holly never told her who he was, only that she hated him for betraying her.

Holly, too, had tried to escape. She had not wanted to return to Cornwall, but felt, as a single mother, that she had no other option. A council house and a job as the school nurse in St Piran Sixth Form College proved her decision was sound. Hannah never felt the lack of brothers and sisters because she had her Aunt Loveday, and Loveday's husband Sam, her uncles and all her Penrose cousins, especially Mor, who was closest to her in age. But there were no books in any of their homes. Apart from the Bible there were just two in her mother's bungalow: a Reader's Digest selection of best-sellers by James Herriot, and a cloth-bound copy of *Great Expectations* in such poor condition that it was years before Hannah could bear to open any Dickens at all. Yet she still loved books, and for all Holly's complaints about how they took up too much space, returning to this room felt as if she was returning to the hidden core of her deepest self. These were not the set texts she had taken to university or stud-ied for exams, which remained in London in a reproachful huddle. Here were the myths and fairy tales, children's books and poems that had made her who she was.

Only Mr Kenward understood this.

"'People say that life is the thing, but I prefer reading",' he'd said to Hannah when they first became friends, and although she later came to know it as a quotation it had struck her with an electrifying force.

'That's how I feel, exactly.'

'Then you must borrow whatever you can't buy, my dear. Not the living authors – they must be paid for, like any worker – but the dead don't.'

'I should like to read both,' Hannah answered. Her love of books became her ladder up and out of the land where she was born. All the Cornish young knew they must leave, because there were no jobs if they stayed.

'I know I'll lose you too, once you grow up,' Holly told her. 'As long as you come back often.'

'I will, Mum, I promise,' Hannah would reply; though ever since she had been with Jake, her visits were fraught with mortification.

'Oh God,' she said aloud.

Outside was Mum's car, a little hatchback the colour of rain – for Cornish rain has its own colour, a soft greenish grey. Normally, she would have worried about the battery running down, but the garage had installed a big red key in the passenger footwell which she could turn to cut off the power – a kill-switch it was called. If only there were one for the human heart, too.

The last time the car had been driven was Easter, because Holly, already pale and frail, wanted to go out to a favourite spot on the cliffs.

'I want my ashes scattered here when I go.'

Hannah brought Maisy that time; it was easy to pretend that Jake was once again too busy. They sat there, three generations, watching the sea crinkle beneath them like tin foil. Maisy made a crown for her grandmother out of daisies.

'I'll treasure that, my lovely,' Holly said, bending her thin neck so it could be looped over her head.

'I hope you feel better soon, Granny.'

Holly smiled with an effort. 'My father, your great-grandfather, would have loved you.'

Having a kind father, or even a good grandfather, is one of the worst things a girl can have, because it gives a woman the delusion that all men are like that. Her grandfather Dan was almost illiterate, but he could and did turn his hand to anything that had gone wrong in the home and he helped Holly so much that it was thanks to him that her mother's bungalow was snug and nicely painted, with shelves and cupboards and storm windows to keep out the gales. He was the sort who, when he found a stray kitten, or a fledgling bird would put it into his breast pocket and carry it home to safety. She was twelve when a lorry driver from Humble Pies crashed into him, killing him instantly.

The compensation money took a long time to come through, and when it did, it was shared among his four children as his wife died soon after. But it was enough to reassure Hannah that she could leave for university. Her mother wanted her to aim high, though she also tried to warn her when she went to Durham.

'Remember, we're not English, we're Cornish.'

'Mum, I'm sure that the north-east won't be all that different from the south-west.'

It was, of course. Hannah had never felt so foreign in her life, but then she had never met anyone black or Muslim or posh or northern before, and now she had friends who were at least one of these. Everything was new and exciting, but especially the knowledge that she could spend the next three years reading and thinking. She plunged into Chaucer, Malory and *Sir Gawain and the Green Knight*. At last, she had arrived in a place where her mind could expand like a foot released from a too-tight shoe.

Most of all, she liked living in the Castle, a place that not even communal living could strip of romance. Every student wanted to live in the Castle, in the heart of the medieval city, and everyone applied for it, but she had been one of the lucky ones.

'You know bits of it were in the Harry Potter films?' said her new friend Nazneen. 'How cool is that?'

Places change personality. Hannah lost her Cornish accent; Nazneen ('call me Naz') shed her spectacles; boys

31

who had never thought twice about barging ahead suddenly opened doors for girls; girls who had lived all their lives in a mould of studious shyness became outspoken and outgoing. Hannah cycled through being an aspiring actor, a student journalist and an activist for Labour in her first two terms. Of course, Castle students were different from the rest. Its splendour of high ceilings and arched windows, thick granite walls and ornamental plaster gave them the feeling of belonging to an elite body. Even in her fondest fantasies, she had never imagined living in such grandeur.

Many of them were born to this world anyway. Well over half had been privately educated or had gone to pushy state schools where everyone got three A*s at A level. Nobody came from the south-west. When they learnt that Hannah came from Cornwall, these same people often grew misty-eyed over summers at Rock, Fowey, St Ives and Fol.

'Such a lovely part of the world,' they would say. They imagined that she must live in a whitewashed fisherman's cottage just like the ones they had rented and spend her life surfing and eating cream teas.

When Hannah went back at Christmas, she saw her home with new eyes. She had never found it beautiful, but now she perceived that St Piran was sordid. Her mother's bungalow wasn't shabby-chic, just shabby. Her uncle's pub was hideous. Above all, she was ashamed because it was unworthy of Jake.

Jake strode about the Castle as if it were his own. He looked like King Arthur in *Merlin*, spoke in the loud, confident voice of those bred to call across rolling acres and wore a gold signet ring on the little finger of his right hand. Hannah didn't know what this meant but he'd been to a famous school and lived in a large house in the Home Counties with a swimming pool and a tennis court to which some students had been invited for his birthday party. Even for Durham, where many students were unusually large, loud and ebullient, he seemed sophisticated. The first time she saw his bright blond head it gave her a strange feeling. Very soon, it became the only thing she took any notice of.

Yet, being Hannah, she could not help being sardonic.

'Another one taking his degree in beer,' was what she said when she saw him vomiting in the street. 'Don't worry, mate, the white wine came up with the fish and the red wine came up with the meat.' The friends she was with thought it hilarious, but secretly she only wanted him to notice her.

Her mother could see that she had changed. They had always enjoyed chatting, but suddenly they had nothing in common. Hannah hated phrases like 'turkey with all the trimmings', and slumping in front of the TV, and she was mortified that they had plastic windows. She loathed the way all her relations failed to put a hand over their mouths when yawning, thought burping was funny and demonstrated a hundred other instances of coarse behaviour. They knew she was different, and Mor went so far as to call her a snob. She couldn't help it.

'I'm sorry, Mum, but I think I should go back early,' she said on Boxing Day.

'I expect you want to get back to your studies, don't you?'

'Yes.'

Her experience of sex was minimal. Geoff and Hannah were the only two geeks in their year, friends who rid each other of their virginity after A levels. The experience had been painful and devoid of any emotion but embarrassment, but at least she did not have to worry about seeming like an innocent. Sex with Jake would be different. Night after night she dreamt of him, with such vividness that she felt as experienced as the most promiscuous of her new friends. Possessed by longing, she hung around him, picking up scraps of information, and rereading Jane Austen for guidance. She imagined saying to Jake, 'You are a gentleman; I am a gentleman's daughter.' It might even be true.

Yet Jake's canon was so different from hers that they might as well have been studying different subjects. He hated Hardy, laughed at D. H. Lawrence and dismissed all women writers. Anyone who was not white and either American or European did not exist. Conrad was his man, alongside a handful of other authors like Byron, Waugh, Amis and Nabokov, whose chief characteristics seemed to be aggressive virility or aristocratic lineage.

'The novel is an outmoded form, like the railway,' Jake said in a seminar. 'We should be studying film instead. Or, ultimately, video gaming.' He had a languid, drawling way of speaking that seemed to her the quintessence of posh.

'But don't you think that there's something about putting thoughts and feelings into language that is important?' Hannah asked. She wanted to be challenging but it came out as diffident.

'Why bother? The only stories people remember are what they read as children.'

While other students either laughed or bristled, Hannah was fascinated. She had never encountered anyone like him. She longed to be in love; in her imagination she was a sister to Elizabeth Bennet, Dorothea Brooke and Jane Eyre, and this is only a small step to falling in love with the most arrogant man who happens to be around. From fiction she had learnt that nothing was impossible to women with intelligence and application. It did not occur to her that the stories about poor, plain women winning their heart's desire had been written by poor, plain women who had nothing but genius to recommend them.

The idea that she had applied to university to learn became almost quaint. Why should she read about heroines, instead of becoming one herself? What she had come to Durham for, she believed, was to find her soulmate, and this was unmistakably Jake. She began to study how she could elevate herself to his notice. After scrutinising Jake's many girlfriends, she deduced that from now on she must wear plain fabric, wedge heels, discreet make-up, and no glitter. Her hair should be lighter, and above all she should have less flesh on her body. It was easy, as a student, to lose 10 lbs and at the end of her first year, her cousin Mor (who still used her qualification in hairdressing, though she was now training to be a chef) transformed her to a blonde.

'Is it all right?' Hannah asked anxiously. Mor was the closest to her in age, but (not being academic) was another Penrose failure, though the cousins were still friends.

'You look amazing, Han. Go get him!'

Hannah blushed, and tossed her head. 'We'll see.'

Her real masterstroke was, however, house-hunting.

Every winter, university towns go into ferment as students compete for the best places to rent in their second and third years. Lulled into a false sense of security, Castle students were especially prone to being late, so Hannah made it her business to look early. She unearthed a narrow Victorian house whose landlord was prepared to let to three under-graduates because of its poor insulation, dismal condition and storage heaters. Even so, her mother had to guarantee the rent; all summer in Cornwall, Hannah cleaned houses, pulled beer and waited tables to pay back the deposit, risk-ing disaster if two other students wouldn't rent with her.

Everything was staked on the anticipation that Jake would leave it to the last moment.

She changed her Facebook image to show her new, blonde look, and after many attempts to sound casual, messaged him.

Hi! We have a spare room in town that we're looking to fill. Interested?

'Are you sure?' Naz asked. She'd agreed, much to Hannah's relief, to be one of the other co-tenants after working all summer as a mother's help. 'He's quite . . . well, entitled.'

'He'll be the most fun,' Hannah said.

'That's what I'm worried about,' Nazneen muttered. 'Still . . . I feel like an impostor here anyway.'

'Do you? I don't,' said Hannah, surprised.

'You don't feel it because you are one. An impostor.'

Hannah was hurt by her friend's bluntness. 'Am I? How can you tell?'

'I'm a Londoner,' Naz answered. 'We are born with bullshit detectors.'

September came, and, as hoped, Jake accepted the offer. Hannah raced round with fresh paint and bleach, dressing the house as if making the set for a play, and even planting flowers in a pot by the front door. After he moved in – his mother rolled up in a Range Rover, bulging with a goose-feather duvet, a pad for the mattress, a giant TV set and a coffee-maker – they had a house-warming party. Hannah wore a sprigged white cotton dress with a low-cut bodice, a vintage Laura Ashley find that she knew suited her. He told her that she looked 'like a milk-maid waiting to be fucked'.

'I am,' she said, gazing up at him.

How she found the nerve she could never quite believe, but it was as if she were possessed by a different personality.

She was appreciative and accommodating, flexible and naughty, and the next morning she brought him a full English breakfast in bed.

'You're a sweet girl, Han.'

'I like you too.'

'Cool.'

For six weeks they did little but stay in bed. The sex was all she had hoped, and she felt her assumed persona become real. He was romantic, taking her out to dinner, to see arthouse films in Durham's cinema, to clubs on evenings that played the 1980s music they both enjoyed dancing to. He liked buying her books that taught her more about his kind of family and class, and it never occurred to her to wonder why he was not equally interested in her own background. By coincidence, it turned out that he'd spent many summer holidays at Fol as a child.

'Really pretty place. My grandfather, Lord Evenlode, has a place there. Maybe we met before.'

'Let me think ... No, I don't remember cleaning his toilets.'

Instead of despising her, he loved the idea of her being so different.

'You're a barmaid? Sick. Mummy will hate you,' he said. 'But that's fine, because I hate her.'

'Why?'

'She thinks I'm still a little boy. She's always interfering and nagging.'

Hannah resolved never to interfere or to nag.

Gradually, almost all the friends she had made in the first year drifted away. It didn't matter, because she had Jake's instead. They had charming manners and liked her because she cooked them hot dinners and sweet, stodgy puddings.

The boys were enthusiastic and cheerful. They met up to play sport or video games, and when a new one came out, Jake would be lost for hours. Even Hannah lost patience.

'Do you really have to play those things?'

'*Victory Cry* is amazing. Why don't you try?'

'I don't like violence.'

He patted her head. 'Of course not, babes.'

She cooked dinner every night and did his laundry and was grateful when he came to bed.

'You need to be careful of having a kind of starter marriage,' Nazneen said quietly, seeing her struggling with a bag of empty bottles and beer cans.

Hannah bridled. 'Just because *you've* never been in love.'

'I'm only trying to give you good advice. You need to think about your own life, not his.'

Hannah told herself that Nazneen was a virgin, and could know nothing about love.

'Naz, your soul is desiccated by Law.'

She knew she should resist this, but – as is the way of all warnings from friends that we know in our deepest hearts to be true – she couldn't forgive her for what she'd said.

Jake hardly noticed her, but when Naz was mentioned at all he'd say, 'Is the nun at home?'

'Who?'

'Your Muslim friend.'

Hannah bristled. She didn't understand Naz's religion, but she understood it was despised just like her own family's Methodism.

'Naz is in the library. I should be too.'

'You've got the rest of your life to read books in.'

It was a surprise, as well as a relief, when their household stayed the same for the final year, but Nazneen had the cheapest room, and earplugs. She had told Hannah that she needed to get a First.

'Does it matter?'

'It does if you want a career in Law, yes. I have to be independent as soon as possible; otherwise I'll be back at home until I marry.'

Terms at university seem to last a year not a few weeks. It felt as if she had been with Jake forever and going back to spend two months with her mother in the summer was a penance.

'Why don't you invite him to stay?' Holly asked.

'Oh no,' Hannah said, horrified. She had spent a weekend at his house, which to her terrified eyes seemed as grand as Buckingham Palace. His mother Etta had asked if she were related to the Welsh Penroses. His father Jolyon addressed everything to her breasts. His sister Saskia ignored her completely. When she offered a box of Ferrero Rocher as a gift, Etta said, 'Too kind,' before putting them away in a cupboard clearly meant for re-gifting.

'Bendicks next time, babes,' Jake said, with a snort of laughter.

'If there is one,' muttered Saskia.

Hannah's marks had been falling ever since the start of the second year. She wrote her dissertation (*Jane Austen's Cinderellas*) over the Christmas holidays, but her brain felt blunted and dull.

With Finals approaching, everyone was frightened about employment and student debt. People had stopped talking about a downturn and were calling it a recession – how deep and long it would last, nobody knew. She had no work experience of the sort that professional employers would take seriously, only the menial jobs she had done back home. She needed to get a proper job, and an English degree didn't seem like the best choice now.

'What would you like to do when you leave?' Naz asked her.

'I don't know. Once upon a time, I'd have said publishing. Or journalism. But everyone says there's no future in those, and if you don't have rich parents with a home in London . . . '

'Does it have to be London?'

'Yes. It's where Jake is going, and it's where I've always wanted to live. Nothing ever happens in Cornwall, and there are no jobs.'

Sometimes, a future is decided on the flimsiest things. The TV series she and Jake most enjoyed watching together was *Mad Men*. Advertising appealed to them for different reasons, but when the annual milk round for graduate trainees opened, they both applied to the same agency.

Hannah was interviewed by a woman whom she instantly took to. She had been honest about her lack of work experience, saying that, having worked as a cleaner ever since she was fourteen, she used many of the products the agency advertised. They discussed not only which campaigns she liked (one of them, luckily, her interviewer had been involved in) but Hannah's theory that each of Jane Austen's heroines dramatised a different way of getting a husband. After this, her interviewer said, briskly, 'There are three different options in advertising. One is super-fun and quite childlike, which is being a creative. One is being responsible and powerful, like a parent, which is an account executive. And one is like being the stroppy teenager in between, which is being a strategist. Which do you think sounds best for you?'

'The strategist,' Hannah said. She understood that this

was a choice of three, just as in a fairy tale, and she must choose wisely. 'How do you become one of those?'

'You have to learn from someone who is a strategist already, like me.'

'What do strategists do?'

'Mostly tell clients where they are going wrong, and what they should do instead. Nobody understands us.' The woman pulled a tragic face, then laughed. 'But we are the most important people in agencies. You can use your brain.'

Hannah left feeling exhilarated. Maybe she would be able to spin her English degree into gold after all. Otherwise, she had no idea how she would ever pay back her debts.

'It's all very well for you,' she said to Nazneen, who had already had three offers from top City law firms. Of course: she ticked all the boxes for equality and diversity, and she had done a vocational degree. What could Hannah say? She had studied what she loved, she was from one of the poorest places in Europe, she'd gone to a state school where most pupils barely scraped three Cs, and she was the first person in her family to go to university: only because she was white, none of this was supposed to count. Yet both she and Jake received offers, conditional on achieving at least a 2:1.

In the last term, with no more lectures or seminars, Jake decided to go back home to revise.

'Mummy thinks I'll do better without distractions,' he said.

Hannah accepted this almost with relief. It was up to her to save her future in the only way she knew how. She almost lived in the library, writing an essay a day and staying up until midnight to read all the texts she was supposed to have got through over the past two years. There were so many of them! Why did people *write* so much? What had once seemed easy and delightful became labyrinths of words in which she wandered, clueless, despairing.

'Are you OK?' Nazneen whispered, and with Jake away, they became friends again.

Hannah, ashamed, said, 'I've been a cow to you, Naz. I'm sorry.'

'It's OK, I understand. Love makes people do crazy things.'

Later, Hannah realised that Finals aren't really a test about what you've learnt or think, they are about whether you could stick at a course of study – any study. All tests used to initiate people into any elite had this in common whether you had to go out and kill a lion or learn reams of quotations that you would never, ever need again. She wrote and wrote until the top joint of her middle finger became shiny, red and sore, then she went back for the next paper, and the one after that. For weeks, all Finals students were zombies and when exams ended, they were all drunk. Hannah wanted to lose herself in love, but Jake couldn't wait to leave a city that he had always described as having 'three prisons, one of which you pay to go to'.

He was driven off to the South of France by his mother, leaving a scrum of plastic and paper in his wake. The girls cleaned up the house then retrieved the deposit, which they agreed not to share with Jake unless he remembered to ask for it. He never did.

Hannah returned to Cornwall to await her results with every expectation of failure. For weeks, she heard nothing from Jake.

'Oh, Mum,' she said, 'I think it's all over between us.'

'It'll turn out all right in the wash,' Holly said. 'Come on, lovely, I'll make you a cup of tea.'

Those days together were both the happiest and the

saddest of times. Holly was not warm and generous, like Loveday. She was brisk, controlled, practical and parsimonious to the point of reusing teabags. It drove Hannah mad. But now she understood that even if they couldn't live together, they were family. People do not have to think alike, live alike or talk alike to love each other deeply. Everything Holly said or had or did grated on Hannah (and quite possibly, she realised, vice versa) yet the bond of trust, affection and loyalty was the foundation of her life.

Not that this made being back in Cornwall any easier.

'Mum, I *have* to go to London. Jake is going to be there.'

'Sweetheart, you're expecting a prince to come galloping along on a white horse to save you,' Holly said. 'If there's one thing life has taught me, it's that you have to rescue yourself. You'll have a degree, and that's the thing.'

'I don't even know I've got that.'

'Yes, you do.'

When her marks came through, she'd done far better than feared. Jake, too, got a 2:1. Hers was high and his low, but who cared? They had nailed it. She was to be a trainee strategist, and he a trainee creative.

Have you found a flat for us yet? he texted.

Not yet, but I will! she answered joyfully.

Three weeks before their internships were due to start, Hannah took the train back and stayed with the Husseins above their corner shop off the Archway Road, sleeping on the sofa-bed and waking each morning to the thrill of being in London at last.

'All I've ever wanted is to live and work here,' she told Nazneen. 'I mean, it's *the* city, isn't it?'

Even then it was very expensive. Nazneen was back to living at home and had a room of her own because two of her brothers were now away at university. One was going to be a doctor, the other an engineer. Naz's sisters were going for accountancy and computer science. Her upbringing could not have been more different from Hannah's, and her father, though he ran a newsagent, had actually obtained a degree himself back in Pakistan. Enormous sacrifices had been made by the Husseins to give each child the best education; talking to these quiet, serious, studious people Hannah was deeply impressed, not least because what little they had came from selling the most basic supplies and staying up in the shop from 7 a.m. to 11 p.m., every single day of the year. She had never known anyone like them, but Naz, too, was desperate to leave home.

'Soon as I've got a deposit, I'm applying for a mortgage,' she said. 'You should think about it, too.'

'Jake and I are going to rent.'

Once again, Hannah found somewhere to live. It was in the Castle Road Estate, a 1970s grid of concrete and glass in the most squalid part of Kentish Town. But it cost £900 a month, and they could afford it.

'A council flat?' Jake asked dubiously.

'Ex-council,' said Hannah.

She could only see the independence it offered, and took the name of their new home as a sign of better things to come. It never occurred to her that it would, in many ways, be her prison for the next nine years.

4

The Lottery of Luck

As soon as dawn came, Hannah drove beneath the gathering clouds to see her mother for the last time. When she had visited before, Holly was still able to speak and to live at home. Now she lay immobile in a hospice, a veil of grey over a skeletal frame. Loveday, who had been with her throughout the past week, had gone home exhausted.

'She won't last the day,' she said. 'I'll be back as soon as I've slept.'

Guilty and heart-stricken, Hannah sat for hours, holding her mother's thin, limp hand, telling her how much she loved her, listening for the faint sound that started and stopped and started. Each time, she held her own breath, willing there to be another, hoping for a miracle at the last moment but knowing there would not be one. The Minister from St Piran's Chapel came and sat with them for a while, praying, before giving Holly his last blessing. The pauses between breaths became longer, and longer, and quieter and quieter, then stopped for ever.

She was alone.

Hannah put her hands up to her face, then lowered them with an effort. She could not break down now, there was too much to do. It was a relief to know it was over, she told herself, that the cruel tubes and cannulas could be taken out; the machines switched off and wheeled away. Nothing could touch Holly now, nothing could hurt her. Hannah knew that the terrible grief she had kept sealed away was rising like a dark tide, that when it reached a certain point it would overwhelm her, but it could not be here, not yet. She dreaded that moment, efficiently ticking boxes on forms, getting the death certificate in triplicate and learning that there was money for a coffin, a service and cremation.

'She was always a good planner, poor dear,' said the nurse. Everyone there knew Holly, for she had been one of their own. Loveday arrived, followed by Hannah's uncles Kit and Ross, and her cousin Mor. They cried in each other's arms and expected Hannah to cry as well but she was too numb. Nothing of this felt real, except the loneliness.

'We'd best be going,' said Loveday at last. 'Do you want to come back to ours?'

Hannah tried to steady herself. She was suddenly cold, having put on the only thing she could find in her wardrobe that wasn't heavy – the white sprigged cotton dress she had worn all those years ago to seduce Jake. It hadn't fitted her after pregnancy, but now it hung loose.

'No – no thanks, Loveday. I need to be alone for a bit. I've got Mum's car.'

Her aunt patted her hand and left.

'Are you sure you're all right to drive?' the nurse asked. 'There's a storm coming.'

'Yes,' she said. It didn't strike her as odd that the walls of the hospice kept shimmering.

Lila was texted the news. She texted right back that all was well with Maisy, and that Hannah should not worry.

A day off . . . A whole twenty-four hours with nobody to answer to. Except, she had.

Long before Hannah had learnt to drive, she cycled and walked the long twisting roads around St Piran, dreaming of escape. She knew where Endpoint was, high on a tongue of land between St Piran and Fol, although you could see the house only when out at sea due to the thick woods that grew all around it. The identity of the owner had been a mystery to her, but that went for so many properties around here, bought and sold in the lottery of luck from which Hannah would always be excluded. Could she walk in and do what she'd promised? She looked at her reflection in the dark glass of the hospice, then checked her mobile again. The battery was now completely flat. She remembered what Jinni had advised: Make sure your mobile is turned off. Surely, if it had no power, it was untraceable?

The last place she wanted to be was the bungalow, with its sad memories of Holly. At the very least, she should call in on Con Coad and see whether he was really as bad as Jinni said. Their plan had been a crazy one, but anything was better than pretending life could ever be normal again.

The wind from the sea was rising, whipping her hair about like frenzied snakes. Yes or no? It was a fork in her life, a choice that would carry her irrevocably one way or another, just as going to university had been. That seemed like an enormous choice then, demanding every drop of courage and determination she possessed; but this was far worse. Was she really going to murder a man she had never met, just because he was an abusive husband like her own? She got into the car and released the handbrake.

The road was ink-black, and all the leaves and verges shone green as if lit from within. Out the other side of town, the woods loomed and in the rear-view mirror the moors behind the town were suddenly illuminated. Seconds later, a distant boom of thunder told her the storm was getting closer. She drove faster, the wind whining at the window. Her mother didn't deserve to die so young. Jake didn't deserve to live. Jinni's husband didn't deserve to be unpunished. Was she the one to punish him? Maybe she should at least have a word, tell him that men like him couldn't go around with impunity. She had the Taser, after all. She could tell him what she thought of him, and if he turned violent, she'd let him have a nasty shock that would serve him right. Through country lanes, the air thickening, the woods closing in and closing in, until rage welled up so powerfully that she stamped on the brake.

In a moment, the ignition was off, and the kill-switch turned. Hard drops of rain began to smack into the windscreen. The gates to Endpoint were open, and she was out of the car, propelled up the long potholed drive by a wind that pushed her as a sail is filled almost to bursting. Shrubs with rustling leathery leaves bulged and swelled, looming like monsters, or perhaps she was the monster. In her hand she gripped the Taser. She could do it; she would do it, she would confront him.

Round the bend was a long stone building swathed in thick vines that stirred and bristled in the tattered light. It had pointed turrets at either end, machicolations and bits of broken masonry scattered all around on the stony forecourt. Facing the house, just before a circular drive with a fountain in the middle, was an enormous beech, so stooped with years that its drooping branches were propped up on wooden posts like an old man needing sticks. Several windows were boarded up. Weeds furred the flagstones, and walls were fanged with grime. Its big front door, studded with giant iron nails, was shut. She yanked on a bell-pull set in the wall beneath a tangle of roses. No sound came, and then the lightning forked with a brilliance that turned the sky violet.

'Hello! Hello?'

No answer. For an instant she was surrounded in a blinding whirl of crimson petals.

'Anybody there?'

All at once, something surged out of the shadows.

'OOOOAAOOO!'

An enormous creature with goggling eyes lunged towards her from the side of the house. Hannah gasped and prepared to use her Taser, conscious that she held an electric charge far weaker than the one searing the night. She shouted in a tremulous voice, 'Stop! Stay where you are!'

She didn't expect it to hear, let alone obey her, but the creature halted and waved a clawed arm in the air, as if in threat. There was a click, and simultaneously a weak, warm security light flicked on. The looming figure resolved into a very large man wearing heavy glasses, headphones and carrying a spanner. He looked furious, or possibly insane.

Hannah shouted, 'Who are you?'

He answered just as the thunder crashed.

'*What?*'

Another blast of alcohol and fury. Hannah gripped the Taser in her pocket, preparing to paralyse him, then hesitated. She couldn't be sure it was Coad. For the first time, it struck her how odd it was to be sent to kill someone without any means of identifying him. What if he were the caretaker? He looked far too ugly and dishevelled to be Jinni's husband.

'My car's broken down at the end of the drive.'

He stared at her. Clearly slow-witted, too.

'CAR!' she yelled.

The rain made it impossible to see or hear or think of anything but the need to be out of it. Already, the drive at their feet had become a torrential river and her shoes were soaked.

'Um-irrgh!' he bellowed and pushed past.

The front door opened, and after a pause, Hannah followed.

Inside, all the sounds were still of water: hammering on the roof, gulping down drainpipes and dripping off them both on to the flagstone floor of a large hall. The man pushed the headphones back round his neck and wiped his glasses. A powerful smell rolled off him – a mixture of stale sweat and a lot of booze. His overalls were filthy, and so were his hands. Dirt or grease streaked the flesh not covered by long tufts of beard, eyebrows and hair. He was clearly drunk.

'What the fuck do you want?'

'My engine has died,' Hannah said. 'I can't get a signal.'

'Phone's there,' he said, with a jerk of his head.

'Great.'

She didn't want to turn her back on him in this dark, strange house, and wasn't sure what to do. But even as she walked to the telephone, she noticed that the shadowy walls were tipping from side to side, as if the storm had somehow made the house float like a boat; and then she was flat on her back, the repulsive face scowling up – no, down – into hers.

'What happened?'

'You fainted.'

'Did I?'

His breath was so rank she had to breathe through her mouth.

'I'll call an ambulance.'

'Don't need an ambulance.' Though maybe it would be wise to get help, she thought hazily. She couldn't trust him, as a man, not to attack her.

'What's your name?'

'Hannah.' She tried to sit up, and immediately the room began to swim again. 'Oh.'

'Are you sick? Pregnant?'

Despite her trepidation, she gave a short, bitter laugh.

'No. I just haven't eaten for two days. I've been with my mum at the hospice. She's – she's – she's dead.'

To her horror, she felt tears spurt out of her eyes.

'Shit,' said the giant. 'Shit, shit, shit. Fuck.'

He stomped off.

Hannah lay staring up at the ceiling, relieved but also wondering whether he was going to leave her on the freezing flagstones. It seemed perfectly possible, and possibly preferable given how angry and unpleasant he seemed. Eventually he returned and dropped something smelly but warm on her.

'Blanket. Drink this. Christ Almighty.'

The cold, which had seeped in with the rain, still shook through her body, though some of that was fear. She sat up and clutched the mug of tea, then sipped. It was hot and sweet.

'Thanks.'

'You must eat.'

She remained silent, both fearful and resentful.

The giant rubbed his big nose.

'Can you get up, like?'

The 'like' decided her. Only Cornish people said this. He could not possibly be anyone but the caretaker.

'I think so.'

She got to her feet. He didn't offer her a hand but shambled rudely through a door ahead.

The kitchen was as chaotic as the rest, a sagging brown sofa as big as a barge down one wall and an enormous dresser crammed with the classic blue and cream striped plates, all cracked and chipped. Everything was dirty, and the oven black with grease. It was warm, however, and didn't smell as bad as the rest of the house. By an Aga was a shaggy grey dog the size of a pony. It rose, stretched, and advanced, growling.

Hannah stood very still. She didn't know which to be more afraid of, owner or dog.

'Deerhound. He won't bite.'

Hannah put out her hand for the dog to sniff, then scratched its long, bony head. Slowly, it waved a tail like a rudder from side to side.

'What's he called?'

'Bran.'

The dog lay down again with its paws over its ears. It didn't like the thunder either.

'What's your name?'

'Stan.'

Hannah felt like giggling. Stan and Bran. It was ridiculous, but also reassuring.

'Are you alone here?'

He paused, then answered, 'Apart from him.'

The thunder rumbled again.

'I'll cook summat,' he said, in an unfriendly tone.

He took a long carton of eggs, cracking them all into a glass bowl. A steel saucepan had a slab of butter placed in it. She looked nervously at it. What if one of the hairs from his horrid beard got into the mixture? What if he put something into the omelette to drug and rape her? The foolishness at having put herself in his power was making her shake. He could be capable of any number of nasty things. The gumboots had come off, revealing mismatched socks, each with a hole in the end through which poked a large, hairy toe. Hannah jumped when there was another thunderclap.

'Storm's right on top of us.'

Just as he said it, there was a popping sound and the house was plunged into darkness. Hannah yelped.

'Don't scream, you silly bint,' he said harshly. 'It upsets the dog.'

By candlelight, Stan looked even more wild. Both front teeth were chipped, and his eyes looked bloodshot and squinting. There was a cut on his lip, and a strange look on his face, the little she could see of it beneath the torrents of hair. Could she outrun him in the pelting rain? Her car at the end of the drive was too far away to make a dash for it. Her mind seethed with possibilities. Maybe he'd be too big to Taser if he attacked her. Maybe she could find a room and bolt herself in for the night.

'Is there a loo?'

'Through there, side of the hall. Take a candle.'

The flame wavered as she walked to the end of the next room, passing large, lumpy bits of old furniture. Even in semi-darkness, the place was in a terrible state. The light caught long, trailing cobwebs, and stuff (she dared not think what) crunched underfoot. It smelt of damp, dirt and bad drains. Wind whined through cracks, ivy had forced its way through windows and she bit back a gasp as something scuttled across the floor in the shadows. How could this be the home of a rich man? Yet there were also traces of luxury. The cloakroom in the turret was covered with pale green wallpaper, on which exquisite hand-painted Chinese birds, butterflies and fish gazed at her in round-eyed surprise between flowering iris and ripples of water. There were worn wool jackets hanging from coat-pegs, a selection of wooden walking-sticks and the hardback books that posh people always left lying around as casually as they left fresh fruit, to rot as often as to be read. Ancient, yellowing copies of the *TLS* were jammed into a magazine rack, bearing the names of long-forgotten authors from her English degree. A bowl filled with miniature tablets of soap swiped from hotels around the world was the finishing touch for a miser. Hannah looked in the mirror. Her face was very pale.

'All you need,' she muttered, 'is a vampire bat.'

There was no toilet paper. She found a sodden tissue in her pocket and did her best. Then she washed and dried her hands and face. It gave her a little courage. I will not run, she thought; not unless it becomes a matter of life or death. There was a bolt on this door, and if all else failed she could stay in the toilet all night and read the *TLS*. But maybe her fears were unnecessary. Even if his language and breath were foul, he hadn't actually done anything; and she was hungry.

When she returned an omelette was forming. Stan had made some effort with his own appearance too, having tied both his locks and his beard back with elastic bands, but the hair swarming down his enormous arms still looked like an army of angry insects. She eyed him, and his dirty finger-nails, with trepidation.

'It's very kind of you.'

He grunted and opened a circular wire rack, flipped out

four pieces of toast, took the pan off the heat and spooned half the omelette on to one plate and half on the other. Hannah felt reassured by this.

They began to eat.

'It's good.'

The giant seemed to become marginally less grim.

'There's sardines. Artichoke hearts.'

'Won't it be difficult to replace?'

'No. Stop fuck – fussing.'

She worried now about what might happen to him when Coad returned. It was always a temptation to steal from second homes and eating from the owner's store-room supplies was theft.

Hadn't she borrowed countless books and DVDs from such places? She'd always replaced them, carefully, but there were stories of caretakers who had made a tidy bit of income renting out houses that weren't theirs. Easy to see why this might seem like a crime that hurt nobody – though of course it was actual stealing because of utilities and wear. Maybe Coad was too rich to notice a few things missing from the store-cupboard. Maybe, given the state of this place, he didn't care.

The rain made it sound as if they were standing beneath a waterfall.

'Storm's not passing. You can try the AA, or you can turn in here. It'll be over by morning.'

'I'm not a member of the AA.'

'Any garage'll be closed by now. And I'm too stank to drive.'

It was a risk. He might be dangerous and was almost certainly untrustworthy, even if the omelette had been good. She could go back to her car, which was not, of course, broken down, and wait for the storm to pass, but after her

55

faint it might be dangerous to drive. Besides, anything was better than going back to her mother's desolate bungalow. Hannah drew a deep breath.

'I'll stay, if it's OK.'

'Fine.' He cleared his throat. 'West wing is on the left, upstairs. End room should be OK.' He belched, and she could not help recoiling. 'I'm the other end of the house.'

Plastic buckets were positioned every few yards to catch raindrops that glittered in the candlelight. At the bottom of the staircase there were piles of stuff, and yet more piles at the top, threatening to topple over in an avalanche. All kinds of junk were mixed up: a bicycle locked in an act of mechanical copulation with a dressmaker's dummy, a deflated football balanced on an umbrella stand, a porcelain teacup with a dead mouse curled inside it. The long Persian rugs were tattered, and blotches of dark mould kept forming into faces that winked, blinked, then slid away into shape-lessness when stared at. Dim old portraits, rusting weapons, heavy wooden chests, a twisted length of bone that looked as if it must belong to a unicorn, dusty peacock feathers and dustier pampas grass in tall vases, brass umbrella stands, plastic ashtrays from pubs, rotting damask curtains, the top half of a Barbie doll, a rocking horse with a cracked leg. At one point, clocks began to strike midnight in frail chiming voices, one after another. Every floorboard creaked.

The sewage smell was the worst. She wondered how she would sleep through it.

Most of all what surprised her were the books – shelves upon shelves of them, paperbacks and hardbacks all jumbled up together in every corridor and room. Without their presence, Hannah would have felt a lot more nervous. She could only glimpse the titles, which seemed to range from

Northanger Abbey and *Crime and Punishment* to titles like *The Left Hand of Darkness*, *Stig of the Dump*, *When I Lived in Modern Times*, *The Little White Horse*, *The Bell Jar* and *Possession*. Someone in this house was clearly a reader or had been. She didn't think it could be Jinni: a reader is never without a book, a real paper book, and Jinni had travelled with nothing but her handbag, her iPad and the wine.

Of course, reading is no guarantee of virtue, but an addiction. Hannah, who had once prided herself on being special simply because she read early and ardently, had to remind herself of this. Jake had, in his way, been a reader – and it did not seem to have given him the slightest degree of empathy. Yet she felt comforted, as if her life had slid back into a genre that she recognised and liked.

The west wing seemed in slightly better condition than the rest of this malodorous mansion. The smell vanished the further she walked. She counted six bedrooms, maybe more; just how big was this place? It seemed to be a minor stately home. One room had already been used, for its door was open. Hannah knew, immediately, that this was where Jinni had slept for her sweet, heavy perfume still lingered. Cautiously, she tried the light switch, and to her relief the room sprang into stark detail. A drawer was pulled out. A lamp lay on its side on the floor, its shade askew. Was this the way it usually was? Could there have been a fight before Coad left? The mirror over the fireplace, a big gilt-framed one lavishly adorned with swags and bows, was cracked across one corner and had obviously had something thrown at it, a lump of sea-smoothed granite. Fearful, she went further. In the bathroom cotton-wool pads smeared with make-up were scattered around, but no blood or, as she briefly feared, body. The bath, a white roll-top had a towel draped half into it. Urine stained the toilet bowl. Wrinkling her nose, she flushed it away.

Maybe it hadn't been Jinni who had left it like this, however. Not flushing a toilet was what men did, as if the seat left upright was a kind of benediction on whoever came next. It must have been Coad. Unless – and she felt another tremor – it was Stan. She thought of his puffy face and bad temper, wondering whether she had locked herself in with a psychopath. But it was too late to back out now. She hurried down the corridor, glad the lights were working again, and determined to block the bedroom door.

At the end of the corridor was a room with a big window. There was nothing to see through the streaming glass but her own reflection, so she pulled on the cord and thick linen curtains swished across the storm. This room was as promised, clean and tidy, its walls papered with an old William Morris pattern of twining green seaweed and pale blue flowers that was both graceful and sinister. On the walls were botanical prints, mounted and framed, and to one side a full-length oil portrait of a dark-haired young woman wearing long evening gloves that matched her sleeveless yellow dress. She, at least, had a friendly smile. There were hardbacks in a big bookcase, all women authors Hannah particularly enjoyed, like Frances Hodgson Burnett, Edith Wharton, Alison Lurie, Alice Munro and Eva Ibbotson, plus, of course, Jane Austen. It was a room that was feminine without silliness, with a clean bathroom and old-fashioned brass taps. She turned the heavy key in the door, however, and pushed a wooden chest in front of it. She then reached into her handbag, found the charger for her mobile and plugged it in.

Her last thought, as she climbed under the sheets, was relief that she had not yet murdered a man.

5

A Walk in the Woods

A blade of sunlight came through the gap in the curtains. Hannah rose, and opened them.

No trace of the storm remained. Outside, waves glittered and crinkled; inside, there was the possibility of breakfast.

It was after 10 a.m. Embarrassed, she showered and dressed rapidly, stripping the bed and bathroom before unlocking her door. On the way to the kitchen, she paused and removed the other bedlinen from Jinni's room as well, descending with a big bundle under one arm.

Stan was washing up and listening to Radio Cornwall. He still looked awful: he wore a ragged red T-shirt in which his belly was distinct, and long baggy shorts which revealed a blue tattoo of twining vines up one shaggy calf. His hair was now tied back in a bun, and his beard straggled over his chest, with bits of stuff caught in it. When he turned, his eyes were concealed by dark glasses. Of course, he must be hungover.

'Oh.'

'Where should I put these?'

'Don't bother,' he said. 'That's my job.'

'It's nothing.' She drew a breath, and told him the secret that nobody but her employers knew. 'I work as a cleaner in London.'

'You do?'

'Yes.' Hannah flushed. 'I used to work in advertising, but when my husband left, it was the only thing I could find that fitted with child-minding.'

'Cheers.'

She wondered whether he was being sarcastic.

'I can put the sheets on to wash, if you tell me where the machine is. I stripped the other bed too.'

Something that might have been surprise crossed his sullen face. Stan pointed to a door that led to the utility room.

'She was in a hurry to get back. Don't know why she came down.'

Hannah knew why, of course, and knew the 'she' was Jinni. As the Cyclopean eye of the washing machine began to roll this way and that, the folly of their plan shook her. What on earth had they been thinking? She'd been fired up by fear, anger, grief and wine. Now, after a good night's sleep, she was sane again. Thank goodness she had agreed to kill first, because it meant that nothing would have happened to Jake. Yes, if her husband were to drop down dead, she'd be relieved. But he was also Maisy's beloved father. Losing him would devastate his daughter. All she wanted was for both sides to be civilised, and to not be so miserably poor. Sometimes she felt that she had become two people: one the good, gentle, sensible mother and the other the fury driven to the edge of reason.

Or was she crazy, as Jake kept insisting?

This was the trouble about a marriage that had gone bad. You didn't know who was mad, who was bad and who was just sad. To hear Jake, you would think that she had planned on getting pregnant all by herself. He'd been involved too. He'd been the one who had wanted to keep the baby, even though she'd offered to have an abortion. Sometimes, she thought she would not even have minded so much were he to admit that he had wronged her. But the only way that he could be the hero of his own life was to make her its villain, and the only way she could survive was to make him so. And he did hurt her, physically and emotionally. They were locked in an endless struggle of loathing and recrimination, not just because of Maisy but because of money. It was a struggle as sordid as it was desperate.

There was no legal aid for divorce, and most women – even ones who had been beaten black and blue, or given a sexually transmitted disease – were punished by the law because they were almost always economically inferior. A decent man, the kind she should have married, would have paid for her lawyer as well as his own but Jake was not decent, and she had no savings left, just debts. If you earned at least 8 per cent less than a man for doing the same job, that was the inevitable result, and if you took time out (as it was euphemistically called) to have a child, even more so. She remembered saying airily to Nazneen at university that since women had won equal rights and equal education, feminism was no longer needed, and her friend saying drily, 'Just wait.' So here she was, almost thirty, and she understood that however pleasant men might make themselves to women when they were young and pretty, there was no justice for her sex.

She returned to the kitchen scowling.

'Bacon? Croissant?'

'I shouldn't impose on you any longer.'

He shrugged. 'The croissants will only go stale.'

She was still hungry, so took one, an orange and some coffee. The taste of real coffee was one of the things she missed most about not having money. The croissant was a crescent of crisp, buttery flakiness and the apricot jam made it ambrosial.

'Did you buy these in Fol?'

'Made them.'

No wonder Coad let him have the run of the house, even if his housekeeping was atrocious.

'Sorry it's all such a mess,' he said, as if he had just noticed.

Hannah replied, with sympathy, 'It must be a lot for just one person to keep clean.'

She stared through the grimy French windows, at the ruined kitchen garden, its raised beds plumed with tall fennel and cow parsley; along the brick walls where unpruned apples, pears, cherries and plums were trying to ripen. She glanced up at Stan. He'd lifted his dark glasses in the shade, and now she saw that one swollen eye was turning black.

'Oh, your face! What happened?'

'Walked into a door.'

'Bad luck,' she said. He'd been so drunk last night, it wasn't surprising.

'Yes,' he said, grimacing.

'Have you tried aloe vera?'

'What?'

'Some of that, over there.' She pointed to a spikey, speckled plant on the windowsill. 'If you cut a bit off – may I? – the goo inside will help soothe it.'

62

'I didn't know it had a use. Go on, then.'

She took a knife, split open a fleshy stem. He sat down and turned his face up to her, reluctantly. When she touched him, he flinched. She flinched also: he was the first man other than her husband she had touched in years.

'I'll try not to hurt you.'

She patted the green jelly around his eye gingerly. It felt hot. His lashes were tangled, and very long. If he ever had a haircut, he'd need an electric hedge-trimmer.

'You sure this works?' he asked in a suspicious voice. 'It's fucking sore.'

'Yes. My mum was a school nurse. Used it all the time for burns and bruises.'

'At St Piran College?'

'That's right. Holly Penrose.'

'I remember her. She patched me up a few times after a match.'

Hannah nodded, swallowing.

'Seems to be working.'

'It ought to. Mum taught me a bit about plants.'

Had he really walked into a door? Remembering the state of the other bedroom, she couldn't help but wonder. Maybe there had been a fight between the Coads and he'd intervened. Maybe he'd assaulted Jinni himself. Her fearfulness returned. She was alone in a strange house with a very big, bad-tempered man.

'Is there somewhere with good reception where I can call my daughter in London?'

'Garden is probably best.'

Outside, Hannah tried to chat brightly.

'When are you coming back?' Maisy said.

'Tonight, sweetie. I'm in Cornwall because of Granny.'

What could a six-year-old understand about death? Hannah wasn't even sure she understood it herself. She would have to explain tomorrow, without telling lies about heaven.

'Is she poorly?'

'Not any longer.'

'Will I be able to be in Cornwall soon?'

'Of course,' said Hannah, although whether she would in fact be able to return, and how she would get through the long summer holidays in future was something she dared not address. 'We can come down together next month. All the cousins will be there.'

She had her back turned to the house and Stan, self-consciously. Perhaps she should warn him that his employer's wife was going around plotting murder . . . Would he believe her? Hesitantly, she texted Jake. After all, Holly's death would affect their daughter. Maybe it would make him kinder. He hated his own mother but knew how much Holly had meant to Maisy, and to her.

Mum died yesterday. Not told M yet.

No answer. He often didn't answer for hours or days. She went back indoors and said to Stan, 'She's fine. Sorry to be a nuisance.'

'You're not. To be honest . . . ' He paused. She couldn't see his expression behind the beard. 'I was thinking of swimming out to sea last night.'

Hannah stared at him, shocked.

'You could have drowned in the storm.'

'Yes. That was the plan.'

Had she really interrupted an intended suicide? Hannah raised her eyes to his and saw their expression. He looked like someone without hope.

64

'I feel like that, sometimes,' she said, on impulse. 'Only I couldn't do that to other people, especially not my daughter.'

'It must be a comfort to have a child.'

She said, 'Yes. Didn't stop my ex from having affairs.'

'Mine too.'

So he was married. It was hard to think of any woman who wouldn't be repulsed by him. Still, there was no accounting for taste, and maybe his hairy heart was a good one. She had not been wise enough to choose a kind man, so how should she know?

'The thing about suicide is you don't get to find out what happens next. It's like never finishing a book or walking out in the middle of a film. Things change, and look how lovely it is today.'

Hannah knew she was talking to him as if he were a child, but he nodded slowly and said,

'I'm going down for a swim now. I can show you the woods, if you like.'

Even though her return didn't have to be until the afternoon, she hesitated. To stay any longer was not wise. There would be people to inform, a mountain of dismal duties. But she didn't want to leave him alone … She shivered. Having come intending to kill one man, she seemed to have saved another.

'Sure.'

They walked down the straight stone path flanked by lavender bushes spiked with sweet indigo. At the further end of the kitchen garden was a solid wooden gate in the brick wall, with a latch. The hound was quivering with eagerness to be off; once through, it bounded away. Stan followed, moving without a sound on rubber sandals. Out in the light his skin glowed a dark amber. Maybe he was one of those Cornishmen who was part Breton, or part pirate.

Beyond were billowing, brilliant flowers – violet-blue iris, tall cream fox-lilies and everywhere more roses. It was riotously overgrown, with foxgloves and ox-eye daisies and long silky grasses spurting through the beds in exuberance. The air shimmered.

'My goodness, it's hot.'

'Soon be midsummer.'

'I'm glad Mum died before it,' she said, blinking. The pain kept welling up just when she thought she had it under control.

'Come on, I need to get out of the glare.'

The path drew them deeper and deeper into the cool, winding down along the sides of a deep gorge. There seemed no end to it, the monumental trunks spraying a glassy transparency of beech leaves, the undulating oaks and pale birch, the crevices where a few last primroses fainted palely, the high banks plumed with soft shuttlecocks of green fern, not just the ordinary kind but the primordial tree fern that, like giant cedars and other semi-tropical plants, reminded her that everything here was unlike the rest of Britain. Tiny streams chattered and dripped, the ground steamed and streamed with collected rain, and the rich scent of the soil was almost overpowering. Birds visible and invisible sang above and below. It seemed enormous, as though the strange geography that makes the hilly southwest so much bigger than it seems on a map was playing tricks on her senses.

'It's like a jungle.'

'Just heat and water.'

When she and her mother had the time, they would go off to visit the great gardens that Cornwall has in abundance, each glorious in its own way if you liked rhododendron and azalea. But this gorge was different. It seemed to have grown into beauty by itself, in the dawn of the world.

A fat furry bee lay prostrate in the sun.

'Look at that! Blissed-out.'

'Least they're safe here,' he said. 'We used to have red squirrels, too. One of the last places in Britain to have them.'

One blink, and he'd be indistinguishable from the mossy granite boulders. Every now and again he would pause, twining roses and honeysuckle around young trees with his huge yet delicate fingers. There was a clump of wild garlic leaves and he put some in a bag, clearly for consumption later. An odd creature, she thought, even in a part of the world where oddity was not unusual. Perhaps he was more hermit than housekeeper, a green man in a green shade.

'Did you make all this?' Hannah asked.

'No! It grew long, long ago.'

'It has a personality,' she said, then immediately felt stupid.

But he answered, 'The spirit of the place, it's called. Some people think it is haunted by Tristan after he lost Isolde, who appears in the shape of a white stag.'

'Do you?'

'No. But what do I know? If you see the white stag, you're blessed for life, they say.'

Out of the bird-ringing wood, through a wooden fence with a stile and on to a broad cliff-side stretch of short turf, smelling of sheep and specked with tiny yellow tormentil.

She walked to the cliff edge.

'Careful!' Stan said suddenly. 'That goes all the way down.'

There was a jumble of rocks sticking up.

'What is it?'

'Blowhole. When the tide is high, the spray shoots out from below. You don't want to fall down it.'

Hannah listened. On a calm day like today, she could hear nothing.

'It looks too small to fall down.'

'It's not stable. Should be fenced-off, I suppose, but people don't tend to come along this way. We're on a peninsula. It's what makes Endpoint special. You can walk all the way along the sands from St Piran to Fol when the tide is out, but it's cut off otherwise except by the inland road.'

A narrow, stony path wound down to the beach. Each turn brought a different view of fluorescent coconut-scented gorse, navy sea. Above, skylarks evaporated into light, and below was a crescent of pale sand.

'There's somebody in the water – oh, it's a seal!'

'My mate while swimming, though Bran gets jealous.'

The hound turned and grinned, then surged forward again, long tail whirling. The fearfulness of the night before had gone.

Hannah said, 'Didn't you think of Bran, last night? How lonely and frightened he'd have been when you didn't come back?'

'Humans don't deserve the love of dogs,' Stan muttered.

'No, I suppose not. But that doesn't mean we're not responsible for them.'

'I can't even be responsible for myself.'

'You're not just here for *yourself*, though.' She couldn't help the sharpness in her tone.

'My family are all dead. My wife hates me.'

'Then your wife doesn't deserve you,' Hannah said. 'Why give her the power to hurt you?'

'It's not about giving her anything. She just does—'

'Have you talked to anyone else about the way you feel?'

He shook his shaggy head.

'Well, I'm glad you told me. But you should see your GP.'

'I don't think I have one.'

'Of course you do. Even in St Piran there's still a doctor's surgery. What about friends?'

Stan sighed. 'I'm not sure I have any left.'

She wondered what he'd done to believe this. But then, when she was at her lowest in London, she had felt the same. It was easy to lose friends, especially when you had a child. People like her former boss Ali Gold, with whom she had been close, had vanished from her life when she gave up her job; Naz had moved on, and Lila was just a neighbour. Apart from her family, she had no one.

There was a pause, and she said, 'Promise me you won't try again. If you don't care about other people, then think about your poor dog.'

Bran lolloped along the beach below, barking joyfully at gulls.

'Fuck,' he muttered. 'She'd have him put down.' There was a long pause, then he looked at her with his sad, puffy eyes and said, 'A'right.'

'Good. You must keep your promise. I'm coming back here, you know.'

'To live?'

'No, for Mum's funeral, next month. We'll stay for a couple of weeks, if I can afford it. After that, I don't know. The council will want her bungalow back.'

Just above the final flight of steps, set back in the cove, there was the ruin of a granite cottage. The stream from the ponds above ran to one side of its small strip of land before clattering down on to the beach.

'Is that Endpoint's too?'

'Yes.'

'My dream house,' Hannah said, caught between irony and longing. She could see – she could always see – exactly how lovely it could be, the solidity of the granite walls and fish-scale slate, the rotten windows made whole, perfectly snug even in a gale being sheltered by the cliffs as if by loving arms. It was the kind of house she'd drawn as a child. 'What a shame it's falling down.'

'No money to rebuild anything here,' muttered Stan, with a return to his surly manner. 'It's all fucked.'

The heat of the day was intensifying. The sea and the sky merged their broad bands of blue.

'Oh, how perfect,' she said. 'I wish I'd brought a costume.'

'You can swim without. In underwear, I mean.'

His skin seemed to get even darker.

'Um ... No,' said Hannah. The idea of baring any flesh made her shrink. 'I'll paddle.'

He shrugged, pulled off his ragged T-shirt, kicked off his sandals and, dropping his sunglasses on top of them, waded in without a backwards glance, still wearing his shorts. She looked at his retreating form with envy and exasperation. No woman would ever have stripped off so casually. What must it be like to not have the strength and confidence drained from you by biology? To be, instead, big and strong and convinced the world was yours? Hannah stared after him. Above the baggy shorts his back was blotched with black marks, probably more hair. The dog stood still, whining as its master plunged into the waves, then trotted off to chase the gulls.

Hannah took off her shoes and wandered along the beach too. She was glad to have it to herself. Solitude was her greatest luxury, although these days she rarely had the energy to read.

There were some long, jagged dark rocks like upturned boats sticking out of the sand. Here were pieces of sea-glass, polished into opaque jewels by the tumbling waves. Maisy would like these, and maybe Lila's daughter would too. She filled her pockets. Eventually, she sat down above a rock-pool, cooling her feet and washing the tiny grains out from her toes. A waterfall, the collection of all the streams above, cascaded in ribbons of green weed from the cliff-face, then wriggled on to the sand and out to sea.

Her grief felt like something falling down a long, long hole. Eventually, she knew, it would become less acute, though it would never entirely leave. But there was consolation already in the knowledge that Holly had perhaps been able to sense a few final moments of comfort and love. It was the lot of parents to give more than they received. She would always love Maisy more than Maisy would love her, and it was the same with her own mother, whose courage she was still only beginning to understand. Holly would have been horrified to learn she had turned up at a stranger's door, intending to kill him out of, what? Although she never talked about the man who had impregnated her with Hannah, she had a strong moral compass.

'There's only one rule in life worth keeping, and that's: Do as you would be done by. Everything in the Bible comes down to that,' she'd told Hannah. It was a simple philosophy, and, like her belief that 'it'll all come out in the wash', hard to prove as efficacious.

After a while Hannah let her thoughts drift, sitting completely still and watching the shapes of light and water waver and melt. Encouraged by her immobility, a small yellow crab was walking sideways across the sandy floor, its claws held up in a formal gesture, as if about to dance. Shoals of tiny fish needled this way and that over tented limpets. A miniature world, surviving from one tide to the next in its enclosed space, never aspiring to what lay beyond its confines. The lost joys of her childhood returned, made more precious by the knowledge of how temporary they were.

Could she and Maisy repeat what her own mother had done and come back to Cornwall to live? St Piran was cheaper than London. (Anywhere was.) She could continue the lease on Mum's bungalow, and maybe retrain as a teacher – it was a job that would allow her to earn and look after her child. But that kind of life would require the total immolation of Hannah's own hopes for herself; and in London Maisy had a chance of a better education, more stimulus, more variety of friends and opportunities. You don't go tombstoning off a harbour wall unless it is literally the only entertainment you can find.

When she looked up, she could see a paraglider hovering above the cliffs like a giant butterfly.

I must tell Mum about Endpoint, she thought, then remembered she could not.

Her mobile buzzed.

Need to discuss somewhere cheaper to rent. You've had a free ride for two years. Time to move on.

6

Poisoned Darts

All Hannah's pleasure in the beach vanished instantly, along with the rock-pool creatures. She stood up, head throbbing. To send such a message when she'd told him that her mother had just died . . . How could anyone be so heartless?

Only a short while ago, she had felt strong and confident, telling Stan not to kill himself, but now she could feel it again, the grip of rage squeezing her like a great fist.

A *free ride*, was that what Jake really believed was going on? She would never be free, whether she stood up to him or let him bully her into a worse and worse situation. Without the money for legal advice, she was powerless to stop him harming her and her child. It was all hopeless, hopeless – unless she did as Jinni suggested.

Wouldn't it be so much simpler if he were dead . . . ?

Her brain felt as if it were boiling. It didn't feel like she was planning a crime, so much as if she were fighting for her right to exist. She suddenly had no doubt that, if she did kill

Con Coad, Jinni would carry out her half of the bargain. The offer had been a serious one, not a joke.

'Bastard, *bastard*,' she muttered.

It had been a drip-drip-drip, and for years she had excused his temper and remarks as being due to stress, or the drugs that had been all too readily available to a creative. Then it was her own fault for making him angry, and she would do anything to win back his affection, abasing herself and flattering his ego as if she were his slave.

She was not yet thirty but felt like an old woman.

Once, after three broken nights in succession, she lost her keys to the flat and had to call the estate agent to get back in. She turned up at their office with Maisy in a buggy, frantic.

'Don't tell my husband,' she begged the agent.

He looked surprised. 'Anyone can lose keys. Happens all the time,' he said, and this ordinary kindness had restored her for a few minutes.

Jake's criticisms over the smallest error seemed to sink into her blood like poisoned darts, robbing her of all rational thought. Only with Maisy could she feel brave. To protect Maisy, she'd face down a man-eating tiger, even if it meant putting her own head in its mouth.

Hannah now believed that she had never felt confident, but in the brief time when she was getting away from Cornwall she became so. There had been a person formed out of stories who had flown on borrowed wings to look down on the smallness of her life in St Piran and searched for a bigger horizon. She loved heroines like Jane Eyre who spoke their minds fearlessly. *Do you think, because I am poor, obscure, plain and little, I am soulless and heartless? You think wrong! I have as much soul as you – and full as much heart!*

She had barely discovered who she was when she gave it away, without stopping to think that to give all of yourself to another is to make yourself defenceless. For a part of every person must remain forever hidden from everyone else, including the one you most long to trust, locked away like a secret garden behind a high wall and a strong gate. Given the chance, most people would always destroy another person. That was what she had learnt from love, rather than literature.

The noise of the waterfall, so pleasant a few minutes ago, now sounded like breaking glass.

'Hannah?' Stan asked. 'Are you feeling faint again?'

He had come out of the sea without her noticing. The water made rivulets down his chest and legs.

'No. It's just stuff from my ex-husband.'

He crouched beside her. 'Can I help?'

Taking refuge in irritability she said, 'No. I'd better go back.'

'All right.'

He put on the T-shirt without bothering to dry himself, strapped on his sandals, and set off, moving almost as swiftly as the hound. She followed, as fast as she could.

It soon became evident that, despite his puffy face and beer belly, Stan was much fitter than she was. He stopped.

'Would you like a dog sleigh?'

'A what?'

'Here.' Stan gave a sharp whistle, and Bran came racing back. The lead was clipped to his collar and given to Hannah.

'Hold tight. Ready? Home!'

Bran bounded up the stairs again, pulling. It was like being attached to a coiled spring of endless energy. Her feet flew, and she laughed despite herself.

They moved fast, past the ruined cottage, across the cliff

75

path and through the woods, this time from a different angle to the path by which they had descended. There was a long dark pool fringed with iris and bobbing with fat buds of water lilies; a tunnel of gigantic gunnera leaves with spiky stalks; a sprawling magnolia tree covered with pink blooms the size of salad bowls. Hannah barely had time to notice any of it before it was past. Bran was tireless and her legs could hardly keep up.

'Long climb.'

'I'm very glad you showed the woods and cove to me. It's . . . very special.'

'Yes.'

'I've collected some treasures to take back.'

She showed him the sea-glass. He nodded.

'How old is your little one?'

'Six.'

'Come back with her when you're down again. If you like.'

Hannah wondered whether he meant it.

'Wait a moment.'

He disappeared for several minutes, and returned with a bunch of roses, tightly wrapped in newspaper.

'I don't deserve these.'

'Take them.'

She felt worse than ever at deceiving him. 'Thank you. I really do need to go now,' she said abruptly. 'I must get the train back to London.'

He nodded. 'Of course.'

She remembered her lie. 'I'll call the garage.'

She walked back to the car with him and turned the kill-switch key just before the ignition.

'Success!'

'Well,' he said, 'it must have dried out.'

'Maybe,' Hannah answered, revving the engine. She was slightly ashamed that her ruse had worked. 'Are you sure I can't give you some money for bed and breakfast?'

'On the house . . . '

He stood there, shifting from one elephantine foot to the other.

'Bye.'

Hannah nodded, released the handbrake, and drove off.

Strange man, she thought, probably a bit on the spectrum. His suggestion that she swim in her underwear had been a bit creepy, though logically there was little difference between this and a bikini. She hoped he wouldn't get into trouble for raiding his supplies and even more that he'd get help for depression.

Back at the stuffy bungalow, she got out her laptop and began to do all the chores that needed to be done – writing to the bank, and the funeral parlour, emailing relations whom she couldn't bear to talk to. Loveday had texted, *Call me when you want to talk, dear heart.*

She didn't expect any replies, but some got back at once. *Sorry for your loss, Holly was a lovely person . . .*

Plenty of people had been fond of her mum, perhaps because she was kind without ever expecting anything in return, which is the secret of being liked in a small town, or indeed anywhere. A wave of nostalgia for this life swamped her. To be somewhere that you could be liked, and known, and even a little protected . . . but London was where she lived now. If she gave that up, she might as well never have left and got into debt for a degree.

She loaded a wheeled suitcase with as many books as she could manage, mostly the fairy tales that Maisy also loved, and her copy of *Persuasion*. It was her least-favourite Austen novel, its heroine a passive sufferer who had lost her looks through sheer unhappiness, but also, of course, genius.

Nazneen had always had a much more practical attitude to love and marriage.

'Course you were going to be disappointed, Han, because you didn't understand that men aren't our friends. You know they've found that the time of life when women are happiest is eighty-five, because that's when they are widows.'

'Don't you want to meet someone?'

'Not a man, no.' This was the closest Naz could come to admitting what Hannah half-suspected. 'You?'

'I have enough on my plate. Besides, who would take me with a child?'

She was lonely, even though her old housemate got in touch every few months. They met in a local café, and although it was one of the smarter ones on Kentish Town high street, with fresh coffee and an artisan bakery, she could feel Naz looking down on it: Nazneen, who now had a flat of her own in Hackney and a flourishing legal career.

'I know, I can't believe it either. But the moment I earned over £30k, that was it.'

Hannah swallowed her humiliation and listened. Nazneen was very full of what she could afford, and unlike herself had kept in touch with the old university crowd. Eventually, she said, 'Maybe I'd have a flat by now if I hadn't had Maisy.'

Nazneen turned on her with sudden, startling anger. 'Of course, you're one of those people who seem to think that having a child is the *only* worthwhile thing for a woman to do.'

Taken aback, Hannah said, 'I don't. A lot of the time, it's totally boring.'

'And you feel superior, don't you, to women like me?'

Hannah looked at her – the tailored taupe suit, the white silk blouse and immaculate haircut – then down at her own worn jeans and faded T-shirt. She smiled, wryly.

'I'm wearing the only clean clothes I have, and they've got holes in. So do my trainers. My hair is a mess. I don't know how I'm going to pay my rent next month. How am I superior?'

'Because that's what my family says,' said Nazneen. 'Why aren't I giving them grandchildren? Why aren't I bringing home any nice boys? What's *wrong* with me? And on and on.'

Hannah saw that her friend, too, was unhappy, and her eyes filled with tears.

'Naz, what you're doing is important too. Really important. To be a lawyer, or a doctor or something professional is ... You've got a future that isn't just biology.' She wiped her eyes, humiliated. 'You have made your life, and it's a good one. Maybe you'll meet someone, and maybe you won't – but what matters is that this is *your* life, not theirs. I don't feel superior to you, I admire you.'

Nazneen sighed, and the harshness left her face. 'I admire you too, you know, Hannah. I couldn't possibly do what you've done.'

They gripped hands.

'I had one shot, and I threw it away. I mean, I wouldn't be without Maisy now, but if she hadn't come along ... I don't know if Jake would have left, but—'

'Hannah, do you need money?' Nazneen said. 'Because I can give you some. Not as a loan, just to help.'

She shook her head; though of course she did.

'I'm OK. Really. It's done me good just to talk to you.'

If only she had stayed in proper employment just three more years, enough to get a solid CV. Such a stupid mistake, as if she didn't live in an age of contraception and choice. And now she had lost her best and dearest friend, her mother.

Hannah remembered the first night she had come home from hospital, in agony from the birth and the stitches in her groin, to find that her baby would only cry and cry and cry. That noise had gone through her like a jet-engine taking off with all her freedom on board. It had been bad enough for Jake, who at least got away from it at work, but for her those early days had been an unending torment of guilt, fear, adoration and bewilderment. People without babies feared the torrents of shit, but people with them knew that it was the loss of sleep and liberty that was the real torture. Jake tried to help, but he didn't understand that this was the new normal, for ever. She thought she would go crazy until Holly had driven up to see her grand-daughter and found her own daughter still in her pyjamas in the afternoon, sobbing, and the infant Maisy howling.

'Don't worry, my lovely, you're going to be fine,' Holly had said, and she had turned round within the hour and driven the pair of them back to Cornwall for two months, giving up her own bed, and rest, so that Hannah could heal. It was the greatest thing her mother had ever done for her, and Hannah often wondered how she would have coped without it. From then on, all summers had been spent at St Piran.

'I can't give her a Cornish childhood, but I can give her the next best thing,' Holly had said.

Jake had visited, at least the first two summers, but after that it had always just been Hannah and Maisy. She'd lied that her husband was too busy at work, and her mother never questioned it.

'You're a city person now, I suppose,' Holly said once. 'Always busy.'

The bungalow was filled with stuff Hannah knew too well and had spent many years disliking: the Pleather sofa and armchair, the old wool blankets that her mother went on using despite everyone else having duvets, the drooping spider plants by the window, melamine plates, blue toilet bleach and jars of nameless slime. No wonder so many cultures burnt people with their possessions. How would it ever be cleared? She would never see her mother again, never talk to her, hear her laugh, touch her hands or smell her special smell, and yet somehow these ugly things had survived her. She would always think of her when she saw holly, or bit into a crisp green apple; she would think of her when she saw Maisy's cheekbones and heard her laugh. Guilt added to her sorrow, for her mother must have been lonely and frightened, dying, and she had not been able to speak to her.

Yet the truth was that Hannah couldn't have afforded to take a month off work, or to plunge further into debt on her credit card. Even with Jake paying the rent, and £120 a month in child maintenance, there was food, heating, council tax, water, broadband, Maisy's shoes and the many things that needed to be covered just to have permission to live. All of these she had to earn through hard labour, cleaning other people's homes. She was under no illusions that, were she to find a cheaper rental, she'd get more money from her husband; on the contrary, it would cost her a great deal to move, and most private landlords wouldn't accept a tenant like her anyway. She lived in terror of eviction, and in even more of becoming homeless.

You've had a free ride . . .

If only, Hannah thought.

7

A Slum in the Sky

She dreaded returning to London, where even a used bag from a posh shop felt like a necessary lie.

'Do you mind if I take that?' she'd ask, seeing one in the recycling. Her employers didn't understand that a bright yellow bag from Selfridges or even a green and white plastic one from Waitrose made the difference between appearing respectable, and not. People with everything laughed at being anxious over appearances, but that was because they had no need for them. Hannah hated St Piran and hated being poor. The more she saw of Fol, the more she understood what was wrong about the way she lived. She had seen this even as a child.

'Can't we just have white lights?' Hannah would beg every Christmas.

'Don't be silly, Han,' her mother always answered. 'Why have white when you could have rainbows?'

Holly had unerring bad taste. If there was a choice

between two objects she could afford, the one that was fussy, inelegant and superfluous always won. Even her name was embarrassing. All Hannah's relations were given proper Cornish names, but her mother had been born on Christmas Day, and so, of course, was called Holly. But why hadn't she called her daughter something romantic like Demelza or Endellion? Hannah, humiliated by everything, was mortified even by this. As soon as she escaped, she told herself, she would make a life of her own, the way she wanted it to be.

The flat in the Castle Estate had all kinds of things wrong with it when they first moved in, including a smoke alarm that didn't work, and rats, but it represented what both she and Jake longed for above all: independence in London.

'Fantastic location,' said the agent.

'Buy-to-let is the only show in town,' the owner remarked. 'Not that I need to tell a couple of young professionals like yourselves that, do I?'

It was by no means the worst rental property they had looked at, but still pretty bad. Doors were warped like damp cardboard and the toilet (separate from the bathroom) had no basin. The walls were painted the colour of lard, and electric cables looped and snagged round skirtings. The ceilings were low and the windows, though double-glazed, had frames of white PVC just like those in Hannah's mother's house. The only furniture was a pine double bed, with broken slats and a thin mattress, and a shallow MDF cupboard. The gas and electricity had to be fed with a card. It had once been quite a spacious three-bedroomed flat, but the owner had carved it into two to make it more profitable, and this was let to students.

Jake called it 'a slum in the sky', although in those days he said it with irony. The difference was that to Jake the discomfort was a form of tourism, whereas to Hannah it was a chance to show that living in a council ('ex-council', Jake reminded her) property did not mean living without style.

It was true that their neighbours were not like themselves, though initially their only contact had been when one of them, speaking in a heavy Asian accent, rang the buzzer to complain about Hannah hammering in picture hooks at 9 p.m. because his child was trying to sleep. She apologised profusely, but Jake was furious.

'You don't want to upset chavs,' he said. 'They turn their dogs on you if things get nasty. Council house and violent, you know.'

'Hey, I grew up on a council estate. They're just people like me and you, Jake.'

He answered, 'The sooner we're out of here, the better.'

It was in an ugly building, looking out on to other ugly buildings, a place where generations of Irish, Greek, Spanish, Caribbean, Bangladeshi, Pakistani and Somali immigrants had congregated for want of anywhere better. However, the flat itself was full of light. Even the wood laminate floors were a lot less bad than the wall-to-wall carpet-tiles and lino she had grown up with. She rejoiced in the space, the privacy, the fact that with two starter salaries it was easily affordable.

'We can change it. A room is just an empty box. We can redecorate.'

'The landlord will have a fit.'

'He won't even notice.'

Hannah had learnt a good deal from her Uncle Kit, a builder, plumber and decorator. Jake, though unable to use a screwdriver, was a willing pair of extra hands. The walls were now the soft cream colour that is produced by a half-and-half mixture of magnolia and white trade emulsion, and the low ceilings made to look higher with plain polystyrene coving that, once painted white, improved the proportions. She tacked the electric cable to the skirting, put up red roller-blinds above the squat windows to make them look taller and tiled on top of the bumpy bathroom tiles with smooth white ones. She even plumbed in a narrow sink beside the toilet. The black mould on the ceiling had been scrubbed away with diluted bleach and hot water, the chipboard kitchen units given navy-painted doors and kick-plates. It looked and smelt clean.

'It can all be changed back, if need be.'

'You've worked miracles, babes.'

Jake's respect and enthusiasm were reward enough. At such moments she saw the boy he might have been – affectionate, spontaneous, innocent, good-hearted – before he had been sent to prep school.

She blamed his mother for burying this; but then Etta was an Evenlode, a member of a minor aristocratic family of which Jake was immensely proud. Tall, pin-thin and immaculately dressed, she arrived at their door with her face stiff with endurance beneath hair frozen in its blonde-grey curl.

'Darlings, you are brave!'

The flat was inspected with determined interest, its geographical location declared 'very convenient'.

'I don't really know north of Harley Street. Kentish Town, hmm. It's the sort of place where villains in John Buchan live, isn't it?'

'Mummy, that was a hundred years ago. Now it's got Anima e Cuore, the best Italian restaurant in town.'

'It looks bad, but its food is amazing,' said Hannah shyly.

'Marvellous! Let's go there.'

'You can't. It's always booked up for weeks in advance.'

'What a shame,' Etta said, touching her pearl necklace. 'Well, I can see you've both been very busy here.'

'Han has. I've just been the slave labour.'

Every day, they scrambled into their shiny new professional selves, convincing older people that they were serious, talented and worth their salaries. Hannah particularly liked her boss, Ali Gold. She had been the one who interviewed Hannah during the milk round and was now the agency's senior strategist.

'We are the people who straddle the business and creative sides in advertising,' she told Hannah. 'We're about merging emotion and logic, dreaming and doing, theory and reality. I think you have potential because although you've spent three years studying, you have experience of doing all the menial, practical jobs that too many students avoid. I'm not interested in applicants with a Duke of Edinburgh Gold Medal or a week's work experience in Daddy's company. I want imagination plus graft.'

Glamorous, robust, witty and maternal, Ali was her first encounter with the professional classes, whose members Hannah looked at with aspiration. She seemed to have travelled everywhere, read everything, seen everything and now lived in a large semi-detached house in Highbury with her husband and twins.

'She's rumoured to have taken client calls even while in labour,' Hannah was told.

Ali, like herself, had come from humble beginnings, though she had gone to Oxford. She had no time for either philistinism or pretension. When Hannah said something about the absence of poetry in business, Ali retorted, 'There's nothing wrong with making money. Just you remember that the Renaissance was founded on banking and the discovery of double-entry book-keeping. Art needs money, and money needs art, and both need advertising.'

In those early days, everyone in advertising seemed pleasant and interesting; even the creatives' habit of snorting cocaine before meetings was accepted as cool. But when the Christmas party (which lasted from 10 a.m. until 6 a.m. the following day) came along, Hannah saw a different side.

'Be careful,' Ali told her. 'Just don't let any of the seniors get you in a room alone.'

'What about the CEO?'

'Especially not him.'

Hannah was soon experiencing levels of harassment of a kind she had never known, even as a barmaid. Middle-aged men plunged their hands up her blouse and down her trousers, slapped her bottom and told her that she could serve them a cream tea any time. The evening meetings in top restaurants and clubs were an opportunity for more comments and groping, and when Hannah objected, she was told to stop being prissy.

'You're not on campus now, sweetheart,' one man told her.

Hannah was appalled.

'Is it just me, or does "We're all one big happy family here" sound sinister?'

Jake said, 'Flirting doesn't mean anything.'

'Haven't you noticed how most of the young women leave the agency?'

'They probably get better offers,' he answered. 'Anyway, people know not to mess with you because you're my girlfriend.'

It was true that everyone in the agency (which prided

itself on being known in the business for 'hunting, shooting and advertising') seemed to know about his relations. The younger men were slightly better but those over forty all seemed to regard female staff as fair game. Hannah tried everything, from chewing a clove of raw garlic to keeping a record to show to HR. None of it helped. Men who were affable, sensible colleagues to other men believed that they were Don Draper to her.

'I'm afraid you have to grow a thicker skin,' said Ali, when confided in. 'Grit your teeth and think of being able to afford a home of your own in seven years.'

Hannah half-laughed. 'I have about as much hope of that as I do of winning the lottery.'

'I know, it's tough for you Millennials,' Ali said. 'Be patient. We couldn't buy until we were thirty.'

'I don't think I'll be able to buy even a studio until I'm fifty.'

Still, being able to rent a flat to themselves made up for a lot. Inevitably, it was Hannah who raced round when she got back, tidying, cleaning, ironing shirts and cooking. Jake had never been good at the domestic side of life, but he did try, and Hannah was in the grip of a nesting instinct so strong that she could not quite understand it herself.

'Look, the nasturtium seeds we planted are flowering!'

'Can we eat them or are they just to look at?'

'Both.'

Whether they would eventually buy together was not broached. Theirs was a modern relationship, in which either party was free to go. If Jake wanted to take off for weekends to cycle or go rock-climbing with his mates, he went.

'There are three of us in this relationship, and one is a bicycle,' Hannah said. She felt that if she gave him maximum freedom, he would want to return to her.

One mystery to her was that, no matter how hard she worked, she always earned less than Jake. She discovered this quite by accident.

'How come you get an extra £600 a year? We're both graduate trainees.'

'I don't know. Ask them for more.'

She didn't dare. She lived between two worlds, at ease in neither. Every so often, Jake's sister would audibly mock her accent, while her Cornish family told her that she sounded 'posh'.

After two years, Jake moved to another firm for more money; Hannah stayed. They worked long hours, but with two salaries and a small raise, felt rich. Foreign holidays and bottles of wine became almost normal. The rent crept up by another £20 a week, then another £20; they were too busy to look elsewhere.

'We're like those squirrels in the tree opposite, running up and down,' Hannah said. She liked to watch them, in the one bit of green her eyes could rest on in all the concrete and tarmac. 'If we had a giant hamster wheel, we could power the whole block.'

It was not easy, however. With Jake gone from her agency, the groping immediately increased. Balding, red-faced men told her that they thought they'd 'be a good match'. One told her, 'Do you think, when I could hire anyone, that I don't hire girls I can fuck?'

Shaken, Hannah's reaction was to work even harder and to dress as plainly as possible. She tried to make allies among other young women, talking to them under cover of the noise from the hand-dryers in the toilets, but one by one they left, signing Non-Disclosure Agreements. Her nickname was 'Boadicea' for insisting that using models in underwear to sell everything from ovens to vitamins was not a good strategy.

The CEO of the company took her out to lunch and said, 'I'm trying to help you out here, Hannah. Stop being so shrill. A strategist is all about instinct. What are your instincts telling you?'

He smiled at her, and the smooth, slightly heavy face she had believed to be kindly became that of a satyr.

When she complained again to HR, she was told she was imagining it all. Increasingly, she spent her lunchbreaks (all fifteen minutes of them) sitting in the loo, crying. The perks of her job included gym membership, massage, expense accounts; now she was invited for a session with a therapist to see whether she was losing her mind. She was asked about her family background, and naively told her inquisitor about being the child of a single parent. The conclusion shocked her.

'Your psychological problems are making it difficult for colleagues to work with you. Maybe it's because you never knew your father.'

That summer, Hannah tried to ask her mother to at least tell her the name of her father. Holly, usually so kind and calm, almost bit her head off.

'Ask me no questions and I'll tell you no lies. It's none of your business.'

On many mornings Jake walked her to the bus stop like a prisoner.

'I don't know how long I can go on taking this.'

'Just suck it up for a bit, and it'll blow over. Loads of graduate trainees get this.'

'Do you?'

'I learnt to look after myself at school,' he said.

What did she know? There were other Durham graduates from their year in London, all embarking on fledgling careers, and being in their early to mid-twenties they drifted together in a superficially friendly mass, meeting for parties, pub crawls and picnics in the park.

It was after one of these, walking past the heavily scented white blossoms of mock orange, that Hannah said, with trepidation, 'Jake, I have some news.'

She was pregnant. How it had happened was a mystery: but they were young and maybe she had forgotten, just once, to take the Pill.

Hannah was prepared to have an abortion, but instead Jake said, 'Why don't we get married?'

'Really?'

Jake went down on one knee on the pavement with a flourish.

'Miss Hannah Penrose, I am asking you to marry me.'

Hannah was conscious that she had never loved him so much as at this moment. She had sometimes wondered whether he loved her as she did him, but here was the proof of it. He was sacrificing his independence in order to save her from the fate that had almost destroyed her own mother.

Still, she said, 'We don't have to rush into this, Jakey. Mum told me so many times how hard it was for her.'

'But that was because *she* wasn't married,' he said. She could see him falling in love with his own nobility. 'You've got me, babes, and you've got a job with maternity leave. You don't want to be one of those awful career women, waiting until your eggs have withered, do you?'

Hannah thought of Ali Gold, whose agonies with IVF she had been told all about. 'No.'

She did not have morning-sickness but became tired.

He showed a new gentleness and consideration, signing them up to Ocado so that she wouldn't have to carry heavy shopping bags, buying her books about babies and childbirth and ringing her every day from work. He looked more like King Arthur than ever, pacing the third floor of John Lewis with his golden head deep in conference with the sales team. They began talking more seriously about finding a home of their own but help with a deposit was hopeless as far as Hannah's family was concerned, and Jake refused to ask his.

'They have the money, of course, but then my mother would have won.'

Hannah did not quite understand what the war between Jake and Etta was about, but of course sided with her future husband. She had not forgotten their sneers. Etta's excitement over the prospect of her first grandchild was something that Jake regarded with grim satisfaction.

'They can fuck right off,' he said. 'I'll get my trust fund when I'm thirty.'

Hannah had only the vaguest idea what a trust fund was until he explained that it was what had paid for his expensive education, and that there would be enough left over for a flat, provided property prices didn't go up too fast. It sounded like something out of the Victorian novels she loved, but this was one of the many differences between them.

'Imagine an actual *home*,' Hannah said, longingly. 'With a garden.'

'I'm not going to let her win,' Jake said.

Hannah persuaded herself that she would continue to work just as before only with a beaming infant balanced on her hip. Her boss regarded her with concern on being told the news.

'Have you thought how you're going to keep working? You're a good strategist, but this is very early in your career. You need to have a plan – several plans, in fact, because nothing about children goes as expected. Remember, it's all about how to direct resources to make the biggest impact. And don't, whatever you do, give up work.'

'It can't be that difficult, can it?'

'You have no idea,' said Ali.

'Are you sure you really want this?' Nazneen asked. Hannah had asked her to be a bridesmaid at their wedding, but Naz had refused, saying that as a Muslim she could not be part of a Christian ceremony. (Hannah, who remembered how her friend had enjoyed the carol services at Durham Cathedral, wondered at this.)

'Yes, I do, I really do.'

'Then congratulations; I'm happy for you both.'

They decided to get married at Jake's family home in Middlesex, as they had a large garden which could accommodate a marquee for 120 guests. It was all to be very traditional, an Anglican ceremony in the village church followed by a wedding breakfast, and if Hannah had secretly wished for the chapel at St Piran, she knew she could not possibly invite the Arabellas and Sebastians of Jake's world to The Jolly Lobster after. The obvious solution of asking his mother's parents if they might be married in Cornwall, was the last thing he wanted, and in the event Lord and Lady Evenlode declined to attend on the grounds of ill-health. Loveday was one of the only people from her old life, alongside her mother, her cousin Mor (who was one of her bridesmaids, and by far the prettiest) and Mr Kenward, who gave her away.

The wedding, organised by Etta, went smoothly but Saskia

remarked after it, 'To think that of all Jake's girlfriends, he chose *you!*'

Hannah felt as if she had been slapped. She told herself now that she had done nothing wrong, except to fall in love with the wrong person, but even she could not be sure, because of what she had absorbed from Jane Austen. What she knew for certain was that she had offered him an escape, and he had not taken it. He had risen to the occasion – and she had sunk.

But the rich are different precisely because they have more choices. People loved to pretend they were above money, that it was sordid and evil – but it was only so if you lacked it.

If I had just £1000 I could afford a lawyer to fight my case, Hannah thought, staring out the window as the countryside rewound itself back to London. If I had £5000 I could move flat. If I had £10,000, I could pay off my debts. Every £5000 was another rung in the ladder that was missing. Rent was what was draining the life-blood from her generation. In every part of the developed world, housing had become a problem, but now the city that, ten years ago, had prided itself on being the international leader had become a place of sink-holed streets, buckling bridges and burning tower blocks. She was returning without anything but the knowledge of her mother's death and the ignorance of her father's identity.

It was close to midnight when she got back, but she raced up the dirty concrete stairs to knock on Lila's door, after texting her. Lila would never answer the door unless she knew who was on the other side.

'Sorry I'm so late,' she whispered. 'I had a lot to do for the funeral.'

Lila's face scrunched up with sympathy. 'It's fine. Maisy's asleep.'

The flat was stiflingly hot. She opened Maisy's window and her own, trying to create a draught. The air smelt vile.

Her plants on the tiny balcony were all wilting. Hannah went around frantically watering them, laying the table for breakfast, trying to prepare for the next school day, trying to brace herself. A siren wailed up Kentish Town high street, and the orange streetlamps throbbed like a headache in the plane tree opposite.

But the bunch of Stan's roses filled the room with scent. It was years since she'd had any, but she remembered how to arrange them, an inch of stems cut off with a sharp knife, all the foliage stripped off below each bloom, and never an even number in the vase. They fell into a beautiful shape, even as they were dying.

What an odd man, she thought again; but then Coad himself must be strange too, if he were as rich as Jinni claimed yet lived in such a ruin. She itched to Google him, but hesitated. Even if she were to go incognito online, she had an uneasy feeling that it might be traceable by the police if anything were to happen to him. Surely, the plan she and Jinni had hatched would fall away now that she hadn't done her own part?

The electric buzz of the city grated against her eyeballs. She must try to rest, because of the next day and the next day and the next day. London was all about work. On her way to bed, she picked up the mail. Among the fliers for deep-pan pizza, a small padded envelope lay on the mat.

Puzzled, she opened it.

Inside was a chunky old Nokia mobile.

She knew at once who it was from, even without the printed slip.

TURN ME ON.

8

A Space in Which to Think

Hannah stared at the mobile as if it could explode.

How had it arrived in her flat? She was sure she had not given Jinni her address, but then she had told Jinni her surname and so anyone could find her on the electoral register. But to gain access to the block, which had a special entry-pad with a fob and post it directly into her flat door was frightening. Had it been delivered earlier, or just now? She looked through the spyhole at the landing. There was nobody.

Hannah's stomach roiled.

It was one thing, after all, to discuss how much they each wished to be widows, and even to accept the Taser. It was one thing to trick her way into Coad's house. This, however ... This was *insisting* she commit a murder. If she turned on the mobile, then what had been a fantasy would advance another stage, and another, until there would be no going back.

But do I want to turn back? Hannah thought.

Sometimes she could see sanity as if it were a cliff, where the turf curls back from the stone like the lip from a snarling dog, giving way to empty air and black jagged places. To resist madness and despair seemed to take almost all her reserves of energy, just as looking after Maisy took all her reserves of patience. There might be a gorgeousness to abandoning all responsibility and caution. Yet caution was what dogged her every thought and action now that she was a mother.

Hannah considered dropping the mobile to smash on the concrete below. If she destroyed it right now, the temptation would be stopped. That would be the sensible thing to do; yet she hesitated.

She was curious. Very little in her present life was interesting or exciting, apart from her daughter, yet from the moment she had stepped out of the overcrowded train carriage into First Class, things had changed. Someone had listened to her story. Jinni was the most intriguing person she had met in years. Being with her, talking to her, had made her feel as if she were living again.

In many respects, she was lucky. She didn't have to deliver meals on a motorbike or work shifts in a nursing home, and although she had no job security, sick-pay or holiday leave, the going rate for a cleaner in Kentish Town was £12 an hour, cash, with a week off over Christmas. The work was tiring, repetitive and isolating, but she had a degree of mental freedom. On the other hand, if she made a call on hands-free while vacuuming or ironing, it was looked on with disfavour, as if her labour must include complete subservience.

'Can you make your calls in your own time, please?' said one employer sharply, when Hannah had been trying to deal with her mother's illness. She was supposed to be a domestic machine without thoughts or feelings or sensation. She could never be ill and must work even when bent double from period pains.

The cash she earned never went into her bank account, but it was vital to survival. Armed only with her yellow Marigold gloves, Hannah trudged all over Camden, Islington and Highgate, hoping each home would be properly equipped with the right detergents and e-cloths, longing for professional steam irons that helped save her back and arms, wrestling with vacuum cleaners that coiled like snakes and toilet brushes with moulting bristles. She felt herself becoming bitter and hard as she flushed away her youth. Sometimes she would sing, under her breath,

> *A good sword and a trusty hand*
> *A merry heart and true*
> *King James's men shall understand*
> *What Cornish men can do.*
> *And have they fixed the where and when?*
> *And shall Trelawny die?*
> *Here's twenty thousand Cornish men*
> *Will know the reason why.*

It always cheered her to think of the Cornish standing up to the King in London for their unjustly imprisoned compatriot and marching across the Tamar to free him from the Tower. But nobody now had the spirit or energy for protest about anything. Her generation might be roused to protest about Trump, or Brexit, but not about their own lives. She felt she had fallen very low and could fall even further, and the fear made her shrink inside herself, like a snail whose fragile shell could be crushed by any passing weight. Every day on her way to and from work, she passed people begging or sleeping in doorways. Armies of people like Lila still cleaned offices at night, for less than the minimum wage after their agency had taken its cut. To them, the idea that someone from Cornwall might also feel underprivileged would have seemed absurd ... All her relations had voted Leave. Here, they were derided as ignorant bigots, but the problems were still there.

Meanwhile, there was the burner phone.

Hannah shoved it into the bottom of that saggy, shapeless bag all mothers of young children carry, a kind of kangaroo pouch containing everything from a sewing kit to a box of raisins. The pink Taser was still there, too. What should she do next? She'd heard of animals that chewed off their own paws to escape traps. Ever since Maisy was born, Hannah had felt herself become two people: the good mother who organised everything, and the woman silently screaming and raking her nails down the walls. Sometimes she heard her employers complaining to friends that 'effectively, I am a single mother', and it made her want to say, 'Why don't you try my life, then, just for one day? Why don't you try living on one tiny income, and doing *absolutely everything on your own*?'

The smallest things could derail her. She was obsessively careful with money while also seeing her credit card debt rise due to a hundred unforeseen circumstances. Whenever she could, she smuggled in a bag of her own laundry to wash at an employer's because it saved her £4 a month on electricity. When alone in the house, she would lock the shower-room door and quickly wash herself and her hair, for the same reason. She hated doing this, but still walked along with her gaze fixed on the pavement in case anyone should have dropped some loose change.

Many of her worst struggles revolved around eating. A few months after Jake left, she lost her shame about using food banks, even if their tins and packets were hard to make appetising. It wasn't just the young who were using them, but a number of middle-aged people whose pensions had somehow been delayed an extra seven years by the government, and the disabled denied benefits because they were deemed fit for work. She knew better than most how to manage because she still had a functioning cooker, even though it had to be pre-paid to work. A big bag of oatmeal could be turned into porridge or, when baked with sugar and marge, flapjacks. Pasta sauce made from an onion, carrots, a tin of tomatoes and a stock cube could thicken into stew if flour, potatoes and leeks were added. With pastry, it could become a pie. She bagged up the out-of-date fruit and vegetables that were being thrown away by her employers and haunted the cheapest supermarkets just before closing time, pouncing on a bag of frozen chicken wings because Maisy had to have meat. Even a wilting lettuce could go into a soup or sauce. Every meal was a test of determination and ingenuity. She was thinner than she had ever been, but she and Maisy ate hot meals.

Jake, exasperated, said, 'Why don't you get off your arse and try copywriting? You could be earning twenty quid an hour as a freelance instead of sponging off me.'

'I don't have the time to even look.'

Hannah was too ashamed to tell him she had returned to cleaning, the final mortification. She had, in fact, done her best to get work as a freelance, but the work was so erratic that she couldn't rely on it. She was a strategist, not a copywriter, and she dreaded returning to the predatory sexism she had encountered before. The only thing she could rely on was what she had done previously: cleaning.

Even those jobs hadn't been easy to get, but by means of leafleting every house within a mile radius, Hannah had found clients. Most lived only a couple of blocks away, but on the other side of the gulf that was the high street, and they belonged to the professional world she could only see at night, before curtains were drawn: those terraced and semi-detached Victorian houses that had been built for the humblest kind of clerk or book-keeper but which were now, with their high corniced ceilings, sash windows and garden, worth well over £1.5 million, and rising. Everyone wanted one of these, and so the most modest dwellings had been stretched and excavated and dissected, transformed into bigger houses or smaller flats. Nothing was more desirable or more durable than bricks and mortar; only investors from the Far East bought the shiny steel and glass high-rise apartments built as deposit-boxes in the sky, because they did not understand history and, besides, nobody lived in them. The continual flow of foreign money into the capital was carrying the city further and further away from the lives of its ordinary inhabitants with their ordinary earnings, and the foreign labour that made much of this possible only added to it.

'I thought you'd be Polish,' said the first woman who employed her. 'I've never had an English cleaner.'

'Well, I'm Cornish,' said Hannah, trying not to sound truculent.

'You don't smoke, do you?'

'Never have, never will.'

'Any references?'

Hannah had never expected to need them. 'Here.'

The woman nodded distractedly. 'Fine. I don't care, provided you save us from our filth. I'm Polly, by the way.'

Polly was a lawyer, and she helped Hannah get a job

cleaning for another neighbour, Katie, a magazine editor, and with Katie's colleague Sebastian and his partner Justin, both in Islington. Katie had a toddler, whom Hannah sometimes babysat on a Friday night because she could put her own child to sleep on the sofa and push her home in the buggy that at four, then five years old, she still just fitted into. It was worth carrying Maisy back up the three flights of stairs on the Castle Estate at midnight to get another £25.

Other clients used her, but she barely saw them. Polly was the only one who, because she worked from home sometimes and Hannah was in her house twice a week for six hours at a time she dared ask if it would be all right to have a short break for food and drink. Of course it was, and Polly also passed on her own copy of the *Observer* and the *Sunday Times* on Mondays, before the bin collection came.

'Does your little girl enjoy looking at the pictures?'

'Yes,' Hannah said, not wishing to say that she read the newspapers herself.

But there were other, altogether less pleasant employers.

'Take that expression off your face,' said one, who saw her reaction after he had struck his son for breaking a bowl. 'How dare you look at me like that?'

Others followed her round, pointing out any cobwebs she had missed; some screamed at her.

'You've broken the Dyson, you silly girl,' said one woman in Islington. 'Don't come back.'

As a cleaner, she was expected to be all-seeing, yet inaudible and invisible. Even though she went into other people's houses and dealt with the detritus of their private lives, exchanges with other adults were mostly things like, 'We need more laundry tablets' or 'There's a stain on the stair carpet'.

'Every woman who cleans other people's homes for a living goes crazy,' said one client. 'I don't care if you're bi-polar, anorexic or find God, as long as you don't steal and remember to wipe the skirtings.'

It was the sort of thing they felt entitled to come out with.

She cared for the furniture that she would never own: deep sofas upholstered in velvet; inlaid tables; linen sheets; tall, button-backed headboards; bamboo towels and heavy glass doors opening on to decking and semi-tropical plants. Each house, with its engineered wooden floors, its spiralisers and coffeemakers, was curiously alike, affluence layered on affluence like polish on furniture. Taking in the Ocado delivery, scouring the bath and mowing the grass was part of it; she vacuumed and mopped and wiped until her back felt like breaking, always quiet and polite.

Hannah knew how soundly her clients slept, how often they had sex, how well their bowels functioned, how frequently they changed their clothes, what they ate, what they read, where they banked and even what (if any) pornography they watched. A ghost in the house of capitalism, she was supposed to live without needs. Even Polly didn't understand that when she went away in winter and turned off the heating to save on energy bills, it meant Hannah had to toil in a house as cold as a tomb. What Hannah did was a job, but because it was domestic work, the women who employed her were ashamed of not doing it themselves, even though this was plainly impossible if they had careers.

'I don't have time to clean my own home,' Polly said. 'No man would expect to.'

'Do you work out?' Polly's daughter Tania asked her once, seeing her bare arms.

'No, I just work,' Hannah answered shortly.

Hannah worked five days a week, six hours a day. Then she collected Maisy and went back to the flat to feed, comfort, entertain and encourage her child to believe that she could do or be anybody she wished.

Every so often, her mother-in-law came to visit, bringing silly soft toys and frilly dresses for Maisy. The last time had been when Holly was still alive. Hannah had not mentioned the illness; withholding information felt like the only way she could keep some dignity.

'I am sorry about what has happened with Jake,' Etta said. 'But please don't let our granddaughter grow up without knowing us. She's the only one we have.'

She looked so unhappy that Hannah almost relented. But then she thought, If you really cared, you'd make your son pay what he owes us. That was all she wanted – not gifts, not riches, just what was fair. Yet her pride and mistrust lay on her tongue like a scold's bridle.

'Do you have any coffee?' Etta asked.

'Sorry, tea is all I have,' Hannah would say.

Even if she did tell her how desperate matters were, what could Etta do? Jake was an adult, and this was his responsibility. But another part of Hannah could not help blaming her mother-in-law for his selfishness. It is a parent's first duty to keep a child safe, and it is their second duty to educate us into better versions of ourselves. Etta was incapable of having any real conversation with her children, skating on the surface of life with her long legs, without any apparent thought of the murky depths below.

'You Millennials!' said Etta archly. 'I suppose you're spending it all on avocado toasts.'

Hannah once tested Etta's grasp of the real world by asking her what she thought the minimum wage was and had been told it was £80,000 a year. As if! At least she didn't bring Jake's sister with her when she visited. Saskia was married now, too, to a property developer. (Hannah had been invited to their wedding but declined.) There were no children, and allusions to 'difficulties' with fertility. Etta looked at her granddaughter with yearning.

'If you ever need a break looking after her—'

'Sorry,' Hannah answered. 'She's too little.'

'How is she doing at school? You're sending her to the local primary, Jake says.'

'She's fine.'

One afternoon, soon after her mother's death, she had a visit from the landlord, Tod. There was no warning, not even a text. He was standing in the kitchen when they got back from Maisy's school. Hannah almost fainted from shock.

'What are you doing here?'

'Your rent's late, darlin',' he said. 'Two weeks.'

They both knew he was breaking the law by letting himself in without twenty-four hours' notice, but she was a world away from the professional of nine years ago.

'I'm sorry, my husband must have forgotten. I'll get on to him.'

'If you don't pay up in the next week, you're out,' he said.

Tod didn't need to make any threats. Lila told her he was a minor gangster, though it might just have been his shaved head and gold jewellery that gave this impression. He was known to have bought up four of the council flats in the estate as buy-to-lets. The three-bedroomed flat above Hannah's, where the annual turnover of UCL students lived, was another one of his. Every year she heard the same complaints about it echoing up the stairwell, but they had parents who could force him to buy them new mattresses and mend broken washing machines in return for an exorbitant rent. When they had parties or played loud music after midnight, nobody rang their bell.

'I'll make sure.'

Tod leered and said, 'There are plenty of ways a young woman like yourself could pay me back.'

Hannah flushed with anger. 'I'll remind my husband today.'

'Fine. But if it's not paid, you're out.'

The first thing she did after he'd gone was to call Lila. The sounds of her friend's gentle knock on the door felt like rescue, though all she could do was sympathise.

Hannah found she was shaking with fear and fury.

'Oh, Lila! It was horrible. He was suggesting I – you know – with him.'

'What a creep.'

Lila had moved into the flat across the landing with an elderly woman she called her auntie when Maisy was three; it suited them both because of the bedroom tax, and by the time her own daughter Bella was old enough to need a room of her own the auntie had died. Whether she was a real aunt or not was unclear, but she had given Lila the refuge she most needed when she fled her husband Ahmed.

'I just don't know what to do,' Hannah said, trembling.

'He can't throw you out,' Lila said. 'You're a single mother; you're only late with one payment. You have rights.'

'I think Tod could put me out on the street any time. I'm a private tenant.'

'Tell your ex. He's got the money, hasn't he?'

'Yes, but he won't give me enough. '

She texted Jake, increasingly desperate messages. No reply. Then, on the following Friday, he rang the buzzer.

'Is Maisy ready?'

Hannah said on the intercom, 'You can't take her until you've paid the rent, Jake.'

'You've got to be kidding.'

'No, I'm not.'

A stream of filthy language was shouted over the intercom, in between leaning on the buzzer. Maisy began wailing. Hannah said fiercely, 'Put your fingers in your ears, sweetie, and go to your room.'

When Jake stopped his tirade, she said, 'All you're doing is making your daughter frightened. Go and get our rent money out from a cashpoint.'

'I can't get that amount out in one go.'

'Yes, you can. You have at least two cards, you can take £600 out on each. It's £1200, in case you've forgotten.'

'Ask me nicely.'

She counted to ten. 'I am asking nicely.'

The only card she held was that he loved their daughter. She hated using this against him, but what else could she do? The loving father and the hating husband were like two different people. He didn't see that she was poor because he didn't wish to see. The kind of family he had grown up with, the sort who genuinely believed the minimum wage was £80,000 a year, could not conceive of a life that was different from their own. Jake had once lived on the earnings of a graduate trainee, but now he must be on four or five times that amount, and the more he earned the worse he behaved. All the patience and kindness he had shown when she was pregnant had vanished. He could lose his temper in a flash, clapping his hands sharply and loudly as if she were his slave, before sneering at her for being neurotic, stupid, inattentive, fat and (of course) low born. She had used the depreciating assets of her youth to trap him when he had been naïve and immature, and his reward for doing the decent thing in marrying her was that she would have her hooks into him for ever. On and on and on it went, and all she could do was keep silent and suffer. When in a real rage, he would attack her, apparently on impulse but always so that he left no mark. These experiences were so appalling that she tried to forget them as soon as they occurred; it was what he said that hurt most. How could he look on their daughter with such devotion and never remember who had brought her into the world with so much blood and effort? How could he not see that Maisy was half of her as well?

'She's too small for her age. Why don't you give her more meat?'

'Because I can't afford it.'

'Bollocks. You're just a terrible mother.'

Hatred seethed in her veins as milk had once done in her breasts. Had Hannah been able to keep Jake away from Maisy for ever, she would have; but she needed his money. It made her feel like a whore, and yet she would even have had sex with him if he'd demanded it in exchange: not that he did; not now he had Eve.

Sometimes, Hannah wondered whether Eve knew what kind of man she was sleeping with. Presumably, Jake was as charming and gentle as he had once been to her. Or perhaps he had changed; perhaps his violence reflected a much darker strain of sexuality. She couldn't begin to guess, just hoped that her successor was wiser and better defended than herself.

Ten minutes later, he returned with a roll of cash. Still she wouldn't open the door to the building.

'Post it through the letter flap so I can count it.'

'How do I know you can be trusted?'

'Let me think: because I'm not like you?'

'Bitch.'

Hannah took the money up to her flat to count it. She had made herself completely cold and hard in order not to let him get to her, and her hands did not even shake. Even so, she was taut as a hawser. She could feel her neighbours listening on the other side of their own doors all the way up the stairwell. Later, she knew, they would complain to her about the noise and bad language, and she would have to apologise as if it were her fault, though most of them probably knew her situation thanks to the thin walls. They were quiet people, who probably had their own reasons for not wishing to draw attention to themselves. Not one would help her if he snatched the cash back, but what he did when she opened the main door was almost as bad.

As soon as the door opened, Jake seized her forearms with both hands, so hard she yelped, and pulled his face close to hers.

'Never, ever, do that again, Hannah. D'you understand? I won't answer for the consequences if you do.'

'Let me go! Take your hands off me!' she shrieked.

His response was to push her so violently that she fell on to the concrete stairs, banging her knee and her lip. Her mouth filled with the taste of coins. Even that wasn't enough to slake his rage, and he raised his arm to strike her. Hannah cried out in involuntary anguish, and suddenly Lila erupted on to the landing.

'You! Stop! Leave her alone!'

Her voice was full of fear, but she had a mobile in her shaking hand and she showed him that she had taken his picture. Jake looked at Lila in astonishment.

'What?'

'I'll call the police.'

More doors in the stairwell opened, and brown or black faces looked down at them. Two of them belonged to UCL students, and one (who had introduced himself as Xan) called, 'Hey there, Hannah, do you need help?'

His ringing voice, or rather his accent, acted on Jake like a bucket of cold water.

'Oh, for fuck's sake. Is everyone here completely mad?' He pushed past Hannah, his voice ringing through the stairwell. 'Maisy! Maisy, where are you?'

'Daddy!'

The little girl ran down, delighted, although tears still streaked her cheeks.

Jake picked his daughter up.

'Hello, sweet-pea,' he said. He looked so loving that nobody would believe how he had just behaved. 'Let's get you out of here.'

Maisy nestled into him, and Hannah tried not to sob as they went past because her daughter forgot even to say goodbye. As soon as the front door clicked shut, Lila called to Hannah.

'Are you OK? Is anything broken?'

'No – no. Thanks, Lila. I'm fine, really.'

'Women in our situation would be happier as widows.'

Hannah grimaced. It was so close to what Jinni had said that she wondered whether all women longed for this. 'I'm fine.'

'OK,' Lila said, and went quietly back to her flat, as did the other residents.

Hannah wiped her eyes, mortified, watching her husband through the glass.

Triumphant, as if he had just saved their daughter from

danger, Jake carried her to his car. It was a smart new Audi – another sign of how well he was doing. When he saw her watching, he put the window down and stuck his hand out with one finger up. A second later, he swerved into the middle of the road with a screech of tyres, then straightened and roared down the street.

In his wake was a small, furry form, twisting on the tarmac. Hannah ran out, limping. It was one of the grey squirrels that scampered around the scrawny maple tree below her kitchen window.

The squirrel was shrilling, a sound she had never heard before, its large liquid eyes dark red.

Had Jake done this deliberately, had he aimed to run it over in a fit of spite and bad temper? Hannah stared, aghast. Its agony was so pitiful, and unnecessary, and there was nothing she could do. Even if she had the money, a vet could not save it. Its back was broken. She picked up one of the bricks that were left scattered on the pavement and smashed it down on the squirrel's head, again and again, until it was a mush of blood and fur. Then she bent over and vomited.

The burner phone was in Hannah's hands as soon as she had washed them.

9

A Walk in the Park

'I was wondering when you were going to call.'

'I wasn't able to do it. He was out.'

'Ah.'

Jinni sounded light, amused, as if they were friends discussing something entirely ordinary. On the mobile, her voice seemed creamier than it had done on the train.

'How did you get into my block?' Hannah asked.

'A nice young man let me in. Mixed-race, student.'

It must have been Xan, Hannah thought. He was always friendly, once even carrying her shopping upstairs. In turn, she sometimes took in Amazon deliveries for him, and had learnt that he was studying English, as she had once done. Though she did not think that Xan would be cleaning other people's houses for a living when he graduated. He had grown up in Hampstead, he'd told her, though his family now lived in Devon.

'Did he see your face?'

'I doubt it. I was wearing a helmet.'

There was a pause, in which Hannah tried to imagine what Jinni would look like dressed as a dispatch rider. She was tall, and slim enough to pass as a man.

'How are you?'

'I'm ... ' Hannah couldn't speak for a moment. 'Things are pretty bad.'

'Oh?'

Hannah chose her words carefully. 'My situation needs to be resolved.'

She had at last looked Coad up on Google, taking care to go incognito on the library computer. There was very little about him – no Facebook profile, no Instagram, no LinkedIn, no photograph, just a short Wikipedia entry. He was thirty-five and a games designer, worth an estimated $5 million after his work on *Victory Cry 2* for some American company. She read the amount again, staggered. Five million dollars! Yet why should it be surprising, considering what games cost to buy, and how popular they were? She thought of Jake and his mates screaming with laughter as they pressed their controllers, spraying pixelated pedestrians with virtual bullets, roaring and grunting as if reverting to the most primitive version of masculinity, completely addicted. She was sure that the first *Victory Cry* had been one of the games he had played at university. Anyone who made those games was little better than a drug dealer, she thought.

Jinni said, 'Mine too. So?'

'I think we ought to meet. There are things I'd like to know more about.'

'But that could be unwise.'

Hannah, however, insisted. 'We could have a walk in a park.'

'We could,' said Jinni.

She suggested Regent's Park, and the long path known as the Broad Walk. Its advantage was that it could be approached from so many directions that any encounter could seem incidental.

This time, Jinni was in white: narrow linen trousers, a sleeveless top – both exquisitely cut – and a jacket of transparent fabric so fine it almost floated as she walked. There was a wide straw hat on her head, and black sunglasses obscuring her eyes. Around her long neck was a choker of polished crystal, like lozenges of ice, and to match it the drops that hung from her ears were also crystal, or possibly diamonds. Her skin seemed to be almost luminous. She was the kind of figure you might expect to see posing against a turquoise sea in a glossy magazine, not walking through a dusty London park; but then maybe this was just what being married to a multi-millionaire looked like.

'Hello.'

Once again, Hannah felt herself small, sweaty, frumpish. She had come straight from work and was hot and tired. Her plastic trainers had made her feet swell, her washed-out T-shirt had a hole under each arm, and her bra was by now a grey twist of nylon. Her ponytail lay lank on her scalp, she needed a shower, and she was bare of a scrap of make-up. Jinni's scent, heavy and sweet, washed over her, reminding her of the bedroom at Endpoint.

'Well,' said Jinni, 'here we are again.' She gave a sudden, dazzling smile.

'I only have an hour before I have to pick up my daughter.'

Jinni raised her eyebrows slightly. 'It won't take too long.'

As before, Hannah felt the force of her personality. Very few people give their whole attention to another; Jinni's dark eyes looked at her with an intensity usually reserved for lovers. Hannah felt her heart thump in her chest. She was frightened yet fascinated, wanting above all to be worthy of this regard and yet fearful, feeling that she was in the presence of someone both magnetic and extraordinary.

'You have some questions.'

'Yes.'

'Why don't we find some shade? I know we should be glad of every scrap of sunshine in this country, but even so . . . '

They walked towards the Inner Circle of the park where, years ago, Jake had asked her to marry him. Today, he had texted her that she was *a stupid fucking cunt*. Remember this, she told herself. Remember that someone who seems like the best person in the world can be the worst.

'What do you need to know?'

Hannah asked, at random, 'Why does Con live in Cornwall?'

Jinni sighed through her nostrils, releasing a stream of steam from her e-cigarette. 'His father was Cornish. They made a fortune from china clay. Hence the house.'

'It's falling down.'

There was a pause. 'How do you know?'

'I could see from the outside.' Hannah did not want to examine her motivations for keeping her encounter with Stan secret. It was none of Jinni's business to know that the caretaker had been suicidal. The place lingered in her memory. It was difficult to sleep in the heat, but when she did, she found herself wandering down winding paths and cool avenues. 'I couldn't do it.'

'Damn.' Jinni breathed out a stream of vapour from the stick she was holding. 'It was such a good plan.'

'I'm going back to Cornwall soon, though,' Hannah said. 'Because of my mother's funeral.'

'I see. And? You still have the Taser?'

Playing for time, Hannah said, 'I don't know what your husband looks like. Do you have a photograph?'

Jinni nodded.

'It's quite hard to find pictures of Con. Avoids the camera like a vampire avoids mirrors.' She reached into her bag, taking out a large folder. 'I thought of this. Here.'

Hannah put out her hand, and Jenni opened the folder. Inside was an envelope, which she shook into Hannah's hand.

'Open it later. Then destroy it.'

Hannah hesitated. Jinni's caution about touching the envelope made her understand, yet again, the seriousness of what was being proposed. If she went through with this, if she actually murdered a man in exchange for her own husband being killed, it must not be traced back to them both. It would mean not only a life sentence for her but devastation for her daughter. Hannah's mind flip-flopped between the horror of this and the horror of what men like Jake did to women like her. She had always thought of herself as gentle and honest, and yet ... She thought of the grey squirrel in the street. What was the difference between killing a wounded animal and putting a toxic marriage out of its misery? Jake was determined to take Maisy away from her, saying that she couldn't cope because – in an unguarded moment – she had told him she was on antidepressants. Even though she had stopped taking these now, she knew he'd find a way to bring this up in a battle for custody.

'Do you want one of Jake?'

'I don't need one. He's on Facebook.' Jinni paused. 'Handsome.'

'He has hidden shallows.'

116

An amused expression slid across Jinni's features.

'Everyone sees different things in different people, don't they?'

Hannah said, 'I believe he's the worst person I've ever met.'

'Surely everyone is somewhere along a line between good and bad.'

This was the kind of thing people said when they had no experience of spite.

'No, believe me. Jake is off that line.'

'Why did you marry him?'

Hannah gave a bitter laugh. 'I suppose I wanted my life to be perfect. I believed in Jane Austen.'

'Even though you know that's impossible?'

'Maybe. The heart says one thing and the head another.'

So, which do you trust?' Jinni asked.

A dog raced past them, barking.

'I have to trust myself,' Hannah said. 'But I don't know whether I can trust you.'

Jinni took off her gauzy jacket. 'This is what he did to me.'

There, on her companion's forearms were five fading bruises that looked identical to hers. Silently, she rolled up her own sleeves and showed her own forearms in turn. Jinni looked at them, inscrutably.

'Men think they can do anything to us, so they do.'

'Is that the only reason why anyone behaves well? Out of fear?'

'Don't you think?'

'Maybe.' Hannah sighed. 'I used to think men, most of them, were OK. That they had the capacity for decency and self-sacrifice. That they respected women and understood we deserved respect. Now I think that is just a myth they told us about themselves. They're just bullies, rapists and shits.'

Jinni smiled slightly. 'They hate us too, you know. Especially if one is attractive.'

'But why, when we haven't *done* anything to them!'

'They hate us even more for not doing anything to them.'

They had walked around the greater part of the Outer Circle, past the formal flowerbeds, past the playground, past the curve of palatial Regency terraces, ornamented with the white draped figures of goddesses representing Peace or Mercy or Justice. If I were to do this thing, Hannah thought, if I were to kill a man and nobody else knew, who would punish me?

'You really think we can do it? And not be caught?'

'Sure,' said Jinni. 'Don't you?'

'All I want is to have him out of my life.'

'Nothing connects us,' Jinni said. 'That is the key. But I won't do yours until you do mine.'

'I understand,' Hannah said. She drew a deep breath, and looked at the bruises on Jinni's forearms, then her own, and the shock and fury and humiliation she had felt were as vivid as ever. She could feel the crack in her mind spreading. 'I'll find a way.'

When she got back to the flat, she opened the envelope. The face that looked up at her was smiling and clean-shaven, yet not completely unfamiliar. She examined it, frowning.

Con Coad looked very like Stan.

10

The Ingredients of Happiness

The more she looked, the less sure she became.

Everything about Coad's face and expression was so very different from the rough, bloated, scowling man she had encountered on the day of her mother's death. He was slim, better-looking, younger, and smiling. Yet the eyes were a similar shape, and maybe the mouth, too – it was hard to tell without all the hair.

Family features tended to be repeated in small communities, however, and it was entirely possible that Jinni's husband had relations not just living nearby but working for him. All the rich old families in Cornwall were reputed to have had children by their housemaids. Stan must be a Coad by-blow. As soon as this idea struck her, she felt relieved. Of course, that would be it. St Piran was almost infested by Penroses all bearing various degrees of resemblance to herself. Why shouldn't it be the same with Coad?

Besides, why would someone called Con introduce himself

as Stan? Stan was a poor, rough labourer, not this smooth, confident creep with that indefinable air of entitlement. The drunken, dirty, despairing bloke she had roused could not be the same man.

I was thinking of swimming out to sea last night . . . that was the plan.

People said that money couldn't buy happiness, but this was the sort of thing that rich people said to deflect envy. From where Hannah stood, the reason why money was worth having was precisely because it *did* buy you the ingredients of happiness even if some were too stupid to assemble them. Why pretend otherwise? She thought of Jake and his friends, born with silver spoons not so much in their mouths as up their noses. In London, a dealer would turn up on a moped with as much cocaine and ketamine and weed, ordered by credit card, as they wanted. That was where a chunk of Jake's earnings had gone, and she might as well have blown hers on drugs too instead of sitting there, stone-cold sober, while he and his mates giggled and talked nonsense.

'Don't be a prig, it's no different from wine or coffee,' he'd said when she objected.

How stupid of me to have believed I could get anywhere by doing what people told me were the right things, she thought. That you could pull yourself up by your boot-straps, that you could work your way up, that there was a trickle-down of wealth, that it didn't matter where you had come from but where you were going to – all these were lies, repeated throughout her adolescence until people believed them. Back when her mother had been a child, there were enough traces of the gigantic national sacrifice of the War to produce a more equal society, but now only money got you everything worth having. Why else did the rich want tax cuts? Money bought better healthcare, better education, better living conditions, more respect, advantage and comfort. If you couldn't be happy with all of those things then you probably weren't meant to be so in the first place.

People played at looking poor, as they had once played at being shepherds. The fashion among the young and rich for wearing ripped jeans filled her with silent fury. Half her life was a struggle not to look like this. Polly's daughter was always throwing out clothes, most of them almost unworn.

'Could you drop these off at Oxfam?' Polly would say.

'Actually, I could use them, if you don't mind, Polly.'

'Yes, of course. Freecycling, isn't it?'

Polly spoke humorously but she had no idea what these nearly new garments meant to Hannah. How could she? She was a lawyer earning well over £150,000 a year and would be surprised to know that a Russell Group university graduate was keeping her house spotless. The receipts for Tania's Deliveroo meals totalled more than Hannah's weekly shop. Yet Polly was, miraculously, going to pay her wages for seven whole weeks of holiday. There was no point in Hannah coming in twice a week, not for such a stretch of time.

'It's not your fault we're all going to America until September, and you haven't had any time off in two years, have you? I've got a sprinkler system for the garden, and the house will be fine.'

It meant that Hannah could go to Cornwall for the whole summer. She informed her other clients that she'd be away for July and August due to her mother's death; though they were disgruntled, they couldn't stop her, but unlike Polly they didn't give her holiday pay.

'Lucky you,' said Lila, when she asked her neighbour if she'd mind watering the plants on her balcony. 'Though you could probably do with a break. I've been worried about you.'

Hannah flushed. She was still unsure whether they were friends or just neighbours. 'I'm OK, really. You were so brave to defend me as you did the other day.'

Lila looked at her sympathetically. 'I know what it's like to live in fear. When I first came here to live with my auntie, I was almost out of my mind.'

For this cheerful, proud woman to tell her such a thing was a mark both of trust and of concern.

'I feel like that, sometimes,' Hannah answered carefully. 'Things have become nasty with Jake. But ... ' Then she added, on impulse, 'Lila, would you and Bella like to come to Cornwall for a visit? There's enough room, and we have an inflatable mattress.'

Lila refused, and Hannah was relieved because she knew that however courageous and warm her neighbour was, an observant Muslim wearing a hijab in Cornwall would probably not feel at her ease. Also, Mor's kids might not accommodate a strange child. Maisy was brimming with excitement at seeing them again.

'Can I see my cousins?'
'Yes.'
'And go swimming in the sea with them?'
'Yes, sweetheart.'
'And bake cakes?'
'Lots.'
'Are we nearly there yet?'

Hannah looked out at the frothing white flowers along the track, and said, 'Soon.'

The train journey was long, but it felt very different from the one she had spent with Jinni.

'We can do this. We can set each other free,' Jinni had

said; and put that way, there was something noble about their joint enterprise.

In their second meeting, Jinni had revealed more. She might be married to a rich man, but if they divorced, she would be poor, too. Could this be true? Hannah had no idea what it was like for the wives of rich men, but Jinni said that because she had been unable to have children any settlement would be negligible.

'Do you work?' Hannah asked tentatively.

'I did. You don't, do you? As a mother.'

'Of course I do. I have to.'

'But your husband must pay you maintenance.'

'He barely even pays the rent.' Hannah had told Jinni this before, and it was no less humiliating the second time. 'I get a bit of maintenance for my daughter. But there's everything else.'

'How do you manage?'

'I clean people's houses.'

'Surely not.'

Hannah bridled at the disbelieving tone.

'Feel how rough my hands are.'

Jinni took her hand. Her own was cold, despite the heat of the afternoon, and as marble smooth as Hannah's was not.

'What does your lawyer say?'

'I can't afford one.'

'It'd be worth borrowing to get legal advice.'

Exasperated, Hannah cried, 'I have nothing to borrow against!'

It was hopeless trying to explain her situation, she thought, as the train carried her to Cornwall again. Rich people didn't believe that poverty still existed. Even intelligent ones, people like Polly who read newspapers and listened to Radio 4, somehow failed to notice stuff, or if they did they could do nothing about it. Polly often worked for free for illegal immigrants, but the idea that someone British might be too poor to be able to afford a train fare or a meal was completely alien to her: Hannah was able to make this trip with her daughter partly because Polly had paid her wages in advance, and this was an enormous and unlooked-for relief. Every so often, one of Hannah's employers would forget to leave out her weekly wage, or be short, and then the delicate balance of her finances would be thrown into chaos. Whenever this happened, Hannah would have to say, politely, 'It doesn't matter, pay me next week.' But it did matter, terribly.

London was emptying for summer, as it always did. In affluent streets, scaffolding went up as builders and decorators moved in to make homes even more perfect, but even on the estate flats, many people left. The rich went south and west, the rest north and east, but nobody stayed if they could help it. The air was too dirty, too hot and too foul. All great cities experience this flight, but Hannah was relieved to be in the advance guard, for once, even though it was for her mother's funeral. Maisy's school had given her permission to start her holiday early, under the circumstances.

Hannah looked across at Maisy, bent over a colouring book, wholly absorbed. This time, she had brought water, sandwiches, hard-boiled eggs, apples and, above all, books, for beneath Jake's golden hair, Maisy took after her. Their favourite times together were still those when, for twenty minutes before sleep, Maisy lay in her arms sharing a story. They both loved these moments of absolute peace and pleasure. Hannah had no energy to read to herself, but revisiting her own favourites was compensation enough; and now they were on to *I Was a Rat!*, it hardly mattered.

'Mummy, I want you to go on reading to me even when I can read all by myself.'

'All right. Does Daddy read to you?'

'He's no good. Eve is, but she only does it to show off to him.'

'Ah.'

Hannah never asked directly about Eve. Though consumed by curiosity, she felt that it might damage her child to do so.

In her worst moments she wondered whether the love of reading was not a curse. Parents now fretted over their children not reading enough (or not reading at all) but what practical benefit, really, could literature give a person in the modern world? Fewer and fewer pupils even chose English as an A level, let alone a university degree; Jake himself had only read it at uni as a soft option, he'd told her, because courses were desperate for boys.

'Why didn't you do Law, like me?' Nazneen had asked her once. 'You've got the brains.'

'I did it for its own sake. Follow your passion, only be sure never to put that word in your personal statement! Besides, I don't have a legal brain like you.'

'Do you really think that's what I was born with?' Nazneen had shaken her head. 'I couldn't waste time studying a subject that wouldn't lead to a career.'

'Literature is what feeds my spirit. Dreaming of the real life I do not lead.'

'What use is feeding your spirit if you can't feed your body first?'

'I don't know. But we are more than bodies, Naz, don't you think?'

'If your body is hungry, that matters more.'

Hannah looked out at the landscape, the fields turning pale in the parching heat, the cattle clustering under the shade of oak and ash, swallows dipping into fast-shrinking rivers. The air conditioning was working this time, but even the sound of the train on the track seemed to be repeating to her, endlessly, *There is no hope, there is no hope.*

She could not tell where mourning for her mother ended and mourning for herself began. She had been loved, and not known it any more than a fish knows it lives in water until exposed to air, thrashing and gasping in its desperation to inhale an element not its own.

Sometimes, Jake tried to justify the change in himself.

'Every cell in my body has changed in seven years, so why should my feelings be the same?'

'Because you could change with me?'

Even when she discovered the existence of Eve, she had not hated him instantly. No woman loves without the hope of permanence, and Hannah had once thought that if he was desperately in love, she could accept it and wait until it burnt itself out – coming from an old-fashioned community, she knew of wives who had done just that. But there had been others, both before and after marriage, several at the agency.

'You don't understand, Han. Every man wants to fuck a woman on his desk. It's a universal fantasy.'

'But why couldn't it just stay a fantasy? Why make it *real*?'

It was what men did, however. She had never been like other girls; perhaps if she'd watched *Oprah* and read *Marie Claire* magazine, like her cousin Mor, she'd have been smarter about the opposite sex and not idealised them.

The train went into the first tunnel, reminding her of the moment when Jinni had suggested their plan. The cold

126

despair and hot anger that had made it possible to smash the squirrel to death was still in her. Hannah leant her head against the window and felt its vibrations going into her skull.

Her poor mother had died believing that Hannah and Maisy were enjoying a good life.

'At least I know you're safe,' she said in the last year, repeatedly. 'That's all I wanted for you.'

Rooting around in her handbag for a tissue to blow her nose with, her fingers touched the Taser, and recoiled. What if Maisy were to find it and turn it on? A charge that could knock out a grown man could be lethal for a child. It was pink, Maisy's favourite colour. She was fascinated by electronics, all children were. It was madness to keep it.

Really, the sensible thing would be to get rid of it altogether, but she pushed it back down again, like her conscience.

11

The Funeral

Arriving at St Piran in the afternoon was very different from her midnight trudge. Loveday was there beyond the cindery platform, scooping Maisy up in her plump arms, while her dog, Pisky, barked and Loveday's son Cadan beamed. He was another Cornish giant, with the flat face, slanting eyes and loving heart of someone born with Down's syndrome.

'Hi,' he said, as they hugged him.

'Hello, Cadan.'

Cadan lifted their suitcases. He was almost as big as Stan and carried them without effort.

'Car?'

'Oh, thank goodness, yes. Down, Pisky!'

Her aunt chatted on in a continual flow.

'Now there you are both of you my lovelies and goodness Maisy you've grown at least two inches since I set eyes on you last not that we're supposed to call it inches any more are we, five centimetres then and is that all the luggage you've brought from England? Mor's kids can't move without half a toyshop but I dare say you've left stuff at Holly's haven't you and if not then I'm sure Jago and Tressa have plenty when you get together they're looking forward to seeing their cousin again as soon as you're rested, don't worry about food tonight I put milk, butter, bread, cheese and eggs in the fridge and a nice lettuce that the slugs didn't get to, you'll be wanting to do some shopping of your own tomorrow though there's all the sad business of your Mum's funeral thank goodness it happened so close to the summer holidays but Cadan mowed her lawn so it's not looking too bad or we'd all be at sixes and sevens what with preparing and now then buckle up my loves because the road is worse than ever and we're off . . . '

Loveday had always been the more confident and outgoing of the sisters, never seeming to pause for breath in the flow of chat except during a religious service. She was the lollipop lady for the primary school, and a classroom assistant, and ever since she had become a widow had also started doing Meals on Wheels. Everybody knew her, and during their ride up the hill she beeped or was beeped at by half a dozen friends and relations. The Penrose family lived in Cornwall like a nut in its shell, and the moment Hannah told Loveday anything about herself, it would be all over the peninsula from Truro to Penzance. Coming back reminded her of all the reasons she both loved and loathed this place. Her aunt brought her up to speed with all the doings of her uncles, aunts, cousins and second cousins, none of whom seemed to be doing anything special but all of whom were naturally of intense fascination down to the last ingrown toenail.

'Thanks ever so much for collecting us, Auntie.'

'Well, it can't be easy for you up in London with your busy

life there, and Holly, bless her, planned it all, you know how she liked everything organised in advance.'

Maisy, bouncing about on the back seat, said, 'I can see the sea! I can see the sea!'

As Loveday's car ascended the sprawl of the town, the Atlantic slid in and out of sight in the great arch of England's foot.

'How many people are coming to Mum's funeral?' Hannah asked.

'Oh, only about a hundred.'

'Really?'

'Don't worry; she left some money for the wake at the pub. You look tired, my lovely. I dare say that city life does that to a person,' Loveday said. 'Are you still in that agency doing the advertising? Work you to the bone, do they?'

'I am very busy, with work and Maisy.'

The lie was yet another circling round her head like gulls waiting to land. Hannah hated lying, yet pride kept her silent. She had grown up with both, after all. If only, she thought, I'd found out who my dad is. Maybe I'm not an orphan – that romantic figure in children's books because being without parents seems so desirable when loved.

The funeral was held at the Methodist Chapel where she and her mother had spent many Sundays. It was at the end of a long lane shaded by limes, in a beautiful granite building erected when St Piran had enjoyed its brief period of prosperity. Everything was simple and designed to reflect peace and light and calm. The battered pews could seat up to a thousand but were rarely filled except for weddings, funerals and Christmas. It was Grade 2 listed and even changing a light bulb was a risky business. The carved banister to the gallery above finished in a curl of oak that was almost the only ornament, besides the organ above the pulpit and the one stained-glass window.

'So sorry.'

'So sorry.'

'So sorry for your loss.'

People she didn't recognise kept coming up to kiss and hug her. She felt numb, nodding and thanking them.

'At least she's out of her suffering, poor woman,' Loveday said. 'It was the same for my Sam. There's nothing more you can do for them, and that's a comfort of sorts.'

Her mother's coffin, a plain pine box, was carried in on the shoulders of four shuffling men in suits. Up until this moment, she had half-hoped for it all to be a mistake, for Holly to hop out with her usual brisk, bird-like movements before setting everything to rights.

But the church organ was swelling, and all eyes were streaming, and instead it was the congregation that rose up.

And did those feet in ancient time
Walk upon England's mountains green?
And was the holy Lamb of God
On England's pleasant pastures seen?

The idea of Jesus being (just possibly) in England was gloriously eccentric, Hannah thought, and an image of Him dressed in German tourist sandals skipping gingerly through the prickly gorse on Bodmin Moor came into her mind so she caught her breath in a half-laugh. He'd probably fit right in down here. Loveday squeezed her hand, and the horror of death abated a little.

The smell of damp and polish and mothballs and bats was as familiar as her own fingernails, and so were the hymns,

131

because they were Methodists and music was what they were best at, along with heartfelt prayers for help and guidance and faith. Hannah had been to this church every Sunday until she left home. In London, the only time she went inside a church was when they went to the food bank.

> *Bread of heaven, bread of heaven*
> *Feed me till I want no more . . .*

The organ and the singers seemed to make the rafters shake, and the stained-glass window depicting Jesus as a fisherman in a boat whose sail was the Cornish flag with the white cross of St Piran quivered in its lead. They followed the coffin out to the hearse. Away from all this, Holly would be cremated, something nobody but Hannah and Loveday wanted to watch. Then they were back among the living, heading down the road to her uncle's pub. The faces of those gathered round were a blur, and yet somehow, they must all eat and drink and pretend that death would never happen to them.

'A'right?'

A very large man in a suit stood before her. Had he been one of her mother's pallbearers? One of her many cousins? She tried to think, but her brain was fogged with sadness.

'Fine, thanks.'

'Long day for the little one. Your daughter?'

'Yes. Say hello, Maisy.'

Maisy put out her hand, politely. 'Hello. Are you a giant? You're even bigger than my Uncle Cadan.'

The man crouched down before her and raised his dark glasses. 'Hi, Maisy. I'm not a giant, no. I'm Stan.'

Hannah tried, and failed, to hide her surprise. Though

scarcely kempt, the long straggling beard had been hacked in half, and the hair on his head was washed and tied back. His black eye was a faded yellow. He now looked less like Hagrid in *Harry Potter* and more like a bouncer in a particularly bad night club.

'It's good of you to come.'

'I know what it's like to lose a parent.'

'How is Bran?'

'Fine, thanks. Too hot for him to leave the garden.'

'I don't blame him.'

There was an awkward silence. Hannah broke it.

'Stan gave Mummy the beautiful flowers.'

'I did,' Stan said. 'From the garden at Endpoint.'

'They were nice.'

'There's plenty more. You can come and see it any time.'

'Can Jago and Tressa come too?'

'Who are they?'

'My cousins. They're proper Cornish. I'm only half.'

She was only a quarter, probably, but Hannah didn't want to remind her of this.

'Well, I'm only half too, so that makes two of us. Yes, of course they can.'

All around them, her mother's friends and relations churned, and Hannah was conscious that many were giving them sideways glances. Maybe Stan didn't go out much, or maybe it was her own reappearance that was causing the mosquito buzz of gossip to which all people who live in a small town are attuned.

'Are you better?' she asked.

'Getting there.' Stan shifted from one foot to the other awkwardly. 'So . . . you down here for long?'

'Yes. I've got seven weeks off, so Maisy and I can have a

proper summer down here. It's what I've longed to do for ages, only I couldn't afford it.'

'Ah.' Stan rubbed the side of his large nose. 'If you don't mind my asking, are you looking for work?'

'I was thinking of asking if my uncle needed someone to pull pints. Why?'

'Thing is, I could do with some help at the house.'

Hannah couldn't believe it would be so easy to regain access.

'What sort of help?'

'Organising and er, cleaning. You may have noticed that it's not in a good way. It's going to be put on the market in August, but it's too much for me on my own. I don't want someone local, even if I could get them at such short notice.'

'How much?'

Stan furrowed his brows.

'Say, twenty pounds an hour? As you'd be giving up your holiday. I'd need about twenty hours a week, at least, if you don't mind. It's a big job.'

Hannah nodded, trying not to show her astonishment. Coad must really be paying him well if he could pass up on so much. In high summer, St Piran wages did come close to those in the city because of all the Londoners who decamped to places like Fol for their holidays – but this was a godsend. At the very least, it would mean she'd return to London without her credit card debt. There were so many things she had longed to buy for Maisy, from better food to sensible shoes, and it was one of the things that made her cry with frustration when alone that, so often, she simply could not do so. There was a downside, however. If she wanted to go ahead with the plan to kill Coad, it wouldn't be quite as easy to leave no trace – but then who would suspect a temporary cleaner? She'd still be a total stranger. On the other hand, spending almost every day with such an odd man made her pause. He might be benign, but she had forgotten quite how big he was – at least a foot taller than herself – and how hirsute. Even washed, his dark hair flowed down past his shoulders, and his face was obscured by his beard and heavy eyebrows. He had hair on the back of his hands and boiling up through the neck of his shirt. He still reminded her of an animal.

'Let me think about it,' she said.

Maisy began to complain about wanting to be with her cousins.

'*Please*, Mummy?'

'All right, sweetie. Off you go.'

It was such a relief to let a six-year-old run along a street and know there would be no cars.

'You really would be helping me.'

'As long as it won't get you into trouble.'

'I think I'm in enough trouble as it is.'

Hannah smiled at him. 'You and me both. Are you coming into the pub?'

'If I'm invited.'

'You are. After all, you said my mum patched you up after rugby.'

'She did.'

They walked down the lane after the crowd of Holly's family and friends, bent on consuming enormous quantities of beer and sandwiches at her uncle's pub. The Jolly Lobster was pleasant enough on the inside with a beer-garden out the back and a hedge of red and blue fuchsias. The buzz of the congregation was rising by the minute.

Stan nodded. 'What'd you like?'

'Lemonade, Cornish Orchards, if there's any.'

'Right you are.'

Loveday bustled forward as Stan went off.

'Hello, sweetheart, didn't that go off well, lovely service I thought with all Holly's favourite hymns and such a good turn-out and how did you get *him* to come along?'

'Who?'

Her aunt jerked her head towards Stan.

'He's offered me a job, actually.'

'He has? My goodness! Will you take it?'

Hannah, accustomed to the way her aunt over-reacted to everything, said, 'Why? There's nothing wrong with him is there?'

Loveday's eyes seemed to spark.

'Don't you know? That's the owner of Endpoint, Constantine Coad.'

12

Dirty Work

Hannah was appalled. So, *this* was the monster? Of course, she should have guessed ... but even though Jinni had told her that her husband would be alone that night, she always called him Con, not Stan. She had said he was good-looking, not ugly and hairy. What a fool Hannah had made of herself. She had turned up intending to murder a man, and instead stopped him from killing himself. Her thoughts were once again in turmoil.

'Are you all right, my lovely?'

'Yes, thanks.'

How could it have crossed anyone's mind that Stan was *not* the caretaker? A fat man could be comical or frightening or jolly or unpleasant or intelligent or delightful company but the one thing that he could never be was an acceptable partner to someone like Jinni. It was incomprehensible how two such very different people had come together, let alone married. Hannah knew without knowing quite how she knew that appearances mattered to Jinni enormously. Everything about the way she dressed, moved, spoke signified this, and it was not the unthinking elegance of Jake's mother, who could and did wear jeans and a charity-shop shirt with style, but that of someone who had considered the effect she made even before she got up. In days gone by, Hannah had once been a little like this herself, which was how, perhaps, she knew.

Or perhaps Coad had changed, as Jake had changed during their years together. Hannah did some frantic thinking. Nothing about this made sense.

'He's a bully and a miser,' Jinni had said, but what he was offering to pay her didn't fit that. Maybe he was the sort who would offer a high salary then refuse to pay the full amount on some spurious ground? She'd had one of those, in her early days as a cleaner.

'Why is Endpoint such a mess?' she asked.

Loveday gave her a shrewd look.

'Oh, you've been there, have you? Well, several reasons. One is that Coad's father had dementia for many years.'

'So he let it start to fall down around him?'

'There's not much a child can do when their parent goes doolally,' Loveday said. 'Especially if he was a curmudgeonly fool in the first place. But the Alzheimer's brought out the worst in him, though he was sweet before that.'

'What about the new owner? Is he mad too?'

Her aunt looked dubious. 'I haven't seen him since he went away to America. He's supposed to have come back to look after his dad, but he's hardly been seen. He used to be a nice kid – played rugby with your cousins. I don't know whether he took better care of his dad than he did of the estate, but he and his wife, well, they didn't make themselves popular. Some nasty rows, people said. Police, even.'

Hannah thought of one of the mothers she'd met at Maisy's school, a pretty woman with two young children and a third on the way. She drove a smart car and her husband was a surgeon, one of those professional men whom everyone regarded with awe. The wife seemed perfectly happy until the day when she didn't turn up at school: her sister brought the kids instead.

'In hospital, poor cow, after a miscarriage. He kicked her in the stomach.'

She couldn't work for Coad. It was a crazy idea. He was a drunk, a lout, who had shouted at her and he might think that if she came to clean for him, he could bully and rape her just because she was poor and female. On the other hand, she had the Taser, and the means to carry out her promise. What better chance could she get?

'All right?'

Stan – or Coad, as she must now think of him – stood before her with the lemonade she had asked for. Hannah said abruptly, 'You let me think you were the caretaker, not the owner of Endpoint House.'

'Ah.' He held out the drink to her, and she took it hesitantly. 'Well, I won't be the owner for much longer, if that makes you feel any better.'

'Why not?'

'Lots of reasons. I have to pay death duties. Also, my ex is claiming everything once we're divorced.'

'How come?'

'She thinks it's worth millions.'

'Is it?'

'To a developer who'd put in plastic windows and rip out the woods for luxury holiday flats.'

Hannah thought of Endpoint, its green mystery. She had

seen it for less than a day, but it had sent tendrils into her own imagination. Many other grand Cornish houses were open to the public, though always with a feeling of sadness at the loss of something. So perhaps this was part of his miserliness. He was yet another rich bastard who hated paying up, whether it was taxes or alimony. He was glowering just at the thought of it, she could see.

'It is a very big house for just one person.'

'I know. It was meant for a family, not just one man and his dog.'

Hannah sipped her lemonade. It was slightly tart, fizzy, fruity, delicious, the kind of treat she could never normally afford. Coad, she noticed, was also having one, which suggested that he was either off the booze or already tanked up.

'So, in a way, I *am* nothing more than a caretaker.'

'Surely you can get other cleaners?'

'The ones I had weren't really up to it, as you might have noticed.'

Hannah stiffened. Every single cleaning job she'd ever done had been introduced with these words, because everyone who had the money to pay someone else for their dirty work was never satisfied. Mostly, it was because they never booked enough time. Did they really believe that *any* family home could be kept immaculate with just five hours a week of cleaning? Polly's house – four bedrooms, three adults – needed twelve. A two-bed flat took three. A house the size of Endpoint would need something like thirty hours every single week, even if it were not in its present dreadful condition.

'For what you're offering, you could get an army of people to help.'

'Yes, I could. But I don't want just anybody to just clean

140

and pack. Half the contents need to go into a skip, and then it needs to be made to look better for the photographs the agent is putting online and into *Country Life*. For that, I need someone intelligent.'

'What makes you think that's me?'

'Because you are.'

Hannah felt herself flushing. *Your face makes you look more intelligent than you are.* Of all the things Jake had said to her, this was the most hurtful – and he'd said it when supposedly in love with her. Men said things like this as if women were just projections of whatever they happened to be feeling, not people with feelings of their own. Clearly, Coad thought he could flatter her.

'That doesn't make me any good at presentation.'

'You worked in advertising, right? You know how to present things.'

'I suppose so. Though how do you know?'

'I know something about the media. I used to work in it.'

Hannah suddenly felt a little faint. Was she really going to march in and do this?

The noise of the wake had swelled to an almost deafening clamour of chat and music.

'Sorry, I know it's not a good time. Why don't you give me your number?'

She found her mobile, and gave it to him, thinking how his wife had given her another. Coad entered his name as Stan in her contacts list and pressed 'Call'. It rang.

'Got you.'

A dart of unease went through Hannah. Maybe it wasn't a good idea for him to have her number. It took away the lack of traceable contact if . . . if . . . She didn't want to finish that train of thought.

'Just one thing,' Hannah said, flushing. 'My relations don't know that I'm not working in advertising any more. Would you mind not telling them?'

'Of course.'

A hand brushed her arm.

'Han! I wondered if I'd spot you.'

She turned and saw her old schoolfriend and first boyfriend.

'Hi, Geoff.'

'Hello, Stan.'

'You know each other?'

'Yes,' Geoff said. 'Stan . . . we, sort of, work together.'

'You do?'

'Remotely. We're working on a new game together. We met at uni.'

Once again she was surprised. 'At Imperial?'

Stan's eyes had a glimmer of humour. 'We both read computer science, though I read Philosophy at Oxford first.'

No wonder he looked more like a fifty-year-old than a man in his thirties.

'I'm really sorry about your mum,' Geoff said. 'She was always kind to me.'

'Was she?'

'Yes. She was the first person I came out to.'

Hannah blurted, 'I'm sorry, I had no idea.'

'Yes, well, neither did I. Sorry.'

He smiled at her, and it was obvious now, and Hannah smiled back. As a boyfriend he'd been gentle, at least, and clean, and they had been kind to each other. She'd been fond of him, and sorry they had lost touch; goodness knows, she had few enough friends as it was. She could see Mr Kenward, angular as a heron, approaching. She wondered whether he was there out of courtesy or curiosity: he seldom left his bookshop to go out into the world.

'How are you, dear child? This is a sad time. Holly was far too young to go.'

'It hasn't really sunk in.'

Geoff said, 'It's better when you can do something with the ashes. I sent my father up in fireworks.'

'Mum wanted to be scattered into the sea.'

'She was always a romantic,' Kenward said. 'Afternoon, Stan.'

'Afternoon, Bill.'

Hannah was surprised again. How did these two happen to be on such terms?

'You know I'm an executor of her will?'

Hannah moved away a little to talk to him. 'No. I don't know what an executor is.'

'It means I can sort things out for her estate, which always takes many months. You're her only heir, of course.'

'I see.'

Hannah was puzzled, because her mother could surely have no estate. The bungalow would revert to the council; the little car could only be worth a few hundred; the bits of furniture were all junk.

'Don't worry, it's just a formality.'

'Well, at least Maisy and I will have a summer here. Stan – Mr Coad – has offered me some work at Endpoint. How do you know him?'

Kenward gave her a quizzical look, as if wondering why she was so interested. 'I bought my bookshop from his father. There wasn't a bookshop then, but he thought it'd be a good thing for Fol to have one.'

'I wondered who the reader at Endpoint was.'

'Oh, the Coads all are – or were.'

Hannah was used to middle-class houses with every accoutrement of affluence. Home cinemas, corner fridges, underfloor heating, walk-in wardrobes, remote-controlled sound systems, wine-cellars, swimming pools in the basement, paintings by Jack Vettriano, kitchen equipment by Heston Blumenthal, and much more. The one thing that was almost always missing in such households was books.

'How peculiar.'

'Why?'

'Because usually it's only people like me, the freaks and loners, who read,' she said, with a touch of bitterness. 'You know, the people who never have money.'

Kenward's fine, wrinkled face sharpened with amusement. 'Indeed?'

'It's certainly how other people see it.'

'Then you know the wrong people, my dear Hannah.'

'Are there any other kind?'

After a pause, Kenward said, 'Stan is a good person.'

Hannah regarded him with scepticism.

'Men are completely different to men. You need to be a woman to see the other side. Or a servant. Or both.'

Coad's house *must* be worth a fortune, she thought. No wonder Jinni wants her share of it, because even if it were closer to St Piran than Fol, it was still an extraordinary place. Every house with a sea view on the Cornish coast had long ago become unaffordable to ordinary people, and Endpoint had a coastline of its own. A landlord could make three times the money in just two months of the summer renting to tourists, so most didn't want to let their property to anyone local for the other nine. There were local people living in caravans, while family homes stood empty. Inland, where buses came once a day and even the Spar shops were closing, it was different – but who wanted to live there?

Hannah sighed. She really had no option in this. She went and found Coad.

'I'll do it. When would you like me to start?'

13

The Angel of Death

There was no problem about who should look after Maisy in Cornwall, so Hannah turned up at 9 a.m. to begin cleaning Endpoint, marvelling once again at the potholed drive and large, crumbling house. What had been sinister at night was just neglected by day, and as she turned the corner, she saw that Coad had a long steel ladder up at the front to attack its wild tangle of roses and wisteria. Mounds of cuttings lay on the ground, but what he was doing was shouting into his mobile.

'Why don't you get off your arse? You're a grown-up, get back to work.'

Hannah froze. She could hardly believe that the same words she had heard Jake shout at her could be repeated to Coad's wife.

'All you ever do is leech off me.'

His enormous frame seemed to vibrate with fury.

'I don't care. You've got to stop running up bills. I'm not paying any more, do you understand?'

There was a pause, then he yelled, 'No!'

He threw his mobile violently against the wall, where it bounced off the granite and fell. Hannah, not without trepidation, walked up to the ladder. Coad was still halfway up it, groaning and putting his head to the metal rungs as if in pain.

'Bitch, bitch, fucking bitch,' he muttered. 'Oh God.'

Hannah's impulse was to turn around and run away, but instead she made herself pick up the mobile. It was the latest model of iPhone, the large unwieldy kind designed for the male hand. A person who could afford this could afford to pay his wife's bills.

'I *think* it's still working,' she said.

He looked down at her, face flushed.

'It, er, fell.'

He began to step down. It struck her that she could push the ladder sideways to make him fall, but he was too heavy to push.

'Thanks,' he said, with an effort. 'I, um, decided to have a go at the front of the house and chop a lot back. People make their minds up about a property in the first three minutes, apparently. It's like falling in love.'

He looked around at the bits of fallen stone dotted around the drive, then up at the crumbling castellations.

'Probably a hopeless job.'

Hannah did not want to get involved in discussions.

'Have you ordered skips? You're going to need at least seven, big ones.'

'No, not yet.'

'I would,' she said. 'And I'll need a delivery of bleach, bin bags, Astonish, e-cloths, vinegar, baking powder and a Henry hoover.'

'Er – right. Why vinegar and baking powder?'

'If you soak your oven in it, the old grease will come off. It's the best and cheapest cleaner there is.'

Encountering the reek inside was worse than recollected. She wished she'd thought to bring pads for her knees. Her job seemed more suitable to twenty maids with twenty mops than just one small, weary woman. She gathered her courage, determined not to succumb to hopelessness.

'How many rooms are there, altogether?'

'I never counted. I suppose, about twenty. It depends what you count as a room, really. There are rooms just for flower-arranging and wrapping presents. And then there's the attic.'

Hannah sniffed. 'Drains?'

'The plumbing is a nightmare,' said Coad. 'I don't know if you noticed, the water that comes out of the taps in the bath is brown. It's from the house well, and I think it's clean despite appearances. But the stench ... I'm afraid that's probably my father.'

'Are you keeping his corpse here?'

'Um, no, he liked to er, stuff his droppings in strange places. Umbrella stands, coat pockets, bookcases. I haven't managed to find them all.'

'I see. A lovely game of hide-and-seek for me, then.'

In the course of the next few days, Hannah was to uncover a quantity of dried turds, some wrapped in old newspaper and tissues, others not. Demented he might have been, but Coad's father seemed to have been malicious as well as cunning, for in some cases the deposits were concealed inside the hems of curtains, up chimneys, on top of toilet cisterns and in between books. Only the west wing, where she had slept, seemed free of it, and the kitchen.

This was Coad's domain, and to her relief it was reasonably clean. She got to work on the oven and fridge and turned the Aga off because in the heatwave it was unbearable as well as wasteful. As soon as the skips arrived, she began to throw out bag after bag of rubbish. It was lonely work, and she spoke as little as possible to him. His words to Jinni meant that she could not see him without fear and dislike, for she kept expecting to be shouted at and was perpetually on edge. She thought of what Ali had said to her about not getting trapped by an employer and how much worse it would be to be crammed into a small space with someone the size of Coad. Perhaps he sensed her hostility, because he, too, seemed awkward. Hannah reminded herself to be blandly polite. However stupid someone may be, everyone is exquisitely sensitive to their own self-love where other people's feelings towards themselves are concerned. Coad brought her mugs of tea like a cat bringing in a mouse.

Go away, fool, she wanted to say. *Don't you realise that I'm here to kill you?*

Yet to her annoyance, he kept trying to resume their earlier friendliness. It made her even more uncomfortable and wary.

'I've made us lunch.'

'You don't need to, Mr Coad.'

'I've laid the table outside. And I'm still Stan.'

Hannah hesitated. She didn't want to get to know him, but whenever she remembered her situation, she would flip-flop between resolution and indecision.

'All right.'

They sat in silence for a few minutes, eating a mixture of dips, eggs, slow-cooked chicken and lamb kebabs, so spicy and richly flavoured that at first she wasn't sure she would like it. There was rice, chickpeas and bulgur wheat, and tiny chopped tomatoes with mint and fresh parsley, sweet and sour okra, finely sliced cucumber salad and mango pickle. It was colourful, strange and delightful.

'This is very different from the food I'm used to.'

'Didn't you have Middle Eastern food in London?'

'No, never. Jake didn't like garlic and I'm not very adventurous, I suppose.'

He said, 'I've been thinking, this is a lot to be doing by yourself. I can help – unless you think I need more people.'

'Depends what you can afford,' said Hannah. She did not want other cleaners around if she was going to fulfil her mission.

'I'm haemorrhaging money as it is. And I don't want lots of bloody busybodies talking about my dad and this place. Do you think the two of us could do it?'

Hannah gave it some thought. 'I think it's possible, with two of us, over a month. We've filled six skips already, and if we get those back, the worst of the rubbish will be gone. It won't be perfect, but it won't stink.'

'My father was a good man,' Coad said, 'until the drink, and dementia, changed his personality. Then – he was ashamed, I think, and frightened, and wouldn't trust anybody but me. Mr and Mrs Bolitho, the caretakers, couldn't cope; they're getting on, too. I couldn't just leave him to rot here, you see.'

Hannah was silent. Information like this made her uneasy, because Stan made himself sound kind.

'Whatever you decide, I think there's a blocked drain somewhere, but I haven't discovered where it is yet. I think you should call in a plumber.'

'I've tried. Hundreds of pounds later, there's no difference. They even put cameras down.'

Hannah said reluctantly, 'Ask my Uncle Kit. He's a builder and he won't rip you off.'

By now it had not rained for weeks and weeks, though there was still a heavy dew in Cornwall. Hannah worried about her plants in London. Her tiny balcony felt like the one bit of beauty she had managed to make in a canyon of concrete. She was as proud of its morning glories, snapdragons and nasturtiums, and of the bees that somehow found them, as Coad was of his acres. Prouder, because everything there had been made with her own efforts.

All the same, the woods were lovely. The twisted trunks, mossy boulders and silvery streams seemed those of an enchanted world. It was here that Hannah found her opportunity to kill her new employer.

Once again, she was toiling in a haze of bleach and water, her anger being turned to some practical use, but now Coad worked beside her when he wasn't tackling the garden. He had cut down the rhododendron and camellias and ferns along the drive, saying they'd all bush back out in a few weeks. He was an oven of energy, or perhaps it was fury too, and he still drank, even if he sweated much of it out. When he spoke to her, she made sure she looked him in the eye and answered calmly, determined never to show her fear as if he were a big dog that could turn nasty.

She often overheard other exchanges with his wife. He would pace up and down, usually outside the house, but his voice floated up quite clearly.

'No, no! You still aren't listening!

'Can you stop screaming at me and see sense?' After a pause, 'I need time. The photographer is coming. Jesus, how much more of this do I have to take? Yes, I've got someone new in to help. She's a local girl, Hannah. Why? No. She's not. Oh, for fuck's sake, suit yourself.'

That's given me away, Hannah thought. Jinni will guess that I'm inside Endpoint.

She checked the burner mobile when she got back to the bungalow, but there was no message, so she turned it off again. Maybe Coad's wife understood that she was waiting for the right moment; and just five days into her new job, Hannah saw her chance.

The heat and humidity caused plants to spring up from one day to the next. Nothing, however, appeared as quickly as fungi. The bases and trunks of trees were ridged and spattered with strange growths, some the conventional umbrella shape like the one her mother's concrete gnome sat on, but others like undulating wooden steps or stiff outcrops of coral. Yet the peculiar heat of the Cornish Riviera brought on seasonal changes quicker than in other parts.

'Chanterelles!' said Coad, returning from one of his runs. In his hands were bright yellow mushrooms, fan-shaped with deep gills, and some smaller white fungi. 'Delicious. And look, field mushrooms too.'

Hannah eyed these dubiously.

'Are you sure?'

'Absolutely. I pick them every summer, they're a real treat. Can you find some parsley? I'll fry them up for a special risotto.'

She'd heard the saying that the definition of a wild mushroom expert is one who is still alive but thought no more of it until she went out into the kitchen garden and saw, poking up in a shady corner, another entirely white fungus. It looked very like the button mushrooms that were sold by supermarkets all year round. But it was not.

Many years ago, her mother had pointed out something very similar to her.

'Never even touch that one,' she said. 'That's the Angel of Death. It looks pretty, doesn't it? Like something a pisky would sit on. But just one of those could kill a whole family. We had a case of a father and daughter who ate one in a stew. She died, and he had to have a kidney transplant. Every bit of it is poison.'

Hannah looked at it out of the corner of her eye. It seemed to glow with a neon glare, as if inviting her to take it. Coad had picked the rest of the mushrooms himself. His foraging habit would be well known and having just joined him she would hardly come under suspicion. It would be the perfect murder, right there on the spur of the moment. All she had to do was make sure that she ate none herself.

How easy it was to kneel and pluck it out of the earth. The soft, silky fungus held its shape for a moment then crumbled in her hand as if eager to disappear into its harmless relations, smelling delicious as sautéed in butter and garlic they turned a faint, pale gold. The panful of poison was tipped into the saucepan of risotto rice, by now a plump, pearly swell with butter, stock and a glass of white wine. Her parsley was the finishing touch.

'Almost ready,' said Coad.

'I'm not sure I want something hot, actually. I've got a headache.'

'Do you need an aspirin? You've gone pale again.' He filled a glass with water and fished a packet out of the kitchen drawer. 'Here.'

Hannah took them and swallowed but was suddenly pulled apart by conflict she never expected to feel. Death by poison would not be a calm, serene passing into unconsciousness.

Long ago, writing an essay on Keats, she had looked up hemlock, and found that far from a philosopher's rational exit from the world, or the Romantic poet's dreamy descent into Lethe, the poisoned are gripped by violent vomiting, diarrhoea and muscle spasms. If Coad ate a mouthful of the risotto, this would happen to him, too.

'Smells good.' He paused, and said, 'Any better?'

His concern was like a slap. Hannah began to panic.

What to do? What to do? He had taken the pot off the hob and was grating parmesan for it. The pips to *The World at One* were sounding and as soon as the headlines had been read, he'd want to eat. He loved eating as much as he loved cooking, with an innocent sensuality that reminded her of when he had first made her an omelette.

If she said that she thought one of the mushrooms wasn't safe, he might not listen. He'd picked them himself, after all, and he would be as stubborn as all men.

Wildly, she looked around. Her impulse to commit this crime had subsided into flat despair.

'Wait a moment, I'll just scrub down the surfaces,' she said.

She seized a bottle, unscrewed the cap and pretended to trip, squeezing the bottle. An arc of bleach squirted out, spattering the cooker and splashing into the pot.

'Oh no!'

'Fuck,' said Coad, putting down his wooden spoon. 'It's ruined.'

'I'm so sorry,' she said, and waited, cringing. There was a pause. Coad looked thunderous. He lifted a plate as if about to smash it; then belched.

'Sorry.'

Still Hannah waited.

154

'Let's have salad,' he muttered. 'You're right, it's too hot for this anyway.'

Limp with relief, Hannah was even more silent than usual, uncertain of everything. Had she just made a terrible mistake – or averted one?

She could not make up her mind. Each time she received another unpleasant call or text from Jake, she felt the pain, anger and stress jab her like a cattle-prod. What mercy did any man deserve? She remembered how she had loved her job until the men started circling and bullying. The worst of the lechers was 'too brilliant to sack' and had been promoted, whereas she'd been told to shut up.

'Do you get harassed by guys here?' she'd asked Ali. 'Does it wear off?'

Ali had looked at her with narrowed eyes.

'It helps being married to a lawyer,' she'd said. 'And being older.'

'So that's the answer? Wait until I'm too old for them to hit on me?'

Ali had said, 'This whole industry is riddled with sexism. One day, there'll be a reckoning.'

That had been years ago, and nothing seemed to change. Generation Rent posted pictures of the perfect life they did not lead on Instagram, and these were perceived as boasting, not images of hopeless yearning. Whatever they did, whether it was protesting about climate change or trying to find a little bit of joy in life, they were mocked.

Even her cousin felt it.

'Mum says things like, "By your age we had a home of our own". She doesn't think that in her time there was affordable housing and banks that gave mortgages. She even thinks that having a mobile is a luxury, although I have to have one for work. Ben and me work all the hours God sends, and we can never save enough. We're desperate to move out but we just can't budge.'

'Is the council not able to help?'

Mor snorted.

'They're bloody useless. They're more interested in homing incomers and immigrants than people like us, and the rest are being sold off to developers for yet more luxury second homes.'

'Mor, I'm sure that's not true,' said Hannah uncomfortably.

'It is, Han. You don't live here any more. You wait, some developer will be buying up the land at Coad's.'

The news that Hannah was working at Endpoint could not be kept secret, of course. She had to tell her aunt and cousin, although she pretended that she was sorting out the library.

'Some of the books might be valuable,' she said, but when she asked Stan if this were the case he exploded.

'Believe me, I had Sotheby's all over it. They thought the Chinese vases might be worth something, but no. My old man sold everything of value to fund the all-important business of getting pissed every day.'

'Didn't you realise it was all falling to bits?'

'No,' he said. 'After I went away, I didn't feel like coming back. I love the woods, but it isn't home.'

It was a house that had lost its heart, Hannah thought. Coad would work and work until he streamed with sweat, returning with twigs in his wild hair. She kept finding bottles of beer, and although he had sweated some of his flab off it looked as if he was going the same way as his father once the job was done.

When she went back to St Piran to collect Maisy, her relations could not disguise their curiosity.

Her aunt said dreamily, 'I remember when we used to go into the grounds at Endpoint as kids. They used to have the summer festival there – a big tea party with music. Everyone went. It was the big event.'

'I don't remember ever going.'

'It must have been before you came. Later, it became a jungle. Everything went to pieces when poor Mrs Coad got sick.'

'Did you know them?'

'Oh, no! They were far too posh for the likes of us. The Coad family goes back hundreds of years, like the Evenlodes, though without a title. Old Mr Coad was a real catch, back in the day. Nobody thought he'd marry a foreigner. Very beautiful, mind, and kind and clever too.'

'Where was she from?'

'One of those faraway places,' said Loveday, to whom everywhere outside Cornwall was off the map. 'Lots of wars. Africa? Arabia? I think her people were refugees at some point. She said they'd lost everything. Mind, they still seemed to have money from somewhere.'

Hannah thought, So his dark skin isn't just a tan, then. She felt foolish for not realising.

'Did you ever meet Con Coad's wife?'

Loveday's expression changed. 'Once or twice. She didn't like it here.'

'And?'

'Your Uncle Kit has a story about her. He was driving his van and trailer along a bit of narrow lane, and met this swanky car, a Mercedes. You know how it is with a van and trailer, you can't reverse, and there was a lay-by right behind her. So he sat there, waiting for her to go back and she wouldn't. Too high and mighty.'

'What did he do?'

'Well, *he* didn't do anything, but she leant out of the car and shouted, "Do you know who I am?"' Loveday paused, enjoying herself. 'So, he said, "Judging by the way you look, you're nobody very important. Now you go back, because if I squeeze past you, I might dent your motor."'

'No!'

'He did. And she was in such a temper that when she reversed, she went straight into the fence and dented her car anyway. But she was that vindictive, she took his number and reported him to the police for fly-tipping, which he had a hard time proving he didn't do.'

Vindictive? Hannah pondered this, too. But almost everyone could be so, if sufficiently exasperated.

14

The Dragon

The summer weather was drawing more and more people to the coast, and the Cornish were not happy. They never were, of course, but some reports claimed that an extra five million tourists were now in the county, and that towns by the sea were bursting. Reservoirs had sunk to half, and the river that usually emptied into St Piran harbour was now a shallow trickle.

The Jolly Lobster was doing a roaring trade.

'As long as we don't run out of beer and sausages, this'll be the best summer we've had for decades,' said her Uncle Ross. 'Who needs foreign travel if the English weather is going to be like this? Bring on global warming!'

Hannah was glad for him, though everything she hated seemed to congregate around tourism. Noise, pollution, crisp packets, sunburn, the absence of shade or grace or peace. Increasingly, Endpoint felt like a refuge. Even St Piran did, protected by its ugliness.

The drought that turned moorland into tinder was never going to penetrate too deeply here, however, and every day she and Maisy woke to blue skies and the cry of white gulls over the sea was a blessing. Her mother's bungalow ached with absence yet felt like the place to be. She watered its hydrangeas and spent weekends with her mother's family.

'Mummy, why can't we stay here for ever?'

'The house isn't ours, my love.'

'Why?'

'We live in London.'

'Why do we?'

'Because we do.'

St Piran had a clean sandy beach where kids of all ages were able swim. Maisy could run around with her cousins, and her strength and confidence grew. Hannah, too, relaxed. Loveday would keep an eye on them all.

'Are you sure you don't mind? Can I give you some money for her food?' Hannah asked.

Her aunt burst out laughing.

'We see little enough of her as it is,' said Loveday. 'Stop worrying.'

'How can I repay you?'

'If Mor needs an extra pair of hands for a dinner, I'll let you know,' she answered. 'You know she's made quite a name for herself as a cook?'

Hannah's hands were aching from all the work she was doing already. No amount of bleach and black bin bags seemed enough, and despite the skips of rubbish piling up, the awful smell still came in gusts. Her uncle was coming the next day to open up the drain in the forecourt.

'Bound to be a dead rat. Unless my ex prawned a curtain-pole for me.'

'Would she do that?'

'Jinni believes in a scorched-earth policy.'

It was the first time he had mentioned his wife by name. Hannah felt uneasy, as if two separate spheres were touching.

'Why?'

'I've no idea. Some people feel that the world owes them. When she got pissed-off with me she'd slash my clothes. I didn't care about those so much, but I did when she threw out all my old notebooks of ideas for games.'

Hannah side-stepped this piece of information. 'If you're throwing these out, may I take some?' she asked, spotting some tattered old paperbacks.

'Of course. These were ours as kids. Here.' He passed her one with a picture of a dragon on the jacket. '*Green Smoke*, one of my sister's favourites. It's set in Cornwall. In Constantine Bay, no less.'

Hannah asked, 'Is that why you were called Constantine?'

'Maybe. There was a Cornish saint and a Byzantine king with the same name. My mother liked to think that our cultures would learn from each other.'

'It's an interesting name. Mine isn't even Cornish.'

'It's still a good name, a palindrome, the same backwards as forwards. It means you are without deceit.'

'Like Eve?'

'Yes, I suppose.'

How odd, Hannah reflected, that she and her rival should share this, too.

'I didn't know you had a sister,' she said, 'What—' She stopped when she saw his face.

'Drowned,' he said.

'Oh. I'm so sorry.'

161

'Yes, well. I'm the last of the Coads,' he said. 'The last of my mother's family, too. So you see why I thought—'

'No,' Hannah interrupted. 'You must not think that again.'

'What I was going to say is that, I thought your daughter should have her books, if she'd like them.'

Green Smoke was a great success with Maisy. It was about a little girl who met and befriended a dragon. In return for a share of her biscuits, the dragon told her stories about his past in the court of King Arthur and took her on short magical adventures. Every word of it seemed to sink into Maisy's skin, and after Hannah had read it to her once, she read and reread it with intense fervour. She was now determined to explore every cave along the coast, just in case it yielded a dragon. When she came to Endpoint, she sat for hours, drawing pictures of herself and a large, smiling monster on the beach.

'These are for you and Bran,' she told Coad. The dog followed Maisy around like a protective shadow. When they had romped to exhaustion, the little girl would lie in the kitchen garden with her arms wrapped around the hound, each wearing an expression of total contentment.

'I'll put them up on the kitchen wall. I used to look for R. Dragon too.'

'Did you ever find him?'

He smiled at her. 'That's a secret.'

'Did you? Really and truly?'

Hannah wondered whether he would lie, but he said, 'Everyone has to find out for themselves.'

He would have been a good father, she thought, caught off-guard.

Maisy exclaimed, 'So you did, you did, but you can't say!'

Coad smiled at her, and his grim face was lightened for a moment.

'I hope she's not bothering you.'

'No, not at all. She's a nice child. You're a good mother.'

Hannah turned away at the unexpected compliment. It hurt her almost as much as Jake's spite, because, after all, she still intended to kill him.

He paid Hannah without fail, counting out the notes on the kitchen table. She never had to remind him or wait. Every day she was so exhausted that she could hardly crawl into her car, but her labours had so far earned £700. It felt like a miracle. Another fortnight, and she could start to build up a small savings fund: exactly what she most needed before winter came. She was weary, but in a different way from before.

'Do you want a receipt?'

'Not unless you want to give me one.' He looked down at her sweaty face. 'I hope this isn't too much for you?'

'I'm used to it.'

'This is not the sort of mess you can get used to, though.'

The decrepitude of Endpoint was striking. Bushes grew out of its stonework, and ivy was spreading across window-panes and even into rooms. As room after room was cleared of decades of accumulated dust, she could see, outside and in, that the house had the wildly eccentric grace of fine architecture that did not disguise large stretches of decay. Pictures showed their absence with rectangles of vivid silk damask among the faded grey, mirrors were speckled and freckled with damp, and crystal chandeliers dulled to dirty opalescence. Mice had destroyed many soft furnishings, and spiders spun banners of filth. It would take another fortune to restore this for future generations; she was surprised that it hadn't been flagged up as at risk by some historical association but there were so many grand old houses rotting away in Cornwall that perhaps nobody noticed. The 1970s kitchen – all varnished pine like a sucked toffee – was the only half-decent room besides the bedroom that she had once slept in.

'How did it get to be like this?' Hannah asked, though it was clear from the empty bottles everywhere that there must have been at least one reason. 'Did you run out of money?'

Coad rubbed his nose. 'Partly. But a house, any house, needs love and energy to live. My dad sort of lost heart after Mum died.'

'How old were you when that happened?'

'Fourteen.'

'The worst time. Not that there's ever a good time, as I'm discovering.'

'Yes. It was.' He was silent. 'She was just, you know, the best. So funny, and beautiful. I thought all women must be like her.'

Maybe this was why he was so horrible to his wife, she thought: Jinni couldn't live up to Mummy.

'When did you inherit it?'

'Last year. Dad should really have given it to me long before, to avoid death duties, but he didn't.' Coad added, with diffidence, 'That probably sounds like a nice problem to have.'

'Yes,' said Hannah. 'I wish my mother had been able to leave me something more than a fifteen-year-old car.'

She never spoke to clients like this normally, but Coad wasn't a normal employer. No matter that her ultimate intentions towards him were malign: spending time toiling at the wiping, scrubbing, hauling water and carrying out of huge bags of rubbish together created a kind of truce. She could not decide whether he was simple or complicated. His accent was mostly Cornish, but sometimes slid into something else, as if he were truly two people in one body.

'Why do you call yourself Stan not Con?' she asked suddenly.

'Only my ex-wife calls me Con. Probably because it means something rude in French.'

'What did you do to her to make her hate you so much?'

For a moment, she feared she had been too impertinent, but he said after a silence, 'Ask her. I'm just the boring man who pays the bills.'

This was the way all men saw themselves, no doubt. Hannah had once asked a group of men, for research purposes, what they thought on seeing their reflection in the mirror when they got up, and been told, by one and all, 'Not bad.' It still made her smile, because there probably wasn't a woman in the world who thought this of themselves.

Sometimes Coad went off with an airgun to hunt vermin.

The first time Hannah saw him plodding back with a limp bagful of small corpses, she was appalled. Those furry faces, the tiny paws, emptied of life, made her think of what Jake had done in London. He saw her expression, and growled, 'If I don't shoot them, they'll kill hundreds of trees in the wood by gnawing through their bark – plus any chance of red squirrels returning to Cornwall. Far as I'm concerned, they're just fluffy rats.'

'They're still living creatures.'

'They were brought in from Canada a hundred and fifty years ago. They're not native.'

'By that logic, you should be exterminated too.' She couldn't help a note of acid entering her voice. 'You're as foreign as they are, here.'

'Maybe so. But I'm a dead shot – they never know what's hit them.'

'Even after a couple of beers at lunch?'

'Yes.'

It was probably just another video game to him, she thought.

Yet he never stood too close to her, his dog adored him, he loved Nature. So, she reminded herself, did Hitler. He was kind to Maisy and her cousins when they came to Endpoint, not seeming to mind when a ball was thrown too enthusiastically into a window. Maybe his cruelty only applied to women.

When he went off to hack and rend at brambles and bushes she could never be sure whether he might see her as another bit of vegetation in his way. After a row with his wife, she could feel his rage. Maisy, however, was irrepressible. The child who was so quiet in London chattered away to him unstoppably.

'You have a lot of books,' Maisy said. 'Even more than Mummy. Are they all stories?'

'Not all. There are lots of other kinds. Here's one you might like.'

He pulled out a big book of Renaissance paintings, once an expensive volume.

'This is by someone called Uccello, of St George and the dragon.'

'It's in the National Gallery,' Hannah added. She remembered when she had seen it with Nazneen, on first coming to London. 'I'll take you there when we get back.'

Maisy gazed at the reproduction: the pale princess in a pink dress, the winged green monster, the armoured knight on horseback rushing forwards to thrust his lance into the dragon's goggling eye.

'Poor dragon,' she said.

'I often thought so.'

'But he was keeping the princess a prisoner,' Hannah objected.

'No, Mummy.' Maisy pointed. 'She's got him on a lead, just like Bran.'

'Look at his teeth and claws, though, and his horrible great big legs. That lead won't hold him for a second.'

'Well,' said Coad, drily, 'she might be the dangerous one. Women usually are, in my experience.'

Hannah glared. Her neighbour Lila had taken her husband to court after he had tried to strangle her, she'd had a doctor's report on her injuries, but the Crown Prosecution Service had deemed it inadmissible and after a hearing it had been dismissed.

'They will believe me only if they find me dead,' Lila had said.

However pleasant Coad was to Maisy, he was still the enemy. He made it clear by a hundred remarks that he neither liked nor trusted women.

'Why are you so angry with your ex?' she asked. 'Is it just the affairs?'

'Yes. Those, and the fact she only married me for my money,' he said. 'I was a fool to believe otherwise. That's what women do, isn't it?'

Dripping with sweat, Hannah could not remain silent.

'No. Some of us do it because, fools that we are, we are in love with the men we marry. I was. Plenty of women get betrayed too. And more of us find ourselves punished through no fault of our own.'

He looked at her with a sort of sneer. 'But you're still supported by men, aren't you?'

'If only,' she replied. 'Do you think I'd be doing this job if I were?'

'No,' he said. 'I suppose not.'

She had an uneasy sense that, just as she was overhearing bits of his divorce battle, he was overhearing hers.

Once again, she'd heard from the estate agent that Jake had not paid the rent. She had rung him from the kitchen garden, just as she had rung Maisy on the day of her mother's death.

'I can't believe you're doing this to us,' she said. 'I *need* that money.'

She had heard Coad mutter, 'The eternal story.'

How could he be so stupid? Remarks like these, as if she were some sort of parasite, made her hate him. What did men think a mother and child could live on, air? He was probably one of those rich people who'd say things like, 'But you could be buying loads of *lovely* vegetables for just £3 and make a delicious soup'; or, 'How about spaghetti with a dash of olive oil and parmesan cheese, that costs practically nothing?' But try living on these for day after day after day, and you'd see why fish and chips was a treat.

One afternoon, when Maisy was in St Piran, Coad invited Hannah to come for a swim. He had been drinking and growling, and at first, she refused.

'Come on. It's too bloody hot for this.'

Hannah was caught between her fear and longing to swim.

'We've been working all day without stopping. I'll lend you a towel.'

'All right.'

Once again, she followed him down the path through the woods. It was so hot that the air seemed to throb. The little streams she had seen on her first visit had vanished beneath

168

dead leaves. Out on to the coastal path, and her heart begin to hammer. It was deserted. Even the skylarks were silent.

'How much beach is there? Can you see?'

He leant forwards to where the grass grew in tussocks, interspersed by pale rock. Her eyes dazzled. This was the moment to keep her promise. She could do it at last.

She tensed, preparing to push him over the edge, and in the second just before she did so a vast figure rose up out of the empty air between land and sea. Bigger than an eagle, bigger than an angel, its ridged, rainbow-coloured wings vibrating on the wind, it hovered before them. The shock was almost paralysing but Coad threw up his hands and staggered forwards.

Hannah could see him going over the edge of the cliff, his huge ungainly form with its arms and legs flailing, hair streaming behind him and a deep groan dwindling as he smashed on to the rocks below. Down, down, down, and then she blinked because although she could see it happening right before her eyes, it was not yet the case.

She cried out and grabbed his belt. He rocked on his feet, enormously heavy. For a terrifying moment she feared that he would drag them both over the edge, then he sank to his knees, dragging her down behind him and almost collapsing on top of her. They lay on the turf, dazed. The figure swooped on along the cliff edge, oblivious.

The only sound was that of the sea and panting. The deerhound raced up to them, anxious, lavishing both with kisses. Then Stan said, 'I thought that was going to be the end of me.'

Hannah was furious with herself, yet also profoundly relieved.

Her eyes followed the paraglider, now a distant figure swooping along the cliffs towards Fol.

'Unbelievable.'

'How did you see it? He came out of nowhere.'

'Instinct, I suppose.'

Coad said, 'I should never have got so close to the edge, especially with a drink or two inside me.'

'Who was that lunatic?'

'Didn't you recognise him? That was Bill Kenward.'

'Good God!'

Had she pushed Coad over the cliff, she would have done so in front of someone who had known her all her life. There could have been no question that he would have failed to recognise her, and she knew that he would have reported it.

'He's mad for paragliding, at his age. Bloody lunatic.'

'Yes. I must go and visit him,' she said.

'Anyway, thank you,' he said. 'That's the second time you've saved my life.'

When they continued down to the beach, she bent and picked up the Taser that had flown out of her hand.

15

At the Beach

How much the episode affected her employer's behaviour towards her was hard to tell, but from then on, his manner to her was less guarded.

'I suppose the good thing about a near-death experience is that you're forced to realise you don't really want to die.'

'Yes, it concentrates the mind wonderfully,' Hannah said.

She had failed for the third time, and it felt as if it was fate. Why should she be any more successful at murder than she was at marriage, motherhood or a career? Although she had probably committed a crime just by conspiring to do this in the first place, the feeling of relief that swept over her when she decided to cease from further attempts was a powerful one. Maybe Stan wasn't as bad as Jinni had made out. Maybe she could find a way round her own predicament with Jake. The fear she felt of destitution had gone, and she was sleeping better and eating better. The more her savings mounted, the less desperate she felt about the future.

'I've stopped drinking. It wasn't good for me.'

'No, it usually isn't.'

'If I seem to be slipping back, say something.'

'I can't be responsible for your behaviour, you know.'

He grimaced. 'I did as you suggested and saw a GP. She was better than I expected – I suppose depression is one of the commonest complaints round here.'

'Yes. Mum always said that half the people in St Piran are addicted to anti-depressants.'

'That bad? I had no idea. She prescribed me some pills but said to try running first. So I did, and it helps.'

'Bran must enjoy that.'

'He does.' He was sweeping up some glass. That morning, they had opened a cupboard and several empty bottles of spirits had tumbled out to smash on the stone floor. 'Jesus! How many more of these did he leave? No wonder my ex couldn't stand it.'

Hannah winced.

'How long did she live here with you?'

'Ages. About a month.' He saw her expression. 'Jinni didn't sign up for looking after a demented old man in Cornwall. Not just because it was stressful and boring but—'

'Did she ever love you?'

'I expect not. Jinni, well, it's always about her. She wants to be the centre of attention, always.'

Hannah asked, knowing all too well what the answer was, 'Is she?'

'Always. She's very beautiful, and . . . you want to please her, to be worthy of her attention except you can't be, not ever. But if you deny her anything, she never forgives you.'

'How do you mean?'

Stan shrugged. 'She does stuff, like changing my

172

Wikipedia page. It's protected now, but she wrote some nasty things.'

Or plotting to have you murdered, Hannah thought. Ever since the cliff edge, she had begun to feel doubt about Jinni. Why had she trusted a complete stranger? That meeting on the train had been so intoxicatingly strange, she almost wondered whether she had been hypnotised as well as tipsy. But it turned out that there was a difference between thinking about murder and doing it. She had been shocked by her hallucination of Stan's fall. It had been so vivid that she still couldn't see him without a feeling of guilt and shame. A part of her believed that she had murdered him already.

Sometimes Hannah thought of Jinni as a friend, or at least an ally; sometimes as an enemy. Her glamour, her sophistication, her air of mystery that might or might not include sympathy all held a charge that was almost irresistible. It consumed her imagination to such a degree that she wondered whether she was, for the first time in her life, attracted to another woman; or whether she had somehow been overawed by her as the incarnation of all that she was not. As she worked her way through the first pair of new Marigolds, two bottles of bleach, three pots of Astonish, four rolls of black bin bags and five old sheets ripped into rags, Hannah found herself becoming less crushed and more curious about her employer's marriage.

It did not escape her that by not killing Jinni's husband she was also saving her own. Jinni would not kill Jake unless Hannah killed Stan, and however angry, wounded and badly treated she was, Jake did not deserve to die for his actions. The further she stepped back from this state of mind, the more relieved she became. Yes, it was probably true that most divorcing people found themselves wishing their former partner would drop down dead, while also fantasising about going back to the time in which they were still happy. People were capable of having two or more completely contradictory feelings about each other and not acting on them, because they were (usually) rational beings. It partly came down to this: she didn't want Jake to be harmed, just for him to come to his senses and stop behaving like a monster. Death was an excessive punishment for disappointment on her side and meanness on his.

Room after room yielded to her labours. Once her Uncle Kit had cleared the drain, the smell vanished and before long was replaced by fresh air and the scent of beeswax. The house would still leak and creak, and was unmistakably shabby and frail, but freed from its piles of clutter, excrement, mouse-droppings and baroque cobwebs it regained something of its former grace.

She wondered how Coad's wife had ever coped, because Jinni was not the kind of person whom she could imagine outside London, though mail still came for Mrs G. Coad. Mostly, they were invoices. *I'm just the boring man who pays the bills.*

'So why did you get married?'

Stan sighed gustily. 'Because when she fixes people with the tractor beam of her attention, they almost always do as she wants. Have you ever met anyone like that?'

'Yes,' said Hannah truthfully. 'Why you, though?'

'I have no idea, except I happened to be around, and I must have seemed more successful than I was. And it was New York, where apparently there aren't too many straight single men around. I was this geek who got lucky, or that's what it felt like.'

'I felt the same with my ex, I suppose,' Hannah said. 'It

wasn't just first love, I was afraid to let go. But you were a grown-up; you must have had some idea?'

'Who is ever grown-up, deep down? I'd had other girl-friends, but not like her, and I was living in another country and culture, far away from everyone ... Some colleagues tried to warn me, only I didn't listen. I thought they were envious, or just didn't know what she was really like. I was so tired of being alone. I wanted a family, a life together, and I stupidly assumed she did as well. But she didn't.'

'Didn't or couldn't?'

This had been the part of Jinni's story that had particularly excited Hannah's compassion.

'Didn't. Maybe we should have discussed children before we got married.'

'Er – yes, you should.'

'Well, my bad. She told lie after lie; first that she wanted them, but not yet, then that she couldn't have them because she'd had cancer treatment. Only she hadn't.'

'She lied that she'd had *cancer*?'

'Yes.'

Hannah did not know what to think. Of course, women should not be pressured or coerced into having babies if they didn't want to, nobody should, but this was still disturbing. It struck her that Stan might be making this whole story up to justify himself.

'Maybe she couldn't bear to tell you the truth. Lots of women are terrified of childbirth. It's no picnic, you know. Well, you don't, but take it from me.'

'No. I asked her if it was that. She said she just didn't want a family.'

'So why did she marry you? There must have been plenty of others.'

'Oh, there were. But not ones who had more money than sense.'

It sounded close to the kind of thing Jake accused her of, not that he'd ever made the kind of money that Coad, presumably, once commanded. But all these things could be true, Hannah thought. It was entirely plausible that he had taken out his frustration on his wife. She had seen the marks of this, after all.

It was not, in the end, her problem. Her main concern was to keep her daughter safe. Maisy could accompany her to Endpoint whenever she wished, and being besotted with the deerhound, she often did. Hannah had no fear as long as Bran was beside her, a grey arc of fur and friendship. At low tide Hannah swam with her in rock pools while Stan went off into the deeper waters, ploughing into the waves without a backwards glance. His indifference was welcome. Ever since Jake had left her, and perhaps since she had given birth to Maisy, she wanted only to make herself invisible. The dark streaks on his back had taken a long time to fade, and it was not until she saw they had become olive that she realised they were bruises.

The fight with Jinni must have been violent indeed, yet oddly mismatched. Stan's strength was not in question: she had seen him chop wood, heave boxes, wrench up fence-posts almost without effort. He could have snapped any woman's arm like a twig, but she now wondered whether Jinni's bruises might have been caused by him preventing blows rather than giving them.

Apart from his labours, he locked himself away in his workshop in the stable block for several hours a day. He was working on a new game, his first in seven years.

'All by yourself?'

'I work remotely with other designers like Geoff. It takes so long, that's the problem.'

'So, not like writing an actual book, which only needs pen and paper?'

She meant it sarcastically, but he responded with more enthusiasm than she'd ever seen in him.

'You do need those, for ideas, yes. But a lot more besides, like coding and artwork and music and ultimately actors reading a script. A lot of people are involved in every game. It's not like anything else, except perhaps a movie.'

'It sounds complicated.'

'It is, and if I can get the central character right then everything might change. The last one, well, it got me kicked off the company.'

'Why?'

'They wanted a shooter game, and I was through with those.'

'I thought they were all about running and killing.'

Stan shook his head. 'That's like thinking all films are James Bond.'

'What's your new one about? Does it have a plot?'

'A game doesn't have one plot. That's what makes it interesting.'

Hannah found herself smiling. 'I could never find a game more interesting than a good book.'

'How do you know? You've said you never played one.'

'It seems a waste of time.'

'Well, that's just what people thought about novels when they first became popular.'

She longed to have the leisure to read again, but most days there was no time. And if there was she preferred to spend it larking about with her daughter. The steep, rocky cliffs and the shining sand watermarked by the tide, the white gulls calling overhead, the navy waves frilling on to land were a place outside time in which they could just enjoy each other's company, being silly together. Just as she had once dreamt of doing, Hannah showed Maisy the rock pool and when its tiny creatures palled, they became absorbed in building a large sandcastle.

'If we add sea-glass, it could have windows.'

'And a garden of shells.'

They were exquisitely at ease together.

'Are you going to make a moat for the tide?' Stan asked. He'd come back, unnoticed, and squatted before the sandcastle.

'What's a moat?'

'A deep ditch around a castle that you fill with water, to stop enemies from getting in.'

'OK,' Maisy said.

Together, they carved a deep moat all around the castle, then watched the tide foam in, encircling the sandcastle with water, making it instantly, gloriously real just before it slumped back into formlessness. The next time a wave surged up the beach, Hannah picked up their bag.

'Time to go now.'

'Goodbye, sea, goodbye,' Maisy sang, as they ran ahead of the racing, frothing water. 'Can't catch me, can't catch me!'

The sea chased them to the edge of the cliff path. Maisy shrieked with delight, but Stan bent down and said, with great seriousness, 'Maisy, promise me you'll never go on to a beach without a grown-up. It may look friendly now, but when the tide turns, it can kill the strongest swimmer.'

Hannah glanced at Coad. He'd said his sister had drowned, and she assumed from his expression that it must have been here.

'I won't,' she said; then, 'Mummy, I think my tooth might be a little bit wobbly.'

'Do you? Maybe you'll be getting a visit from the Tooth Fairy soon then.'

'Will the Tooth Fairy visit me even if I'm at Daddy's?'

'Yes, I'm sure she will,' Hannah said, quashing her resentment at the thought of anyone but herself taking charge of her daughter's first milk tooth.

The climb back up always tired her, and seeing Maisy lagging Coad said, 'I can give you a piggyback to the house, if your mum allows.'

'Yes! Say yes, Mummy.'

Hannah paused, weighing up her mistrust with the effort of carrying her child up herself.

'Can't she have a dog-sleigh?'

'She's too light. Bran will pull her over. You could have one again, though.'

'Um. All right, then.'

He handed her Bran's lead then scooped her daughter on to his back and continued up the steps.

'Home, Bran!' he said, and the lean shape surged ahead, pulling Hannah up. She remembered her first visit, and a pang of sadness rose in her. If only he were just Stan the caretaker.

'You're very kind.'

'She's as light as a feather.'

Maisy chatted the whole way up. She never stopped asking questions, which ranged from what was inside the TV to whether people could be lonely when asleep.

'Do you think I could find the dragon? The real R. Dragon, like in my book?'

'Maybe,' Coad said. 'He lived in a Cornish cave, didn't he?'

'I've saved a biscuit for him, just in case.'

Hannah heard the yearning in her daughter's voice. At least dragons could not be bought, although an ominous obsession with a hideous concrete ornament in St Piran's garden centre that could emit smoke from its scaly nostrils was currently preoccupying her.

'I don't think it's very likely, sweetie,' Hannah told her.

'You're not looking.' Maisy pointed. 'There!'

Something strange was happening near the top of the cliffs. A spray of glittering water spouted out of the ground in a veil of sparkling drops; it subsided, then puffed up again.

'What's that?' she asked.

Maisy wriggled off Stan's back and darted forward. 'It's dragon-smoke, Mummy!'

'Stop!' he shouted.

The child took no notice. She was running for the pile of rocks where the spray emerged, as quick as her thin little legs could take her.

Coad lunged forwards and caught her in a rugby tackle just before she got to it. Maisy, greatly shocked, opened her mouth to cry.

'I said stop, Maisy.'

His voice was very stern.

'I *want* to see him.'

Hannah was furious.

'Let go of my daughter, please.'

He glared at them both, and she was reminded for a moment of their first meeting.

'That's a hundred-metre drop into a cave, right there.'

'But there are *rocks*.'

'They aren't stable. She could have fallen in and been killed.'

'I want to see the cave.' Maisy's lips trembled.

Stan drew a deep breath.

'I'm sorry I frightened you. That's not a friendly dragon, but a very dangerous one. Do you understand, Maisy? If you get any closer, you'd fall right down his throat and be killed.'

The water sprayed out again, an enchanted fountain.

'What causes it?'

'At high tide, the waves are forced up the chimney. That's why it's called a blowhole. I think the author of *Green Smoke* must have got her idea from the phenomenon.'

Hannah said, with an effort, 'You must listen to Stan, darling. He grew up here. Stay away from these rocks.'

Maisy asked, 'Have you ever been into its cave?'

'Yes.' He nodded. 'When I was a boy, I used to be fascinated by this, just like you. So I went into it, as far as I could go, and it almost caught me.'

Maisy's face pinched. 'Does that mean it might eat me? When I go for a swim?'

Stan rubbed his nose – Hannah now realised that he did this when he was worried. 'No. Not if you're with a grown-up. Look, why don't you let Bran guide you through the woods? You might get to see the white stag.'

Hannah watched her daughter run ahead, then said, 'Can't you just tell her about the tides?'

'I don't think she'd understand yet. But she'll understand dragons.'

'She will.' Hannah paused, then said, 'Thank you.'

After this, their conversations became more informal. The lunches he produced kept surprising her: fried aubergine, marrows stuffed with fragrant rice, meat and pine nuts, salad in pitta bread, square parcels of spicy mince, bright mango pickle.

'What sort of food is this?' she asked.

'It's Iraqi. My mother taught me to cook. It's the greatest comfort an exile can have.'

'What are these red things in the salad? I know I should recognise them, somehow.'

'Pomegranate seeds.'

'Will I have to spend half the year with you if I eat any?'

She didn't expect him to understand, but he responded, 'Winters aren't long here, Persephone.'

'I know. I miss Cornwall most in winter.'

'So you're not tempted to come back?'

Hannah paused in swallowing.

'Yes, of course. Mum's family are all here. I could walk round town with my eyes shut. Only . . . I want *more* than Spar shops, and everyone being like something left over from the nineteen fifties.'

'Places move on, though. For instance, I bought the ingredients for this in the local Waitrose.'

'Maybe,' said Hannah, unconvinced. She didn't want to say that only yesterday, her uncle had referred to him as a 'darky'. It wasn't meant nastily, but it had sickened her all the same. Stan would always be different here, simply because his skin was a few tints browner than the undiluted Cornish natives. Out in the south-west you never saw a single black or brown face except on TV, and yet people were convinced the country was being over-run by foreigners.

Few here paid much attention to the national news, and especially not anything to do with politics. Hannah knew without asking how her mother's family had voted: the same way that their parents and grandparents had always done, believing they were protecting their communities and the seas that they had fished in for generations and could now no longer look to for a living. Every year, St Piran became poorer, and it only added to their fear and anger.

It was the same all over the country. People had always had quarrels, but now the gulf between old and young, rich and poor, city and country seemed deeper, and each side was fiercely entrenched. Cornwall had voted overwhelmingly to Leave – though the very next day after the Referendum, the story went, it asked if it could still get the grant money it had been given by Europe. Londoners loved recounting this, though it added to their fury and incomprehension about why half the country – or just over half of it – had such different politics.

'It's pure racism,' Polly had said, and in a way it was: but the race the Cornish most objected to was Londoners.

Coad was an odd fish to find in this place. Gradually, she gathered a few more details about him. He'd taught himself to code at fourteen, being obsessed with the particularly noxious shooter game *Victory Cry*, set in the Iraq War. No surprises there, she thought; he'd gone to America to work for the company that made it, risen rapidly and then he'd developed *Victory Cry 2* with online modifications that had made him a celebrity of sorts in the gaming world. Unknown to his employers, he had put hidden content which allowed players to find a room with a door. When opened, it revealed the Iraqi widows and orphans of all those you had killed and made you follow their stories. Gamers world-wide had been outraged, and Coad had been fired.

'What I did was give it emergent properties, something that's since become cool but they hated me for it,' he said. 'Too much like criticising America.'

He had set up as an independent, producing a single game,

Pilgrim, which asked players to make increasingly difficult choices about who they saved on a journey escaping from a murderous kingdom, and who they allowed to die. It had been put out for free online, and nobody had made money from it but Coad had been hailed as an artist revolutionising gaming. It was all very confusing, and the only thing Hannah was sure of was that she would never want to play it.

'But why not?'

'I'd rather see a story through my imagination and the language.'

'Which is only one way to enjoy it.'

'It's still the best way. Just one person putting down words on a page, and one person reading them. Like a message passed across space and time, from their heart and mind into mine. It's different for every single person who reads it, but it's still pure.'

'A game isn't impure because it's more complex, any more than a film or a play is.'

He seemed less frightening and bad-tempered now he wasn't drinking. When not working at the cleaning, or in his office, he would doodle images for the new game that would have 'a kind of Albrecht Dürer meets Mervyn Peake look to it'.

'What?'

'Beautiful but sinister. Like the architecture in Prague.'

'I've never been there,' she said. 'I've hardly been anywhere. You don't realise that someone like me must hunt every bit of information down on the internet if we have access to a computer and learn it all by ourselves. It's not in the air we breathe. We'll never be at ease with culture in the way you are, we'll always be despised for it.'

Stan looked at her in mild surprise.

'Why would anyone despise you?'

'Oh I'm sure you do.'

'No. Why would I?'

'Because that's what people like you, born into privilege, always do. But someone like me might as well stay ignorant because all it does is show us a world we can't ever enter.'

He rubbed his nose, thinking.

'Well, firstly, as you say, most of it is online now, and secondly a lot of people who have access to high culture don't value it. Whether you love books or art or music is as much to do with your temperament as education, surely?'

'But you still know it exists in the first place.'

'So much is luck. What your parents do or enjoy. Teachers at school. Friends you make.'

Resentfully she said, 'I didn't meet those kinds of people here. I grew up in a bookless home. The only books I had were the ones Bill Kenward gave to me, or that I bought myself. You've no idea how desperate that is – if you love reading.'

'I do, too. He was important to me as well, you know. Like an adopted godfather, not that we did God in my family.'

Hannah thought, I bet you had only to point to a book for it to be bought by your parents. Then she felt guilty, because her own home had been nothing like as dirty and chaotic as his.

'How do you know him?'

'Bill was a friend of my parents'.'

'He's a mystery to most.'

'Why a mystery?'

'Nobody knows why he came to live here.'

'Do people need a reason? Plenty just love Cornwall. But he had connections here, didn't he?'

'I'm not sure. I never felt he and Mum were friends, really. They'd both worked at the same public school, ages ago.'

'Knotshead. Yes. I was a pupil there for a few years, when Mum became sick.'

Immediately intrigued she asked, 'What was it like?'

'It had good parts and bad parts. Mostly bad, because I was so worried about my mother. But when she was dying, I came back to St Piran, and after GCSEs I stayed here.'

'I'm so sorry,' Hannah said, and despite herself her eyes filled with tears.

'Yes, well.' He fondled his dog's ears. 'The people you love never leave you. Even if that's no comfort to you now, it will be.'

Jake had seemed kind, too. When they had gone on their first summer holiday together, Hannah had broken her leg and he had risen to the disaster magnificently, staying with her to talk to the hospital staff in almost-fluent Spanish, impressing everyone with his patience and consideration.

Hannah clenched her fists. Coad might not deserve death, but she must not feel sorry for him.

16

A Cold Eye

High summer, and in the main streets of Fol you couldn't park or walk, just shuffle. There wasn't much to do apart from sail, sunbathe, shop and swim, so the next most popular entertainment was entertaining.

'You free to help serve at a private dinner?' Mor asked.

'Sure. How many?'

'Nine. The Sponges. Cadan is helping me in the kitchen but I need an extra pair of hands.'

She could do it, of course she could, even if she was beginning to get twinges in her back and knees that would make it less and less easy to earn a living as a cleaner. It meant borrowing a black skirt and white shirt (just in case any of the guests could possibly mistake her for one of themselves) and scraping her hair back into a tight ponytail. There was a perverse comfort in this, because as soon as she put on a uniform, she might as well have become invisible.

People believed that servants no longer existed in Britain,

and it was true as far as the sort that were shown in television series of the kind adored by foreigners as the essence of England. Hannah couldn't bear to watch those feasts of nostalgia. Everyone fantasised about having staff, whether these were butlers, nannies, cooks, chauffeurs or cleaners – but everyone who was not like herself believed that the servants no longer existed. What had happened was that the cooking, cleaning, driving and child-minding was no longer the responsibility of a resident household but outsourced to people who had all the responsibility and no security. It was supposed to mean that people were 'free to negotiate better conditions', but in practice the young, the powerless, the indebted were just hired and fired on the spot.

After cleaning and caring for their families, what rich people hated most was making their own meals. Somehow Mor had been smart enough to switch from hairdressing to cooking, and managed to build up her catering business on the back of this. Gentle and unpretentious, she'd been employed in one of the best restaurants in the south-west. Now she was working for herself, out of her uncle's pub. Hannah suspected that a fair bit of extra sea-bass that EU regulations demanded should be thrown back dead into the sea somehow wound up on the table this way; but the fame of the food at the Jolly Lobster had grown to such an extent that food critics from the national press had ventured down to taste it and pronounce it worth having – 'even if', the *Telegraph* could not help adding, 'the décor is deplorable'.

Hannah knew who the Sponges were: Ivo was the editor of the *Chronicle* newspaper, and Ellen an American shoe designer of some fame. They had bought a cottage in Fol a decade ago as a holiday home and were almost local celebrities.

Beaufol House overlooked the Fol estuary. It had been expanded upwards, downwards and sideways until it was three times its original size. Inside, everything was painted, furnished and upholstered in navy – this colour having replaced grey as the current shade of luxury – although the floors were all limestone. There was plenty of thick rope, decoratively twined, and a generally nautical air.

'See that yacht?' her cousin murmured. 'That belongs to one of the guests, Philip Wu – a billionaire, from Singapore, nickname Panga – and his wife Cecilia.'

'Is she from Singapore too?'

'No. Some sort of Anglo-German princess. The other guests I know about are the Evenlodes. Lord and Lady.'

'No pressure, then.'

Ellen Sponge was clearly feeling the strain but Mor was calm, putting food in the oven or on to the Sponges' platters. It is always disconcerting to see someone you think you know well show their professionalism, and as Hannah began circulating with canapés, she felt real pride in her cousin. Mor had succeeded by a different route, one that was not academic but which was every bit as demanding as the one Hannah had believed in, and it was she who was the real star of the Penrose clan. Dressed in spotless white, her eyes luminous with concentration, she was as dedicated to her craft as any artist. Indeed, she *was* an artist, even if the guests barely even seemed to taste or see Mor's exquisite confections, consumed in a single swallow. The quail's eggs, the caviar, the lobster and vegetable *amuses-bouches* were more like punctuation to conversation than food.

'Who's that?' Hannah asked, spotting someone vaguely familiar.

'Benedick Hunter.'

'Not the actor we all used to fancy in *Slapdash*?'

Hannah peered through a large floral arrangement that shielded the kitchen area from the rest. He looked like a magazine that had been left out in the rain.

'Himself. Now the face of Stannah Stairlifts.'

The guests were almost all Londoners, dressed in the relaxed way of people whose whole life was, as far as she could see, a holiday. Thinner, livelier and smart even in casual dress, their faces wore the expressions of amused cynicism that made their tribe distinct. Hannah's gaze flicked over to the women's jewels, the men's linen shirts and deck shoes. Money like this had leached the life out of Fol, as surely as the warming seas were bleaching coral. Ever since the town had become fashionable, its rents had soared, so that only coffee shops and knick-knack boutiques survived in what had once been a place with real businesses like a butcher, a baker and a hardware merchant.

'Such a charming place.'

'Yes, on a good day, it could be mistaken for Italy.'

There was a general murmur of complacency, for this year the fall in sterling meant Europe was out of fashion for a holiday, even for the rich.

'Besides, our grandchildren keep lecturing us about being more environmentally responsible and not flying.'

'Don't for goodness' sakes go to Padstow. It's just one pasty shop after another.'

'Absolute rip-off. I mean, it's one thing to put Cornwall on the map and another to make it an extension of Chelsea.'

'Poor Cornwall,' said an elderly woman in a deep voice. 'It has no choice but tourism now.'

She and her husband were by far the shabbiest of those present, with teeth like faded yellow dusters on a washing line and long, sad faces. He wore what looked like his old school tie, a fraying black fabric with pale blue stripes and she a necklace of cough sweets that were probably amethysts, and an air of ruined beauty that was indistinguishable from pride. Hannah guessed these were Lord and Lady Evenlode. So these were Jake's grandparents. She had never met them. They had been too snobbish to come to her wedding, but the excuse had been bad health and hip replacements. Jake had visited them when staying briefly at her mother's in St Piran. They lived in a huge old pile near there; the gardens, which were famous and occasionally open to the public, had been landscaped by Humphry Repton.

'Summer like this is bound to put prices up next year. We feel we got in just in time.'

'I prefer Devon,' said the actor, 'though everywhere is bursting at the seams now.'

'I'm just glad to be out of London,' said Ivo. 'The pollution has become quite appalling.'

'So is the traffic along the A30. And the trains keep breaking down.'

'Really, the *only* thing is to fly to Newquay,' said Ellen.

It was not these people's fault that they were multi-millionaires, that they had got on to the housing ladder decades ago and had no idea what it was like for anyone under thirty. It was not good to hate, it made her feel sick and miserable, but it was better than feeling she had no right to exist.

Every time she glimpsed the assembled party on the other side of the elaborate floral arrangement, it crossed her mind that, had she remained with Jake she would not have been serving them but among them. Though she would never have been accepted. To them, the only thing worse than being a Londoner was coming from a town.

She could overhear snatches of conversation.

'What the people down here don't understand is that Britain's economy depends on services, not goods—'

'Of course, London is the new oil, and its wealth should be shared more fairly, but they'll ruin everything—'

'You wait; we'll run out of everything, food, medicines, paper, cars—'

' . . . used to come here every summer when we were little. My brother even married one of the locals.'

Hannah's heart jumped into her mouth. She knew that voice.

'Really?'

'Frightful mistake.'

'Why?'

'Total pramface; got her hooks in at university—'

'Many get carried away by a pretty face—'

'I thought you said it was the tits,' said a male voice.

Hannah retreated to the kitchen area. There was no doubt that the speaker was Jake's sister Saskia, and the pramface in question was herself. She had never heard the expression before but knew instantly what it meant. Even though she gained a degree identical to Jake's she had apparently been one, simply because she'd grown up on a Cornish council estate and fallen pregnant by mistake.

Rage and mortification hurt her head. No wonder they looked down on her.

'All right, Han?'

Mor had noticed her distress.

'Um, no. Someone I used to know is a guest here.'

'Who?'

Hannah grimaced. 'They won't recognise me as a waitress, don't worry. The Wilcoxes never notice staff.'

'Do you want to leave?'

'I just need a moment.'

Cadan went out to pour more wine. He managed it beautifully, but one of the guests registered his face and flinched. It was Saskia, naturally. It was an offence to disturb the bubble of perfection in which these people lived, Hannah thought. Her cousin noticed, of course he did. He returned to the workstation.

'They don't like me,' he told Mor, his mouth trembling.

'I think she noticed you're doing so well.'

'I am?'

'You are. You were so quiet that you made her jump, that's all. But that's fine.'

Hannah patted his shoulder, thinking to herself that if her cousin ever lost his temper he would be as terrifying as Stan. But wasn't that the case always? The bitter lines from one of Shakespeare's sonnets came back to her. *They that have power to hurt, and will do none . . . They rightly do inherit heaven's graces.* Jake had talked of his temper with affectionate regret, as if it were a dog over which he had no control.

Every time she was sent another vile text by him, she felt herself going mad again. She had buried the memory of all the bad things he had done to her – the hair-pulling, the red-hot potato, the arm-twisting – and then wondered why. But she knew why. What was the point of remembering unless you could change your life?

The meal flowed on. Serving dishes were brought, circulated, removed. Hannah listened without showing she listened. People did not look beyond the candlelight, and in her waitressing gear she was invisible.

'We couldn't decide between oak, mahogany and walnut for the fittings in the yacht, so in the end I asked Cecilia—'

'Impossible to find a decent hotel with a helicopter pad—'

'Montenegro has been ruined, Kazakhstan is the place. You can hunt wolves there from a helicopter. Simply marvellous, darling.'

Hannah tried not to stare at her sister-in-law. Saskia's face was already pouchy with discontent, her fat rows of cultured pearls and her large diamond rings not disguising this. Jake's sister had never uttered two words to her that were not spiteful or dismissive, and yet she was putting herself out to try and be charming to Cecilia. She is unhappy, Hannah thought, because she has never learnt to be kind, which is the very worst sort of unhappiness because nobody will ever feel sympathy for you. Cecilia, who was used to having people suck up to her, was clearly not impressed but too polite to be snubbing; and Saskia was too stupid or too desperate to perceive this.

' ... why the proposed development should be turned down, as long as they call it Fol Bay not St Piran.'

'But will he sell?'

'I don't think he's got any choice,' said Saskia's husband.

'He's some sort of video games bore, isn't he?'

'Yes. Briefly successful, something like *Soldier* or *Assassin*.'

'*Pilgrim*, I think,' said Ivo. 'Our eldest son played it for months. Says its coding is extremely elegant and spare, whatever that means.'

They had to be discussing Stan, and Endpoint. Hannah hovered with her platter.

'Such a weird sub-culture, though it's worth billions.'

'It's not a sub-culture any longer. Gaming is bigger than movies now,' said Wu.

'Don't you find that depressing?' said Ellen.

'Oh no!' said Cecilia. 'You're thinking of the early games. Now it's more like improv theatre, because tiny choices, like shaving or picking a flower, make an enormous difference to each outcome. I used to review them for the *Rambler* magazine.'

'The last time I played *Red Dead Redemption*, I was in a beautiful moonlit forest and killed one bear and the game generated a whole pack of them, and they killed my horse so I couldn't get away and had to spend the whole night shooting to stay alive,' said Philip Wu. 'It's like throwing dice with a hundred functions. The kind of mind that can think of all that has me in awe.'

'I can't believe a game could ever have the complexity of a great novel,' Ivo said. 'Being inside a character's head, feeling their feelings and understanding their motives.'

Hannah nodded silently, but Cecilia said, 'I used to think like you, until I tried gaming.'

'But there's something so infantile about dying and coming back to life at an earlier point,' said Ivo. 'What gives a novel depth is what gives our lives meaning.'

'Which is what? Money?' asked Saskia, with a touch of unpleasantness.

'Why no,' Ivo said. 'Death.'

Wu said, 'It's still an interesting philosophical experiment to imagine alternatives, however. There are novels and films with split endings, after all.'

'Yes,' said Ivo pleasantly; 'but it is a lie. Life has only one direction.'

'Did you ever meet his wife?' said Saskia. '*What* a woman!'

Hannah felt the pang of some emotion she could not quite identify.

'An odd couple,' said Lady Evenlode. 'I could never see what they could possibly have in common.'

'I worked with her once, years ago,' said Benedick.

'In a play?'

'No, a very bad TV series.'

Ah, Hannah thought. So Jinni was an actress. It made sense, in a way; not that she'd ever met any actors in real life.

The chatter rose: the talk of people who didn't really know each other but who were trying to make themselves agreeable by finding common cause while drinking too much wine. Hannah retreated to help her cousin. Mor was focused only on ensuring that every dish she sent out was exquisitely cooked and prepared.

While the second course was being eaten, Hannah went out to the side of the house for some air. Cadan was there, sitting on a steel dustbin, looking up at the night sky. He gave her the beaming smile that made her love him. Loveday always called him her special child.

'A'right?'

Hannah nodded. 'You?'

'I like the stars.'

'Me too.' They were quiet for a little, looking up. 'Do you often help Mor?'

'She's training me,' Cadan said, with pride. 'I can make may – mayo.'

'That's more than I can do,' Hannah said.

Inside, the diners were increasingly animated, even if much of their animation seemed to draw on animosity towards the political issue that was dividing counties and families the length and breadth of Britain. As the wine glasses were filled and refilled, she exchanged glances with Mor, knowing that her cousin probably shared some of her private irritation. They needed this money, of course they did, and dinners like these were what kept paying the bills through the lean winter months. Mor would be charging £80 a head, clearing about £35 of that given how cleverly the local lobster and crayfish were eked out, but the price for it was their pride. At least her uncle Kit was now a home-owner. He had teamed up with four other young couples, one of them a farmer's daughter gifted with a plot of land a couple of miles from the coast. They'd built five houses for themselves, each couple providing an essential service for each dwelling: masonry, electrics, carpentry, plumbing, and digging the foundations. Unless you inherited, like Ross and the Jolly Lobster, it was the only way ordinary working families could possibly buy their own homes.

She knew what Loveday would say: why shouldn't rich people as well as poorer ones come here on holiday? Surely it was better they should spend money in Cornwall than in St Tropez or Florida, especially if it meant they didn't fly there? If you lived and worked in a place blessed by nature, you had to accept the summer crowds as the toll. You didn't have to be born in a place to feel some connection to it, or to want to retire there. If only they didn't also kill the thing they loved.

She glanced over at her former sister-in-law, in between stacking dishes. Saskia really did not look happy, and neither did her husband – what was he called? Rupert? No, Hamish. The property developer, whom Jake had called with a curl of the lip, 'a Surrey Scot'. They were quarrelling in the way of posh people, which meant talking with shocking frank-ness and controlled venom about each other in front of an audience.

'You only married me because nobody else would have you,' Hamish was saying.

'Oh, don't be absurd. I could have married anyone.'

'As long as they weren't poor. My wife can't abide anyone with an income of less than £200k.'

'What's wrong with that?' Saskia drew herself up. 'You're not suggesting that *poverty* is an essential part of marriage?'

'Oh, surely not. Just think of the school fees!' said Ivo Sponge, with a touch of irony. He glanced at his wife, who raised her eyebrows. Of all the couples present, Hannah thought, they were the only ones who looked as if they might genuinely like each other.

'No, you're not so stupid as to believe for richer, for poorer is anything other than a formula.'

'I wanted *children*,' said Saskia, in anguish.

'Really? They're so exhausting, darling,' said Wu's wife, yawning. 'Ours woke me up last night, and I had to wake the night nanny to see what was wrong.'

There was a ripple of laughter at this, although Hannah could tell that it had not been said as a joke.

'Do you mean, Panga, you have *two* nannies on board?'

'Why not? Otherwise, where would be the holiday?' said Wu's wife.

'Where indeed?' said Ivo, with the blandest of expressions.

'Do you take all your holidays on the sea?' asked Lord Evenlode, with creaky politeness. Hannah looked at him with interest:

'Oh no, of course not. For one thing, I get seasick. Even with pills. So darling Panga—'

'Cecilia is asking me to buy us an English country house,' Wu said. He smiled, showing teeth that had probably cost a fortune in orthodontics and made quite an ordinary face into one of dazzling good looks. 'She feels that now the twins can run around, it would be better to stick to the land.'

'Are you looking down here?' asked Lady Evenlode, suddenly waking up. 'There are plenty of fine Cornish houses.'

Hannah paused while trying not to scrape the remains of the dinner too noisily into the Tupperware she was taking back home. Three of the women there had barely touched it.

'Really?'

'Yes. Like Endpoint. Lovely house, decent estate.'

'Cornwall is heaven, if you can stomach the rain and the locals,' said Saskia.

'Frankly, they should be lined up against a wall and shot for tanking the economy,' said the actor. 'Why did anyone think a referendum is ever a good idea? We all know what would happen if there were one on capital punishment.'

'Quite,' Ivo answered. He sounded bored, probably because conversations like these were too familiar.

'That's why democracy is such a bad idea,' Philip Wu added. 'What would people rather live in, India or Singapore?'

'I do adore India, though. Such wonderful people,' said Ellen.

'Yes but those dreadful drains! And the roads. Singapore is completely twenty-first century.'

'One simply has to have a helicopter in India,' said Wu. 'Much, I suspect, like Cornwall.'

There was general laughter, though the actor said, 'I'd rather have bad plumbing and freedom.'

'Aren't you interested in the land at Endpoint, Hamish?'

'If I were, I would hardly say so,' Saskia's husband answered. His face was mottled with red, like the left-over Eton Mess Hannah was decanting for the kids to enjoy the next day.

'It has views across the bay – or would do if most of the woods were felled,' said Lord Evenlode. 'Always been the drawback of that place, the lack of a decent sea view.'

Hannah heard this in horror.

'Why's it for sale?'

'The owner's father neglected to make provision for death duties,' answered Lord Evenlode.

Saskia said, 'And he's divorcing. Not a nice man, by all accounts.'

Lady Evenlode gave her a piercing look. 'There are two sides to every story in a marriage, aren't there?'

'Oh, yes, but I had this from the horse's mouth.'

Hamish snorted. 'Women are such champions of their own sex, aren't they? I suppose you never, ever lie.'

'Only about the cost of clothes,' said his wife.

Hannah went on with the washing-up, her thoughts churning with the dishwasher. So Saskia knew Jinni, somehow. She must know a great many people, of course. Over time, it had become painfully clear how most of Jake's world knew each other and had done so for generations. They went to school together, or on holiday, or bought homes in the same place, and everyone else didn't exist except as servants and functionaries. She might as well have been living in one of Jane Austen's villages, except that as a working-class Cornishwoman she wouldn't even have been a governess.

All the false confidence that education had given her was stripped away. She could read and read and work and work and would never be one of them. If she were to reveal her presence to Saskia as her sister-in-law, it would upset only herself. She remembered what Naz had told her, when she'd dismissed impostor syndrome at university: *You don't feel it because you are one. An impostor.*

Quietly, she, Cadan and Mor packed everything away. The white quartz surfaces of the kitchen would be left spotless, the bottles removed to recycling bins and the dinner left to run its final course. Ivo's wife Ellen came over to thank them and press an extra £20 each into their hands; like all Americans, and unlike the British, she seemed to understand what a difference a tip made instead of thinking money was indecent, like sex.

'Well done,' she said.

'A pleasure,' said Mor. Hannah thought that had she poisoned this crew with mushrooms, they would almost have deserved it.

17

The Cellar

Driving back, Mor said, 'They're not all bad.'

'I didn't say they were.'

'No, but I could see you thinking it. Without people like the Sponges, Fol would still be a half-dead fishing village.'

'I know, Mor, I do know. Maybe if I had a home here that I could let out to tourists in the summer I'd feel a bit different, but I don't. We should do what they're doing in St Ives and stop incomers from buying properties.'

'Would that solve anything? If you ask me, it'd simply push the problem further down the coast.'

They were passing one of the hidden eyesores of the coast between Fol and St Piran: a valley of static caravans whose plastic sides gleamed faintly in the moonlight. It had no view, and only locals even knew it existed, but like an increasing number of seaside towns it was a dumping ground. Addicts, alcoholics, the mentally and physically disabled, the unemployed and the unemployable had washed up there for years. Even as Mor drove, a thin figure lurched out of the verge, drunk or drugged or crazed into carelessness. She swerved to avoid it, and both women drew breath sharply, then swore as they jolted over a pothole. There was a whimper from the back seat.

'It's OK, Cadan.'

'Oh my God. It's like living near zombies,' Hannah said.

'They're mostly harmless, poor souls. Or would be if they weren't addicted to spice.'

Hannah shivered. 'How long until all of us are living like that? I used to think that homelessness and begging were things in Victorian novels, things we'd left behind, and yet it's all come back.'

'In Fol, we have the luxury of the rich attracting the rich.'

'Leaving St Piran with the dregs. Mind you, we've got legions in London, too.'

'Yes. But at least if we get money coming into coastal towns, there's some hope, unlike the inland areas. What we really need is to be allowed to hang on to more of what we pay in taxes, not send them to bloody London. But we're just this olde-worlde place of cream teas and fucked-over fishermen.'

It was the same quarrel that had been going on over the dinner they had just left.

'Only everything that actually brings money – agriculture, tourism, the fisheries – is going to be destroyed.'

'We did without the EU before, and we'll do so again. So what if we go without for a few years? We don't need tomatoes in the middle of winter. Those people – the Germans, the French – they've always been our enemies down here. Always.'

'Oh, Mor,' said Hannah. She hated quarrelling with family, but the pain of the Referendum was felt on both sides.

'History moves on. But if you feel so angry, why stay? Why not move to Exeter, at least?'

'If I stay, I can make a difference to five people who wouldn't otherwise have jobs here, including Cadan,' Mor said. 'I just wish we could get a council house.'

Hannah thought of mobile homes, their plastic sides almost bulging with hopelessness. She didn't want to think about the homeless, any more than the people in Fol wanted to think about St Piran.

'I still hate them for not knowing, or wanting to know, what it's like not to be them.'

Mor was silent. Then she asked, 'Was that your sister-in-law this evening?'

Hannah had forgotten that her cousin had been her bridesmaid.

'Yes. About to be ex sister-in-law.'

'I thought so.'

'You have a good memory.'

'It was my first time out of Cornwall. I thought it was dead cool.'

Hannah smiled wryly. She'd always liked Loveday's daughter, though the liking had been tinged with slight envy due to her cousin's happy, solid family. That Morwenna had repeated this pattern was no surprise, any more than that she should have repeated her own solitary childhood. Divorce and single parenthood were, she now thought, transferred down the generations like a curse.

'I hope the Wilcoxes weren't as foul to you as they were to me.'

Mor laughed. 'Were they?'

'Saskia hated me the moment we met. As you may have heard, they thought me too common for them – a pramface.'

204

Mor stopped her car in a lay-by. Like so many around St Piran, it was littered with plastic bags, cardboard boxes from takeaways, aluminium cans, old tyres, even condoms glistening in the headlights like giant slugs. How could people be so careless?

'Babies never arrive at convenient times, like, do they?' Mor said, handing her a tissue. 'Mine didn't. We're bursting at the seams at Mum's. But it's probably better to have them when you're young and have enough energy to enjoy them.'

'Oh, I do, I love Maisy to bits. It's only that – well, if you want to know, I gave up my job to look after her. And then I found out Jake was having an affair, and he moved out, and—'

It came out in a great clot of misery. Telling her cousin was very different from telling Jinni, where she had been able to keep her grief checked by anger. Hannah cried until her face felt raw, apologising and blowing her nose then crying some more. From the back seat, Cadan silently put out a hand, and stroked her cheek.

'You should have told us.'

'How could I? I didn't want to upset Mum, especially not when she was dying. Besides, it's so humiliating.'

'But we are your family, Han. Families don't judge.'

'Lots do,' Hannah said, hiccuping. 'Jake's do.'

'More fool them. The way I see it, family is what has your back. Always. You want to know why every organisation tries to undermine it? Families are what stand against them, Cornish families especially.'

'Next thing you'll be saying I should never have married out.' Hannah gave a watery smile.

'I'm worried about you, Han. We all are. We can see you're running on empty.'

This was the moment in which to tell her cousin about Jinni, and the murder plot. Yet she also knew that if she were to disclose it, then not only would Mor immediately condemn it but she would lose some source of inner strength and determination.

'You're very kind to listen to my moaning,' she said. 'Sorry.'

'So, what are you going to do? If there's nothing for you in London, will you come back?'

Hannah sat up straighter.

'I didn't say there was nothing. I do have a life there. Just not the life I hoped for.'

'Is Jake supporting you, at least?'

Hannah sighed. 'He gives me money for the rent, and a tiny bit for Maisy. But nothing near enough. That's why I still need to work, even when I'm supposedly on holiday.'

'I see. We wondered why you were up at Endpoint. Strange place.'

'It is.'

'All those roses, and rhododendron. Old Mr Coad was a drunk, they say.'

'But it's beautiful, too.'

They passed the entrance just as she spoke, and she looked down the long, dark drive.

'How do you find him? People liked him, but then he went away to America and came back unfriendly.'

This was Hannah's chance to find out more, even if local gossip was always partial.

'He seems sad.'

'That'd be his dad dying, I shouldn't wonder. Or maybe his mother. They were close, by all accounts.'

'What did she die of?'

'Cancer. Though some would say heartbreak.'

'Why heartbreak?'

'She had a daughter, Stan's little sister. She died young, poor child, drowned, and Mrs Coad never got over it. Well, how would you?'

Death surrounded him. Every day, going to Endpoint, Hannah thought about how she had tried to kill Coad, and could not bring herself to do it. Had she won, or failed?

She was very tired the next day, but the dinner party had made her even more curious about him. Instead of avoiding Stan, she began to seek him out.

He was working in his studio – the stable block from which he'd emerged that first night – but it wasn't easy. Occasionally she could hear him growling and groaning through the open windows. It surprised her that it sounded so effortful, even painful, to create a form of entertainment.

'I suppose it's a quest, isn't it?'

'Yes. It's what suits the form best.'

'Even though that has severe limitations?'

'Does it?'

'Yes, because not everyone can move purposefully through life, can they? Some people just want to be allowed to live in peace.'

Coad rubbed his nose. 'But that can be a quest, too, can't it? It's certainly what I'd like most.'

They had worked through all the ground floor and now reached the bedrooms. These were simpler, and the labour of stripping off ivy and sweeping up dust and cobwebs less provoking because there wasn't as much rubbish left to throw on to the skips. She guessed that Stan's father must not have come up there. In a cupboard in the room she'd slept in, in the west wing, Hannah found a treasure trove of dresses, many from the 1940s. Shrouded in moth-proof coverings they looked sinister, but unwrapped they revealed glimpses of silks as subtle and delicate as the wings of a new butterfly.

'If any of them fit you, take them.'

'Oh no! I couldn't possibly.'

'Why not? They've sat here ever since my grandmother died.'

'Was she the Cornish one or—'

'The Iraqi one, yes.' He grinned suddenly. 'My Cornish granny lived in tweeds and wellington boots and said the English were German. My Nana, she was a great beauty, and she loved fashion. When her family left Iraq she insisted on bringing some of her dresses with her. She was right to do so, because her father, my great grandfather, was one of the greatest tailors in Baghdad, and when they got to London it was the foundation of their fortune.'

'She must have been tiny,' said Hannah, unable to resist holding up a dress against herself. It would fit her, she knew.

'She had a waist that my baba – my grandfather – could circle with his hands.'

'Did she wear a veil over these?'

Stan laughed. 'No! She was Jewish, not Muslim. You look surprised, but there were Jews in Baghdad for over two thousand years before we were forced into exile by the Farhud – the massacre. Iraqi Jews are Sephardic, not Ashkenazi like the ones from Europe. You probably don't know the difference, most people don't. People often mistake us for Arabs. Our people were at peace with each other for hundreds if not thousands of years. My mother's family spoke Arabic, Aramaic, French and English, as well as Hebrew. They were the most cosmopolitan and sophisticated people you could possibly imagine.'

'Did you ever visit?'

'No. I never knew it, except through their memories, and pictures. They escaped in 1943, long before I was born. It took many trials to get to Britain. But they were successful, and this is something from that time. My Nana gave these to my mother, in case that fashion ever came back.'

Hannah looked at the dress in her hands, a silk and net confection embroidered with tiny roses and bearing a label saying Dior. Even without trying it on, she could see that it would suit her, being made (unlike so many modern garments) for a woman with a waist, breasts and hips. She thought of how doubly isolated Stan was, not just bereaved but without family. He must be the loneliest man in Britain, out in this remote part of a remote county.

'I'm glad they got to safety.'

'My grandmother had nightmares about being smuggled out over the border. She never liked being confined. Even having her nails painted made her feel she was being shut up in her body.'

'That sounds pretty extreme.'

'Yes. The trauma of being a refugee . . . My mother always kept a packed suitcase under her bed. And . . . ' He paused. 'Sometimes she and my sister and I would hide in the cellar. Just, you know, in case.'

'There's a cellar here?'

'A very big one.'

'How romantic. May I see?'

'If you wish. It's below the kitchen.'

The door was just a plain wooden door in the kitchen. It could have been a cupboard, but when Hannah opened it she saw stone steps curving down.

'Where does that go?'

'I don't know exactly how far it reaches – all the way under the house.'

'No smugglers' tunnel?'

She was teasing, but he answered, 'Maybe. I never explored.'

Hannah saw a light switch and flicked it. 'Look, it's not dark.'

Curiosity led her to descend the steps. They were the colour of old bone. Thick beams, or rafters, carried the floor overhead. Slabs of stone struck a chill through the soles of her sandals.

In the bleached radiance of the lamps she saw pillars of brick, and a jumble of old tools, a bicycle with rusting pedals, two old suitcases, a deflated beach ball, a blue kayak without a paddle, a life-belt and many cardboard boxes which appeared to be packed with tins. There was also row after row of wine-racks, all empty. Presumably, Stan's father had drunk everything there was to drink.

'Goodness, you could have a big party down here.'

'My parents used to have parties, but I never have,' he said.

There was a faint smell of mould but not damp, many cobwebs, and a thick layer of dust, but the cellar went on beyond the reach of light. Even allowing for the footprint of Endpoint, it did seem to be very large. She walked to the edge of the light and peered into the shadows.

'Hannah?'

Suddenly she was nervous, and angry with herself. What was she doing down here? His silences, his reserve, his impulsive acts of generosity and his brooding were all things that should make her wary. What if he trapped her, in a place where she couldn't escape? Hannah could hear his rubber flip-flops following hers across the stone floor, and they sounded like the smacking lips of a monster. Her skin prickled, and she stepped into the shadow, heart thumping. She had stopped carrying the Taser in her pocket, and now wondered whether this was a mistake.

'Hannah? Are you there?'

His bulk seemed even more looming in the confined space. She thought of all the giants in stories, of their taste for human flesh and extreme violence, of their heartlessness and greed. Almost, she could believe he was one of these. But Stan said, in a voice that sounded half-strangled, 'Hannah, I really don't like being down here. I have – I get – I—'

'I'm here.'

She stepped round a pillar of brick. Stan was blinking and shivering, his face a moon of fear.

'Claustrophobia. You should have said.'

'Yes. Stupid to follow you.'

All at once, her fear was replaced by pity. He couldn't help being large, any more than she could help being small; and he was so horribly alone.

'Can you move? I'm here.'

Slowly, he put his hand in hers. It was cold and clammy, like that of a drowning man.

'I'm not good in confined spaces.'

'Don't worry, Stan. The door is close by.'

He seemed turned to stone.

She put a hand on his arm, afraid now that she would not be able to get him out again because he was far too big even for another man to lift, but then he seemed to gather new strength.

'Just keep going; look, we're almost out.'

It took an age, and the whole time she feared he might fall backwards on top of her. Once they emerged at the top of the steps he went straight for the table and sat down on the big wooden chair with his head in his hands.

'Jesus. Sorry about that.'

'It's OK. I faint in thunderstorms, remember?'

He half laughed. 'Only you're a woman.'

'So?' Hannah said crossly. 'Everyone is afraid of something. How are you feeling now?'

'My vision is coming back to normal.'

'I'll make us some tea.'

She chatted, casually, while the colour came back into his face. Knowing that he had this phobia made her wonder whether Jinni had ever discovered it. She thought not: for if so, what could be easier than locking him in the cellar until he died of fright?

18

Vanished

Hannah now moved, as she thought of it, between not two but three worlds. There was the world of Endpoint, with its crumbling walls, overgrown gardens and winding woods. There was Fol, with its luxurious shops and holiday homes that were now as expensive as Hampstead and Notting Hill. Then there was the world of St Piran, with its discount supermarkets, tanning salons, betting shops and boarded-up high street. It, too, was subdivided between people like Loveday's children who had employment, and people like those in the Fol valley, who did not. Sometimes, these two tribes would cross paths, but not often because even to afford the bus fare out of the Fol valley was more than most could manage. Valley people lived one benefit payment away from total disaster, and sometimes not even that if they fell into gambling or drugs.

Here, too, a food bank had been opened, although this was not popular because it attracted more poverty. The nature of work here brought in those from outside the county, or from the desolate inlands where even to get to a place for education was a struggle. Those drawn to the coast by the promise of seasonal jobs inevitably washed up in winter like so much sea-wrack; and if they did not move away again, they had to be accommodated for the rest of the year, living on what benefits they could get.

Loveday was infuriated by this.

'It's a total disgrace. We never used to have all these drifters and druggies. When my grandmother was a girl this was one of the richest small towns in England. But as soon as the mines closed and the china clay industry went, everyone young left. Even the fishermen can't make a living.'

'There isn't any fishing in St Piran, though, is there? It's all lobsters.'

'There is further along the coast. Besides, it's the whole county that matters not just our little bit of it. We can't live on tourism for three months a year and fresh air for the rest.'

Just five miles away from St Piran's shabby pebbledash, Fol's stone and plaster, paint and wood were all immaculate, the front gardens and public spaces vivid with flowers, and people eating and drinking, talking and walking or just looking at the lovely scenery before them. The blue waters bobbed with sailing boats that clinked and tinkled as if freighted with jewellery. The green hills rising behind them, ribboned with dry-stone walls, were gift-wrapped luxuries, ornamented with decorative cows. In those streets, people who strolled along dressed in flattering garments, tanned and healthy and wearing pleasant expressions. Naturally: it is easy to be pleasant when life treats you kindly. The real test of character is when it does not. Hannah knew she must not succumb to envy, but it was hard to resist.

Nobody ordinary lived in Fol any more. Its butcher had been replaced by a tearoom, its baker by an ice-cream parlour, and although it still sold candlesticks they were made on the other side of the globe. In one street, three pasty shops next door to each other were staffed by young people in blue and white striped tops; another shop sold exotic shells whose attractively speckled, mother-of-pearl or pink-flushed surfaces had caused them to be ripped from the dying waters of tropical oceans, and yet another sold children's clothes of the kind that, once soiled would never be worn again. Yet the people who toiled to keep its shops open, its drains clear, its streets swept and its lights on had to catch buses at dawn from places that were as lonely and ugly as Fol was not.

The Fol Bookshop was off one of the main streets, but in an angle that meant its dark green bay window caught the eye of passers-by. Hannah, feeling guilty that she hadn't visited Mr Kenward before, dropped in one day with Maisy.

'You must have been the same age as your daughter when you first started visiting,' he said, greeting them both.

'I suppose I must. I can't remember much before then.'

'Nothing at all?'

'I think there was a white building with columns. Or maybe that was a dream.'

'No, it sounds like one of the temples in the grounds of Knotshead.'

'Do you miss it?'

'Only the library. Much of which I carry in my head. I hear you've been sorting through a lot at Endpoint.'

'Look, Mummy, *The Gruffalo*! May I read it?'

Maisy had become uncertain about whether she was allowed to enjoy picture books, a dismaying change that Hannah ascribed to the influence of her cousins. Kenward answered, 'You may. There are lots of others you might like as well.'

While Maisy took down her favourites, Hannah and Kenward chatted about books, because talking about books is, for passionate readers, the next best thing to reading them. Even if two readers will rarely if ever agree (even about books they both love), discussing books is an infinite subject: as Kenward used to say, 'If there are only four letters to the genetic code to life on Earth, how many more worlds could be created with twenty-six in the alphabet?' Of course, he was just as interested in biography, history, archaeology, biology, psychogeography and a host of other subjects, but they exchanged ideas, information, opinions and enthusiasm with much vigour and laughter. Ever since Maisy's birth, Hannah had had very little time for her own reading – a complaint that she had never understood before, because you could read in the bath or while waiting for a pot to boil or a bus to come, surely? But the combination of physical labour and the continual interruptions caused by a small child had meant that mostly, she was living off the memory of books, as a bear lives off its fat in winter. Even so, it was a pleasure to discuss them.

Their relationship, though spasmodic, had changed over the years from that of master and apprentice to one of equals, even if it was unlikely that she would ever be able to read as much or as widely as him. Yet the delight of talking about what they had read and liked (or read and disliked) was just the same. When Hannah ever felt regret about her marriage, she remembered how Jake had simply stopped reading once he started work. To him, books had always been a means to an end not an end in themselves.

'So how are you getting on with clearing the library at Endpoint?'

'I'm finding it very difficult to put books aside for throwing out,' she confessed.

'Yes, that does tend to be the problem,' said Mr Kenward. He was taking away a good many from the Endpoint library to sell, as some were valuable enough to be worth doing so. 'I expect a few thousand will end up in storage until Stan finds somewhere else to live.'

'Does he read?'

He seemed startled. 'Dear me, yes. Why do you think he doesn't?'

'I've yet to meet a man of my age who does.'

That morning, an email from the letting agent arrived. Nine years ago, they had drawn up the contract for the ex-council flat, but the contract rolled on from one year to the next, the agents always pressing for a rent increase that she didn't dare object to, for if she had to leave then she would never find the money for a new deposit now.

```
FLAT 4A, CASTLE ESTATE
Outstanding arrears £1200

Dear Jake and Hannah,
   We regret to inform you that the
rental monies due have not been paid
this month ...
```

Hannah read the now-familiar warnings with dread. Once again, Jake had 'forgotten' to pay the rent. Why couldn't he have a standing order? She knew why.

To have her beg and plead with him for money each month in order to keep a roof over their heads was humiliation piled on humiliation. Well, not this month. For once, she could pay the balance herself, thanks to her labours at Endpoint, but it meant that the advance she had hoped to make in clearing her debts was negated. It was infuriating, and unjust, but she was a little less desperate.

Once again, she texted and rang his mobile repeatedly, leaving messages. She rang his office, and left messages there too. Two days passed without reply, so she gritted her teeth and rang his mother.

'Etta? It's Hannah.'

'Is everything all right?'

'No, not really.' Hannah tried to keep her voice even and controlled. She was, after all, asking for help and her dignity was all she had. 'I'm sorry to trouble you, but Jake has forgotten to pay the rent on the flat. Again.'

'Oh dear. Have you tried calling him? Hello?'

Hannah waited until her rage subsided. 'He's, well, vanished. My mother died recently so I'm in Cornwall, but I can't get hold of him.'

Etta sounded surprised.

'How awful for you and Maisy. What was it?'

'Sorry?'

'Your mother.'

Why did people ask this?

'Cancer. But the rent is why I'm ringing.'

'It's probably an oversight.'

Hannah sighed. Her mother-in-law's blindness to what Jake was really like was one of her most aggravating features. No matter how vile he was, she went on making excuses for him. But then, so had she.

'We really do need him to pay it.'

Did Etta really need to have this spelt out?

218

'He's always been terrible at answering calls.'

Hannah counted to five. 'I was wondering whether he's blocked me.'

'I'll call his number.'

A few minutes later, Etta rang back.

'I've left him an urgent message. Maybe he's abroad.'

'He's supposed to be at work until the end of the month, when he's collecting Maisy.'

Negotiating the holidays was always hellish with young children. Hannah knew that many working couples tried to stagger their own leave so that they could look after their kids in a kind of relay race, booking a fortnight each that overlapped in the middle. If one half was not working, then it was supposedly easier. But look how that panned out for me, she thought.

Etta asked, 'Do you need help?'

Yes, Hannah thought silently. But she'd have to be home-less before she took money from the people who called her a pramface.

'Just let me know if he contacts you.'

'I will. And I'm sorry he's being so irresponsible.'

Etta was not so bad, really, Hannah thought. She was sorry for her, as a mother. Her in-laws had given him an excellent education, opportunities and formal good manners, but somehow all this had done was spoil him. She could see how it had happened: Jake had been strikingly beautiful as a child and good things do not happen to such boys.

'What did she think? That middle-aged men teach in prep schools because they really like the way little boys think?' Jake said once, with withering sarcasm.

'Was it her decision?'

'Of course it was! My father defers to her on everything to

do with the family. It's traditional to send sons away at eight if you're an Evenlode, and we all went to a prep school that was a haven for paedophiles.'

'Maybe she genuinely didn't know.'

'Don't be an idiot, Hannah. She has a brother, my Uncle Andrew, the one I'll inherit the title from if he doesn't have a son. He'd been there too. Maybe he liked having grown men stick their hands down his shorts. Some boys did. At least it meant they were getting some love and affection.'

Hannah did not know what to make of this; he rarely referred to it again, and she hoped that this meant he had come to terms with it. Nobody she knew had experienced abuse as a child; it was one of those curious features of a certain kind of public schoolboy that was only gradually coming to light. Eventually, she read more and understood more about how it must have affected their marriage, but by then it was too late.

It seemed as if Jake never grew out of his schooldays. Whenever he got together with his friends, it was all they discussed, joking and reminiscing as if it had all been the most glorious fun. You could not complain to anyone else who had been through what they had been through, and the irony was that people who hadn't been were envious of their education.

'It's just a British tradition,' he said once, dismissively. 'Send your children away to be abused by strangers instead of their relations.'

However harsh her own childhood had felt at times, however anxious and deprived, nothing bad had happened to her like this, ever. She had once thought that if she gave Jake unstinting love, it would heal him, only he hadn't wanted that. He wanted whatever it was that Eve could give, presumably undiluted attention, or perhaps the narrow body of a woman who looked like the boy he no longer was.

'Why don't you get down to the gym? You disgust me,' he'd said in one of their rows. His favourite adjective for her was 'fat', although she was thinner than she had ever been. But she had no interest in her body as anything other than the thing that stood between her child and destitution.

When she thought of what would happen the next month, the fear rose again. She could cover the rent, just, though it would leave her with almost nothing once again. Only Mor knew how desperate her situation was, and she couldn't say anything to her cousin or aunt because they would insist on trying to help, and they were poor as well. Her short nails got ever shorter because she could not help tearing at them in nervous self-disgust.

'Stop hurting yourself, Hannah. It won't make you feel better,' she could hear her mother's voice say.

She still couldn't bear to tackle her mother's clothes, sad assemblies of brown, beige and grey that even charity shops were reluctant to take, including a couple of things she had bought as presents in the days when she had a proper job, that her mother had barely worn. She thought of the exquisite couture dresses Stan had kept in his mother's bedroom and thought: We can't bear to lose our mothers' smell.

She was hunting for clues about her father, though she didn't want to admit it. At the back of a drawer, she found an envelope of tiny sepia family photographs of her long-dead grandparents, some of Hannah herself as a small child, Holly as a young woman in her grandparents' pub. With a slight shock, she realised that her mother had once been very pretty.

At all costs, Hannah told herself, I must not turn into my

mother. Even if she loved Holly and understood more about what she must have endured with every month, her rebellion against her was one of the driving forces of her life.

'Oh yes,' her aunt told her. 'Your mum was the same as you, desperate to get away.'

'Did she ever tell you anything about my father?'

'Nothing except the usual.'

'The usual?'

'He was married, wouldn't leave his wife. Wanted to have his cake and eat it.'

'Poor Mum. How did she meet him?'

Hannah had always longed to ask this.

'He was a teacher.'

'Oh.' All her dreams of discovering that she was the child of someone rich and famous – like Gore Tore, the rock star who made sure that every child he had sired was given £250,000 – shrivelled in an instant.

'We never knew his name, or even what he taught. She wouldn't say anything else.'

'What a bastard.' Yet Hannah pitied the wife, too: for wasn't she in the same position?

There had always been a hardness to her mother, as well as an obsessive fear of poverty, for even when she became the school nurse at St Piran Sixth Form College, she watched every penny to a degree that drained joy out of life. ('What's the point of doing anything to a place that isn't your own?' she'd said, just like Jake.) It was the same with buying books, or pictures, or anything pleasant in life. Her mother had not even thought to buy her a bra as a teenager. The times in which she had been born, a time of greater optimism and less austerity, had not really touched their lives, though Loveday thought things had become worse.

'At least the council gave my poor sister a home – which is more than they've done for Mor and her family. We're on to them every month about how badly she needs a place, but they'll probably be with me till I drop dead.'

Holly went on searching and was able to throw away her mother's macramé plant holders, fridge magnets and accumulated tat, making weary journeys to the town recycling centre with her car full of bin bags. The sheer quantity of stuff accumulated even by a modest life like Holly's astonished her. Why had her mother needed three potato peelers or two vacuum cleaners? She would never know. Slowly, the bungalow, like Endpoint, became less cluttered. Every day, she expected to get a call from the council demanding that she vacated it but perhaps August was a busy time for them, too. She was glad: it gave her time both to pack and to mourn the only true home she had ever had. Ugly and graceless though it was, it still felt safe, and somehow a place of refuge. Once it was gone, she might never be able to revisit Cornwall, and that thought pierced her to the heart.

Maisy loved it as much as she did, or possibly even more because of her devotion to her cousins. In London, she was the only child of a single mother, but here she was part of the Penrose clan, something that fostered her confidence. Loveday was the unofficial guardian of all the cousins (or, to be accurate, second cousins) and their games on the beach and picnics in that endless summer had Maisy swimming like one of the ducks in the harbour, unaided by water-wings, and body surfing. She seemed to have grown, and her thin little body was looking more robust under the influence of better food.

Hannah and Stan went on toiling in the heat. Together, they had managed to clear and dress three of the main rooms and one bedroom at Endpoint for the photographs that would go online and into *Country Life* to sell it. She sometimes smiled at the irony that she, who had grown up on a council estate, could somehow see what it needed, but then she had spent decades of her life dreaming of the life she did not have.

'It has to look dishevelled in a romantic way, not as if it'll fall down the moment a drill touches it,' Hannah told Stan. 'Don't repaint anything, but do have big vases full of big flowers, and the one good rug in the drawing-room. People aren't buying your furnishing; they're buying something they can project their fantasies on to.'

Sometimes, just doing things like rehanging curtains so that the sun-rotted damask was turned inward to the wall or reversing faded sofa cushions to reveal their original colours was enough. Paintwork could be scrubbed down, and dirty wallpaper cleaned with soft bread. Hannah moved tall vases full of peacock feathers and bulky antique furniture to conceal the worst.

'How did it get to be this bad?' she asked.

'It's just the usual story of the past hundred years,' Stan said. 'There were no men left to work the land or look after the house after the First World War, and three out of four sons were killed. The good farmland was sold off. And then in the next War, it had soldiers billeted here who thought it fun to put bullets into the walls. Then came crippling post-war taxes, and the collapse of the china clay industry. My dad was the last one left, and although my mother's family paid for the plumbing to be modernised as a wedding gift, it wasn't enough. After she died my father never saw the point of looking after anything. A house is like any relationship: if you don't bother to keep it in good repair, it decays. It wasn't too bad when I left for America, but once the roof started leaking, it accelerated. "It can be a problem for my heirs," he'd say, meaning me. I think he hated me. He blamed me for my sister's death.'

'Did you blame yourself?'

'Yes, of course. We were each other's greatest friends, but like all children we also fought sometimes. There was a four-year age gap, and at twelve, that starts to feel like a lot. The day she died I didn't want her to come into the cave with me, I wanted to go exploring by myself. I shouldn't have left her alone on the beach; I was old enough to know better. But I thought I knew the tide times, and I didn't even realise she hadn't gone back, and then—'

'You were both children. A child can't be responsible for another child,' said Hannah. She wondered whether his own air of something almost unfinished about him, something odd and vulnerable, came from this. But maybe it was this same flaw that made him lose his temper and neglect himself.

'My parents never forgave me. It killed my mother.'

'People don't get cancer and dementia from grief.'

'You think so?' He was silent for a while. 'Maybe not, but that's what it feels like. That's why I don't mind about selling this house.'

Together, she and Stan unearthed lamps in undamaged shades to switch on, moved half the furniture, re-hung pictures and discussed a hundred other details that would make the photographs look better. It did not have to last; it was like dressing a stage set, in which pleasing impressions and temporary appearances were everything. Hannah understood this, because it was the same as advertising.

She even tried to persuade him to buy silk wisteria blooms to twist up the front of the house, on the grounds that there

225

was a real wisteria there, just not one that happened to be in flower in August.

'But it's a lie,' he said, and refused.

When the photographer from the estate agent came, he snapped away.

'A certain sort of buyer will be interested in run-down properties,' he said. 'It's not the worst house this size I've seen, not by a long chalk.'

It wasn't much, in return for their labours so far, but when Hannah thought of the chaos she had first encountered, it was praise enough.

'Maybe someone will take it on,' Stan said, after the photographer had left.

'Of course they will!' she said. His gloom, though understandable, annoyed her. 'It's a wonderful house, just one that needs millions spending on it to put right. Maybe if your new game is a hit ... '

He shook his head. 'It won't be.'

'How do you know?'

'It's not commercial enough. I'm not motivated by money. All I want is to be free. For my ex to be truly my ex.'

'What's stopping it?'

'Money. She thinks there must be more, even though I've explained about the death duties.'

For weeks, Hannah had not thought of the mobile that Jinni had given her. It lay in her bag, a small slab of rubbery plastic and metal. She wasn't even sure whether, without a charger, she could still get it to work. Later that day, having collected Maisy from her cousin's, she held down the button.

The screen lit up and the instrument buzzed.

Your turn now.

19

Changed with Every Tide

Hannah felt her cheeks turn to marble.

Had Jinni really gone ahead without waiting? Surely that was what her text implied, that it was now Hannah's turn to murder, because Jinni had already killed Jake. An eye for an eye. Yes, she was convinced, and with this came terror of an order she had never experienced before. She had agreed to something unutterably foolish, crazy, criminal; and now, though she had been unable to kill Stan herself, a man was dead, and not just any man but the father of her child. Oh God! What had been a mad fantasy was real, and what should have repelled her had been made to seem perfectly natural. Even if she found Jake loathsome, even if he had been cruel, unjust, mean-spirited and vile, she did not wish him to have met with a violent end.

'Until now, I never knew myself,' she muttered.

But she had accepted the Taser, and she had rung Jinni on the burner mobile. How had she not seen that her former travelling companion was a lunatic? Yes, Hannah answered herself; there had been flashes of unease, but she had chosen to ignore her instincts. She had been susceptible to beauty and glamour and sympathy. Why had Jinni beckoned her into the first-class carriage, why pick *her* of all people? Was she mad enough to have taken a chance, on the spur of the moment, or had she somehow *known* that Hannah was in the same situation? But how could she? Hannah thought of the long white finger beckoning, the flowing green dress and magnetic gaze. She had been seduced by an enchantress, as surely as a character in a fairy-tale. Nothing would stop Jinni from doing what she had decided to do. It was all in her walk, so confident and purposeful.

What should she do? What *could* she do? What if she were to profess complete ignorance and astonishment and grief when Jake's body was found? She could ditch the burner mobile; there was nothing to connect her to Jinni apart from working in Endpoint while she was away. After all, she had tried to ring him often enough, and her mother-in-law had been alerted to his disappearance by her. Nobody could prove that she was anywhere near Jake. She had spent the past month in Cornwall. Yet she remembered Jinni sweeping up the rubbish from their drinks together. If Jake's body were to be found then there would be evidence planted there to incriminate Hannah, somehow.

She had expected her life to belong to one kind of genre, but instead it had twisted into another, something darker, nastier and less predictable. Yet whose life stayed on one track, from birth to death, ever? The comfort of reading was that it persuaded you that everything would conform to a particular pattern, that there would be tropes and coincidences and characters obeying certain rules, and even though it was clearly labelled Fiction you still expected it to be telling the truth, not just about life but about yourself.

How could I have been so stupid? she thought.

Sweating with fright, Hannah told herself that even if she went to the police, they'd think her deranged. Where was her proof? She had not thought to record their second conversation, and if she had, she couldn't remember whether Jinni would have said anything definitively incriminating. On reflection, she thought it unlikely. Her texts were ambiguous, and she had been careful not to say anything specific on their second meeting.

Even if Jinni had hand-delivered the burner phone to the Castle Estate and been let in by Xan, Hannah had little doubt that she would not have been identifiable, especially as she had been wearing a helmet. An actress, the kind who could change her appearance, would have taken good care of it. Perhaps she wasn't even dark-haired and brown eyed. She could be anyone. The only thing Hannah could be sure of was that she was mad – or bad. No wonder Stan was so desperate to be rid of her.

Could she tell him the truth? It was tempting but the moment she did so, she knew he would recoil. It had taken these days and weeks of toiling together over a common project to establish a kind of trust, even liking, for although he had always been kind to her, she knew he had also been wary. They were becoming friends. These days, he made small jokes, and allowed her to tease him. He had stopped making sexist generalisations, and she had modified her own views about men. Confidences had been made, and hopes shared. All that would vanish if he knew what she really was.

All through the short, tepid night, she paced up and down

the bungalow, until sheer weariness forced her to bed. Her mother's mattress had always been too soft and now she dreamt of sinking lower and lower into a swampy marsh, suffocating by inches as she strained to find a foothold. The mud forced its way between her lips, then up her nostrils and into her ears and eyeballs until, at dawn, she sat bolt upright, terrified.

That morning, when she drove Maisy to her cousins, Hannah was so exhausted and preoccupied that she almost drove into the back of another car.

'Look where you're going, stupid!' shouted the driver.

Hannah gave him a blast of her horn that made Maisy jump.

'Sorry, darling, it was just a nasty man.'

'I don't like it when you get cross, Mummy. Your face goes all horrible.'

Maisy's eyes were filling, she could see in the driver's mirror, and her lip was quivering. Hannah's conscience, like a piece of tired elastic, still had a little punishment in it. She was trembling so violently that for a moment she couldn't drive.

'I can't help it,' Hannah gasped.

'Mummy? Can we go now?'

Maisy's imperious little voice grated on her nerves.

'Not yet. You must give me a moment.'

'Mum-my! Let's GO.'

'Be quiet, Maisy! For heaven's sake.'

Maisy began to cry, and said, 'You're a nasty mummy. Mean, nasty mummy.'

Hannah bit her lip, trying not to swear. A dozen times a day she had to restrain herself with someone she adored but who had not yet learnt empathy. She was frightened sometimes that Maisy might become like her father, charming when she felt like it but utterly selfish and spiteful when not.

This was the trouble with parenthood: you had to present the best possible version of yourself as endlessly patient, polite, loving and kind and then, inevitably, that failed so that you were always being held to account to live up to this superior version which couldn't exist. Many people believed that having a child was a lifestyle choice, like buying a smartphone or subscribing to Netflix, but it demanded an endless self-sacrifice. If people, especially women, understood what they were giving up with motherhood, maybe it wouldn't come as such a shock. She thought of Jinni's remark – clever of you to get a baby *out of him* – as if a child was merely a bargaining chip for more money.

What if I am convicted, thought Hannah, and go to prison? If Jake was dead then her child might go into care, a punishment worse than any other.

Maisy was dropped off at Loveday's and ran into the house without a backwards glance. Hannah sighed with relief. The comforting thought that Jinni's text was a lie occurred to her. She had not heard back from either her mother-in-law or Jake's office, but in August the whole country went into a kind of fugue state. Surely if Jake had not turned up for work, somebody would have noticed and got in touch? But maybe they wouldn't. Offices had changed, even since she had worked in one.

That afternoon, the cleaner who had looked after Endpoint made a visit. Mrs Bolitho, who was not the sort of person anybody, including her husband, would dream of calling by her first name, had wanted to see the house 'before it gets ripped apart'.

She was very complimentary about the effect of their labours, though sad at the end of an era.

'Never thought we'd see this place without a Coad in it,' she said. 'Though so much of my family's blood, sweat and toil has gone into Endpoint, it feels like we're losing something too.'

'Whoever buys this will have to be someone who restores it,' Hannah said. 'There's no point, otherwise.'

Mrs Bolitho gave a grudging nod.

'I'm glad young Stan has seen sense about getting help,' she said. 'So, you're Loveday's niece, are you? Good to see someone local doing some work around here. I'd forgotten what this place looked like underneath the mess.' She added, in an undertone, 'You keep an eye out, my lovely, won't you? Is that wife of his still around?'

Hannah, blushing hotly, said that she thought not.

'Well, here's hoping,' said Mrs Bolitho. 'That one, she'm headed for Bodmin.'

It was what Cornish people said when they thought someone should be locked up as insane. But then, why would someone from St Piran like Jinni? She was everything they were not. Hannah could not help feeling defensive, even now.

These days, when she walked along the long, creaking corridors, they no longer frightened her. The floors were not sticky. The toilets were clean enough to wash in. Light bulbs had been replaced. Even the creepers up the front of the house looked fresh and bright. Of course, she herself looked worse. She left a change of clothes hanging in the cloakroom that she had used the first time she had come to Endpoint, and nowadays the round-eyed Chinese birds looked friendly as she took off her marginally more respectable dress, put on her oldest jeans and T-shirt, scraped her hair up into a knot and slipped on flip-flops.

Stan padded along behind her, accompanied by the castanet-like click of his hound's claws.

'So many things,' he muttered. He kept a bottle of water with him, and at times was morose, but he hadn't touched a drop of alcohol since the day when she had almost pushed him over the cliff. The puffiness had left his face and hands, he was clearly having a shower each morning, he was keeping his hair tied back and his beard and nails short. He still had terrible teeth, but she couldn't believe she had ever mistaken him for the caretaker.

They were still sorting through cupboards and shelves, now they could actually access them.

'You know what to do,' Hannah answered. 'Not two but three piles, one for Keep, one for Throw, and one for Maybe. It's a much easier way, and you usually end up throwing away the Maybe pile.'

'I suppose the paperbacks are for Throw,' he muttered.

'It's up to you. I'm doing the same thing at my mum's. All the books there were mine, though. It's strange, I seem to have been given books pretty much from the start, although she never had any herself.'

'That'd be Bill Kenward, I expect. He liked giving children books.'

'Did yours come from him as well?'

Stan nodded. 'I was about seven when he came to Fol, and you must have been, what?'

'Three, I think.'

'I always loved that shop. The bell on the doormat, the wooden shelves like a labyrinth inside and the displays in the green bay window.'

'Yes! It's one of my earliest memories.'

'All our best books came from there, mine and my sister's.

The Dark Is Rising, The Weirdstone of Brisingamen, Tintin, The Hobbit . . . He gave us that copy of *Green Smoke*, because of it being set in Cornwall.'

'Maisy is obsessed by it,' said Hannah.

'I hope she doesn't take it too literally.'

They were cleaning the west wing together. Hannah drew a deep breath and asked, 'Stan, the night I arrived, you had a black eye. You said you walked into a door, but . . . had you been in a fight?'

He said nothing, and she said, 'I saw a lamp on the floor, too, and a broken mirror.'

There was a long pause. Then Stan said, 'She has a temper.'

'Are you saying *she* attacked *you*?'

He flushed. 'I know. Here I am, a hulking great lump, and yes, she hits me.'

Hannah said, with a note of scepticism, 'You're sure that you don't hit her first?'

'No! God, I'd snap her like a twig.'

'That doesn't stop plenty of men.'

Stan made a growling sound. 'Maybe. But I'm not one of them.'

Hannah gave him a long look, trying to weigh up whether he was telling the truth or not. She thought of the bruises on Jinni's forearms. 'My husband has hit me. And other things.'

'Then he's a bastard.'

'Hitting anyone is wrong, isn't it?' she said pointedly.

'Usually, yes.'

'So you didn't do *anything* to her?'

'Why would I?'

'I don't know,' Hannah said. 'Because you could?'

'I would never, ever hurt a woman. It's just not . . . manly.

Men are people, too, Hannah. Most of us learn how to behave. You seem to think we're all brutes.'

'So what happens if you lose your temper?'

'The person I'm most likely to hurt is myself. Though she had a fair go at it too.'

Hannah could imagine Jinni having a fierce temper, and yet so did Stan. She had been terrified when she arrived the first night. She'd heard him shouting at her. 'How did you meet?'

He gave a harsh laugh. 'I wasn't always as I am now. When I was in America in one of the top gaming companies, it was a very different environment.'

'I imagine it's full of grunting men whose knuckles drag on the floor.'

Stan glared at her. 'Then you could not be more wrong. It's one of the most creative and successful industries that exists. A game design uses artists, actors, composers, classical musicians, mathematicians, even philosophers. It's very, very cool.'

'But it's not like literature or painting or opera or film.'

'No, it's not those things; it's a fusion of all those things. There are as many kinds of game as there are films or books or music. *The Last of Us* is a bit like Cormack McCarthy's *The Road* – lots of issues about whether it's right to kill one person to potentially save humanity. *Fable* allows you to choose both good and bad actions throughout the story, and your choices have implications for how your character appears as the story progresses. *Senua's Sacrifice* has a main character who has schizophrenia, and voices that talk and whisper to her all the way through her journey through a sort of afterlife realm to save her friend's soul – it's eerie and brilliantly acted. The artwork is beautiful. Even *Victory Cry* looked beautiful. The main thing stopping games being high art is the money needed to make them. The system is stacked against individual vision.'

Hannah remained sceptical but couldn't help being moved. When he spoke like this, she could believe he had once been attractive to Jinni.

'Was your wife a gamer?'

He grimaced. 'She did the voice for one minor character. By the time I met her, it was obvious that her career wasn't going to pan out. She was looking for a change of direction.'

'In video games?'

'In marriage.'

Hannah said, with asperity, 'Do you really think women today see marriage as a career?'

'It depends, doesn't it? If enough money is involved . . . '

'We aren't living in Jane Austen's world.'

'Well, I hate her books. The laureate of female helplessness.'

Hannah could not believe he had said this. 'She is not!'

'Yes, she is. There are dozens of things she could have written about – and she didn't. She's no feminist, and a sight too interested in marrying money. The Brontës were braver.'

'Braver, maybe, but not better.' Hannah was furious. 'I'm not one of those sillies who want to prance about in bonnets, but you're just wrong. Her heroines are brave, because they marry for love not money, which believe me was pretty revolutionary for a woman in her day. She was realistic about the few choices we had then, but she never pretended otherwise. Maybe if you'd read her more carefully, you'd have spotted Jinni coming. And maybe if I'd understood her better, I'd have found someone better than Jake.'

'But do you think you can apply what you learn from art to life?'

'Yes,' said Hannah, 'I do. Even if I've made the wrong choices, there are things that should have warned me, most of all about myself. I wasn't a good enough reader. I didn't examine what the best literature was telling me.'

'I should have been more cautious too,' Stan said. 'Only I'd been working too hard to think about dating, and I was suddenly . . .' He stopped, stammering slightly. 'There aren't, aren't many women in my industry, and there was this stunning woman who seemed genuinely interested in me. I was flattered, I suppose. Anyone would be . . . Six months after we met, we were married. I thought I was the luckiest man in the world.'

'What went wrong?'

'I brought her back to London, which she liked, and then Cornwall, which she hated.'

'Even though you had just got married and your father wasn't kind to you?'

'Yes. He was still my father, and all that I had left of family. I wanted her to meet him. It was a disaster. I'd left him a strong, active man who liked a drink or two of an evening. I came back and found him an alcoholic, raving, demented and living as you saw. He hoarded everything. I tried to make him more comfortable, less aggressive, stop his drinking. I hired carers but he kept driving them away so a lot of it I had to do myself. It was a dreadful situation and Jinni—'

'Hated it?'

'Yes. I couldn't blame her. She had married me to live the high life, not to look after a demented old man in Cornwall with someone who stopped making money from one month to the next. She was very angry.'

Hannah said, 'My husband hated Cornwall too. Hated my mum, hated St Piran.'

'So why did you marry him?'

'I thought he was the love of my life – until he met someone else.'

'My wife met several of those,' Stan said. 'We'd be divorced by now if she'd agree to a settlement.'

Once again, there was that treacherous quiver of sympathy. Jinni had made no mention of other lovers, though it was inevitable that someone so attractive would have them. In her account, the fault was all Stan's. Hannah could well believe it might be – and yet Jake, who had seemed so beautiful, loving and perfect, was vain, selfish and cruel. Stan, who looked wild, coarse and frightening now seemed gentle and even civilised. But just because he claimed not to hit women didn't mean that he didn't bully them. A man could intimidate someone smaller and weaker just by raising his voice. He could be one person to his wife and another to his cleaner.

People had affairs for all kinds of reasons, including desperation to escape a bad relationship. Hannah remembered the bruises, the distinct finger-marks on Jinni's arms. On the other hand, Stan's black eye and bruised back would have been counter-evidence. The more she thought about it, the more confused she felt, as if the truth was something that changed with every tide.

'Why won't she agree?'

'She wants more money than I can give,' he said. 'Isn't that always the way?'

'Not in my case,' Hannah answered.

Stan paused. 'You are not like them. Other women, I mean.'

'No, I am *exactly* like other women. I'm being divorced, whether I want it or not.'

'Would you want to stay married?'

'No,' she said. 'Even if divorce is never a good thing for children, I know what he's really like. He hates me.'

Stan sighed. 'I ought to hate my wife, but I don't.'

'Really?'

'Yes. It was a choice we should neither of us have made. Getting married, I mean. She never loved me. She believes that all her problems can be solved with money.'

Hannah felt a flash of anger. 'Well, an awful lot of mine could be.'

'I don't doubt it. But Jinni already has the flat in London and a lot of maintenance.'

It sounded like the kind of thing Jake would say about her.

Stan rumbled on, oblivious. 'Once this house is sold, I'll be free. She's spending a fortune on lawyers and forensic accountants because she thinks that I must be hiding money from her, but there's nothing else. This'll probably go for the price of a two-bedroomed flat in Notting Hill.'

'But the land . . . Someone said there's a developer who's interested.'

She didn't want to tell him about Saskia's husband.

Stan snorted. 'To cut down the woods and put up another bloody development of luxury holiday homes that nobody lives in? Over my dead body.'

Maybe, Hannah thought; but not if I must do it.

20

Another Story

Hannah was no longer sure what she felt about Stan, but she could not kill him. The situation with Jake might be desperate, but however angry she was, however maddened by injustice and unkindness, she couldn't use Jinni's husband as the lightning rod for her emotions. He was not what she had been led to believe, and even if he were guilty of cruelty towards his wife, it was not for her to punish him.

She had found a copy of *Strangers on a Train* in the shelves at Endpoint – it was well thumbed, possibly by Jinni herself – and the Highsmith novel, even more than the Hitchcock film, had left a most disagreeable impression. The Catholic wife who would not divorce the hero had been portrayed as a promiscuous alcoholic who somehow deserved her murder. How convenient, she thought, for them all. How devastated their child would be if Jake were really dead. Maisy loved her father, and (when he remembered her existence) brought out the best in him. There *was* good in him, even though he no longer showed it where she was concerned.

Whenever she held Maisy in her arms, she felt the weight of loving someone who would forever be a blend of both her parents. She could not untangle her own DNA from that of her husband, or even edit out what was good in herself and what was bad in him. It was not only physical resemblances, his long legs instead of her shorter ones, there were also emotional characteristics. Maisy had Hannah's stubbornness and Jake's charm, but her pout of shyness was all too like that of Etta, and her occasional prickly temper outbursts like Holly's. She thought again of the father she had never known, wondering what he had been like and whether her own love of reading or distaste for loud music came from him. There was so much that she didn't know and hadn't dared ask while Holly had been alive.

'Are you sad again, Mummy?'

'Yes, sweetheart. Just a bit.'

'Is it because of Granny? Loveday says she's watching over us from Heaven.'

'Does she? That's nice.' Hannah often wished she could share her aunt's faith, the simplest kind of story to live within. 'We need to put her ashes into the sea, you know.'

Maisy pondered this. 'Doesn't she need them?'

'Not any more. It's what's left over of her body, that hurt when she got very sick. We can have a special tea, with cake. All the cousins and Loveday can come.'

'Can we invite Daddy?'

'No, sweetie. He's away.'

'Where is he?'

'I don't know, exactly. But you'll see him at the end of the month, I'm sure,' Hannah lied.

'Can we invite Stan and Bran?'

'Yes, maybe. And some other friends, like Mr Kenward.'

Hannah had been meaning to visit the bookseller again. Apart from anything else, she wanted to ask him more about the school where he and her mother had met, and which Holly would never talk about.

Getting to see him was not easy, given that his busiest days, like most shopkeepers', were Saturday and Sunday. Eventually, she asked Stan if she might leave an hour earlier on Friday.

'You don't need to ask.'

'Thank you. I'll make up the hours.'

'I know you will.'

She wanted to trust him, too, but employers could turn nasty on a hair.

Loveday, however, would say, 'If you believe you are lucky, you will be.'

'But, Loveday, if I believed that I was going to get £20,000 it wouldn't just happen.'

'Never give up hope, my lovely. It's hopelessness that is the death of the soul.'

'What if I don't believe in souls?'

'It doesn't matter; your soul will still be in you.'

It was good for Maisy to spend time with her great-aunt, and when Hannah left Endpoint an hour earlier than usual in order to catch Mr Kenward, she didn't feel a moment's anxiety. Loveday's cottage was not at all like the romantic places snapped up in Fol; it was built of harsh red brick, its roof tiled in concrete and its windows plastic. Yet apart from being overcrowded by having Mor, Ben and their two young children living there too, it was still a real home for real people.

Fol was a fantasy, a seaside idyll with properties that had sold for a million pounds now being torn down to sell for three times that. It could not go on like this, everyone agreed, and yet somehow it did. Its bookshop was the kind of place that tourists used to stop at and peer into with loud expressions of ecstasy that such a quaint old place should still be in existence. Whether the tourists bought so much as a postcard was another matter, although the business did its best to entice them to do so with monochrome photographs of what they believed to be Old Fisher-Folk (actually a group of local people dressed up in oilskins and sou'westers in return for a pint of St Piran beer).

As Mr Kenward observed drily: 'They would sooner buy a map showing where famous books had been inspired or written than any of the books themselves.'

Yet occasionally, one of these casual passers-by would find him- or herself not only buying but reading a book. Kenward was quite ruthless about persuading them and had even established a book club that sent a monthly choice out to Fol's burgeoning population of retired people. Somebody had only to enter the shop for his tall figure to unfold, then, after a period of profound stillness, pounce on the unwary.

'Every time a reader is born, there is joy in Heaven,' he told her when she was a child. 'You may not think Heaven exists, but it does, it's full of readers.'

'What about people who don't read?' Hannah had asked.

'They read in other ways. Everything tells a story.'

He was different from everyone else she talked to. Holly would only say that he was 'connected'. To what, or whom, she never explained, but he seemed to know everyone. Later, when Hannah was in the throes of the exams that would give her the ladder out of Cornwall, he, not the poor harassed women at St Piran Sixth Form College, had been her true teacher.

'You will go to university,' he told her. 'And you should go away to do this, as far away as you can get.'

'But that's so expensive!'

'Not in the long run. The expensive thing is not becoming who you are meant to be.'

'I don't know what that is yet.'

'Nor will you for a long, long time.'

'How long?'

'Oh, half your life. But it's worth finding out, don't you think?'

Every year, until she was eighteen, he had given her books and she always found that they suited her perfectly.

'You always seem to know what I'd like before I do myself. How is that?'

'I've known you ever since you were a tiny child. Also, I am fond of you, and when you are fond of a person you can know things about them without being told.'

'Is that true of everyone?'

'It depends whether you think with your heart or feel with your head.'

Hannah did not like to interrupt her mother's friend when he was selling to some hapless tourist, but he had just released a regular customer (Ivo Sponge, staggering out with two bulging cloth bags of hardbacks). She stepped inside as a child steps into a sweet-shop (or perhaps an addict into a crack-den).

'Hello, Hannah. I was wondering when you were going to drop by again.'

'I couldn't get away before now, at least not to see you without interruptions. There are things I want to ask you about my mother.'

'Ah.' He gave her a piercing look. 'Yes. Why don't you come upstairs for tea? I've sold so much to that Sponge chap, I can shut up shop early today.'

She nodded, and he opened a panelled door she knew well. It was the entrance to a narrow hall. A small staircase patterned with harlequins of light from the sun penetrating through red and blue coloured glass squares set in the window led to his home above the shop.

Upstairs was the familiar kitchen with a round deal table, three bentwood chairs, a dresser with blue and white striped Cornish-ware, an old electric stove and a fridge. Next door, over the front of the shop, was a sitting-room with a big Turkish carpet and a wood-burner, and up the final flight of stairs, presumably, his bedroom and bathroom. It was very obviously the home of a man living alone, for all the prints on the walls seemed of a strictly Classical kind, featuring plenty of broken columns and drapery but no people. For the first time, she wondered whether he might be gay.

Hannah took a deep breath.

'Do you know who my father is?'

'I do.'

'Then tell me, because I need to know.'

21

At the Cliff Edge

'He was called Martin Mortmain, and he was an English teacher, and my friend.'

Already things looked different.

'Was? Does that mean he's dead?'

'I'm afraid so, yes. He died twelve years ago.'

Hannah felt a mixture of sadness and relief. She was an orphan after all, and her life would always be lopsided from this loss, but at least she had some information at last. 'So I will never know him, then. Not that I expect he wanted to know me.'

'Actually, he did, but your mother prevented it.'

'Why?'

'Holly was a brave woman in so many ways, but she couldn't let go of her feelings for him. Denying him any contact with you was the one thing left that she could control.'

The old man took a gulp from his mug. Hannah did the same; the suppression of strong emotion by means of tea was always correct procedure. The sensation of hot liquid travelling down the throat was remarkably similar to sorrow, she thought.

'I can understand that, in a way. Jake and I are divorcing. He's found somebody else, and I feel, I feel so angry and powerless – but I do let him take Maisy, every other week. My daughter loves her father, you see, and that's more important than what I feel.'

The bookseller nodded. 'Then you are a bigger person than Holly managed to be. She hated him for choosing to stay with his wife. It wasn't easy for him to do that, but he had a particular reason.'

'What was that?'

'She had multiple sclerosis. The cruellest disease, bringing paralysis and death by inches.'

'Poor woman.'

'Yes. Martin and Jessica were quite young when it struck, young enough to hope for a family. That never happened. He adored her, but – you can't expect someone to live like a monk.'

No, thought Hannah, though I bet that if it was a woman in this situation, she would be expected to.

'His wife offered him a divorce, but he refused to abandon her. Perhaps it was that they were Catholics, but he was a devoted husband and an honourable man. Then, when he was forty your mother arrived at the school, as lovely as the spring, and she and Martin fell in love. Everybody could see it, and being a boarding school made it very public. It was a dreadful situation. Holly thought that when she became pregnant with you, he would do what most men do in his situation and leave his sick wife to marry her.'

'Only, he didn't.'

'No. I can't tell you how rare that is. So instead your mother was the one to leave, returning to St Piran. She adored you but she was bitterly disappointed. She'd been determined to leave Cornwall, and yet there was nowhere else for her to go. It was less bad than it might have been for her as a single mother because of changing attitudes, but she was a proud woman and from that time on, she hated him. "You have had what you wanted, but I haven't," she said. He wanted to help her, to give you money, only she wouldn't accept a penny.'

Hannah felt a tumult of emotion. How could her mother have been so selfish? She had longed and longed to know her father, even if he was a pig, but it seemed that his story was more complicated than this. Then she thought of what her mother must have suffered to make her so bitter, and her eyes filled with tears. 'Oh. I wish I'd known. I knew she was unhappy, and I thought it might be my fault. What a sad situation for them all. *I* would have seen him.'

'Of course you would.' Kenward seemed about to say something more but checked himself. 'Holly meant no harm, but once she had made up her mind, that was it and she would never see or speak to him again. She was stubborn to a fault. Every letter he sent was returned unopened. Martin blamed himself. He saw a good deal of you when you were very small, before she gave him the ultimatum to choose between her and his wife, and he loved you very much.'

'I have no memory of him or that time. None.'

'She forbade me from ever talking to you about him. Maybe I should have, but I find it hard to break promises. I came to Fol soon after. I was looking for somewhere to retire to, and although I didn't come as a spy, I was able to pass him news of you, and even a few photographs. He sent money for me to buy you books, you know, not so many that Holly would have been suspicious, but certain things.'

'Do you mean, he *directed* my reading?'

'Nobody can do that. You can no more force a child to read than you can make a horse drink. But you were so hungry for them, you were a born bookworm, and it was the one thing he could do for you, at a distance. Martin was just like you. He knew that you'd got into Durham before he died. He was so proud. He left some money in his will for you to have when you turn thirty. I don't know how much, but it should help. There's never a time in anyone's life when money isn't needed.'

Hannah looked at his gentle, anxious face beneath its halo of fine white hair. He had always reminded her of a monk, though she doubted many monks went paragliding.

'I'm glad I know. Thank you for telling me. Poor man, poor wife, poor Mum, poor all of them!' What a miserable story, she thought; and was grateful again to Jake for marrying her and sparing her this, at least. He had done one good and generous thing. Then she remembered that he was probably dead, and her own future was in danger as, quite possibly, was Stan's. She must pretend not to know this, to carry on as normal, hoping for the best while fearing the worst. 'I came to ask you if you'd join us in putting Mum's ashes where she wanted them. We're going to have a small tea party this Monday on the cliff before Endpoint.'

'Yes, of course. If it's not a presumption, have you thought of inviting Stan?'

She had, of course, but not dared to.

'Do you think he'd come?'

'I'm sure he would. He was fond of her too.'

'Was he? I know she was the school nurse when he was a teenager.'

'She also babysat him, before you were born.'

Hannah gave a short laugh. 'Everyone's lives here are so intertwined. It's like trees in a forest, talking to each other through their roots. I never feel that in London.'

'You probably will if you live there long enough.'

Hannah collected her daughter and returned to the bungalow, where she sent a dozen emails, inviting her aunt, uncles and cousins to the cliff edge that Holly had asked for just a few months ago. She texted Stan. All replied that they would come, and so she and Maisy spent the afternoon baking.

Together they creamed the sugar and the butter, cracking in eggs and sifting flour, adding the ingredients one by one until they could rise and rise into a mound of golden glory. It was such a simple kind of magic, yet deeply satisfying in all its stages. Hannah never followed a recipe, for the quantities were so familiar to her that they seemed as instinctive as blinking. She beat her sadness into the batter until it almost floated off the spatula.

'Shall we pick flowers to decorate it?'

'Yes, sweetie. Let's do that while it rises.'

Baking was something all three women had done together for as long as Hannah could remember. Even during the worst times, when she and her mother had been on such a tight budget that supermarket shops were a weekly mortification of having to put back items at the check-out because they did not have enough money, there had always been home-made cake once a week, and it was the taste of love.

They sang one of their favourite songs for baking, *Green Grow the Rushes-O*:

I'll sing you one, o
Green grow the rushes-o
What is your one, o
One is one and all alone
And evermore will be so!

The sun had shone uninterruptedly almost every day, and it made the coast of Cornwall look like an advertisement for itself. It felt unnaturally hot and dry, the heat building like a headache, and the roses did need rain, like everything else. There seemed to be fewer insects, and fewer birds, and reports of invasive jellyfish in the sea, and the biggest shark ever seen, ominous signs of change like the ever-bigger storms that lashed the coast in winter. Londoners talked about giving up meat and dairy – as if the soya milk they drank instead did not come from Amazon rainforest destroyed to grow this – and continued to catch planes for their holidays.

'Can we put aside some of the cake for Granny?'

Hannah wiped the sweat from her forehead. It really was too hot for baking. 'That's a nice idea, but she doesn't need cake any more, sweetheart. Her body is gone, remember?'

'I can keep some for the dragon,' Maisy said, as the scent of toasting almonds, vanilla essence and lemon zest filled the kitchen.

'Of course you can.'

At the agreed time on the following evening, family and friends gathered on the cliff top Holly had loved. The grey granite rocks crumpled on top of each other like lumpen idols. It was too hot to be out before teatime: the mists that rose in veils every morning had long vanished. Even the gulls

251

were silent. The colours made Hannah think of the Laura Knight paintings in which women gazed out at turquoise and navy waters from the edge of the land, lost in thought. She'd seen them at Tate St Ives, years ago, and people never believed the colours could be accurate but they were.

The sheep-nibbled turf was deserted apart from their own company. The Penrose clan waited. Hannah clutched the cardboard tube of her mother's ashes, not wanting to release them yet in case they blew back into everyone's faces.

'Go on,' Kenward said, in his quiet voice.

'I want to say something, but I'm not sure what.'

Suddenly, Stan began to sing. His voice was unexpectedly deep and rich.

> *Thou wast, O God, and Thou wast blest*
> *Before the world begun;*
> *Of Thine Eternity possest*
> *Before Time's glass did run.*
> *Thou needest none Thy praise to sing,*
> *As if Thy joy could fade:*
> *Couldst Thou have needed anything,*
> *Thou couldst have nothing made . . .*

Loveday joined in, the hymn becoming a round, and then Hannah, the celebration or lament intertwining and ending until only Hannah's voice was left, and then there was silence apart from the sigh of the sea. It was time. She opened the container and a gust of wind carried the ashes out in a gritty stream, to fall on to the waves far below. One after another, the guests threw bright flowers they had picked on the way, white convolvulus, purple loosestrife, blue geranium, orange montbretia and pink valerian, the wayside

252

weeds of the county that were dearer to her mother than anything from a garden.

'Holly,' they said, one after another. A glitter went over the bay and was gone.

Then a patchwork of old blankets was spread over the turf, and they settled down on it to eat and drink.

It was a very different kind of feast from that laid on at the pub: more decorous, sadder and yet more joyful. There was lemonade for the children and Prosecco for the adults.

'Good cake,' said Stan, tucking into a slice.

'Thank you. I'm not a proper cook like Mor, but I do enjoy baking. And thanks for singing. I love Tallis.'

'You're welcome. I do too, though I am not, of course, a Christian.'

'It sounded as if you were mourning for yourself as well as for her.'

'When we cry at funerals, how much is for the loss of that person and how much is for our own loss?'

'When you lose someone you love, it's both.'

'Yes. And any love involves loss.'

'Sometimes I wonder whether it's worth the price, because of that.'

'It's not a choice, though, is it?' Stan said. 'Love just happens, sometimes like a thunderclap and sometimes like an acorn growing. Maybe it's better that way. If we could choose who we loved, like rational beings, it would be a matter for thought and will rather than feeling and instinct.'

'And yet feeling and instinct are exactly what we blame when our lives go astray and we take a wrong turning. If only we had exercised more judgement! If only we had not let our hearts rule our heads! But given how few people seem to have their heads in the right place, let alone their hearts, it's a puzzle to know which is right,' Hannah replied. 'I'm not at all sure that I do.'

'It's not a choice between one or the other, or it shouldn't be. The head and the heart should work together, not in opposition. But love has its own rules, unfortunately.'

Hannah said, 'That reminds me of the song in the play – *"Tell me where is fancy bred, In the heart or in the head . . . "'*

She remembered the next lines, and flushed.

'*"It is engendered in the eyes,"*' Stan quoted. 'No wonder it's hopeless for the rest of us.'

They watched the sun sink slowly into its own gold. The breeze was stronger, now, and very welcome. All the children ran off to play further away from the unguarded cliff edge and Bran and Loveday's dog Pisky bounded about joyfully, barking.

'My cousin says, "Treat your children like dogs and your dogs like children,"' Hannah said. 'I think that's why hers are so nice. And Bran, too, of course.'

'He goes into mourning on the days when Maisy's not there,' Stan said. 'Do you see how he follows her around?'

'She adores him too. I think when you have no siblings, a dog is the next best thing.'

Was the love of a dog enough to keep Stan alive when and if depression returned? She stole a glance at him. The chipped teeth, the beard and generally wild look were still there, and he was always going to have a big nose, though that suited him. She thought of Jinni's description, and how it had misled her. Had he ever been good-looking? He glanced up, and she blushed and looked away.

'Well, this feels more like a proper send-off,' said her aunt, plumping herself down beside her with immaculate timing. 'Look, the tide is going out again.'

They watched the sea draw back, line after line of placid, silvery water mirroring a sky barely feathered with white. The cloudlessness was disconcerting, as if Cornwall had lost half its landscape, the ever-changing hills and valleys of vapour that made everyone a dreamer. The turf was turning straw-coloured. Even the yellow gorse was becoming less abundant, its coconut-scented flowers turning to peapods on bristling spikes. The murmurous streams at Endpoint had sunk deep into their furrows of dead leaves.

All over the country, people had fled the heat, but the sea-side was little better than the rest. The sun beat relentlessly on every unshaded road and building, desiccating lawns and melting food and flesh into a shapeless, curdled mess. Even Fol was vile, its pretty narrow streets a human lobsterpot where sunburnt visitors struggled to get in or out. The TV showed pictures of London parks looking like deserts. There were fires on moors both near and far. The most popular beaches were too crowded to walk on, and at night filled with fires and rubbish that disgusted the locals.

'Imagine if we were to do that in *your* front garden!' was their exclamation.

At least St Piran was far enough away from fashion to be like this. Shielded by ugliness, it remained the kind of small town that everyone drove through unless they had to live in it.

'Good summer,' Stan said. He was turning darker by the day. 'I hope this hasn't been too painful for you.'

'Yes. And no. I miss Mum dreadfully, but it's better knowing she isn't suffering.'

'Have you ever thought about coming back?' Loveday asked. Hannah's face went stiff.

'Yes, I have. I think if I apply for it, I could go on living in Mum's bungalow, the council couldn't object now I'm a single mother too, and I could live in a house with a garden again, re-train as a teacher, Maisy could grow up with her cousins.'

'But you won't.' Stan said this with an understanding that took her by surprise.

Hannah wanted to say that she'd feel as if she were buried alive in St Piran, but it was too rude to say so in front of Loveday. So she answered, 'I cannot just repeat my mother's choice, and I am not just going to give up everything I've struggled for.'

She knew as she said these words that they were said more in defiance than belief. She might still lose Maisy, if Jinni had indeed killed her daughter's father. She might lose her if Jake was alive and preparing to employ lawyers against her. She wished, over and over, that she had been kinder to and more appreciative of her own mother, thinking that she was making a better fist of life although it had become evident that she was almost certainly doing worse.

This was the terrible paradox of parenthood. You learnt so much, and yet what could you do with that knowledge? Any other field of human endeavour rewarded you for learning more, for specialising and refining, but the next generation was something that punished you, unendingly. There were no degrees, no prizes, no bonuses for feeding, changing, comforting, entertaining, educating, cleaning, protecting or caring for a child until it was old enough to attain independence. All it did was inoculate you against romance, which was certainly something that people needed to be immunised against, like measles. When Hannah thought of how she had idealised Jake, just because he looked pretty, she felt like smashing her head against the walls.

'Oh dear, the cousins are getting a bit too boisterous. All that sugar,' said Loveday, rising.

Maisy, wildly excited, rushed, shrieking, and flung her arms around Hannah's neck. Her cousins Jago and Tressa followed close on her heels and all fell on top of Hannah, pushing her on to the turf.

'Mummy! Mummy!'

'Let go. You're hurting me.'

Hannah struggled to release herself from the scrum, and Loveday tried to stop them but the children, caught up in their own tussle, took no notice. Her discomfort and alarm grew until suddenly, she was released. The relief was instant. She looked up, and saw Stan picking them up and growling. It should have been terrifying, but they were laughing, running back and clambering up him as if he were a tree not a very large man.

'Aargh!' he roared. 'Come here, you pesky varmints!'

Off they all went, until the children tired of this game. He returned, to sit down beside her again.

She smiled at him.

'Thank you.'

'Exhausting. I don't know how you manage even one.'

'I never regret having her; I just wish it hadn't been so soon.'

The deerhound, panting, came back to rest, and Hannah scratched its scruffy grey head.

'What would you do, if you could?'

'Use my degree again,' said Hannah. 'Right now, I'm back doing the kind of jobs I was doing as a teenager, and every year that passes I'm less employable as anything else.'

'Did you like advertising, then?'

'I liked having a job, and some colleagues, and a salary, but mostly it was having ideas and getting people to pay for them.'

Mor came to sit where Loveday had been. She said, 'Those are skills that you could still use, Han.'

'Only if I had two things I no longer possess: time and confidence.'

'Confidence is a hard thing to get back, I know that, but your time will grow now that Maisy is at school, won't it?'

'Not really. Not until she's able to walk herself back home and be on her own, which she's far too little to do for at least five years. That's the problem that men don't think about, the holidays and the hours. If you can't afford a child-minder or don't have a helpful granny, you're stuffed. As with everything else, you need money to make money.'

'I know.'

She shaded her eyes, staring out to sea. A fishing trawler was crossing the horizon.

'French,' said Mor, following her gaze. 'Our men can't afford a big ship like that.'

'It *has* to change.'

'Our granddad died thinking that, and it still hasn't. What's the EU ever done for us?'

Hannah couldn't help it. 'In Cornwall? A university, medical research, superfast broadband, A30 improvements, airport improvement, housing projects, the Penzance Lido, mining aid, tech start-ups, social support, small business support – far more than Westminster has *ever* done for us. Do you think the seven families that basically own this county will ever lift a finger to help us when the grant money stops? Of course not. They want it nice and empty, and us on our knees. Oh, Mor . . . '

'As far as I can see, they've destroyed our fishing industry and given us nothing but a bloody great road we didn't want and too many tourists. The only rich person who seems to care about Cornwall is the Prince. Still, we ought to be able to have a memorial picnic without the national quarrel. At least, unlike many families, we're all still talking to each other.'

'I feel guilty enjoying this,' Hannah said, 'when Mum's gone.'

'Don't be,' Loveday answered. 'All she ever wanted was for you to be happy, you know. Same as any parent.'

Everyone had memories of her mother: how mischievous she had been as a child, how pretty as a young woman, and how determined as a nurse. It surprised Hannah to learn these aspects of her, but then what would Maisy remember of her, in turn? She'd tried to be a very different kind of parent, gentler and more fun, but whether her child would remember this or the long dreary trudges laden with shopping on a day when she was bone-tired was another matter. Only perhaps all she would remember was that her mother murdered her father.

22

Ivy and Honeysuckle

That night, Hannah could not sleep. The heat pressed down on her mother's bungalow like a hot flannel and it seemed as if her mind enacted and re-enacted the crime she had agreed to commit. How simple it had sounded on the train, just two months ago. She still had the Taser, she could still use it to knock Stan out and suffocate him or push him off a cliff or down the stairs. It would be so simple, and she was haunted by the fear she might do it.

When she fell into a doze, she had a dream, so vivid that it was like living another, parallel life at great speed and intensity. In this existence, Jake's passion for Eve had been as brief and searing as summer lightning, over almost as soon as it had begun. He had returned to her, begging forgiveness, and she had given it, with relief.

'She meant nothing to me,' he said. In her dream, she was glad because they no longer hated each other. They could be a family again, and everything could begin afresh.

When Hannah woke, she lay for a moment believing that this was true. At that moment she realised that however badly her husband had behaved to her, however selfishly and cruelly, he had probably never *intended* to be so; and this gave her unexpected relief. In her anguish, she had come to believe that every bad word and action was done voluntarily, out of calculated intent. Yet now she understood that he had been floundering about as blindly and stupidly as she had herself. He could not have been so awful otherwise.

When she had fallen in love with him, it had not been for his looks or charm or self-assurance – all the aspects that had first caught her attention – but for the person beneath that, the boy he had once been. Her love for him had always (she now realised) been partly maternal, but once she became a mother of a real child, he was left abandoned. If only *he* had been able to move on, to put his own childishness to one side and grow into a parent himself, how much good that would have done them all . . .

Had Jake ever asked her for her forgiveness, how willingly she would have given it! Maybe not at once, because the pain had been so great, but it would have come. She wanted so much to get over it, to become a bigger person. This holiday had given her the time and space to recover, as if after a long illness. Each time she plunged into the cold, lively saltwater she could feel that tingling surge of pure animal delight, reminding her that she was still a young woman. Her life was not over – how could it be? One day, perhaps, she might even fall in love and marry again.

Yet if what she feared was true, and he had been murdered, none of this was possible. Instead of the wound healing, it would spread to Maisy, too, and be worse, far worse. Instead of being free, she would be bound to her husband by a deed that would haunt her all her life. She had fantasised so often about killing him, but she had never thought about what it would be like if Jake were actually dead.

Why had she ever agreed on this plan? Jinni had made it seem quite natural, and almost sensible. Even if it was astonishing that more husbands were not murdered by their wives – given how many wives were murdered by husbands, and how much greater the provocation to women so often was – it was a credit to her sex that they restrained themselves. Or perhaps they didn't. Perhaps women were more clever, not more moral. Hannah had been hurt, diminished, tormented, bullied, but it had not altered what she really was. She had been foolish in all kinds of ways but not wicked. At least, not yet.

She slept again, and this time her dreams were full of silvery streams, soft moss and trees twined around with ivy and honeysuckle, half-strangled or lovingly embraced she could not tell which.

She lay on top of the sheet in her cotton nightdress, remembering the picnic.

'You're looking well,' Loveday had said to her.

'Am I?'

'Yes. You've got your jojo back.'

Hannah smiled. 'Mojo, I think you mean. Do I?'

'You're not all grey and thin.'

'Was I?'

'Yes. Don't you think?' Stan, sitting nearby, said nothing. 'You were getting that London look. Like a plant that's been kept in the dark.'

Hannah glanced affectionately at her aunt. To Loveday, any woman who was under a size 16 was in imminent danger of wasting away. ('Absolute rubbish that dairy makes people

262

fat,' she'd say. 'People need it to make their skin nice and their hair shine and their joints work.')

'I do feel better for being out of doors more.'

'You should do something special before you return, my lovely. Don't you have a big birthday soon?'

'Yes. Though it's not something I feel like celebrating.'

'Thirty?' Loveday snorted. 'Nonsense! You're just entering your peak. We should celebrate!'

'That would be lovely, but I haven't a thing to wear.'

Even the sprigged cotton dress, which she was wearing now, was falling apart at the seams.

'You could have it at the pub.'

The Jolly Lobster was not Hannah's idea of a good time. She shook her head.

'It'd remind me too much of Mum's funeral,' she said tactfully.

But Stan, who had been listening said, 'I'm going to have a tea-party at the end of the month. My parents used to have one, and it was a good custom. Why don't you have it at the same time and invite all the Penroses?'

Loveday looked at Hannah when Stan moved off.

'*Well.*'

Hannah said, 'It's not like that, honestly.'

She very much feared it was, however. Hannah gave up the struggle to sleep and paced around the bungalow living room in the sticky dark. Even with the windows open, it felt suffocating. Every morning, between the time that the birds started singing noisily and the sun came in through the thin unlined curtains, she managed a brief sleep but then the light woke her even before her alarm. Those curtains! Whenever she remembered the long, heavy pinch-pleated linen ones framing the windows of Ivo and Ellen Sponge's house in Fol, as luscious as double cream, she felt miserable again. They were only fabric, yet they represented everything that she aspired to.

She thought of the Burne-Jones picture hanging in what was now Maisy's bedroom. It had been a charity shop find, appropriately, bought in her early teens. That poor pale girl in her plain dress in the golden room, looked up to by the king but down on by his courtiers – it was a hopeless situation. Nobody could possibly be happy in a relationship between people who were unequal. The African King could offer her his crown and his hand, but just as easily snatch it back again, put on his armour and gallop off. That was what men did to beggar maids.

The sob rose to her lips, a familiar, sickening sensation that brought no relief. She walked to the window, where the humped heads of the hydrangeas, faintly illuminated by the glow of the town below, were superimposed on her own reflection by the dim indoor light. Everything was doubled, as if she were looking into a secondary world that came into being once darkness fell. A thin moon hung over her head like a knife.

Then she drew breath, because the silhouette of another woman appeared in the black air beside her, small at first then rapidly larger. Even before she turned, she knew who it would be.

'You!'

'You should lock your doors at night.'

'You've got a nerve.'

Jinni smiled. Her face, the high bunched cheekbones and short thin nose, was mask-like beneath the dark hair. Her eyes seemed to glow. She was dressed in black, relieved only by her silvery cuff.

'More than you, it would seem.'

'I can't do it.'

'Can't, or won't?'

'Both. I don't believe Stan is as you say.'

Jinni sat down on the arm of a chair, a long fluid motion. 'Yes, I heard you'd met. My husband seems very taken with you.'

'I'm only helping him pack up before the sale.'

'The sale. I do look forward to that.'

'I'm sure you do. That's what this is about, really, isn't it? It's money.'

Jinni's sneer was unmistakable. 'Divorce is always about money. You know that. He's a narcissist and totally untrustworthy. Just like Jake.'

When women said things like this about men, Hannah had automatically believed them. But now she wondered whether the same adjectives did not apply to Jinni herself. Nothing Stan had said or done had been sophisticated enough to count as manipulation. He had met her, offered her a job, and that was as far as it had gone. When they discussed personal matters, it had been she who asked questions of him, not the other way about. True, this could be because he wasn't interested – and she was wearily familiar with the kind of man who, with a minimum of encouragement, would bore on about himself, his life, his pet, his favourite football or cricket team and more for over an hour without once asking her a question about herself. It was all part of the endless, unquestioning sense of entitlement that the male sex was born with. Yet Stan had, in fact, asked questions, he had not behaved selfishly – and he had not made assumptions about her, as Jinni had.

Why had she believed Jinni's account so readily? There

had been the bruises on her arms, but Stan had even more, and a story to explain them. In any quarrel, there is always a rush to judgement, to pick one side or the other, and whoever got their story in first is always more likely to be believed. Once, a man's story had been the only one to be given credence; now, increasingly, it was the other way about. But women could lie, too. Even if her sex had suffered from prejudice and injustice, and continued to do so, it did not make every single woman a saint nor every single man a monster.

She felt afraid of Jinni, afraid of boring her, afraid of her scorn. Nevertheless, she said, 'I don't believe you.'

Jinni laughed. 'Really? It's all an act, Hannah. He spends his life playing games. If you fall for his lies, you're an even bigger fool than I thought.'

'I don't care if I'm a fool. I'm not a killer.'

'Think what you wish, Hannah. You still have your side of the bargain to keep.'

Dread was making her shake.

'It's a mad thing to have plotted. This whole idea is completely crazy. I don't believe you've killed Jake. Why would you?'

'Presumably you've tried calling him?'

'Yes. But that means nothing.'

Jinni held up an iPhone. 'Recognise this? Its owner was much attached to it, I believe.'

Hannah stared at the black plastic in its white frame. She couldn't be sure, but the case looked familiar. 'Where is he?'

Jinni said, 'The police will find him quite soon. In this hot weather . . . you can imagine the smell.'

Hannah's nausea rose up so powerfully that she knew that she must keep her mouth shut. To think of Jake dead and rotting away, his face turning putrid, the eyeballs dissolving or being eaten, the maggots and worms . . .

'Oh, what have we done?'

Jinni strode forward and seized her shoulders tightly. The shock made Hannah recoil. Her adversary had a kind of griping strength that was frightening, and her nails were as hard as claws.

'It's what you *haven't* done you should be thinking about. If you don't keep your side of the bargain, the police will find evidence that you did it.'

'But how could I? I've been in Cornwall all this time.'

'Why do you think his body isn't in Cornwall, too?'

Hannah gaped at her like a foolish fish. For a moment the two women stood still, almost in an embrace in the darkened room, then Hannah pushed her away with a violent effort.

'Go away,' she said at last. 'Just – leave. I don't want you here. You're evil. I don't want to see you again.'

'Oh, you will,' Jinni said, in her cool, light voice. She turned, and suddenly the room was flooded with harsh, bright light. Hannah, blinded, put her hands over her eyes. By the time they had adjusted, her companion had gone.

What could she do? Who could she tell? Stan, she thought. She must tell him he was in danger, and why. At the very least he must change his will so that Jinni could not profit by his death. Only if he removed the possibility of inheritance could he protect himself. He must do it right away, and let Jinni know, and then he would be safe. Even if he never wanted to see her again, he would live.

She lowered her hands.

'Mummy? Mummy!'

Hannah went into her old bedroom. Maisy was standing up, pale as a harebell in her cotton nightie.

'What is it, honeybun?'

'I saw her! I saw her looking at me!'

'It's just a dream, my love.'

'No, I did, Mummy, I did. She was right there, outside my window.'

'Who was?'

Maisy said, in a whisper, 'Eve.'

Hannah's spine crawled. She picked up the little girl and carried her back to bed. 'Don't worry, darling. A woman dropped by when you were asleep, but it was somebody else.'

'It was Eve, Mummy.'

'It was a dream.'

She was shaking with tension at the intrusion. Why was it that other people seemed to feel free to walk into any place where she was living? But why did her daughter think Jinni was Eve? This faceless adversary she had never met must look like her, or—

'Mummy?'

'Yes?'

'I want to tell you something secret.'

'Tell me.'

Hannah put her ear close to her daughter's mouth, and Maisy whispered, 'I don't like Eve.'

'Mmm.'

'Don't tell Daddy.'

'I won't. I promise.'

Never by one word or deed had Hannah shown her daughter how much she loathed Jake's other woman – if Eve could still be called this. She'd tried not to succumb to it, but of course she did. Even if you couldn't own another person, something very like ownership was implied by marriage, and something very like theft when someone came along and took them away. Though Jake had, apparently, been all too eager to be taken, repeatedly. At any rate, she was relieved that Maisy disliked Eve, yet anxious in a different way because what good would it do? It was clear that to Jake, at least, this was a serious relationship. And yet, Hannah could not help feeling relieved that her child, at least, was not deceived.

She stayed with Maisy, stroking her forehead very lightly in the way that helped her fall asleep. Her child's pale hair gleamed on the pillow like the straw spun into gold. The night cooled, gradually, and she tried to rest.

Scenes of her time at Endpoint kept flitting across her closed lids. The broken cobwebs. The rotting silk curtains. The twisting narwhal bone, so like a unicorn's horn, propped up in the corridor. The room empty but for a large gilt-framed mirror leaning against the floor. The twining green and blue seaweed wallpaper in Stan's mother's bedroom. The stairs piled high with rubbish. The bandy-legged table in the hall with a round brass tray, where envelopes addressed to Mrs G. Coad piled up. G, not J, she thought. Ginny, not Jinni, not Eve. And then the two names ran together, and she realised what she had missed.

23

Atoms of Mistrust

The following day, there was no chance to speak to Stan alone. The house, so long on the market, was being inspected by potential buyers at last. There had been an agent, not an ordinary estate agent but a property finder, a woman so genteel that she could hardly let her words escape through a grille of teeth, who communicated that her clients were interested in seeing Endpoint for themselves while in Cornwall. All there was time to do was rush round, filling vases and trying to tweak every bit of tattered fabric to show its best side.

'The advantage of it looking so terrible before is that the Inland Revenue has valued it at just £700,000,' Stan said.

'So little?'

'Yes. Semi-derelict houses are two a penny down here, as I told you. Most of its value is in the land. But I still owe £500,000 in death duties, all told, because of the London flat. So if it sells for more, it helps.'

Two sleek black cars rolled up the drive, bouncing heavily over the potholes.

One deposited some men in suits, with very short hair and a tightly controlled air of thuggish professionalism that made it clear they were bodyguards. They opened the other car to reveal the Wus.

As before, their glamour was striking. Cecilia Wu was wearing a sleeveless cotton dress printed with enormous pink and red roses that made her even more ravishing than Hannah recollected from the Sponges' dinner. Her husband was also tall, slim, handsome and immaculately elegant. They could have been film stars, or demi-gods, but they were just very rich, which these days, Hannah thought, amounted to the same thing. They advanced, and Wu, beaming, said, 'Philip Wu. You are Constantine Coad, yes? I am an enormous fan of your work.'

Stan blinked. His long hair was tied back in the usual man bun and the muscles in his arms and legs made the bodyguards look puny. At least he was reasonably tidy. If it weren't for the terrible chipped front teeth, he might look almost normal.

'We both are,' said Cecilia, her voice as soft as the cooing of woodpigeons. 'Such graphics! Such imagination! You have truly revolutionised gaming. We loved *Pilgrim*. Even better than *Firewatch* and *Bioshock*. When are you releasing another?'

'I'm working on it,' Stan muttered.

'We can't wait.'

They retreated into the house, and Hannah was left to her astonishment. Was this just politeness? Was Stan really some sort of genius?

It was fortunate that the relentless sunshine continued, for the Wus might feel very differently on a rainy day. Yet despite its distance from London, Endpoint appeared to have ticked many boxes, from anchorage for their yacht to the potential for making a helicopter landing-pad on one side of the house. Most important of all was its isolation.

'We have to be somewhere that isn't overlooked in any way,' Wu said. 'In the modern world, privacy is the only true luxury.'

'And Cornwall, unlike most English counties, has high-speed broadband,' Cecilia added. Her gaze passed over Hannah, unseeingly.

'My assistant, Hannah Penrose,' Stan said.

The Wus inclined their heads with polite smiles, as though they had only just noticed her existence. Hannah asked, 'Shall I bring out some drinks, Stan? Iced tea? Lemonade? Or beer?'

'Beer here,' said Wu.

'St Piran's do a nice light brew, if you'd like to try it.'

'Sure, if you join me?'

'Water, please,' Stan said.

'Just water here too,' said Cecilia. 'With ice.'

'And your, er . . . ?' Hannah nodded at the bodyguards. She wondered whether they were allowed to speak.

'Water. Thank you, ma'am,' said one in an American accent.

She delivered both then watched as Stan (with Bran bounding ahead) took the Wus around the grounds. Looking into the green shade, it was sad to think that if the sale went ahead, Stan and Bran would not be walking these paths many more times.

They were absent for an hour.

She heard voices approaching.

'You do know that the beach is accessible to the public

272

when the tide is out?' Stan said. 'All the coast belongs to the National Trust.'

'Yes. It is very British, but sufficiently far away from the grounds and house to be unimportant,' answered Wu. 'It is the spirit of the place that matters.'

How strange, Hannah thought, that he, too, felt it despite not being English – and yet not strange, if she remembered the paintings she'd seen at the British Museum, with their dreamy mountains, waterfalls and trees. Centuries before the Renaissance, the Chinese had been painting exquisite landscapes, and if anyone would understand the mystery and beauty of Endpoint, it might be someone from the Far East.

'I can see the children being so happy here, especially in the garden,' Cecilia exclaimed. 'And Philip, there is even a Methodist church at St Piran. My husband's family is Methodist, you know.'

'Oh?' said Stan.

'Yes. All the best families in Singapore are.'

Hannah, accustomed to the faint sneer that accompanied her family's religion when mentioned to the English upper classes, was once again astonished. What the Wus would do to the church at St Piran was anyone's guess but it would be quite something if they even helped to mend its roof. Hannah had spent her teens being scornful of religion, but the Christian churches were now the last line of defence against the indifference and stupidity of successive governments of different political stripes. Frail yet resolute, they alone seemed to have a vision of how a society should treat the most vulnerable. Even as an agnostic, she was proud of them.

'If you attended services at St Piran it would be appreciated,' said Stan gravely. 'Apart from resurrecting the traditional annual summer party here, nothing would make you more popular.'

Hannah smiled to herself. She understood that, despite his desperation to sell, he was still trying to do something for the community.

They continued their inspection of the interior. Hannah went back outside, unsure what to do now she no longer had a use. She had left her shabby cleaning clothes in their plastic bag, wearing the sprigged dress in honour of the occasion, but was not sure she had any further business being present. Rubbing cream into her hands, she sent up a silent prayer for the house. Please let these be the people who would make it into a home. If it was bought by the right people, if it were given a new roof, new plumbing, new joists, new stairs, new windows, new everything – that somehow looked just like what it was replacing – it would be here for hundreds more years. Hannah looked up at the battlements, and the creepers swarming up to them, once again laden with roses because they had been pruned and watered. At least it looked and felt very different from the stinking, filthy place she had arrived at just over two months ago, intending to murder its owner.

She could not help feeling that the old house had both burdened and protected the last of the Coads. Had Stan not attempted to look after it on his own he would not have been so monstrously filthy, and then she might not have mistaken him for the caretaker instead of the owner and carried out the plan. It was working in the house that had revealed Stan's character and Jinni's identity as her adversary, Eve. Of course, Jinni had known exactly which train Hannah was catching that midsummer evening: she must have read Hannah's emails to Jake and bought her two first-class tickets at once. Catching Hannah's eye in the crowded standard-class compartment was fortuitous, but Genevieve was a person who would make her own luck. She would always have found some way to offer her the 'spare'.

Pondering this, Hannah's dread increased. Every atom she breathed was mistrust, both of others and herself.

Except – except – the whole point of their original plan had been that the two intended victims were supposedly unknown to them. There could be no link to the killers, but as Eve and Jinni were one and the same, the connection to Jake could be made clear. They had gone away on holiday together, perhaps lived together, and that should be easy to prove and would make Jinni as much a suspect as Hannah if Jake had been murdered. So what Jinni had told her the night before *must* be another lie ...

Hannah drew a deep, shaky breath. Maybe all was not yet lost. She had not killed Stan, because her rage had been contained. Perhaps it was the same for Jinni and Jake.

Inside, the voices of the Wus sounded happy as they toured the house. Of course they were happy, they were handsome, rich and in love ... It was perfect weather for this kind of thing, with a faint breeze stirring the beeches and the lavender beds so that the sounds and scents of high summer gusted across the estate. They were obviously delighted by the house and to meet Stan. How strange to think that, to them, he was like a famous film director or rock star, not the glum, tattooed slob people perceived in Cornwall ...

He sounded relaxed too, his rumblings interspersed with laughter. She hadn't known Stan could laugh, but Cecilia Wu was flirting with him. She was the kind of lovely woman who would flirt with any man, perhaps because she had such an abundance of luck in life that it was small change for her to be generous in this way. Mor (who seemed to know everything about everybody, though it was probably because she read the *Daily Mail*) told her that Philip Wu had been a notorious playboy until he met Cecilia. He was now a completely reformed character. Maybe they would buy Endpoint. Maybe it would be part of their charmed, fairy tale existence.

Hannah stared into her teacup – the one she had first seen with a dead mouse curled up in it. If she told the truth about why she had come into Stan's life, it would mean the end of whatever trust had grown up between them. He would know her for a liar and a manipulator, just like his wife, and his openness would turn to anger and disappointment.

Why did this make her feel so wretched?

You are not like them, he'd said to her; but which of us shows our flaws to another, except inadvertently? The battle to keep them hidden is like the stench of unwashed flesh, a thing as universally despised as it is shared. Maybe Stan, too, was less nice than he seemed. Having been so disastrously wrong about Jake and Jinni, she could have little faith in her judgement again.

Hannah was in an agony of doubt. Her conscious self was like one of those brightly coloured buoys that bobbed on the surface of the sea, its chain corroded by salt, while the rest was sunk on the bottom among black weed and cages into which things crawled and never came out again.

'Let's talk tomorrow,' Cecilia Wu was saying.

The Wus were leaving, and it was clear from the smiles and handshakes that a deal had been struck. Stan disappeared into his office, and she did not dare interrupt him. Besides, she had work to do. The packing up was almost finished; this was her final week, and she wanted at least to get the last of her wages. She would need them.

'That seems to have gone all right,' Stan said, later.

'They like it?'

'Seems so. I'll believe it when I get the deposit.'

'Back to work, then,' she said with all the cheerfulness she could muster. 'I've still got my own life to sort.'

Somehow, she must move out of the flat in Kentish Town. There had to be a cheaper place, even if it meant commuting to get Maisy to school. Just living in St Piran she was on borrowed time. Daily, she expected to get a letter from the council telling her to leave her mother's bungalow. She had sent them a notification of her mother's death after the funeral and was still expecting to be asked to vacate ever since. Nothing came.

'Maybe they're all away on holiday,' she said to herself, though it was hard to believe they could be so incompetent. The local paper had twenty pages of advertisements for holiday homes, and just one for jobs, but everyone needed a place to live. The hidden valley of St Piran, where she had played in woods and rivers as a child with her cousin, now had tents in it as well as mobile homes.

If only, she thought each time she drove past it, I had taken out a mortgage down here when I had a job. Naz had been the only one to see it coming, and though prices in the capital had now fallen by 20 per cent thanks to Brexit, they were still double what they'd been a decade ago. Buying here, she might have joined the ranks of the property-owning class herself, thanks to the gulf that still existed between the capital and the coast. But it was a pipe dream that revolted her, because she could not have lived in it. She'd have become another parasite, and worse, one preying on her own people.

*

277

It was different for the Wus, however. Only people with serious money would touch a house as large and decrepit as Endpoint; even the hotels and care homes hadn't been interested in the present climate. But once they decided to buy the house, matters moved fast. The survey was bad, but not quite as bad as expected, and in any case the whole building would be carefully dismantled to make it fit for habitation in the twenty-first century. The contract was exchanged the next day, and Stan would be out in three weeks. All the sorting and boxing up of possessions was just in time.

'What will you do with all the cupboards and tables and things?'

'Give it away. Nobody wants old brown furniture now, do they?'

'I do,' Hannah said, surprised. 'Why have some bit of rubbish from IKEA when you could have solid wood and details?'

'That's the trouble. Not worth the beeswax you're giving it,' said Stan. They were standing in his mother's bedroom, where Hannah had slept the first time she had met him. Its green and blue wallpaper actually looked cheerful in the sunlight.

'But look how pretty the inlay is on those drawers, and the carvings of flowers and animals on the wardrobe. Look at all the drawers inside for gloves and handkerchiefs, and the lovely shelving and the richness of the wood. You could practically find your way into Narnia from this. It has solidity and character and depth.'

'Exactly. Nobody wants those things.'

'Then they're idiots.'

Stan gave her a long, thoughtful look.

'Tell me what you'd like from here, and it's yours.'

She was embarrassed. 'I couldn't. I have nowhere to put it, and I must find somewhere else to live.'

'Me too,' said Stan.

Hannah raised her eyebrows. 'Where will you go?'

'Once this sale goes through, I can rent. Especially in winter. I can get on with finishing my game.'

'Will you stay in St Piran?'

'Probably. The Evenlodes have a cottage on their estate, I might take that.'

'You know them?'

'Yes, all my life,' he answered absently.

Of course, Hannah reflected.

'And the woods?'

'The Wus aren't interested in those, or the beach. They're going to build a swimming pool and heat it.' He smiled slightly. 'I'm keeping the woods.'

'So all our efforts were worthwhile.'

'Yes. They wouldn't have looked at it as it was before. What they really loved was the eighteenth-century Chinese wallpaper in the turret loo. Cecilia says you can get anything copied in the Far East, even the Palace of Versailles, but what you can't get is authenticity.'

'Do you mind very much?'

'No. They are in love with Endpoint; they'll bring it into the future.'

Hannah hesitated, then said, 'And the alimony?'

'It's worth anything to be free.'

'If you're seeing a lawyer—'

'Yes?'

Hannah could not bring herself to say it. If she were to beg him to protect himself by making a new will, he would want to know why. Or maybe he was clever enough to work that out by himself. She kept forgetting that he was intelligent. He looked so oafish with his chipped teeth and shabby clothes and the hair.

'I'm definitely going to have a party,' Stan said. He stood straighter, unburdened. 'Throw open the gardens as we did in my mother's time and invite everyone who has helped before I leave. So I was wondering if—'

'Of course,' said Hannah quickly. 'I've waitressed for my cousin Mor when she's catered for dinners in Fol.'

'No, I meant as my guest. You, and Maisy, too, of course. You would come, wouldn't you?'

Hannah saw her feet in their flip-flops. 'I have nothing to wear.'

'Why do women always say that?'

'Because, in my case, it's literally true.' She glanced up at his frowning face and sighed.

'Hannah, I don't want to offend you, but . . . are you still in trouble?'

'It's best you don't ask.'

She walked away to her car, on the verge of tears. Even the smell of her own sweat humiliated her. She was a servant, and although he had laboured beside her on this project, he would never feel as she did. Her clothes were falling to bits, with holes under the armpits. When she read about how her generation were spoilt and threw away garments they had just bought, she thought, Who are these people? Her peers were the ones haunting charity shops, and it was the middle-aged who popped cheerily into places like Primark, laughing at its bargains.

Of course, nobody shopped for clothes in St Piran. If you couldn't afford a hand-stitched matelot top from Fol, it meant a journey into Plymouth.

Just in case she had missed something wearable, she went through her mother's meagre wardrobe when she got back to the bungalow. Hannah, who loved clothes with a hopeless passion she usually couldn't dare to admit to, wondered whether Holly had ever yearned for pretty things as well. In the days when Hannah had earned a proper salary, she had tried giving her mother things to wear for birthdays and Christmas, like a blue silk shirt, a brown leather belt and a red cashmere scarf. Each gift had been received with a show of enthusiasm and gratitude. But, as she now discovered, they were never worn, remaining wrapped in tissue paper.

'Why did I bother?' Hannah muttered, remembering with a pang how carefully she had bought each item.

In among these rejected gifts (which at least she could now take back to wear herself) she found a pair of shoes: in creamy satin with low heels, apparently unworn, in a box at the back of the cupboard. She slipped them on. They fitted perfectly, and as she twisted her feet this way and that it came to her that they were the kind of shoes a bride might wear.

Suddenly, she understood that this was exactly what they had been. Holly had bought these, expecting to be married – to her father, Martin. Her foolish mother ... It pierced her heart to think of the unhappiness she must have suffered in her disappointment and pride and loneliness. They were like the incarnation of the whole fantasy that everything was perfect and would always continue to be so if only you got married. If people were to turn up in their very worst clothes, unwashed, unshaven, stinking and sick then at least they would have no illusions about what 'for better, for worse; in sickness and in health' meant. But no.

'Oh, Mum, you poor woman,' she muttered, shoving the box back.

However terrible it was to be betrayed, how much worse it must be to have never been loved enough, valued enough, for that commitment. By Kenward's account, her father had been in an impossible situation, but he should never have touched Holly. He had chosen to do so, and she was the result of that choice.

A party would be good to go to. It was years and years since she'd been to such a thing; and if Stan really was going to invite people from St Piran as well as Fol she might even find some friends there. News of it was travelling around all her relations and creating quite a stir. People were excited at the thought of seeing the old place again; many had memories of visiting its gardens in their childhoods.

'I've been asked to do the tea,' Mor said, predictably. 'Not really what I'm used to doing, as a cook, but I've suggested the Women's Institute for the cakes and scones. There's a frenzy of competitive baking going on, despite the heat. Everyone wants to see what Endpoint is like after being closed all these years. But I'm doing the savouries.'

'I hope he's paying you properly.'

'Oh yes.'

Stan rang her.

'Don't come to work next week. I've got the Bolithos back for the party, and some extra gardeners, and you need a break,' he said. 'It'll be a surprise for you, then.'

Hannah did look round the charity shops in St Piran and Fol. She even looked on eBay, where she had found so many bargains in the dawn of the internet age. But either she was unlucky or she was too picky, for she could find nothing appropriate.

She tried not to mind too much about this. Surely, she

had other things to preoccupy her that were more important than clothes?

And yet – and yet – for a woman there are occasions when clothes are all that stand between happiness and misery, and the older she grows the more these are needed. A very young woman rarely knows that she is already so lovely that she needs little more than a binbag to make her more so. But a woman who has some life under her belt, who has scars and disappointments – that woman needs at least one dress of which she is not ashamed. Hannah did not own a single thing that was suitable for a party.

'I'm sure I can lend you something,' Mor offered. But her cousin had a style tending towards patterned fabric and ornament, which Hannah hated. She would have to wear the blue silk shirt she had once given her own mother, and jeans. If Stan had invited the Evenlodes, or the Wus, her insignificance would be complete.

For Maisy, it was different. Soft, pretty outfits with smocking, pearl buttons and velvet ribbons had showered down on the little girl from Etta, while Holly had knitted her little cardigans and jumpers. Some of these clothes, the ones that Hannah had not instantly sold on eBay, had come down to Cornwall with them and would be passed on to Mor's daughter in turn; they included a dress. Maisy, at any rate, would not be shamed at the party.

Hannah washed her sprigged cotton once Maisy was asleep and tried to get it to look white and fresh once more, but it was no good. Even by the fading evening light, it was almost a rag. She looked at it sadly. She needed her dress of dresses, and she had none. Nothing was left of her dreams.

She remembered what Jake had said about how every cell in his body had changed over seven years, so why should his feelings remain the same; and there was some truth in it. People did change and outgrow what they had been – or shrink into something less. She could never again be a child, or a teenager, or a young bride, and yet she was still made by all those experiences, and also by what she had *not* done. Out of them had come her deepest self, whatever that was now. She could have done it, could have killed a man she didn't know, in the same way that a tree can be bent and twisted into a different shape by circumstance from that which its nature dictated. But she had chosen not to. Sometimes she was convinced that Jinni had spoken the truth, and then her heart would lurch at the thought of all the fear and suffering to come. But then she would think, No. Why should Jinni kill him? He had been a means to an end, the end being getting Stan's money; even if she cared nothing for Jake as her lover, and had been using them both, Jinni would not inconvenience herself by murdering someone – or at least not yet.

One evening, she heard the bungalow doorbell ring – the bing-bong sound she hated above all. Apprehensively, the memory of Jinni's midnight visit still haunting her, she went to open it. Nobody was there, but a long cardboard box with her name on had been left on the porch.

Hannah opened it. Folded between leaves of crackling white tissue-paper was the dress that had once belonged to Stan's grandmother, and a note.

My mother would have been very happy for you to have this. Happy birthday. S.

24

A Cloud of Possibility

Slowly, Hannah unfolded the dress and shook it out. Once again, she marvelled. Its layer upon layer of gauzy knee-length petticoats belled out from a tiny bodice with a boat neck, made of almost transparent cream silk. The top layer was embroidered in a pattern of intertwining red rosebuds and pale green leaves, each stitch so minute that they could hardly be seen. It rustled with luxury.

She turned it over. Even to touch its lush, stiff fabric seemed like a privilege. It was a dress by the only designer ever to love and understand women's bodies as they were, to see their curves as flowers needing petals. It must be worth a fortune. She couldn't possibly wear it.

Yet she *had* to try it on, just once. Her fingers fumbled over the tiny invisible zip at the side, which opened just enough for it to slide over her head. It had a faint, delicate perfume that seemed to come from its depths as from the heart of a lily. The bodice was boned, and she would need no bra. She zipped it up carefully then turned.

The dress fitted perfectly. Underneath all the gauzy layers was a construction like a corset, with a stern set of hooks and eyes that when closed gripped her torso so that the graces of her body were braced and embraced, her breasts pushed up and her waist pulled in. So this was why rich women spent thousands of pounds on couture clothes – this was the elixir which all designers promised but so rarely delivered. Hannah turned this way and that, and the dress swirled out, a cumulonimbus of confidence, a cloud of possibility. She put on her mother's satin shoes, and the look was complete.

'Mummy?'

Maisy was staring at her, open-mouthed.

'Yes?'

'Are you going on *Strictly*?'

'No.' Hannah gave a short laugh. 'No, sweetheart. I was just trying this on.'

'Are you going to wear it to your birthday party?'

'I'm afraid not.'

It was too precious a gift. She took one more look at the vision of what she might be, then carefully unhooked the hooks. The dress clung to her as if it did not want to let her go, and she struggled in a kind of controlled panic to free herself without damaging it before lifting it carefully back over her head in all its stiff, gauzy layers. As she did so, Maisy uttered the cry of loss that was in her own heart. Hannah, standing shorn and almost naked, looked down into her daughter's face.

'It's gorgeous, isn't it?' she said. 'And so kind of Stan to lend it to me.'

'But *he* can't wear it!'

They both laughed at the thought of Stan trying to put it on.

'No, he can't. He probably couldn't even get his arm inside it.' Hannah sighed. 'It belonged to his grandmother, when she was young. But it's not right for me to wear it. I'll put on a nice silk shirt that I gave Granny. All right?'

'But you'll wear trousers, not a skirt.'

'Trousers are very useful when you're running around.'

She wasn't going to a ball. She would never go to a ball.

Maisy put out a hand to touch the dress.

'It's so lovely.'

'Yes. Let's wrap it up very, very carefully and take it back to him.'

For the next three days she took Maisy and Mor's children to the beach. They had a wonderful time, doing all the normal holiday things, like bodyboarding, building sandcastles and playing tag with Pisky. Even her stomach stopped throbbing with anxiety all day. For two hours as the tide went out and two hours while the tide came in, nothing mattered. She felt well again, and the cauldron of fear, guilt and loathing was stilled.

Maisy's obsession with finding dragons continued. Hannah had long since finished reading *Green Smoke* to her, and even found a sequel, but it was the first book that Maisy read and reread to herself.

'I like the stories inside the story,' she said. 'About Merlin and King Arthur and the Dark Tower. But most of all, R. Dragon. I wish I could find a dragon too.'

Every day, she brought along an extra biscuit just in case she met him. Fantasy and reality had blended seamlessly in her mind, and although Hannah had offered to take her to Tintagel it was Constantine Bay she most wished to see.

'I'm sure the dragon is there, Mummy. He might be lonely.'

'Or maybe he's sleeping. You should let sleeping dragons lie.'

Other books were offered, but it was this particular story that had taken root in her daughter's imagination, and as with all first loves, nothing else could equal it. She had even quarrelled with Loveday's son over whether it was better than *How to Train Your Dragon*.

'It's girly,' he said with all the insouciance of a seven-year-old. 'If it had more about fighting, I might like it.'

'Rubbish,' said Maisy, and looked for a moment very like Jake's sister.

Encountering Saskia in Fol was something Hannah dreaded, too. She'd glimpsed her former sister-in-law a couple of times, once going into an ice-cream shop and once sitting alone at a café on the waterfront, scrolling through her iPad, always with the same sullen expression. Was this discontent, or worse? Did she know Jake had vanished? Hannah longed to ask, but knew how she would be received if she ventured to say hello.

Repeatedly, her fingers hovered over Etta's number, just in case her mother-in-law had any news. She resisted. What good could it do? If Jake was still alive, and still with his lover, Hannah could not stop Eve's contact with her child. The ramifications of her foolishness seemed endless: she could hardly tell Jake about the plot, after all. He would assume, reasonably enough, that it was a wild story inspired by jealousy and vindictiveness, and he would (in a way) be right.

'Have you seen Eve again, Maisy?' Hannah asked casually.

'No.'

'If you do, let me know. Promise?'

On the day of the party, she looked again at Stan's gift. It had been well meant, but it was altogether too King Cophetua.

She brushed Maisy's hair.

'Do you want to wear it loose or in a scrunchie?'

'Scrunchie. There's one that goes with my dress. Not too tight.'

'You know your scrunchies always fall out otherwise.'

It was a very pretty outfit, in the kind of hot pink that was currently Maisy's favourite colour. The neck, arm holes and hem were embroidered with mirrorwork.

'Daddy gave it to me.'

'That's nice.'

'Eve helped choose it.'

Hannah was silent.

'You don't mind, do you, Mummy?'

'No, of course not.'

Once her daughter was dressed in all her finery, Hannah put on the blue silk shirt she had given her mother, and the one pair of trousers she had without holes. It looked perfectly nice, but once it was on, she saw that it had a dark stain over the left breast – so it had been worn, after all.

Angry with herself for not checking before, she took off the silk shirt, dabbing at it with detergent and a towel but nothing would shift the stain. It might not be ruined for ever – but it was certainly unwearable for now.

There was nothing for it but to put on the Dior dress. Once again, the intoxication of wearing something exquisite that fitted perfectly coursed through her like champagne. She had not intended to put on make-up, but the dress demanded it.

'Pretty Mummy,' said Maisy, looking at her with an alarmingly practised eye.

'I do my best.'

Even so, she brought her big, saggy bag with her as well as

a little clutch. She could never be without it, and it could be left with her work clothes in the utility room.

When she drove up to Endpoint it was looking very different from the way it had done when she first saw it. The potholes in the drive had been filled in, the verges mown, and the creepers were trimmed back just enough to look romantic in the afternoon light, especially as some of the red roses had returned. (When she thought of her insistence on buying fake wisteria blossoms, she blushed.) The round pond with its winged statue shot a clear jet of water into the sky. The ancient beech tree was still lurching forward on sticks, as if in eagerness to join the party, for the place was deserted no longer. The field to one side brimmed with cars, and instead of the usual air of tranquil decrepitude there were people, talking, laughing and drifting among the flowers. The gardens were enchanting. There were now hundreds of tall white cosmos, Japanese anemone, hollyhocks and gaura in the borders, and the ferns that had been savagely cut back to stumps a few weeks ago were soft with fresh green plumes. The sound of music drifted over, and at the end of one melody there was the sound of applause.

> *A good sword and a trusty hand*
> *A merry heart and true*
> *King James's men shall understand*
> *What Cornish lads can do.*
> *And have they fixed the where and when?*
> *And shall Trelawny die?*
> *Here's twenty thousand Cornish men*
> *Will know the reason why!*

Hannah wondered whether the Wus knew that this was, effectively, the Cornish national anthem. There were people here who believed not just in Brexit but in the devolution of a nation from the rest of Britain. They wanted it for the same reason the Scots, the Welsh and the Irish did, because they felt a people apart from the remote powers of an elite that had neglected and offended them for centuries. Once, she had thought this foolishly nostalgic but now she had more sympathy for their feelings. The centre could not hold, it was rotten to the core, and when people had been given their one chance to protest about it, they had taken vengeance.

> And shall Trelawny live?
> Or shall Trelawny die?
> Here's twenty thousand Cornish men
> Will know the reason why!

'Heart over head,' was what Ivo Sponge had said of their choice to leave the union. It was an utterly predictable disaster that nobody in London had seen coming. To the Cornish, Europe (which was to say, France) had always been the enemy, the invader they had fought at sea and on land for hundreds of years. They couldn't or wouldn't see the enemy now was Putin's Russia, Xi's China and Trump's America; but she refused to despise and disparage them as Londoners did. Maybe the Wus would bring something fresh and good; maybe the economic miracle of Singapore would save this remote county, though how much just one man, no matter how rich, could really turn things around in St Piran was imponderable.

'Isn't this a treat?' said Loveday, spotting them. 'It's as if this poor old place has been woken up and made to remember how it used to be. What a transformation! I can't imagine how hard you and Stan have been working to achieve it all, it's hardly recognisable as the jungle it was, proper job you've done here, even if those rhodies will all be giant in a couple of years though it's lovely to see the fountain back in action in the pond, such a funny little statue of a boy but ever so pretty, I suppose it's a Greek god or something, and the white doves are back in the dovecote too.' She broke off to inspect her niece. 'Goodness, Hannah, you do look nice! What a stunning dress! You look almost like a bride. Where on earth did you find it?'

'It's second-hand,' Hannah said.

'You should wear it all the time,' said her aunt. 'May I see the embroidery? Oh, those roses! My word, they look as if they've been sewn by mice. I've never seen such tiny stitches.'

'I think they were French mice,' Hannah said.

'Were they?' Loveday looked startled, as if believing this possibility. 'A real Paris dress? It's something I'd never have thought to see in a place like this.'

'I'm only borrowing it.'

It was a perfect late summer day. Looking around, she could see children running around the pond in an ecstasy of delight or, more probably, sugar. Long trestle tables draped in crisp white linen displayed every kind of sandwich and small pies, quiches, fruits and urns of tea. From a pistachio-painted van, ice cream was being handed out in cones. How on earth has Stan paid for it all? she wondered. Then she caught sight of the Wus. Of course, this was probably as much their doing as his. They wanted to be popular in the neighbourhood; if they could resume giving the annual garden party and donate money to local causes they would have no difficulty wrapping planners round their fingers. For billionaires, it was all small change. She could see them talking to the vicar, the doctor, a local councillor, her old head teacher and various other people from both Fol and St Piran who probably barely exchanged a word most years. They were radiant, and as their twins played in the great democracy of infancy, she wondered whether this might not be where the Wus would spend most of their time.

'You found something to wear, I see,' said Stan. Loveday melted away, and Hannah looked up at him.

'Yes. It's too generous, and far too precious to keep but I had nothing else.'

'Not at all. A beautiful dress should be worn by a beautiful woman.'

Hannah felt herself flushing.

'I'm not, but you scrub up well too.'

Something else was different about him, she noticed, and couldn't think what. Then he smiled slightly, and she couldn't help but exclaim.

'You've got your teeth mended!'

'I'd been meaning to get it done.'

All at once, she was ashamed of the unkind thoughts she had had about him. How could she have recoiled so much just because of two broken teeth? She was as superficial as Jake.

'I've never worn anything like this. I can't accept it as anything but a loan.'

'Why not? It'll only be lost otherwise. My grandmother would have been delighted.'

Looking up at him, Hannah again felt the turbulent mixture of emotions – guilt, fear, curiosity, gratitude and warmth – she couldn't distinguish between any of them. She half-turned away.

'But I'm only your cleaner.'

Stan said, 'I wish – I wish—'

'What?'

'I wish we could be friends, Hannah, or—'

'You wouldn't if—'

Voices interrupted. 'There you are! We've been looking all over for you.'

'Oh Christ,' Stan muttered under his breath.

Saskia was advancing, like a wasp to meat. She was very dressed-up and slightly drunk although Cecilia Wu beside her was as charmingly poised as before. To Hannah's surprise, Cecilia's smile was directed at herself.

'I *had* to come and ask you,' said Cecilia, in her low, melodious voice, 'is that a vintage Dior dress you are wearing?'

'Yes,' said Hannah, and experienced the satisfaction that accompanies having a garment recognised by one of the most fashionable women in the world.

'My God! I thought so,' said Cecilia. 'I adore Dior. Where did you find it?'

Hannah paused, then said, truthfully, 'In St Piran.'

Cecilia's eyes grew round, and Hannah could see her thinking that perhaps she had found a treasure trove of couture on the doorstep of her new home.

'Impossible!' Saskia exclaimed. 'Nothing good has come out of that dump, ever. Surely you must mean Fol?'

Cecilia ignored her, saying, 'We must have a chat. You're Stan's assistant, aren't you? Such a brilliant man. Here is my card.' She handed Hannah a minute rectangle of stiff embossed card.

Saskia had obviously recognised but was unable to place her, possibly because when they had last met seven years before, Hannah had been blonde. She put out her hand.

294

'We've met before somewhere, haven't we?'

Hannah said, 'Yes, we have. We used to be sisters-in-law. I'm the one you called "the pram-face" last month.'

She turned on her heel and walked off. Later, she heard Cecilia recounting this and Stan giving a great roar of laughter; that, too, was sweet.

Hannah went indoors. She passed Lord and Lady Evenlode, each snoring on a sofa, and yet more children who had settled down in front of a giant TV screen. When had that appeared? Maybe it had been in Stan's studio, and he had brought it out to entertain them. He really did seem to like children. They were pressing buttons on the curved black controls of a video game, shouting delightedly. She wondered whether it was one of Stan's; it seemed to be set in a post-apocalyptic landscape inhabited by sinister beings that needed to be repeatedly destroyed to the doom-laden chanting of a choir.

'Die, sucker, die!' squeaked one of her uncles' kids.

Pausing to watch another monster being blown up in a splatter of gore, she scanned the room for Maisy. No, thank goodness, she wasn't here.

'Have you seen the children?' she asked Mor, snatching at a sandwich on a passing tray.

'I think they were heading for the bottom of the garden. Don't worry, they'll be fine. Look, it's time for your cake to be cut!'

A giant pink and green iced cake studded with roses and thirty flames was brought out, and people began to sing 'Happy Birthday'. Surprised and touched, Hannah took a deep breath and blew out the candles to general applause.

'Happy birthday, Hannah!' Stan said, clapping his enormous hands.

She blushed, and muttered, 'You shouldn't have gone to all this trouble.'

'Why not? I couldn't have done any of this without you.'

The party was so evidently a success that she felt silly for being at all anxious. People she didn't remember but must have gone to school with came up to chat to her, and although some were sad that there would no longer be a Coad living at Endpoint, the Wus were, at least, preferable to another Londoner.

'Have you seen his yacht?' one said.

'Well, you know what they say: a yacht is a hole in the sea into which a rich man pours money.'

'Wait until he starts rebuilding this place.'

'I must recommend an architect to you,' Lady Evenlode, now awake, was saying to Philip Wu in the loud yet muted tones of the slightly deaf. 'Lottie Bredin, splendid gel, lives just the other side of the border but she'd be perfect for a job like this. You know she's been responsible for Gore Tore's affordable housing project in Trelorn? Look her up online, you're going to need a lot of help once English Heritage get wind of this.'

I bet she's another relation, Hannah thought to herself.

Out on the lawn the band were still playing, and some people had kicked off their shoes to dance, twirling and skipping to the melodies of guitar, violin, accordion and drum. The band, all middle-aged men delighted to have such an audience, belted out 'Cornwall My Home', 'Sweet Nightingale', 'Men of Cornwall' and many more.

As we got in the cab, I asked her for her name,
And when she gave it me, well, mine it was the same,
So I lifted up her veil, for her face was covered over,

And to my surprise, it was my wife,
I took down to Lamorna.
She said, I know you now, I knew you all along,
I knew you in the dark, but I did it for a lark,
And for that lark you'll pay, for the taking of the donah:
You'll pay the fare, for I declare,
away down to Lamorna.

It was Celtic music, spirited, honest about the harshness of the land and the qualities its people needed to live there; it got into the blood with its melancholy liveliness. Strange how any drop of something other affected people so deeply, as if being English was somehow a default condition whose dreariness must forever be leavened. Hannah suspected that somewhere, there was a bottle of cider being passed round too.

She knocked on the door of the downstairs loo, calling, 'Maisy? Are you in there?' and was answered by an indignant male voice, 'No!'

Feeling uneasy, Hannah walked swiftly through every room, then out again. It was a beautiful afternoon, and the sun caught the bright yellow ruffles of the evening primroses, the glassy leaves of the beech trees and the floors on which she had laboured so long. But there was no Maisy anywhere.

Stan loomed up. 'All right?'

'I can't find Maisy.'

Hannah's throat was tight with distress.

'Have you looked in the woods?'

'No. She knows she's not supposed to go out of the garden.'

'I'll help you look,' he said. He whistled for Bran, and the dog came at once, which only heightened Hannah's fear. The deerhound never left her daughter's side, so why wasn't it with her?

The afternoon was advancing and the party coming to a natural conclusion. The Wus had long since driven off in their sleek black car, but many lingered. Increasingly worried, Hannah quickened her pace, knocking on the door of the cloakroom in the turret, checking on every bedroom as well as the library, kitchen and ballroom for the flash of her daughter's dress. Mor's kids hadn't seen her for ages, they said; being children, they had no idea how long this was.

'She's wearing a bright pink dress,' Hannah said. 'She shouldn't be hard to spot.'

Again and again people replied, 'Oh yes, I saw her – the little girl with long fair hair ... '

Nobody remembered where she had gone, or when this was. Loveday called to her brothers and children to search as well, without result.

By now Hannah had moved from anxiety to near panic. How could Maisy have vanished in among all these people, many of them relations? Had someone taken her home? Was she hiding? Had she fallen somewhere? Was she up a tree? Sometimes she thought she glimpsed her child's head, but it always belonged to another. The old well was covered with a steel mesh, padlocked, and gave back only her own reflection. The broken glass greenhouses, out of bounds to all, were also empty. There were a hundred places to hide, from hollow trees to little stone huts to the cellar to the stables, but none held Maisy. She crossed and recrossed paths with Stan, whose concern seemed almost as great as her own. Soon the gardens were echoing with calls.

'I think I saw her going through a door in the garden wall,' said a member of the band eventually.

'Which door?'

'In the vegetable garden. There was someone holding her

hand – a woman. Tall, dark hair. Red dress. She had a silver bracelet on one arm.'

Hannah and Stan exchanged horrified glances. 'Jinni.'

'She must have taken her.'

'Why?'

'Revenge, I think.'

Stan looked bewildered. Then he said, 'You can explain later.'

Hannah found the burner mobile in her handbag and switched it on with shaking fingers. As soon as the screen lit up, she texted, *Where is she?*

Almost at once, the message came back: *Beach.*

Hannah felt as if the blood had been punched out of her. She pressed the button again to demand more, but the little mobile went blank. Its battery was gone.

'The wood?'

'No, the beach.'

In seconds, they were through the garden door and out running down the broad, shallow steps made by the tree roots. The wood felt stifling, a swollen mass of heavy fecundity that bulged and stank with dropsical growth.

No glimpse of a bright pink dress or fair hair anywhere. Hannah saw the great spike-stemmed gunnera leaves, the stagnant pond with its fleshy waterlilies, the tangle of weeds and woodland as if in a nightmare. Stan was running down the path, crashing past the great boulders and under the stone arch, though Bran bounded ahead of him. Hannah followed until they burst out on to the cliff path. The sun was sinking across the sea, and everything was turned to bronze. Something else caught her attention.

'Look!'

By the cairn of rocks that marked the blowhole was a

bright pink rosette of fabric. She darted forwards and Stan asked, 'Is it hers?'

Hannah said, 'Yes. We must get down to the beach.'

Below them, far away, a woman was walking back along the shrinking shoreline towards Fol. Hannah couldn't be certain, but she wore red, and she was alone.

25

The Dark Tide

Hannah did not stop to think. The waves were rushing in, no longer soft turquoise but etched by the wind as if made of solid lapis stone. The pale crescent of sand had gone, and the long, jagged lines of rock were barely visible as the dorsal fins of monsters sank beneath the swirling brine. Each suck of the withdrawing waves was like the smack of gigantic lips before another flung itself forward to eat up another stretch of land.

She kicked off her shoes into the lee of the ruined cottage wall and ran down the last flight of steps barefoot. Black bladderwrack was swaying in the surge, a dark tide seething up the thick round cobbles. For a moment she thought of the William Morris wallpaper on Stan's mother's bedroom, those exuberant, snaky swirls of underwater dark and pale green, the drowned flowers and fronds with little specks of white dotted against the black background that looked merely decorative until you realised they were bubbles of air.

The deerhound, greatly excited, barked, running backwards and forwards with its long face wrinkled up as though worried.

'Bran, seek Maisy! Seek, seek, seek!'

The dog ran about, sniffing, then up to the place Hannah dreaded, and barked, urgently. It disappeared into the cave just above the shingle. The sea was already foaming into it, ankle-deep, then with the next wave, calf deep.

'She can't have gone in,' said Hannah; but as she spoke, the wave withdrew from the cave mouth, and carried a pink plastic sandal, tumbling and bobbing. It was unmistakably that of Maisy.

Stan groaned as he, too, saw it. A bigger wave broke against the rock with a muffled roar.

'Hannah, we may not get her out in time. I'm calling the coastguard.'

'I don't care. I'm going in.'

He grasped her arm. 'I know this place, you don't.'

'*Let me go!*'

She wrenched her arm free with violent determination and plunged in. In a few seconds the last of the daylight had gone. The smell of salt and seaweed was overpowering. Beside her, Bran barked and whined.

'Seek, seek, seek,' she said hopelessly. 'Find Maisy! MAISY!'

There was no answer, and Hannah stumbled forward in the dark, slipping on rounded rocks half-submerged in sand that she couldn't see. The walls she touched felt ominously smooth, planed by millennia of tides.

Behind her, she heard Stan calling Bran, and the dog splashed noisily past her, returning to light and safety. She couldn't blame him: why risk your life, and that of your pet, even if you didn't suffer from crippling claustrophobia? Let alone for someone who was not your child but your cleaner's. Only she could do this. Finding her child would be something she had to do alone. She had always feared for Maisy, as if she knew that her life hung by a thread. Hannah went forwards, relieved that the ground beneath her soles, though damp, was not yet wet. She remembered that she had her own mobile phone with a torch, and belatedly turned this on.

The pin-thin beam of light illuminated a small area of the cave, which seemed to go back for several metres. What if Maisy wasn't here, but elsewhere? What if she were risking her life to no end or purpose but her own destruction? But she *knew* that Maisy was inside. A moment later, the torch light caught the marks of footprints on the sandy floor. Some were made by an adult, a slender, bare, high-arched foot, but one or two were smaller, fainter, and unmistakably those of a child. There were other, single footprints, of the adult walking in the other direction: out of the cave.

Utter fury gripped Hannah. This was proof of what she suspected. Jinni had lured her daughter into this place somehow and left her to die.

There was no time to pause. A single swipe of surf, and the footprints were gone. Hannah stumbled on, sick with terror, calling.

How long she had been in there she didn't know, perhaps seconds or minutes. The pinhole torch shone all around. The smooth, glistening rocks were dark red and pale ochre, like the internal organs of some vast creature, but on the ground there was a thing that was not rock.

'Maisy! Maisy, sweetie, it's Mummy! Are you all right?'

There was no answer. She dropped to her knees and felt for a pulse in her child's neck. Maisy was alive. She shook her shoulder gently then harder. The child would not wake.

Quickly, Hannah examined her daughter's head and body for wounds, lifting her eyelids. She did not seem to be hurt, but deeply asleep – drugged, perhaps, or knocked unconscious. She should probably not be moved, but there was no choice if she was to escape drowning.

Lifting her daughter's small, limp body in her arms, Hannah tried to take a staggering step out of the cave. Then another, and another, until even the passion of protectiveness could no longer stand against the force rushing in up to her thighs, then up to her waist, the foam of water meeting the foam of fabric and ruining the beautiful dress for ever, not that it mattered for a single second compared to the precious bundle in her arms. But even if her love was as strong as the sea, her body was not. She was a small, slight woman and would be unbalanced at any moment. How she could possibly carry Maisy out against the oncoming tide? It was likely she would smash her child's skull in trying. Hannah waded back and retreated on to the still-firm sand. In the dim light from her fading mobile, she could see the water sliding towards her, almost gently, before sliding back but coming closer, inexorably, the next time.

Hannah stared into the darkness and held her daughter close. She was cold already and wondered how long it would take them to drown, and whether it would hurt very much. The water touched her foot. The cruelty of doing this to a child, any child, or indeed anyone at all filled her with horror. But Jinni had, and it was a deliberate punishment for Hannah not keeping her side of the bargain. *Do you hate the other woman?* Hannah had asked, and Jinni had answered, *Yes, but not as much as I hate Con.*

More water. It was swirling around her ankles, cold and slightly sticky with salt. The beam from her mobile was already less strong; it was old and didn't hold a charge for long. She turned it down to its dimmest setting, and shivered. Stan had wanted to kill himself this way, but out in the open not trapped underground.

She was covered in shame at the thought of what she had tried to do to him, at what – out of anger, hurt and crazed vindictiveness – she had agreed to. She no longer had any doubt that she had been fed a farrago of lies, and yet even if that were *not* the case, how could she possibly have agreed to kill anyone? Least of all, him.

I wish we could be friends, Hannah, or—

What had he been about to say? Hannah thought of the dreams that had troubled her in the past weeks. She should have told him about Jinni's determination to have him killed, about how nearly she had carried this out. Of all the many things she had failed at, being a murderer was the worst.

It was she who deserved to die; Maisy did not. Maisy, the child who was so gentle that she picked worms off paths with a twig to put them on to grass, who was wholly innocent yet sharing her punishment.

Take me, but save my child, she prayed, the ageless prayer of parents.

The sea roared, and Hannah looked up. The darkness was turning grey, then yellow, then bright with a blinding white light, as if some star had found its way into the cave to burn it with a fierce radiance. Tears streamed down her face, she flung up a hand to protect her eyes and from behind the torchlight from his own mobile Stan's voice said, 'Hannah. It's only me.'

26

The Inner Cave

'You!'

She wanted to ask how he had screwed himself up to do this, despite claustrophobia, and he said, 'I couldn't leave you here.'

'What about Bran?'

'I sent him home.'

Hannah swallowed. 'I'm glad that he won't be—'

Stan said abruptly, 'There's no time. I can carry her.'

'Did you call the coastguard? Is there a way out?'

Stan had lowered the beam, but in the reflected light she saw his face look harsher than ever.

'No, and no – there's no reception. But there is a place where we might be OK, if you hurry.'

Hannah stood up.

'Where?'

'Let's go,' he said. 'You keep the light steady.'

He took Maisy from her. It took no effort, physically, yet

she could see that he was pale and sweating, just as before, deadly frightened, even though the worst was still to come. What it must have taken for him to walk into this kind of place, she could not begin to imagine. Seawater hissed and sucked round his legs.

'We need to go further in.'

'Are you sure?'

'Yes.'

'Is there a passage leading to the cellar?'

'This isn't *Tintin*.'

She followed him up the narrow cave, trying not to slip. There were mussels growing thickly on the walls, and long slimy ribbons of black seaweed showing how far the waves would come. The tonnes and tonnes of rock all around them pressed dreadfully on her mind, as they must on his, but she held the tiny torch-beam steady, and Stan kept putting one giant foot in front of the other. Where could he be taking them? Something like steps rose towards the roof of the cavern. All around was dark, but then it became infinitesimally less so; Hannah looked up and saw high above a dim light. Stan stopped too.

'We're under the blowhole,' he said.

'Can we stay here?'

The air was fresher, and the idea that they were close to the outside world made it tempting to remain beneath the blowhole. He shook his head.

'The spray is pushed up at high tide, remember? We need to get past it.'

There seemed no way out, just a blank cave wall gleaming faintly from all the millions of years of tidewater that stained it. But Stan stepped to one side.

'Here. It's very narrow, but you and Maisy should get through.'

The opening, little more than a foot wide, was behind the wall of rock and must be shielded from the waves. Hannah shone the torch through the crevice and saw only darkness.

'How did you find this?'

'Desperation. There's a ledge you must climb once inside.'

Hannah went through the opening with little difficulty, and Stan handed her Maisy's inert body. They were in an inner chamber of solid rock. The ledge, which she saw by the light of her own mobile, was another two metres up the wall. Slight as she was, the child would be almost impossible to lift there by herself.

'Stan, hurry. I need your help.'

He shouted back, 'I'm not sure I can. I'm a lot bigger than I was when I found this.'

The noise of water was rising, and so were the levels.

'You can't stay and drown.'

'If I must, I must. At least you'll be safe.'

Hannah put all the urgency she had into her voice.

'No, we won't. I can't lift her up without your help, and if she drowns then so do I. We need you. Please!'

Stan grunted, and then put his arm through the gap, as high as he could. Hannah saw that the opening was encrusted with mussel shells. Even without light, they could grow here, black bivalves feeding on what the sea brought them to eat, and they blocked a crucial few inches of the entrance. His arm groped for a stone, found one and smashed at the shells, which fell off reluctantly. There followed a period of more grunting, swearing and struggling. Hannah waited in an agony of apprehension. His head and one shoulder got through and then he seemed to stick.

'The bloody things are like knives,' he muttered. 'Ow, OW! Fuck, damn, bugger, ow.'

Behind him the water mounted so it was trickling over his shoulders, then his head, flattening the long hair like weed. If he didn't get in, he would drown, and his fear was overwhelming him too, his eyes were closing, and she couldn't bear it. Hannah bent forwards.

'You can do this,' she said, and kissed him, because she thought he was about to die.

Stan drew a deep breath, then breathed out, gustily. One more surge poured over his head, and she thought he was going to drown, but with a twist and a heave he pulled himself forwards to land almost head-first into the inner chamber. The surge of water that had been blocked by his body followed.

Hannah helped him to his feet saying urgently, 'Here. Take her.'

She scrambled up to the ledge herself, then reached down for Maisy. Stan lifted the child without a word, and then, with the two of them crammed on to the end, the light bouncing off the roof, stood there with the sea swirling and sucking around his knees. When she looked down, it was into a darkness that glinted like liquid ink.

'Come on!' she urged.

'No room.'

'Don't be ridiculous.' Hannah thought it would be impossible to feel any more fear and guilt that she did already. 'Of course there is! Maisy is tiny, we can squash up together. Oh, hurry!'

She could sense him turning over all the possibilities and said sharply, 'We'll freeze to death if you don't join us. Please, dear Stan.'

With a groan, he seized a spur of rock and hauled himself up. The ceiling of the cave was so low that the momentum nearly caused him to bang his head, but he managed to roll sideways. Once there, his bulk made it instantly cramped. The stone shelf was not quite long enough for him to stretch full length, and no more than three feet wide. They had to lie on their sides like figures in a tomb. It was bitterly cold. Stan was behind her, his back to the rocky wall, then Hannah, then Maisy, gripped tightly in the crook of her right arm, with one leg twined around her legs. To achieve this, the two adults had to make the most minute adjustments, and finally Stan put his chin over Hannah's head.

'Ow!' said Hannah, in turn.

'Sorry.'

'It's like playing sardines. How badly are you cut?' she asked, shining the torch on the ceiling and trying to keep his mind off the rock and dark pressing in all around. 'Bleddy hell, your shirt is ripped to dusters.'

'Lots. The salt makes them sting, but they're clean, I think.'

The ledge, though almost smooth, would feel increasingly hard. It was dry, that was the main thing. Despite the water pouring into the floor of the cave there was no weed that she could see above the shelf, and the crack between the inner chamber and the outer one went all the way up so there should be enough air being sucked from the blowhole on the other side. A thread of hope remained.

'I'm going to turn the light off now, to preserve the battery,' Hannah said. She pressed the button, and the dark was absolute, although her eyes swam with wavering starbursts of phantom radiance. Stan tightened his grip, so fiercely that she was afraid of being hurt. His heart thudded in her ear, systole and diastole, a sea within a sea.

Somehow, she must distract him.

'Let's shut our eyes. How long do we have to wait?'

His voice rumbled in her ear, tickling it. 'Six hours between tides.'

'So, not all that bad, really. We can leave in four. The main problem apart from cramp is not falling asleep.'

'I don't think I will sleep.'

'Keep holding me. Yes, like that. Put your arm around me.'

He was much hotter than expected. It was like lying against a bear, or a lion. She hoped that her own body heat in turn was warming Maisy, and moved her free arm round her, chafing gently. Her daughter breathed but did not stir. She had always been a good sleeper but if she remained unconscious, she would at least not know the terrors they now faced.

Hannah put her free hand further out to feel how near the water had risen. What had been the length of her whole arm was now up to her elbow. Still rising.

'How old were you when you found this place?'

'Twelve. It was one of the worst experiences of my life. My sister—'

'What was she called?'

'Sara. I loved her very much, we all did. She was my best friend.'

Hannah touched his hand with her own, stroking it.

'You shouldn't have come after me.'

'How could I not?'

'Because ... because ... ' Hannah said wretchedly.

'You saved me, so how could I not save you?' said the voice just above her head.

'It's not true.'

'Why isn't it?'

Hannah was silent. The water was quieter now, slapping gently against the sides of the cave. It was pointless to feel

311

how much higher the tide had risen, but she did so. It was now just a hand's breadth from the ledge on which they lay.

Soon, it could rise above the ledge, and then go on rising. They would struggle and scream and choke before they drowned. She would try until her last breath to keep Maisy above herself so that she might have a chance of living, though how her little daughter could ever find her way out in the pitch dark and alone was impossible to imagine. Hannah swallowed back a sob and put out her hand again.

The sea was barely moving.

'How high does it rise? Do you know?'

'It depends if it's a full moon tonight.'

'Is it?'

'Tell me a story, Hannah. It helps to . . . Tell me how you met your husband.'

Hannah told him how she had believed in the stories she had read. How she had loved those poor, clever young women, and how they had given her hope.

'In those days I thought that all I had to do was to follow the rules laid out by literature. That if I was honest, hard-working, kind, etcetera, I would get my heart's desire. I thought that meant someone like him, not what I should have wanted, which was sovereignty. Jake was so handsome, you see, and very much more sophisticated and confident and everything that I wasn't. We were both in love with the idea of being in love, maybe. Looking back, it was probably what I wanted to find when I went to uni. It's very easy to be romantic if you read literature.'

'Yes, you don't have that problem with philosophy and computer science,' Stan said drily. 'I didn't believe that fiction is there as a map to happiness.'

'Well, I know that. It's more like a map that only tells you you're lost when you already are.'

'I don't think fiction is a map at all. How could it be?'

'But if it's not, what's the point of it?'

'What's the point of any art? Here we are, buried in a cave and about to be drowned. Would it be any better if we had beautiful music playing, or could see Botticelli's *Venus* projected on to the walls?'

'It might. To see beauty might distract us a little.'

She could not stop putting her hand out to feel if the water had risen any higher. The anticipation of pain is always worse than the thing itself; that was her excuse, though she knew that it is not, in fact true, pain always being worse than anything that can be imagined.

Stan said, 'Yes, distraction has a lot to be said for it. I've spent hours playing games that took my mind off everything else. But things that are made well, and better than well, they make us more than what we were when we return.'

Hannah could hear the tremor in his voice.

'If you are tired, sleep. You don't have to talk to me.'

'But I like talking to you.' He added, 'I'm sorry about the belly.'

'What belly?' Hannah said, puzzled.

'If I weren't fat, you'd have more room.'

'You aren't fat.' She paused. 'My husband was always telling me that, you know. And I believed him, because when someone close to you tells you something unpleasant, especially about yourself, you believe it, even if you know it's not true.'

'Only somehow, we must resist this without becoming monstrous. That's always the difficulty. Who to believe?'

Or who, Hannah said to herself, to trust.

27

Slack Tide

They lay there, clasped so tightly on the cold, hard ledge that every now and again one or other of them had to shift slightly, always with caution and apologies, in order not to become completely numb. There was a faint green glow from the watch on Stan's wrist. It had luminous hands, and it was all Hannah could do not to stare at it, willing the time to pass more quickly.

'Tell me about the stories in your games. Are they full of muscly men pumping guns, or are they making fountains of blood with swords?'

'I have no guns in my games, now. And my heroes are as often women as men, and black as well as white. You can imagine how well that went down in Trump's America.'

'I think I can, yes.'

'It's so stupid. You could play at being anything you can imagine, and yet the market still wants it to be only about aggressive white men.'

'Does it matter?'

'Yes, of course. I'm not an aggressive white man. People want and need to see characters like themselves.'

'I'd rather read Jane Austen,' said Hannah. 'Even if she only completed six novels.'

'But the problem with a book is that it's always the same. Especially hers.'

'No, it isn't, because each time you yourself are different.'

'Maybe I'm too weak to change.'

'But you're strong enough to have followed me in here.'

'That's not strength.'

'Well, I think it is. But I also think there is something magical about seeing marks on a page and being able to see and hear and think new things because of them. In a game, it's all done for you, but in a book, you are using your imagination. Reading is a creative process. How can a game be anything other than consumption?'

She didn't mean to keep needling him and yet she felt that by making him fight her she was keeping his will alive.

'When you watch a film, are you just passively consuming it or are you bringing your own personality and thoughts to it? I'd say the latter. A game is more than a film. A good game is like being inside a film, and it's different every time.'

'But it's still designed. A book is, literally, a set text but your thoughts and feelings aren't. Everyone reads a slightly different book. Whether they like it or not, whether it speaks to them or not, depends as much on their own experience as the author's. Only my mistake, my dreadful mistake, was to read literature as a form of guidance. I thought that certain books could show me the way out of the world I was born into.'

'Everyone longs for something more than the life they live,

though. I don't see what is wrong with that – how else could any of us become so, other than by dreaming and hoping? I wanted to be all kinds of people when I was growing up.'

'So who is your favourite hero?'

Stan said, 'If I told you that, you'd know too much about me.'

'What's wrong with that? We may be about to die here, and surely it'd be good to have one other person know you better?'

Hannah put her hand over the ledge, very cautiously. She could feel the water with her fingertips, it was hard to be sure, but it was just below the rock on which they lay, and no longer rising. It must have reached the slack tide, the equilibrium in which the incoming forces were equalled by the outgoing ones.

His voice murmured, 'If I had to choose one person to know me better, Hannah, it would be—'

Hannah guessed what he was going to say next, and she couldn't bear it.

'Stan, there's something I must tell you. The night I turned up at Endpoint, I hadn't come to save you. I'd come to kill you.'

He seemed to stop breathing.

'Listen. This is the real story. It's not pretty, but it is true.'

Haltingly, she told him how she had met Jinni, and how they had plotted to murder each other's husbands. At first, she was afraid that he wouldn't believe her. Then she was afraid that he did. She could almost feel him withdrawing.

'That's completely insane.'

'Yes. I know that. Your great love turns out to be one-part Boadicea to two parts Lady Macbeth.'

'Are you referring to Jinni or yourself?'

316

Hannah did not know what he meant by this; when she worked it out, she was even more wretched.

'Well, I'm as bad as she is. All women who are getting divorced believe that we'd be better off as widows. You dream of love and you get a hot baked potato thrown in your face. Hardly surprising if some of us think of homicide.'

'Only you didn't go through with it.'

'Some of that was chance. Maybe I was an idiot not to. When we first met, I thought you were the caretaker. You didn't seem . . . '

He shifted slightly. 'Her type? No. Any more than she was mine, really. But when she smiled on me, it felt as if the sun was shining. Then it began. Bit by bit by bit until I was nothing.'

Hannah said, 'And then, last week, I worked out that in fact the woman Jake was having an affair with, who called herself Eve, was Jinni. Genevieve. My husband's mistress is your ex-wife. It was all set up from the start, do you understand?'

'But why go to all that trouble?'

'Because she wants to get away with it. An exchange of murders is a perfectly good idea if everyone carries the crime through and nobody confesses. I wonder whether Jake was in on it? She knew what train I'd be on because I emailed him, but I can't believe he'd agree to be an accomplice to a murder. However vile he is, he's not like that. If he's still alive, that is. She may have killed him too, as well as attempting to drown Maisy. I simply do not know.'

Stan was silent. Then he said, 'I think the main thing to understand about Jinni is that she hates everyone. You know how the most attractive people are those who are enthusiastic? They embrace life, they're curious and excited about it, and that gives them energy, and everyone loves that. She's the opposite. She's like a black hole into which everything is sucked and destroyed. You feel desperate to keep her attention, to make yourself interesting, and for a while that is what you become; only it never lasts.'

'You mean, you liked having sex with her.'

'It was just sex.'

'I never understand what men mean when they say that. It's so different for women.'

'I suppose it must be.' He shifted uncomfortably. 'Someone who looks like her, well, they mostly just want to be adored ... and I did adore her. She got under my skin and into my brain. I thought she was my chance to make a new life. I know it sounds naïve, but I thought love was about happiness and being with someone who made you feel good about yourself and not lonely.'

'But that's exactly what it should be.'

'Well, not with her. Jinni was sweet at first, so caring and kind and flattering, she made everything feel amazing, and she was very, very good at spending other people's money. But then the mask would slip, and she'd say something so horrible to me about myself, and I couldn't believe that I hadn't made it happen.'

'What a bitch.'

'Well, I am ugly,' said Stan, and the sadness in his voice made her say, 'No, you are *not*!'

'But when you met me, I could see you thinking that I was.'

Hannah said, 'You were drunk, and dirty, and angry. And yes, when you had forgotten how to take care of yourself, you weren't – you weren't yourself, as you are now.'

'What, with half a ton of seaweed in my hair?'

She burst out laughing, and he laughed too. It was an odd

sound in the cave, and she thought that perhaps it was the first time ever such a sound had been made there.

'We probably both look very strange. Your grandmother's lovely dress! I do feel bad about it, though the boning is half-killing me.'

'Jinni was always furious she couldn't wear it.'

'I wonder how she came to be so angry.'

'I don't know. She hated her family, but I never knew them, or even where she came from in America. She would never talk about them. I think maybe they were why she was so hard and cruel, but that's just speculation.'

'She's *American*? I'd never have guessed. She didn't sound like one.'

'She's reinvented herself many times. I was even warned about her by a colleague, someone who had more to do with the Hollywood end of gaming. I should have listened, but I believed Jinni when she told me that powerful men had tried to prey on her in return for work and advancement, and that when she refused them, they spread vile stories about her. Nothing is more plausible, in that industry, and yet not everyone there is a monster. It has its predators but also good people, people who are genuinely creative and idealistic and who just want to do their best despite the system. I believed Jinni, and I stopped believing everyone else. Everything I did under her influence was wrong, although the responsibility is still mine.'

He paused, and they both made the minute adjustments to their positions on the ledge that enabled their blood to keep flowing. She prayed Maisy wasn't also losing heat in this sunless prison and kept trying to chafe her child's thin limbs with her own free hand and leg.

'How did she get to control you?'

'It started with small things, like telling me I shouldn't wear black, it didn't suit me. Or this pair of shoes. Nobody had ever bothered with the way I looked before, so I stopped wearing black and threw those shoes away. I wore clothes she said I should wear and took up mindfulness classes and being woke rather than, you know, having a conscience and trying to be a decent person. Then she wanted me to have my back done.'

'Done?'

'Electrolysis. Because I'm so repulsive,' Stan said. 'She said I couldn't see my back, but it was like having a gorilla. Again, I agreed. I hadn't thought about being hairy; I mean, it's normal for a bloke, but it's also normal to have work done in America and I wanted to please her, or at least not to displease her. So, the fuzz came off my back. But that wasn't enough; she wanted everything zapped, every follicle except what was on my head, including under my arms, and I just couldn't. I am a hairy man, not a smooth man, and I dug my heels in.'

'I'm glad you didn't,' said Hannah. 'You wouldn't be nearly so warm now without it.'

She was surprised to realise that this was the case. It felt like an animal's pelt, and not disgusting at all.

'But it was also part of the way she began to control me. It began with no meat, no alcohol, no dairy, and it became nothing except plants. I lost a lot of weight and went to the gym but I had no energy. She gave me pills to swallow, and some of those, I don't know what was in them, but I began to feel out of it. Then she accused me of fancying other women if I even looked at one in the street. I'm a normal man, of course I *look* but never . . . I tried ignoring her, and her response was to hit me so hard that she smashed my front teeth.'

'Oh, Stan.'

'That was when I should have left. But by then we were not only married but living in Cornwall with my dad, and all I could think about was protecting him. That became her hold over me. We'd never got on that well but I loved him, he was all I had left, and there were still flashes of what he had been like, the parts that the disease hadn't yet eaten up.'

'That's just like me and Maisy. I couldn't stand up for myself because of her either.'

'I understand that completely. Though with a child, you know that one day they'll be strong and understand what was going on, whereas with dementia, there's no hope. He would wander about, especially at night, moving stuff around, piling up mess, and everything just got worse and worse. Mrs Bolitho couldn't help, she had her own troubles and I didn't want to send him to a home, though that would probably have been safer – I wouldn't put a dog in most care homes. It took all my strength to keep looking after him, and I thought I must be getting sick too. She got control of my email accounts, and she got my passwords. Once she had those, she pretty much had control over everything. Anyone who tried to get in touch, she texted them that she – meaning me – never wanted to see them again. They believed it.'

Hannah was thinking about some of the messages she had received from Jake. Even if he had been a pig to her, she wondered whether it was he who had really sent them. Then she wondered whether this was wishful thinking, because he had still behaved abominably. *I deserve to be happy*, he had told her. But who, really, believed this? And what, in any case, was happiness?

'Ironic that she accused you of affairs instead of the other way about.'

'Yes. Believe me, even if I'd been the type I had no energy

for it.' He paused. 'Once she left, I began eating again, but badly. I had months of nothing but pasties and beer. I had to keep going to look after Dad, and my stomach was a sinkhole that had to be filled. I began to feel steadier – just having some peace helped. She only came down to shout at me.'

'But you didn't stop her?'

'No. I realised that we had to divorce as soon as possible, but getting her to agree on the settlement has been an interminable process. That was what the last game I've been working on was about. Two steps forward and one step back.'

'I didn't know you could do video games like that.'

'Yes, why not? But Jinni was just . . . She couldn't see the point of nursing my father. "Why bother, when he's gone?" she said. "Why don't you just put a pillow over his face and put him out of his misery?" And when I wouldn't do this, she began to attack me more seriously.'

'With what?'

'Cigarettes at first. Here, feel.' He brought her fingers to his arms and guided them. The puckered knots of scars were just like those on Lila's arms. So, it was true. Up until now, she had not known whether to believe him or not. 'Here, here and here.'

'Yes,' she murmured.

'She took to jabbing me with a kitchen knife, too. There was a lot of blood. Mrs Bolitho – the lady you met – she called the police. But I told them that I was self-harming, and they believed me. Of course they believed it. A man like me isn't supposed to be abused, especially if he's big and strong and educated. But *anybody* can be abused, man or woman. All it takes is someone who doesn't care, and someone who does. When my father died, we'd just had a great row, or rather she'd shouted and shouted at me about

322

putting him in a home, because he was incontinent and unable to move or speak, only how could I know he wasn't in there still, somehow, unable to move just as we are now? She went into his room, and when she came out – he was dead. Death by natural causes, the doctor said, but I think she suffocated him. The worst thing was that it was a relief, because she couldn't hurt him any more. I failed my sister, I failed my mother, and I failed my father. Do you see, now, why I wanted to die?'

Stan was crying, and Hannah was too. There was so much sadness in him, so much grief, and so much sadness in her as well that it was as if they had become one single sorrow.

'What was the worst thing she did to you?'

'I don't know. So many things. Once, she poured boiling water on my thigh when I was asleep. She wasn't aiming for that, of course. I ran and jumped in the fountain in front of the house and stayed there for two hours. It took the heat out, and that time, I didn't scar. But the fear she might do it again meant that I hardly dared to sleep.'

'Oh, Stan.'

She checked his watch. Another two hours to go. He said, 'I'm not telling you this to ask for pity. I don't deserve pity. I'm telling you because I know how dangerous she is.'

Hannah said, 'She brought Maisy in here. I saw her footprints. And I'm pretty sure I saw her walking back to Fol along the beach just before we got down.'

'But why did she do that?'

'To punish me. You're not the only one whose head she got into. She's . . . Stan, my agreement didn't stop there, you see.'

She told him, haltingly, about the mushrooms and the cliff edge, desperate to unburden herself. At any moment, she expected him to unclamp his arm around her and let her fall from the ledge into the water beneath.

'So what went wrong? What stopped you?'

'I suppose that I began to doubt her. The more I got to know you the more I felt that – that—'

'You don't see, though. You never really wanted to – you *stopped* me from eating the mushroom and from falling off the cliff. It's not what we say or think that counts, it's what we *do*.'

'But each time, it was an accident.'

'There are no accidents.'

'You say she murdered your father. She's told me that she's murdered my husband. I'm responsible for that, if it's true. We plotted together, criss-cross, and even if she kept her word and I didn't, I'm still guilty.'

Stan said, 'Everyone is capable of murder, given the right circumstances. The real mystery is why more of us don't do it.'

28

The White Stag

Time passed, and it was only when Hannah found her foot in a particularly painful seizure that she realised they had both fallen asleep. Somehow, that cold, hard place had become warm enough to grant them a period of unconsciousness. She looked at the luminous face of her watch and felt a fresh jolt of fear.

'Stan! Stan, wake up!'

His leg was lying half on top of her, a dead weight, and she began to struggle. He made no response, and she began to fear he had passed out.

'Wake up! The tide is out now, and we've got to move before it returns.'

Groaning, he stirred, tightening his grip around her waist. Hannah wriggled, afraid of losing her own hold on Maisy, desperate to be free. She kicked him again and again before realising that she had his mobile and could turn the light back on. She shone it in his face, and he blinked and winced.

'Oh, no, no, no. I thought it was a dream.'

She angled the tiny beam of light away. His heart was racing in her ear.

'Look at me, Stan. We can get out now. The sea is out. Come on, we must get down.'

Somehow, she unclamped his arm and leg and slid off the ledge. Though every limb hurt, the floor of the cave felt like luxury because she could stretch and move again. He lowered Maisy into her arms, then landed clumsily on the damp rocky floor himself.

'I'll go through first, then hand me Maisy, then you must follow.'

'Don't leave me.'

He was strong enough to stop her, to clutch her in the deadly grip of a drowning man, but she trusted him.

'I'm right here. I must get her through but I'm not leaving without you.'

He grunted and released her. As before, Hannah slid through the gap into the bigger cave. She reached for her daughter; the limp body came through without difficulty. But the narrowness of the exit was still a problem for Stan.

'Come on. Give me your hand.'

Stan's fingers found hers almost at once. He hadn't uttered a word, but they were clammy with fear.

'Put both your arms, then your shoulders through, like a diver, and suck your chest and stomach in, turn a bit that's it, push with your feet . . . '

He gasped, and she knew that his torso must be being lacerated. There was no water this time to lubricate his passage and the gap in the rock seemed crammed with his flesh, his hair, his suffering.

'You can do it; keep pushing, Stan, that's it, come on . . . '

He squeezed and panted and groaned in a struggle that once again seemed hopeless. She sat on a rock, cradling her child's body, watching him and shining the light into the cave. How long before the tide started to return? They would not last another six hours in here. If she had to save her child and leave him, could she do it? Every moment that Maisy continued to lie in the cold and damp added to her danger, and yet she couldn't bear to make this choice. She wished for soap, oil, forceps, but only he could rescue himself.

Eventually, after wriggling and twisting and exhaling, he got through, panting.

'Can you stand up?'

'Yes.'

'Then do. I can't carry you, dear Stan, even Maisy is heavy, and we still need to get out.'

She kept the torch on full, and its radiance lit the gleaming, glistening rocks ribboned with weed, and the rags of her once glorious dress. It shone on Maisy's long fair hair, streaming over her arm, and on the smooth sandy floor. There was no trace of any footprints. All she could think of was regaining the outer world, however. The closer Stan came to the mouth of the cave, the straighter he stood until once again they were out with the stars prickling the night sky.

'I didn't think we'd make it,' she said.

Wordlessly, Stan took her child, and she felt a great rush of gratitude.

The moon was falling towards the horizon. The sea was black velvet again. It was painful to walk barefoot on the shingle that slipped and pinched. Yet there at the top of the stair were her shoes, kicked off, and beside them, in the shadow of the ruined cottage, a slumped figure that changed in an instant from dejection to delight. Bran bounded forwards, barking and jumping, and Stan growled, 'There, there, you silly bugger. All right?'

Hannah put her arms around the deerhound and was lavishly licked in turn. 'Yes, yes, Bran. I love you too. Shh.'

'I have no belt for Bran to help pull you back up, this time,' Stan said.

'It doesn't matter.'

It was an even longer and wearier climb up through the wood, the dog racing ahead then doubling back anxiously. The great dark canopy overhead rustled and stirred, the ivy twining up the trunks glinting like dim constellations. An owl hooted and was answered by another further off. A fox trotted across the path, not even pausing to acknowledge their presence, and something screamed, briefly. It must have rained, for the little streams were running again, and a mist rose up as the earth exhaled its stored heat, bringing with it a scent of the beginning of autumn.

Hannah heard the slightest noise from Bran and lifted her head. Something was standing in a pool of moonlight. Its antlers were full-grown, a great crown branching from its head, and every hair was rimmed with radiance. The blood in Hannah's body seemed to stop, and her neck prickled. The white stag looked full at them with its black, almond-shaped eyes. Then it flicked into darkness.

They both sighed.

'Well,' said Stan, 'that was something.'

'Yes. I can't believe we saw it, now of all times.'

'Good boy, Bran. You knew not to chase that one, didn't you?'

He was dripping with sweat but plodded on without complaint, carrying the child in both arms. Sometimes Maisy's hair caught on twigs and thorns, and had to be disentangled, patiently, but she never stirred. Hannah, half-running after him on shorter legs, was in a fever of impatience to get her to safety.

The higher up the hill they climbed, the more the wood thinned out. At one point she stopped, terrified by what looked like gigantic figures with pointed helmets and spikey armour, before realising they were echium, pride of the Cornish garden, raising their conical heads of blossom above the brambles. A breeze was gusting through, and with it came mist and the promise of the greyer weather and more normal temperatures that would come as a relief after the endless heat.

A solid darkness stood across their path. They had come to the brick wall of the kitchen garden. She ran ahead to open the door for Stan. Through it shone a warm yellow radiance.

All the windows of the house were lit up, there were several cars still parked in the drive. The kitchen was full of people, and the French windows were open.

Stan walked in and deposited Maisy on the sofa by the Aga with a sigh. There was a babble of voices. Hannah, following hard upon his heels, stood blinking in the light. All was confusion until suddenly, she felt herself gripped by her forearm in a painfully familiar grasp.

'You stupid little bitch! What have you done to her?'

It was Jake. When had he turned up? Saskia must have called him, and his mother, on hearing Maisy had gone missing. Her relief that he was still alive shrivelled instantly before the rage in his face.

'I haven't done anything except find her.'

'Bollocks!'

He was pushing her back against the wall, shouting so loudly she felt his spittle land on her cheeks, and then as his palm swung towards her in a familiar way, she flinched and threw up her other arm to protect her face. The blow made her reel and cringe. She heard people crying out, and then a sudden silence followed by a thud.

When she opened her eyes, she saw something wholly unexpected. Cadan had got hold of Jake by the shoulders and was shaking him backwards and forwards as a dog shakes a rat. Each time her husband's head went back, it hit the wall.

'Don't-ever-ever-do-that,' growled Cadan. He was scarlet in the face. Hannah had never seen him lose control. 'Don't hit Han.'

Everyone froze, but Stan said, 'Leave him.'

Although the two giants looked for a moment as if they might come to blows as well, Cadan grunted, and dropped Jake to the floor. Stan bent over and said, 'You don't touch her again, Jake. You don't touch any women like that again.'

Jake said nothing, but he had been shaken so violently that it must be hard to speak. Stan grasped Jake by his shirt and dragged him to his feet. Then he said in a hard, clear voice, 'Do you understand? Or do I need to drive it into your thick skull?'

There was a yell of pain. Hannah, sickened, put a hand on Stan's arm.

'Stan, let him go.'

'Why? Seems to me this tool needs a taste of his own medicine.'

He had a look in his eye that was terrifying.

Hannah drew a deep breath. 'This is Maisy's father. Stop. Please. I don't need rescuing by the patriarchy.'

After a moment, he let go. As soon as Jake had caught his breath, he said, 'I'll get you for that, you great louts. Both of you. Assault, GBH, threats, everyone witnessed it.'

Stan folded his arms, completely unconcerned; but then another voice said, 'Saw what? I only saw you hitting your wife.'

It was Etta. Jake glared at his mother, but then Loveday joined in. 'Me too. Shocking behaviour.'

'And I,' said Lady Evenlode. 'And as I'm a magistrate, as well as your grandmother, I *think* I'll be believed.'

'Of course you will,' said Loveday. 'Or this room isn't rammed with Penroses.'

Saskia turned on her brother. 'Jake, you *snake*, we all saw you. My God, Hannah, why did you ever put up with this?'

Hannah looked at her wearily. 'I can't begin to think.'

Etta said, 'I'm ashamed of you, Jake.'

'Suck it up,' Jake answered. 'You've made me like this, Mummy.'

'Oh Jakey.' Etta sighed. 'You're over thirty. I stopped having any influence a long, long time ago.'

'Disgraceful behaviour,' said Lord Evenlode. 'Hitting a woman, even if she *is* your wife, is frightfully low.'

Loveday said, 'You'll need some aloe vera on that bruise, Hannah.'

'Don't worry about me; it's Maisy who needs help.'

'What's wrong with her?'

'She won't wake up. We found her in the cave by the beach. We think she's been drugged.'

Loveday said, 'I don't think it's paracetamol, but I'm calling an ambulance.'

'Paracetamol?'

'Yes. That's the worst possibility, but it tastes so bitter that it'd be unusual for a child to take an overdose. My guess is it's anti-histamine.'

'I don't think she did this to herself,' said Hannah. 'I saw two sets of footprints going into the cave, an adult's and a child's, and then the adult's prints going the other way.'

Jake looked up.

'An adult's?'

Hannah said, 'Yes. They were quite distinct. I'm pretty sure from the size, they were a woman's. Other people saw Maisy leave with a woman. She wore a thick silvery cuff.'

She looked steadily at Jake and saw his expression change into understanding, and horror.

'It was pure luck that we found her, with the tide coming in. We were trapped.'

'How did you escape?' Lady Evenlode asked. Her usual vagueness had vanished, and she was looking at Hannah with a sharp, unwavering enquiry.

'We didn't,' Stan answered. 'We had to go deep inside the cave and wait it out.'

'No wonder you both look so dishevelled. You're bleeding, Stan . . . What gave you those cuts?'

'Mussels,' said Stan. He was standing bear-like, wincing and blinking in the full glare of the kitchen lights. Hannah could see Jake looking at the shaggy mat on his chest and the dart of dark hair going down to his waist, and below his waist. She could not pretend it was pretty, and yet . . . and yet . . .

'Stan kept us both alive,' she said. 'He's the bravest man I've ever met.'

Somebody gave her a glass of water, which she drained in two gulps before noticing it came from Cadan.

Hannah touched his shoulder.

'Would you look after Maisy for a moment? I need to get out of this dress before it kills me.'

She retrieved her work clothes from a plastic bag hung

332

in the scullery. The Dior dress she unhooked with relief and hung up. It was salt-stained, but although the net was torn the embroidered silk was tougher than it looked, and maybe some specialist would be able to clean and restore it. She patted it briefly, saying goodbye. Next, she went to find clothes for Stan. She'd never been in his room before, and wondered whether it would be as filthy as the rest of the house had once been, but it was perfectly respectable. She took a fresh shirt from his wardrobe, clean but crumpled, and pressed it to her face.

The paramedic had arrived and began to check Maisy, watched over by her anxious relations from both sides of the family. Her heartbeat and temperature were normal, but her sleep was not.

'I don't think it's concussion,' he said, 'but she should be admitted to the district hospital, just to be on the safe side.'

'Do we still have a district hospital?'

'Yes, just.'

'Thank goodness for that.'

'I'll come with her,' said Hannah, yawning. Now that she was back, she could hardly keep her eyes open.

'I can take her, lovely,' said her aunt. 'You're done-in. She won't wake up until morning now, and she knows me.'

'All right.'

'I can wait too,' said Jake.

Hannah snapped awake. 'You! I wouldn't trust you within a mile of her.'

Etta said, 'We all need to talk once everyone has rested. Jake, it's best you come back with us now.'

Cadan picked Maisy up in his enormous arms, and carried her to Loveday's car with a blanket tucked round her.

'Safe,' he said.

'Yes.'

She knew that if Loveday fell asleep, he would not.

Suddenly, everyone was gone, and Hannah was alone again with Stan. The dog was stretched out on the dog-bed to one side of the Aga, snoring gently. Everything was calm, peaceful, ordinary, as if the ordeal of the past five hours were a lurid dream. There were no dirty pots and pans, no overflowing rubbish bin, no bad smells or layer of filth. The aloe vera plant had put out a new claw of spikes, and the pristine fridge had a platter with a mound of left-over sandwiches under clingfilm.

'We should eat these,' Stan said. 'I'm starving.'

'I can't believe that this is the same day,' Hannah said, between bites.

'It's after midnight, so it's not. It's your birthday.'

'Yes, it is.'

'There should be some champagne left.'

'I'd rather have tea.'

There was a pause. The house, which had been silent apart from the soft puttering of the re-lit Aga, creaked to itself.

'So that's your ex-husband.'

'What can I say? I had terrible taste at twenty.'

'Mine was worse at thirty.'

'They deserve each other, my ex and yours, don't you think?' said Hannah. 'Though Jake may be having second thoughts now she tried to murder our daughter. Pig though he is, he cares about her. I wonder what will happen to Jinni.'

'She'll have no further interest in any of us here now,' Stan said. 'Other people aren't real to her. Only money is.'

What a way to live, Hannah thought. 'She must be very unhappy.'

'No, I think she has no capacity for self-examination, and like too many women a massive sense of entitlement.'

'Strange, I would say exactly the same thing about my ex-husband, and men.'

Hannah looked around at the project on which they had laboured all summer. It would not remain like this. Endpoint would have its fabric mended, re-wired, re-plumbed and whatever else it needed for it to stay intact for another three or four hundred years. The Wus would be spending at least another million on it, and whether they would ever use it to live in permanently remained a matter for much speculation. But it seemed that even if Philip Wu would be flying all over the world for his family business, Cecilia was insistent that the twins would have a 'traditional English education'. (It was being rumoured that Wu had refinanced two leading public schools in order to assure his twins' places there in future.) Having seen how nicely they played with the other children at the party, Hannah couldn't help hoping that they might first also go to the local primary, whose motto was 'Be Kind and Work Hard'. Stranger things had happened, and it would help the Wus be accepted here like nothing else.

'Would you have sold Endpoint if you had the money to keep it?'

'Yes. This house has few good memories for me.'

'I hate to think of her getting away with all she's done to us.'

Stan heaved a sigh. 'It's worth anything to be free of her. I expect she'll leave the country if she hasn't already gone. You can get a flight from Newquay to most places in Europe. This week, I gave her a lump sum as a final settlement, raised against the sale of this place and the London flat. She can't stay in Britain as a divorced American without a visa, and she hates it here anyway. She's done her worst, and she failed.'

'It's still the most appalling thing to have tried to do.'

'Yes. But the main thing is, we all survived. I'm glad you stopped me killing your ex, by the way.'

'I thought you couldn't hurt people?'

Stan's teeth were very white in the darkness of his face.

'I said nothing about other men, especially men who hit women.'

Hannah blushed, and then, to her astonishment, he was on his knees, looking up at her. She felt herself sway towards him, then shrank back.

'Hannah,' he said, 'You know what I feel for you, I think. Can you not trust me?'

She made an irritable movement.

'I'm just so *tired*,' she said. 'What I really want, no what I really *need*, is to have a life of my own again.'

'I see,' he said.

'Do you? I'm not sure you do. You saved my child, and me, from a horrible death and maybe you did that just because you're such a kind, decent man or maybe it's because you think I'm a level in a video game. But there's only one of me. There's only ever one of me. This is *my* story. If I screw up again there's no coming back.'

'You might have more freedom than you think, though.'

She exclaimed, 'How can I? I have a child, and no money, no safety-net, no job, no home of my own, nothing. I don't know what you're offering me—' He made a sudden movement, as if in pain, and she persisted, 'But this isn't the point where you fuck the help just because you think you can.'

'No, it's not. Even if I thought like that about you, which I don't.'

There was a long pause, then Stan yawned suddenly, and she could not help yawning too.

'Sorry ... sorry ... ' she muttered. 'I don't know what to say or think any more.'

'Don't let's quarrel, Hannah. I'm exhausted, and so are you. You can spend the night in my mother's room again or go home.'

'I'm going.' Hannah rose. 'And thank you, by the way. I'll never forget what you did.'

'Don't worry,' he said, with a trace of mockery. 'I did it because I couldn't help myself.'

29

A Fresh Start

As soon as she left, Hannah drove to the district hospital to see her daughter. Loveday and Cadan were both there, nodding off on a seat in the waiting room.

'She's fine,' Loveday said at once. 'Go to sleep. I'll wake you if there's any change.'

Maisy woke soon after sunrise, no worse for her adventure but slightly puzzled about why she was in hospital.

'Have I been poorly?'

'Not really, but the doctor had to check why we couldn't wake you up,' said Hannah.

'I was in the cave,' Maisy said, and stopped, as if uncertain.

'Why were you there alone?'

'Because Eve said—'

'What did she say?' Jake asked. He had walked in without them noticing.

'She said the dragon wouldn't come if a grown-up was there. I had to wait for him on my own, to see him.'

Hannah and Jake exchanged glances. Loveday asked, 'Who is Eve, Maisy?'

'Daddy's girlfriend. She was at Stan's party, and she asked if I was bored. So I said yes, a bit, and she said we could go down to the beach.' Maisy looked at her mother. 'I know you say never to go with strangers, but she wasn't.'

'No,' said Hannah, as Jake buried his face in his hands. 'No, I suppose not.'

'What happened then, Maisy?' Loveday asked. Only somebody who knew her well would know that her quiet voice was a sign of fury.

'We waited a while, and she said she'd brought a magic potion for me. I had to drink and shut my eyes while she sang a dragon-charming song outside the cave. Why am I in hospital, Mummy?'

'Because the drink Eve gave you wasn't good for you,' Hannah said, her voice shaking. 'She's a very bad person, I'm afraid.'

'Like Morgan le Fay?'

'Yes, like her,' said Jake. 'Beautiful but evil. I'm so sorry, Maisy.'

'Did you rescue me?'

Hannah could see the lie beginning to balloon out of his mouth. He so badly wanted to be the rescuer that she almost felt sorry for him.

'No,' said Loveday. '*He* didn't. It was your mum, and Stan. They found you and got you out while you were sleeping. But everything is fine now, so you don't need to worry. You're safe and right as rain. Hannah, Jake, can you just step outside for a moment? Maisy, you will be fine with Cadan, won't you?'

Maisy nodded. Cadan sat next to her, solid and protective.

When they got out into the corridor, Loveday said, 'Right. You *know* this crazy woman Eve, Jake?'

Hannah thought that she had never seen her aunt in full fire-and-brimstone fury.

'Yes,' said Jake miserably.

'She's Stan's ex-wife,' said Hannah. 'Otherwise known as Jinni, or Genevieve, and she's been having an affair with Jake for, ooh, how long is it now? About two years.'

'She's gone,' said Jake. 'We split up last week. It had been coming a long time. She didn't like Maisy being around, and she didn't want her to come on holiday with us. It was an almighty row. But I didn't realise – she was – I thought—'

'You didn't think,' said Loveday. 'That wicked woman, that *tebelvenyn*; it sounds to me as if you were lucky that she didn't try to kill you, too.'

'It's obvious that she had every intention of drowning our daughter,' said Hannah.

'But why would she do all this?' he burst out.

Hannah said, 'Some people are just like that. She wanted Stan dead to inherit all his money. She wanted you for a while because you probably made her look good and because you're always going on about your posh relations. It was always all about her. She's an even bigger narcissist than you, Jake. She didn't want to share you with your daughter. She did it as a punishment.'

She did not add that the punishment had been for her, as much as for him, and that Jinni had nearly succeeded in achieving her original goal of becoming a widow. It was best that Jake never found this out.

'How can she have thought I wouldn't love my own child?'

'But you don't love her, do you? Not properly. You've

340

never bothered to ask how she's living with me. You just have her at weekends, when it suits you.'

'I've been *working*!' Jake said indignantly.

Hannah said, 'So have I. Twenty-five hours a week, cleaning people's houses, scrubbing, hoovering, ironing, washing, taking out the rubbish and dealing with their shit. You think what you do is *work*?'

Loveday said, 'We should report this woman to the police.'

'But what can I prove?' said Hannah. 'I'm the only one who saw her footprints, and nobody will believe me. Maisy's account won't stand up, either. It's an ex-wife and a six-year-old against a rich woman.'

'Well, it's up to you, but I'd get a restraining order against your husband,' said Loveday. 'You'll find that more people round here will believe you than him.' She turned to Jake. 'I always did think you were rubbish.'

She returned to the children's ward. Alone in the corridor, Hannah and Jake looked at each other.

'My aunt is right,' she said. 'I could get a restraining order, given that you struck me before several witnesses.'

He glowered. 'I was beside myself with anxiety, because you'd both gone missing. That was a lapse of temper, which I regret.'

'Over a child whose existence you hadn't bothered to enquire after for many weeks?'

'Eve blocked you on my mobile. I didn't know you were calling. I thought you were ignoring me.'

'Even if that were true, it should have been *you* calling *me*.'

She was calm but relentless, and the more agitated he became the more she felt herself to be in control. Why had this not been possible before? My feelings have changed, she thought. Even when I hated him, I still cared what he thought. The weakness in his face was so clear that she wondered at ever having found it attractive. Layer after layer of silliness, meanness, vanity and spite were laid as if they were semi-transparent sheets over the handsome boy he had once been. Maybe someone else would help him cut free from this; but it would not be she.

'You don't understand; I've had to change everything. She took over my life the moment she got the pin code to my mobile. All she had to do was change your number by one digit, and I couldn't get through.'

Hannah sighed. This was close to what Stan had told her about Jinni's behaviour to him. 'Jake, I know your number off by heart. I don't rely on a machine to remember it. If you had ever cared about us, so would you.'

'I had to ask my mother.' He paused, and Hannah thought with some amusement how much that must have galled him. 'She told me that you'd been trying to get in touch, so I checked and found out what had been done. You're right, Eve's an absolute bitch. Or witch.'

'Whatever,' Hannah said. 'All this was brought about by your own choices. You are an abusive husband. You aren't a fit parent. I've got a record of all your texts, which will make interesting reading for some.' He paled; he was afraid she would send them to his mother, she thought. 'You know I've had to use food banks? You didn't even pay the rent some months.'

'I know – I know – and I am sorry,' said Jake. He did, for a change, look ashamed, though how long it would last was another matter. 'I've done everything wrong. I want to sort out the money. I'll give you half of everything, which is what I was going to do anyway. Just don't take Maisy away.'

'Tell that to your lawyer,' said Hannah. 'I'm getting a

lawyer of my own, by the way. It's not up to you whether you give me half, it's my right. And the way you've behaved, you'll be lucky if you get any contact at all.'

The harshness of her tone was new to him; she could see the shock of it. She did not want to be cruel, and yet she had to put on this armour and wear it, for the weak are the worst adversaries of all, they have no honour and no self-respect, only self-pity. She looked at him with a disgust that included her own behaviour and choices.

I will never again be the person that I was, Hannah thought. She mourned her lost innocence. How was it possible to be thirty, yet not grown up? Was everybody still travelling on this long continuum towards self-knowledge, or did some people just halt, voluntarily or involuntarily? Maybe I will never stop, she told herself; but maybe that is a good thing, because it means my story will go on changing.

'I didn't know you were doing cleaning jobs,' Jake said, adding with a touch of his old disparaging manner, 'No wonder you look tired.'

Hannah would once have been upset by this, but she shrugged. 'I'll be looking for an office job once Maisy is back at school. Though whether I can get back into a professional career when I can only work part time is the question.'

'That director you used to work with, Ali Gold, she's started up her own agency,' he said. 'You should contact her.'

'I haven't got enough experience,' said Hannah automatically.

'Ali's looking for potential, especially female potential, and she rates you. I know because she told me you had more talent in your little finger than ... Anyway, you should email her. She's got an office near King's Cross. I'll send you her details right now.'

343

Ping! Ali Gold's email and mobile number arrived in her phone, just like that.

'How wonderful technology is when it's not used against one,' she said drily; but she would give it a try. Ali was a mother herself. Maybe she'd understand about school hours and working part of the time from home during the holidays. Hannah thought of her former boss, her bright clothes, clacking heels and love of jokes; how much fun it could be to work for someone she liked. And then there was the money, which even for a freelance would be double that of a cleaner ... maybe she could get her life back on track and make a fresh start. She was still a graduate with four years of training and experience. Even if her time out of the professional world had seemed to last for ever, she had only really lost a few years.

'Thanks,' she said. 'Meanwhile, while I'm here, you can also send that email to your lawyer and do a transfer for the rent and child maintenance, back-dated.'

His shame wouldn't last, she knew, but while it was fresh in his mind she had to make his decision to behave decently stick.

'Yes, right away.' He tapped out an email and again did a bank transfer. It all happened so quickly it might almost have been magic. In ten seconds, she had been given – no, earned – enough to live on for the next year. He showed her the screen on his mobile. 'Here, you can check it's gone through.'

'Fine. We can divorce as soon as my lawyer has checked everything. You should be happy. You're getting what you wanted. I wish you well.'

Jake said suddenly, 'You're lucky, Hannah. You're happy because you know how to be good, and you are good. Other people don't find it as easy as you.'

344

Hannah wanted to laugh: he really thought that her life, in which she had suffered so much that she felt herself ageing in dog-years not human ones, was somehow *easy*? To him, the call of duty was a video game, not something that other people, ordinary people, did because they knew the difference between right and wrong. Though as it turned out, she was not nearly as good as he believed.

'Why don't you try it yourself?' she said. 'It isn't easy to be good, it takes a lot of practice, but it's better in the long run. You might even find that it made you some real friends.'

Jake returned to give Maisy a last, lingering hug. His back, when he left, showed total dejection. Hannah sighed. He did love his daughter; and maybe, now that Eve was out of his life, that would grow into something that made him behave better. Contrition – true contrition, rather than superficial apology – is a sort of miracle in an age where shame is an alien concept. Besides, who was she to think herself so much more noble? She had been saved by pure chance from committing the most horrible crime of all.

Stan's words came back to her: *Everybody is capable of murder, given the right circumstances. The real mystery is why more of us don't do it.*

Was it chance, or just instinct, that had caused her to stay her hand each time? She had intended to kill him, after all. Even as she drove Maisy back to the bungalow, she could feel the wild tugging this way and that.

When she thought of what had passed between Stan and herself, her confusion became almost intolerable. She remembered the feel of him pressing against her back, and she thought about what his lips had felt like when she had kissed him in that horrible cave, that strange feeling, like swallowing oysters that might be revolting or delicious. It

345

was no good knowing that he might be attracted to her as well. Any emotional life was focused on her child and would continue to be so for many more years. It had to be so. She was an adult, with an adult's responsibilities.

And yet – and yet – how much she longed for ideas and information, emotions and sensations that were beyond the walled garden of infancy! She had lain in Stan's arms and heard his heart beating, she had felt his truth, she had known him in all kinds of different states, from despair, anger, grief and fear to exhilaration, idealism and generosity, but most of all as that thing she had determined never to trust again, a man. It had become so easy to hate men, to judge all of them as irredeemably coarse, corrupt and vile, to forget that men had ever been responsible for what was also good and honourable and fine. But she had believed that of her husband, once, and look where that had got her.

It was not true that love set you free, any more than truth did. Love had deluded her, turned her into a drudge and a victim, it had made her afraid. It was not that there was anything shameful about being a cleaner – quite the contrary, to bring order and cleanliness into a home was a skill of which anyone should be proud. But her relationship with Stan had not been that of equals. She had been not his employee but his servant, and not his friend but his would-be killer.

London was what would save her, London and work. London made you nobody, and therefore free to become somebody, free to discover who you were, to find other people with the energy and curiosity to want a life that was not the life into which they had been born. It offered people the chance of self-transformation. A single day in London seemed to last twice as long as a day anywhere else, because it was crammed with more incident and effort, interest and stress, than people outside it had in a week. This was the secret of its magnetism even if it was cruel and capricious, as well as brave and steadfast. It was the worst, but it was also the best. She would never not love it.

Hannah remembered someone saying at the Sponges' dinner party that London was the new oil. It wasn't so simple. Its money – and there was a staggering amount of it in a very few hands – should be shared more equally, but its true wealth was its freedom. That was what, unconsciously at first, she had longed for when stuck in Cornwall. But to make it there she had to find what nobody else could give her: the confidence to be herself at last.

Back in St Piran for the last week she felt the days slip down like ice cream, refreshing and sweet but changeless and dull. However friendly, however kindly, however filled with family, she would go mad with boredom if she stayed in a place where tradition was the opium of the people.

Even Maisy seemed to feel it.

'I like my cousins and my aunties and uncles, but I miss Bella, and school,' she announced. Hannah thought: She's a sport of nature like me.

'I miss London too,' Hannah answered. 'Though I think we might look for another home in Kentish Town, one with a garden.'

'If we had a garden, could I have a pet?'

'I don't see why not.'

'A dog?'

'Maybe a little one. Or a cat.'

'No, a dog. A dog like Bran.'

'Bran is too big for London, sweetie. And dogs can't be left alone when I go back to work.'

Maisy showed no sign of the trauma she had largely slept through, but Hannah noticed that she had moved on to King Arthur and the Knights of the Round Table. There was a story called *Sir Gawain and the Loathly Lady* that was her new favourite. It was about a knight, the best knight in King Arthur's court, who sought the answer to a riddle: 'What do all women most desire?' He heard many different answers, but eventually came upon a hideous hag who told him, in return for the knight's promise to marry her, that what all women wanted was their own way. Being a true knight, Sir Gawain then had to marry the hag, but on the wedding night, the Loathly Lady turned out to be a beautiful woman under an enchantment.

'But she can only be beautiful for half the time, so his choice is whether to have her beautiful during the day, when everyone else sees her, or beautiful during the night, when they're alone, Mummy.'

'I see.' Hannah knew this story well but asked, 'So, which does he decide?'

'He thinks for ages, and then says he can't decide for her. It's up to her to choose. Which is the right thing to say, because then the spell is broken.'

She was now reading fluently, and Hannah took her to the Fol Bookshop to buy new books of her own.

'Do you think I love reading because I just do, or because of my father, or because of you?' she asked Mr Kenward. 'My other relations never read anything that's not on the internet.'

'It's half nature, half nurture, don't they say?' he replied mildly. 'Besides, Mor's two seem to like books and stories.'

'Yes, I suppose they do. But only ones that have had films made of them.'

'Who knows where that may lead? Stories with pictures as well as words are as old as, well, stories themselves.'

'I told Stan that I despised video games because they don't get into people's heads.'

'Did you? Well, I'm not a gamer, but from what I've read about them some of them seem to do so. Anything that moves us has some qualification to being considered as art.'

Brooding over this, Hannah sent off her CV to Ali Gold. She expected nothing, but in the afternoon there was a chime on her mobile and a WhatsApp text.

Hi Hannah! Yes, I'm hiring. How are you fixed for a meeting next week? Ali.

She couldn't believe it would be so easy, and it probably wouldn't be. But if she were offered a job, a proper on-the-books professional job then ... A letter from Jake's solicitor came next, confirming his offer to pay her a lump sum, plus child maintenance and (should she wish it) private education for Maisy. It was an astounding £4000 a month, sufficient for her to move out of the Castle Estate.

Some of this, no doubt, was due to Etta. Her mother-in-law had asked to meet her in Fol – she offered to come to St Piran but Hannah had decided against this – before the Wilcox family decamped from Cornwall. They met in a café overlooking the marina, exactly the kind of place that Hannah had never liked but which turned out to be very pleasant if you were no longer worried about how to pay for a cappuccino.

'I want to apologise. I had no idea that you had been left in such an awful situation by Jake,' Etta said, in her jerky, abrupt manner. 'I suppose I should have asked, but it seemed too intrusive.'

'I didn't make it easy for you either, I suppose,' Hannah said.

'No. You're a little intimidating.'

Hannah looked at her in wonder. Etta gave her a bone-china smile. 'We're bears of little brain in my family, as you may have noticed. I thought Jake might be one of the clever, arty ones, like his Uncle Andrew, but we were amazed when he married someone as bright as you.'

Hannah remembered the remark Saskia had made on her wedding day. *To think that of all Jake's girlfriends, he chose you.* It had never struck her that it might be interpreted differently. They were fools, and she wasn't going to forget being called a pram-face in a hurry; but Etta was less bad than the rest.

'I'm not going to stop you seeing Maisy, if that's your worry.'

'Thank you,' Etta said, and the relief was clear on her face. 'She may be our only grandchild . . . and she is such a dear one. We do all love her. We want to help. I haven't been the best mother, but I will do better as a grandmother.'

'I hope so,' said Hannah, and for the first time ever, she gave Etta an entirely unguarded smile. 'We all fail as parents. I know that already. So as far as I'm concerned, the more people there are to spread the load, the better.'

It was true, too. Walking round and saying goodbye to her mother's many siblings, cousins, second cousins and the rest, Hannah felt glad to be a Penrose, from St Piran. It might be the ugliest town in Cornwall, but even if she didn't vote the same way or live the same way, a part of her would always belong to it.

'A'right, Han?' they would ask, and she answered, 'A'right.'

30

A Slice of Paradise

This time, she and Maisy drove back to London rather than catching the train. However expensive a tank of petrol was, it was still half the price of two tickets and it gave them freedom to stop for a break on the way. She was bringing back all her old books, her mother's satin shoes, an aloe vera cutting and the Burne-Jones poster of *King Cophetua and the Beggar Maid*.

The resemblance of Stan to the king did not escape her, and now struck her as comical, as if she had been primed to fall in love with him by the Pre-Raphaelite Brotherhood. The dark curling hair and beard, the sallow skin and the attitude of melancholy and submission were too familiar, as was the pose of the beggar maid, poised for flight from the golden stairs that had elevated her. Where he looked only at her, the beggar maid looked out, wild-eyed from the narrow space that confined her. Although the king had taken off his heavy, ornate crown in humility, there was the great red lance standing suggestively erect up one side of the picture. No doubt about what he wanted, but what about her?

What a poster-girl to grow up with, Hannah thought. She did not even like Burne-Jones, whose flat, genteel figures struck her as watered-down Botticelli. Yet this painting had obsessed her, so much so that she had even visited the real thing in Tate Britain where its life-sized protagonists were a surprise. It was so very conventional; the story of a poor girl and a rich man, it was the same story she had latched on to in Jane Austen and countless other novels, both good and bad. As if all a girl had to be was pretty and all a man needed to have was wealth.

Something about the beggar maid's flowers lying on the golden steps nagged at her memory. Anemones were symbols of rejected love, something that a Victorian painter and audience would have been aware of. Maybe the king looked miserable because his suit, in this version of the story, was not going to be successful.

Hannah clenched the wheel, steering the little grey car up to Plymouth and along the motorway. The reflected sun shone in her eyes as she drove east. In the back seat, Maisy chatted, sang, complained she felt hungry or sick or bored or needed a break, and as ever Hannah replied and responded with the part of her mind that was eternally preoccupied with her child. She wondered whether it was like this for every mother, and whether she would always be divided within herself.

'Yes, darling, I'm sure we'll see Loveday and Mor and your cousins again soon. Maybe they can come to stay with us next time. Do you think they'd like that? Over Christmas, perhaps. London's always lovely then, with the pretty lights. I know it seems a long way off but it's only four months.'

She had said goodbye to everyone at St Piran and Fol apart from Stan. Partly this was embarrassment at the way she had behaved, and what had happened to his grandmother's dress, and partly it was all kinds of other things that she couldn't cope with. The paperwork involved in getting divorced had merged with the paperwork of bereavement, but here, too, there was a surprise.

Hannah had been so used to thinking of her mother as poor that when she was told she had an inheritance of £120,000 it had come as an enormous shock. The solicitor in Fol had got in touch, thanks to Bill Kenward.

'But how did she ever have the money?'

'She had a private pension, and I believe she cashed it in earlier this year. She thought you might like to buy a home here. It'd be quite a tidy investment now that developers are moving into St Piran.'

'Are they? I thought they were only interested in Fol.'

'St Piran has more development potential, I understand. There was interest in the estate at Endpoint, but now that's been sold privately they're looking at rebooting the town. It's not without attractions, the unspoilt beach and so on. It'll bring a lot of employment.'

Hannah thought of the warm Gulf Stream of money flowing along the coastline, pumping out from London. As the next town along from Fol, it was logical to assume that in time even the ugliest town in Cornwall would be transformed by it, especially now that a great many more British people would not be having their summer holidays abroad. Ironic to think that the vote that had convulsed the nation might benefit some. All her life she had been ashamed by the ugliness of St Piran, but what she had really been ashamed of was precisely what its inhabitants could not help: poverty.

If money from tourism and second-home owners now began to flow through it, she had no doubt that its period housing in the old centre would be gentrified and the whole place sanitised, just like Fol. Was it a bad thing or a good one? She thought of the people she had grown up with, and the hidden settlement of caravans and trailers, the desperation of those without jobs or dignity or homes. Money was not magic; but it was perhaps the closest thing, if used wisely and well.

'Will this inheritance affect my divorce settlement?'

'It could, but I doubt the Family Court would think it large enough to make a difference. Especially when you have no other assets.'

Hannah felt the temptation of it. She might be able to stay on in her mother's bungalow.

'Do you think they'd let me stay on? The council, I mean.'

'I think so. She was a tenant for life, wasn't she? That means it can be passed on to you.'

'It's just ... there are so many local people who need a council house. Including my cousin Morwenna and her husband and kids. She's been waiting to move out of her mum's for years.'

'Maybe you'd like to think about asking, then,' said the solicitor, with a slight smile. 'Not that the Housing Department could do any special favours.'

Strangely – or perhaps, knowing St Piran, not so strangely – her cousin was offered the bungalow by the council the very next week. She ran to Hannah, in tears of joy.

'I've always loved this place, but we never thought we'd get a home of our own. You won't mind if we change one or two things, will you?'

'Don't be ridiculous, Mor, it'll be yours to do what you like with. Just promise me you'll get rid of the garden gnome.'

Mor said, 'Oh, I quite like that gnome.' She waited until the horror grew in Hannah's face. 'Only joking! We'll convert the garage and build another bedroom for you and Maisy to come back to every summer. Unless there's someone else you'd rather stay with?'

Hannah had felt herself flush.

'No. He has a *beard*, for heaven's sakes. I've always *hated* beards. Nasty, insanitary things. Men grow them because they think they hide their chins, but they don't.'

'Pity.' Mor gave her a conspiratorial grin. 'I always thought Stan pretty—'

Hannah said, 'It's not like that.' No matter how much she told her cousin and Loveday about her life, her feelings would remain her own business.

On and on and on through the unending hills and valleys and fields, the traffic thickening as more families returned to the city and normal life from their summer holidays. There were the usual crashes and jams, and the fear that her own frail vehicle would break down. Yet this is the price of autonomy, which must always exchange tranquillity and safety for stress and danger. Unless, that is, you found yourself in an empty train carriage with a psychopath.

There had been no further word from Jinni, and Hannah had destroyed the burner phone. It could prove nothing, as far as her adversary's attempted murder of either Maisy or Stan was concerned but linking herself to Jinni was always a risk. She had to hope Stan was right and that, having got her multi-million-pound divorce settlement, Eve would disappear from their lives.

Having been away for more than a month made Camden and Kentish Town fresh and attractive. She had forgotten how many trees there were here, too, the variety and magnificence of them, and the graceful buildings with their gleaming stucco and clean paintwork. To see so many other young people out enjoying themselves in the cafés and shops and parks was to be reminded of why she had chosen to make this city her home.

'Lights!' exclaimed Maisy from the back seat; or perhaps it was 'Life!'

The flat in the Castle Estate was covered with the fine layer of filth that accumulates out of the urban air but it was still familiar and full of the evening sun. Sounds welled from the student flat: music that she recognised as *L'après-midi d'un faune*. Its melancholy sensuality wound around her thoughts, transporting her back to the woods below Endpoint. She had her own plants to look after, though, carefully watered by Lila throughout the heatwave: morning glory, jasmine, nasturtium, sage. They were almost tropical in their flowers and foliage.

'I was expecting to return to a desert of dead stalks,' Hannah told her gratefully. 'Was it unbearably hot here?'

Lila smiled. 'We managed. At least there are the parks nearby, even if the grass has become quite yellow.'

'You should have come to stay with us in Cornwall.'

Lila shook her head.

'I'm still afraid of going to public places. If I didn't have the niqab, I'd never dare leave my flat. I know it makes English people think I must be planning something wicked, but believe me if Ahmed were to see me and track me down . . .'

Hannah could not help feeling some scepticism. Surely, three years later, he must have moved on? But then, she reminded herself, she thought that only because she herself had done so. People for whom a terrible relationship remained unresolved carried round an unhealed wound.

She had been such a person herself until very recently. Poor, gentle Lila was still in the bad place she had just left, and it was like all other forms of suffering, so easy to forget it existed.

'Can't you tell the police?'

Lila shook her head. 'When your husband was threatening you, did you? So if you, a white British woman, did not get help from the authorities, what hope have I?'

Hannah longed to argue but could not. Jake had been shamed into doing the right thing by his family and hers, but she knew too much about divorce now to have much faith in a flawed system. A marriage was a joint enterprise, but still one in which men got richer and women got poorer. She had no doubt that, five years from now, Jake would be earning at least twice what she did.

'If ever you need help, call me. I'll be there for you,' she said.

Lila shook her head. 'You have your own child, and your own life.'

With September came fresher air, some rain and the start of many new things. Hannah was called for an interview with her former boss and offered a job at Gold & Stern, the new agency. The salary was £32,000, just above the average national wage but a fortune to someone who had been earning less than half that. All kinds of possibilities floated before Hannah's eyes: getting a mortgage, getting some paid child-care, but most of all being independent.

'I can't give you yet what you'd have got in the old firm, but I know your work, and it will go up next year,' said Ali Gold. 'What have you been doing?'

'Oh,' said Hannah vaguely, 'freelancing. As you do with a young child.' She added, knowing that it was a half-truth. 'I've been working for Constantine Coad.'

Ali's eyes lit up. 'You have? Wow. The gaming industry is something we'd love to do more with. He's a bit of an iconoclast, isn't he?'

'Yes.'

'I've heard he's going to be setting up a game design company in Cornwall. It could be as big as Rockstar if it takes off.'

Hannah had no idea what she was talking about.

'That'd be fantastic, yes,' she said.

She did not want to tell anyone about her labours as a cleaner, though tidying and cleaning had become the latest hobby of the affluent, with a successful TV show dedicated to decluttering. She had watched a little of it on her laptop and wondered just how long folding fitted sheets with reverence would spark joy in the kind of people in whose homes she had toiled, once the novelty had worn off.

'I'm really sorry,' Polly said when she handed in her notice. 'You've been so reliable, and I don't know how we'll replace you given the current situation. I'll give you a reference if you need.'

Hannah opened her mouth to say that she wouldn't, but then thought again. Nothing was certain in the world, and though she hoped she would never again clean any home but her own, it might be useful to have some testament to honesty and diligence. As for replacing her, she had a suggestion.

'My friend Lila is looking for more hours. She's very nice, and good.'

Polly took her number. 'What are you going to do next?' she asked.

'I'm going back to my old job, in advertising. I'm a strategist.'

'Congratulations.' Polly gave her a shrewd look. 'So those old newspapers, they weren't for your daughter, were they?'

Hannah herself was soon to be crossing the bottom end of Kentish Town Road to live nearby. That journey was less than a quarter of a mile, yet it represented something that had once seemed as impossible as traversing a river guarded by trolls. The flat she and Maisy would inhabit was in a quiet leafy street on the ground floor of a terraced Victorian house. The owner wanted to sell it as quickly as possible.

'Why are you selling?' Hannah asked.

'Divorce settlement,' she said gloomily.

'Ah, I see.' She wondered whether the vendor was the leaver or the left; then whether, in the end, it mattered because divorce was hell, all of it, and there were no victors, just survivors. 'Me too.'

The vendor said with the burst of miserable confidence that was familiar to her, 'I've been taken to the cleaners by my ex's lawyers. This was supposed to be my pension. Give me your offer, I don't care. Anything that means he gets less is fine by me.'

The flat was in far worse condition than the ex-council flat Hannah was still renting, and its price had already been cut from £550,000 to £420,000, which the owner referred to as 'a steal'. Hannah offered £400,000 and wondered whether this was still too much in a falling market, although it was so much money that she felt sick thinking of it. Yet she could, miraculously, afford it. The money from her mother's pension, her father's bequest and Jake's contribution meant that she only needed a small mortgage – small for London, that was, but just possible to raise given what Gold & Stern would pay her. It had a 110-year lease and a share of the freehold.

'I think this will do,' she said.

It was being sold as a one-bedroomed flat, but she could see how, if its bathroom was taken out and a shower put into the separate toilet, it could have two. Its high ceiling was outlined by lumpy plaster strings of sausages that had once been lilies, its floors covered in worn hair-cord carpet, and the walls separating it from its next-door neighbours on either side were one brick thick. The sash windows must leak copious amounts of heating and would need replacing one day. But it had the kind of grace that could never be achieved by post-war housing, and she knew how to fix it, bit by bit. She would have her own bedroom with a proper king-sized bed, and Maisy could have bunk beds so that friends could come for sleepovers. At the back, accessible from the living room, was a long, thin strip of ground, whose soil, stiff with clay and punctuated by brambles and an overgrown apple tree, offered a slice of Paradise.

Maisy loved it immediately.

'Will it really be ours?'

'Yes. No more landlords. No more Generation Rent. We can paint the walls any colour and put up bookshelves and pictures and stay for ever and ever. We'll make a garden. We'll put a playhouse at the bottom of the garden.'

'Can Bella come to stay?'

'Yes, of course.'

Their neighbours would be the only thing she would miss about leaving the Castle Estate. Far from being violent, the only true chavs there – as defined by her ex-husband – had been, in truth, herself and Jake. She had given her notice as soon as her offer was accepted, and Tod the landlord had come around to inspect his property. He prowled around each room, gold chains clinking, failing to notice (as she knew he would) the plain white bathroom tiles that she had tiled on top of the lumpy shiny ones, the cornicing or the electric cables tacked neatly to the repainted walls. It still had rats, though they couldn't get through the steel wool blocking their hole in the kitchen corner.

Eventually, he complained, 'You've put up picture hooks! I didn't give permission for those.'

Hannah sighed and showed him the plastic hooks with their four tiny pins that she had hammered into the concrete walls nine years ago.

'I'll paint over the holes. You won't know they've ever been there.'

'And the floor is marked.'

'The floor has always been marked.'

'Not like this. It'll cost me £800 from your deposit to put that right.'

'Where is your evidence? This is normal wear and tear.' She smiled with the confidence of someone in a professional job and stood her ground. Had she still been poor and desperate he would have gone on bullying and threatening, but she knew that she would get her deposit back.

'You've had a good deal out of me,' he said.

'I've been paying you far more than this . . . place is worth. You'll be lucky to get another tenant for what you charge.'

He coughed. 'As a matter of fact, I'm thinking of selling up. The bottom has dropped out of buy-to-let thanks to this bloody government. I don't suppose you'd be interested?'

31

A Bolt from Heaven

Hannah did not expect to be into her new flat much before Christmas, and she was glad to have a few months in which to prepare. Every moment that her daughter was at school, she was working, and as soon as Maisy had gone to bed, she worked more. Then she thought about what she was going to do to each room in her new home. It was all new, and all a delight, and the hope it gave her made her relax and swell like a shrivelled seed dropped in water. However tired she felt after a long day of using her brain in advertising, she was never as exhausted as she had been after her cleaning job.

She loved working with Ali, who was only hiring women and winning new business every week on the strength of it. There was a nursery in the building, which made all the difference to those with very young children, and to the atmosphere. Hannah had begun by wearing the stiff smart suits she had worn almost a decade ago.

'You don't need to look formal,' Ali said.

'When I turn up for events, I don't want people thinking I'm the secretary or the cleaner,' Hannah said.

'They won't. This is a new kind of business. We don't have to pretend to be men. There is a vast well of talent that has been untapped because employers have been useless at understanding how women work, and if we strategists can't show them how then nobody can. But clients aren't stupid. They know that women are the ones who make most of the purchasing decisions, and if they piss us off it affects their profits,' Ali answered.

A great many of those she hired had been former colleagues, and as they became more successful, so the stories of what they had endured became more widely known and discussed. Other colleagues in other agencies joined in, until it eventually became such a scandal in the industry that some of the worst men (including the CEO of their old company) were eventually dismissed and black-balled from advertising. The rest were sent a code of conduct and stern warnings that bad behaviour would not be tolerated.

Hannah welcomed how busy she was at work and home because it stopped her thinking about Stan. Everything reminded her of him. When Maisy and she went for walks on Hampstead Heath and saw the great oaks and beeches spreading against the sky, they reminisced about his garden. At night, her dreams were all of moss and fur and boulders. Once, she saw the white stag in her dreams, and it spoke to her in his voice.

'*One is one and all alone, And ever more shall be so*', it said; and Hannah wept in her sleep.

'You aren't going to live like a nun, are you?' Nazneen asked. They had met for coffee in the smart café near the bottom of Kentish Town high street, and this time Hannah insisted on paying. Her old friend was ever more successful, and recommended a colleague for Hannah's divorce, 'just to make sure you don't get screwed by him again', but in the event it wasn't necessary. Hannah would be getting half of Jake's pension, half his earnings, half of the trust fund, and enough money for Maisy to last until she was through university. She felt almost guilty about this, now she was earning again herself, until she remembered how he had made her suffer.

'No, but I don't know if I can ever be with another man.'

'Have you ever thought that you might be gay?'

Nazneen had come out, something that had made her so happy that it was a pity it had taken so long. Her family had been astonishingly supportive, and her father had said that he only regretted not teaching her cricket like her brothers. She raised her eyebrows at Hannah, who understood what she was really asking. Jake had always claimed that Naz fancied her, she recalled, though she had dismissed this.

'No. We are as we are. It's not for me, Naz, any more than men are for you.'

She spoke as gently as she knew how, and hoped that it wouldn't affect their friendship.

A month after she began her new job, Jake asked if he might see Maisy again.

'I miss her so much,' he said. 'And I'm having therapy. I am trying to be better.'

'I can't stop you,' said Hannah. 'Legally, that is.'

'I won't visit unless I have your permission.'

The sadness and longing in his voice touched her. However bad a husband he had been, he had always loved their child, and if her own experience of being fatherless was anything to go by then Maisy needed him in her life; also, if she were honest, it gave her time to herself every other week. She had begun to read again, and the pleasure of discovering all the authors she had had no time or energy for before was colouring her life like magic ink. Just now, she was absorbed in Elena Ferrante's Neapolitan Quartet, in between measuring up for the new flat. Half her mind was in Italy, and half on the ill-fitting Victorian sash windows that would need interlined curtains in order not to leave them freezing at night. Finding just the right sort on eBay gave her the deepest satisfaction she had felt for a very long time. Soft furnishings are not a solution to life's problems, she mused, but they do make them a good deal easier to bear; as did thinking how much worse post-war Naples must have been than St Piran.

Sometimes, she thought she saw a tall, ungainly figure in the street, and her heart would lurch, but it was never Stan. Hannah didn't even want to Google his name. She rang Loveday every few weeks to tell her what she and Maisy were up to, but her aunt chattered on about all the works at the big house without mentioning its former owner.

Hannah endured this for a long time, then said, 'How is Stan?'

'Busy with his new company,' Loveday said vaguely.

'Do you know what it's about?'

'Oh no! Well, computer games, I suppose. That was one thing the EU did give us, super-fast broadband, even if they took our fish. The Wus are investing in it. Excalibur, I think it's called. He's working with Falmouth University to train local kids to code, and finding the ones who already can. It could be the new tin.'

Hannah was silent.

'There's an exhibition opening in London about gaming, you know.'

'Is there?'

'Yes. At the Victoria and Albert Museum. He's one of the games designers they're showcasing.'

'I expect it won't be my kind of thing.'

She went on with her moving out, and whether it was because she was saner or because she was over thirty, it made her feel tired. All that she had been through in the summer seemed like a fugue state, and yet knowing what she now did about the way people could behave in the death throes of a marriage, she thought that her experience was probably no stranger than many others. It was the kind of madness that normal people did not discuss, because it was excruciating to recollect. Stan had asked why more people didn't kill each other, and the answer was (as far as she could see) that money prevented it.

Jinni's departure with half her ex-husband's fortune was grotesquely unjust, and in a novel, Hannah thought, she wouldn't have got away with it. She would have been arrested, or swept out to sea by the tide, or crushed by a falling boulder. On the other hand, she had told her the one thing that enabled Maisy to be saved, so perhaps despite her prolonged and calculated cruelty to her own husband, she had not been completely evil. Hannah had to hope this might be the case. Stan had altered his will the day after they got out of the cave, leaving the woods to the Woodland Trust and any other money to St Piran Sixth Form College in the event of his death. (Hannah discovered that this is the same way that local gossip is learnt in a small town, through Mrs Bolitho, via Loveday, who had been a witness.) They all knew about the attempt on Maisy's life. If Jinni ever reappeared in the county, the Penroses and the Evenlodes would make sure that she was brought to justice.

'That bloody woman,' was how Jake now referred to her. 'I dodged a bullet there.'

'You didn't.'

'Yes, I did.'

'Where is she now?'

'America, I expect. Or maybe France. I don't think she'll come back to England.'

'Count your blessings,' Hannah said, adding with a touch of malice, 'I suppose she didn't think it worth her while to kill you.'

It was when she was packing the last bits of kitchenware from the Castle Estate flat, now looking ever shabbier as it became increasingly filled with cardboard boxes, that she had a call on her mobile.

'Hannah?'

It was Lila, speaking very softly, so softly that she could hardly hear her.

'What is it?'

'Ahmed is outside.'

'Oh my God. Have you called the police?'

Through the thin front door that led out on to the landing, there was a sound of a male voice shouting, and repeated thumping. Hannah rang the emergency services, and gabbled the postcode and flat number, then she opened her own door a crack.

Standing before Lila's door, with his back to Hannah, was a man. She could not remember afterwards whether he was tall or short, big or small, only that he was strong and full of fury, hammering with his fist. Already, he had made dents in its flimsy surface, which seemed little more than that of thick cardboard. Its smooth paintwork had a keyhole, a letter-flap, a number and a small round spyhole through which Hannah saw something flicker – the eye of her terrified friend.

'Open up, open up, fucking bitch!' Ahmed shouted.

Move away, lock yourself in another room, Hannah thought, but Lila must be frozen in fear. The lock was weak, and weaker still were its hinges, which Ahmed was now trying to lift and wrench the panel away from. Some of the doors, like her own, had hinge reinforcers, others had metal bolts and panels on the inside. But Lila had nothing. When Hannah herself had suggested improving security on her door her neighbour had shrugged and said that if Ahmed ever found her it would be all over anyway.

'I have dishonoured him by leaving,' she had said. 'That's how he sees it.'

Even then, the door almost held against the assault, until he attacked the lock with a tyre iron. Its lock gave, splintering, jerked forwards a few inches then caught on the chain. Hannah wondered whether she should do what Lila had once done for her and rush out to shout that she had called the police. Understanding what courage this had taken, she felt even more sick with terror: Ahmed would have no compunction about attacking a woman who wasn't his wife. But there was another reason to hesitate, for now the man had taken a white plastic bottle labelled with a bright yellow triangle surrounded in black out from his plastic bag. Hannah suddenly understood what he intended to do.

She had used this same substance to try to clear the drains at Endpoint, wearing rubber gloves and a mask, and even so the fumes had frightened her. Ahmed was going to throw acid through Lila's door. If one drop of it touched human skin, it would burn right through, destroying it for ever. No wonder she was petrified.

Hannah was, too. Scarcely knowing what she was doing, she groped for her handbag on its hook by the door and plunged her hand into the inner pocket. The ludicrous pink ladies' razor thing was still there. Very cautiously and quietly, she opened her door and aimed it across the landing. Was she too far away? Was the Taser still charged? She couldn't wait to find out. When she pressed its button there was a popping noise, and two bright silvery lights cracked across the space to strike Lila's husband in the back.

In an instant he was felled, writhing face-down on the floor. The sound echoed around the concrete stairwell, and Hannah could hear the silence of a collective indrawn breath. Everyone in the building was listening, but nobody else had acted. She knew why – for by now she knew most of them, and their fearfulness of ever drawing attention to themselves – but she also knew they would never tell on her either.

'Lila! Lila, are you OK?' she whispered. There was no answer. She had to hope the acid hadn't touched her – she would surely have heard screaming if it had – and felt uneasy about even getting close to her friend's assailant. The white bottle with its yellow and black label lay on its side, unused, but some of its liquid had splashed out on to the landing, where it foamed and bubbled, lifting decades of dirt.

There was a shriek of approaching sirens, and blue lights blinked through the windows. Hannah, who had been standing stunned at what she had unleashed, realised she was standing on the landing with an illegal weapon in her hand. Two fine wires were dangling out of the muzzle, attached to barbs implanted in the man now lying prone on the floor. If the police found her with it, she would be arrested. She would go to court and be sentenced to imprisonment. After all she had gone through in Cornwall, she had finally used the weapon in the right moment on the right man, but it was still a crime. She would lose everything: child, job, home.

'Lila!' she whispered again, but there was no reply. Perhaps her friend had fainted or was waiting in terror in another room. She must save herself first.

Could her action be concealed? Ahmed was alive but rigid, prone by the splintered door so he could not see her face. She blinked, and just for a moment it was Stan lying there, Stan for whom this blow had originally been intended. But in this case, she had no doubt that Ahmed really was a monster.

She yanked on the wires, and the barbs came out of his back. Trembling with fright at her action or her audacity or both, she stood still. So far, so good, though there must be marks where the barbs had struck that were a giveaway if doctors knew what to look for. Maybe they would think he had just had a fit. Maybe, if he wasn't dead, she might get away with it.

Where to hide the Taser? It was small, but a determined search would still reveal it. Hannah cast around. The floors were concrete, the walls were concrete, if she dropped it out of her window it would still be found. Somebody buzzed the police in; the sound of feet pounding up the stairs propelled her to her own flat and kitchen, and there, in the corner of the kitchen cupboard, she remembered the ball of steel wool that she had pushed down the rat hole.

Unhesitatingly, she fished the steel wool out, wound the wires around the Taser and wiping her fingerprints off, pushed it down the rat hole. Its smooth contours fitted perfectly. There was a faint clunk, followed by an even fainter noise as it fell, down, down, down ... how far did the hole go? Maybe it would go all the way into the ground.

Hannah sat back on her heels, breathing deeply, and replaced the steel wool.

Instead of guilt, or fear, she felt only exhaustion mixed with relief. She wanted to cry, but she also wanted to laugh.

She could not, after all, invent her own life, but she had at least done something that might lead to the betterment of another's.

The steps were right outside on the landing now. There was a crackle of radios, and voices saying, 'Hello? Hello? Can you hear me, sir?' Other voices were calling for Lila, and then there was a knock on her door, the authoritative rap of officialdom.

'And you saw nothing?'

The police officer who had called was very big and wearing a stab vest that strained across her enormous bosom. As soon as the police had seen the bottle of acid, there was no doubt that Ahmed would be charged; Lila's husband was taken away on a stretcher and Lila herself was being interviewed.

Hannah could hear her saying in a tone of near hysteria, 'It was a bolt from heaven! Allah struck him down!'

Hannah said, 'It's all a bit of a blur. My neighbour called me for help. She's always been petrified of her ex. That man was shouting and banging on her door, trying to get in. Then he had some sort of fit.'

The policewoman gave her a look that told Hannah she had seen almost everything bad that human beings could do to each other. She would be very difficult to lie to.

'Any idea why?'

'Maybe stress?' said Hannah. 'If he'd managed to throw acid at her or her kid . . . '

The policewoman tapped her index finger at the

body-camera clipped to her stab vest that was recording their conversation.

'He'll be examined in hospital. It'll take a bit of time to process his case, but if there are marks indicating the use of an illegal weapon, there may be charges pressed. Did you see your neighbour use a weapon of any kind?'

'No, I am sure she did not,' Hannah said truthfully. 'I was watching the whole time.'

The policewoman said, 'I haven't checked the landing yet – that's for the SOCO team, when they arrive. Sorry to interrupt your cleaning. We've taken the bottle away but be careful where it's splashed.'

Hannah swallowed. 'That's all right. I'm just on the point of moving out, as you can see.'

The policewoman nodded. 'Thanks for your help. We'll need a formal statement from you later.'

As soon as she left, Hannah turned on her vacuum cleaner and went out on to the landing. She wasn't sure whether she could remove every single flake of the Taser confetti, but, as a cleaner, she felt sure that she would be better at spotting them than most.

32

The Museum

The clear skies that had lasted into late autumn yielded to the cold and damp of a London winter. It was a relief, for too much fine weather makes Britons depressed, and unable to find other sources of conversation. The move into their new home went smoothly; one of Hannah's neighbours on the Castle Estate had helped with his van.

'Nice,' he remarked, when he saw the street.

'It's still mostly council.'

'Not for long, I bet,' he said. 'The posh is rolling down the hill.'

Hannah laughed. It was a favourite saying in Kentish Town, which lived in perpetual hope that the money from lofty, gentrified Hampstead and Highgate would come to its lowly streets. Change would happen here, as it happened everywhere, but the food bank would probably never be closed. There was poverty and misery in London, too. As soon as she got her first pay cheque, she set up a standing order to pay the food bank £10 a month. It was a drop in the ocean, and yet, what was an ocean but a mass of drops, moving together as a mighty force? The pity was that these people, like those in Cornwall, were so easily overlooked as a disfigurement, a disability that tainted the modern world and its desire for everything to be pretty. Sometimes she thought that the homeless of St Piran had more chance, because it still had families like hers who cared about their community. Or maybe that was pure sentimentality, because St Piran people wanted nothing to do with them either.

When she tried to pay the man with the van, he refused. 'We all know what you did for Lila,' he said. '*Assalamualaikum*. Peace be to you, my sister.'

Many things in her own life became better that winter. She loved being back in an office, and being able to use her brain to tell a compelling story to clients about why a particular campaign would work. The women she worked with were quirky, instinctive, intuitive, curious about people – much like herself, except that, like Ali Gold, they had read psychology at university, not literature. Once a week, on Fridays, they would go out to lunch together, usually sitting in Granary Square if it was fine, eating takeaways from one of the pop-up stalls and watching the fountains spring out of the paving and the canal slide slowly past. A couple of them might, in time, become actual friends – assuming she could ever trust someone new again.

Lila and Bella came to visit them within days. Her former neighbour was a changed woman. For the first time since Hannah had known her, she wore only a scarf round her head, and it was a fine turquoise one that suited her pretty face even if it revealed no hair. She could not stop smiling.

'My husband is going to prison, and we will be safe now,' she said. 'It could all have turned out so differently without you and your friend Miss Nazneen. As soon as I had her on my side in court, things changed.'

'You helped me first,' said Hannah. 'I'll never forget it.'

Lila said, 'If we cannot help each other, there is no *ummah*, no community.'

'Is there a community here?'

'I think so,' said Lila. 'If we want there to be.'

She had brought Hannah a present, a pot with a small shrub with shiny evergreen leaves and a cluster of fat buds.

'A camellia!'

'I thought it might remind you of your Cornwall,' Lila said shyly.

Hannah thought of the shrubs at Endpoint, which by now would be giant bouquets laden with pink, red and white rosettes. It would take years for Lila's gift to become large enough to see from indoors; but she appreciated the generosity of the gesture, and the thoughtfulness. Perhaps, she thought, this is a friend.

'Let's go into the garden and plant it together.'

The two women and their little girls trooped into the long thin strip that Hannah had begun to clear and fork over, and dug a hole for its first shrub, lining this with compost and watering it in well. (Her mother's garden tools were some of the things she had brought back.) She had already taken cuttings of the plants she wanted to put in there – lavender, salvia, rosemary and bay. Maisy had helped her plant dozens of narcissi and crocus bulbs, and once the weather warmed up they would sow a new lawn. She had put in three bare root new climbing roses to go up the old apple tree and the back of the house. The flat, repainted and reconfigured, gave her immense pleasure and a feeling of security, but it was nothing compared to her first garden.

'Mum used to say that I expected to be rescued by a prince on a charger. But the only person who can rescue any of us is ourselves, isn't it?' she said to Loveday during one of their conversations. It comforted her to talk to her aunt, her kind aunt who was so like her own dead mother.

'Oh, dear heart, it is,' her aunt answered. 'Though other people can help, too.'

Hannah did not call Stan, and he did not contact her. She could not bring herself to do so. The rumour that he was setting up his own gaming company in Cornwall was, as Ali had told her, floating around the media, but for now he had disappeared and nobody she knew had seen him, not that she dared to ask. The slightest indication of interest on her part would stoke her family's belief that something had happened between them whereas the truth was either a lot more complicated or a lot simpler. Even if he were serious about her, she had rejected him, perhaps the one man she had ever met who might be worth loving, out of a mixture of shame, hurt, fear and pride. She told herself that she was a cynic, as all romantics must eventually be. She was not sure, really, what she was.

To be both lonely and never alone was the condition of living in the capital. Even in a quiet street such as her own, the city roared and murmured to her like the sound in her ears when underwater. More and more people were leaving it, unable to afford the toll it extracted in both wealth and health; the hours of commuting, the crowds, the bad air, the rising knife crime, the cost of renting and the price of living were all eroding its attractions. It was inimical to families, and to the modest, ordinary life that children demanded.

Yet Hannah continued to love London, as only someone who had come from elsewhere could do. It was, perhaps, her one vice.

Outwardly, her professional persona had settled over her like a coat of varnish. Her former hesitancy with colleagues and clients was completely gone; nothing could be more intimidating than what she had already survived, and she had gained if not confidence then the appearance of it – which is indistinguishable from the real thing, at least in public.

Hannah walked to and from Maisy's school, the Underground, her office, the shops, and then did the whole thing in reverse. Her days went in an ant-like procession of purpose, and in between she read novels. There were so many to catch up on! She could have spent her life reading, if it were not for the demands of the real life she had to lead, the life of responsibilities and bills and parenthood. The pleasure of making a home was comforting, as if she had found a protective exoskeleton for the being she was underneath, and yet not quite enough. She could read, garden, walk, watch films on her new flat-screen TV and talk with colleagues, but it was a life parched of the daily balm of affection except for what her daughter gave her. Presumably, it was the same for her ex-husband. Sometimes Jake took their daughter away for weekends and holidays because she didn't have it in her heart to deny him this; it also, if she was honest, helped her get her domestic life in better order, which was something essential to her stability. He was single too but expressed the view that 'as a natural blond with a title, I don't expect to remain so for long'.

Hannah rolled her eyes. 'Do you really think anyone sensible still cares about that stuff? Titles and class and so on?

In any case, you still need your grandfather and then your Uncle Andrew to die without a male heir before that's true.'

'That's a technicality. How's your own love-life?'

'None of your business.'

Midwinter came and passed, and she could not avoid being reminded of Stan. The big exhibition about video games that Loveday had mentioned kept being advertised on the Underground in lurid, sultry colours. Reviews started to appear in the newspapers. 'Grim smiting versus cartoon spangles apart,' said one, 'video gaming has reached its *Citizen Kane* moment when it will be taken as seriously as film.'

Ridiculous, she thought.

One day in January, an email popped into her inbox.

```
Dear Hannah,
   I'm coming up to town on Saturday to
see the exhibition at the V&A before
it closes. Have you seen it yet? I'm
told it's good. Let me treat you.
   With affection,
   Bill
```

She had never seen Mr Kenward out of his niche in Cornwall, apart from on her wedding day when he had given her away. The idea of encountering his angular figure in the city was faintly surreal, yet his invitation was not one she could turn down without being rude. He was an old family friend (how old? He must be well into his eighties, she thought) and someone to whom she would always be grateful. Even so, remembering how close he had been to Stan, she was suspicious.

'Do you want to come to a museum with me?' she asked

her daughter, but Maisy declined. She had recently lost her first tooth and was now watching the end of *Frozen* with her father, who was taking her to stay with him over half term. It had to be admitted that one benefit of divorce was that Jake was spending far more time with his daughter than he had ever done before. It was almost as good as having a babysitter – better, really, because he paid her rather than the other way about.

Let it go, yowled Princess Elsa in the screen, the frosty fractals whirling. To stop caring seemed the most desirable power of all for her sex.

The film ended. Maisie sighed with satisfaction, and her parents with relief.

'Time to go,' Jake said. Hannah knew they would probably be spending the weekend in his flat, not far away. She had visited it not long ago: it was very sleek and modern but was without charm or personality. The only things that gave it life were Maisy's toys and pictures.

'See you later, sweetie.'

'Bye, Mummy,' said Maisy. 'See you soon.'

Alone, Hannah dressed with more care than usual. A plain black blouse with white collar and well-cut black trousers were rejected as too severe, and a navy suit as too formal. She kept stepping out of her bedroom, catching sight of herself in the full-length mirror opposite and immediately returning to change. All she was doing was meeting an elderly family friend, and yet she wanted to show that she was no longer the poor young drudge she had been in Cornwall. In the end, she chose a new wrap-around dress in fine, dark green wool that she had bought in the sales, and a red woollen scarf. The temperature was dropping; a coat and fleece-lined boots would also be needed. She drew the heavy new linen curtains, so that the flat would not be too chilly when she returned, and left a single light glowing in its orange shade, because, she told herself, returning to an empty flat in winter could be depressing. It all looked as neat and cosy as a nest: her nest, which might as well have been lined like a bird's with down from her own breast.

Trudging along the long tunnel from the Tube station to the museum, among crowds of schoolchildren, tourists, pigeons, buskers and weekenders, Hannah felt a mixture of apprehension and curiosity. It was icy cold, and crowded, and getting dark already.

She almost turned back in the high entrance hall. It was filled with classical statues. In marble and plaster they showed men killing men, men killing monsters, men abducting women, women being raped or just being reduced to torsos without head, arms or legs ... This was art, this was what had survived for hundreds or even thousands of years, unchanging in its celebration of violence, lust and cruelty of one sex towards another. Even where there was beauty, there was so much that was repulsive about it all.

'Hello, my dear,' said Kenward. He was waiting by the entrance with their tickets. Hannah smiled at him, glad to see a familiar face in all this chilly grandeur.

'Did you come up from Cornwall specially for this?'

'Oh, and a few other things. But mostly to see what Stan has been up to.'

'You are a good friend to him.'

He smiled slightly. 'He's a good friend to me, too. He's got the Wus to ask me to curate an entire library for them at Endpoint. It should keep me in business for at least another two years.'

'Are the works finished?'

'No. It's a huge job, even with half the town on it. But it should be habitable by next summer.'

'And to think we cleaned the whole place, just the two of us, to make it saleable.'

'You did more than that. You saved Endpoint, between you, which is worth saving, and that may help save St Piran. And Stan has been restoring the ruined cottage above the beach. That's where he's going to live. It's completely charming.'

'My dream house,' said Hannah, remembering. 'Lucky him. He has the money and the freedom to do anything.'

Kenward shot her a sharp glance under his brows.

'Do you honestly think those are the only things that matter in life?'

'I don't know, but they certainly help.'

Inside the exhibition it was calm and almost austere, as if she had wandered into a cathedral. Sometimes fragments of speech were intelligible, echoing over music; muted voices saying things like, 'Ain't nothin' for it but keep goin'.' What looked like an animated piece of cloth fluttered across endless sand dunes on one screen, while in another a man and a teenage girl ran through a ruined city half-devoured by nature and filled with zombies. A warrior tried repeatedly to get past an enormous monster in a fantastical city drawn with frenzied detail; there were spaceships flying through landscapes melted off a 1970s record cover and images influenced by artists from Magritte to Hopper. Nothing was permanent.

Hannah and Kenward wandered through different rooms, both impressed and depressed by the technological flux on display. The banked screens with their animated avatars and surreal landscapes, the dazzling flashes of bright fluorescent colours and sound effects drew clusters of young people to them like moths to light. So much energy and ingenuity, so many simulations of the natural world, and the unnatural, but where were the personal stories and the emotional response to them? Where was the thought, the interior consciousness, the conscience that had in the end prevented her from committing her own crime?

'It's very busy,' said Kenward, looking rather exhausted. 'I'll just sit here for a bit.'

Hannah wandered on, trying to understand. She had cleaved to a form in which a narrative, like life, had only one direction. You began at the beginning, continued through the middle and came to the end. It could pretend to be otherwise, could offer split time, flashbacks, alternative endings, a stream of consciousness and any number of formal tricks that were by now over a hundred years old but which were still greeted as startling and new, but the momentum was always that of the narrative. A reader might read faster or slower, find slightly different illuminations or details, respond to and interpret scenes differently at different stages in their life: it always offered the same outcome. There was no choice.

Yet the art she loved was about more than momentum. It was not about all the different ways in which a story could play out, but what was imagined in the compact between the author and the reader. The details of what was noticed or (as importantly) not noticed, and the language in which they were described, the way that it made a reader's imagination bridge the gap between minds like an electric current. She could not believe that a game would do as much for a player.

In the last room, there was a wall the size of a cinema screen on to which twelve images of game designers, seated and looking out at the audience, were projected. Each spoke for a short while, then froze. Among them was a face she recognised.

This was a different Stan, groomed and rested and wearing clothes that were not torn or shabby but sharp and new. He looked both like and unlike himself. He was, as Jinni had told her, good-looking, in that he looked like a good person. He spoke.

'To me, gaming is about interactivity, the ability to embody different characters in different stories dealing with different ideas,' he said. 'To fuse ourselves with the virtual self of another must surely increase empathy, and perhaps eventually share the fullest range of emotion of which human beings are capable.'

Hannah stared at his image. Was this portentous nonsense, or not? Above her, the designers talked of how they had not found themselves in existing games, so made new ones. Men and women spoke of being marginalised by race or gender or sexuality or culture, and about playing games in which they could experience not only fear and anger but compassion, guilt, sorrow and bereavement. They spoke of what they were creating as art, a new art that was capable of remarkable things.

Eventually, Hannah looked down; and there, watching her, was the real Stan on a low bench. He was no longer bearded and the clothes he wore looked (as usual) slightly the worse for wear, with a little hair at the top of his wrists. She felt a surge of anger that she had, precisely as feared, been lured here to see him, and then the start of some other emotion.

'I wondered whether you'd come,' he said. Hannah swallowed.

'Why didn't you invite me?'

'Yes, that would have been one possible move,' he said. 'Only I wanted to give you the freedom of choice. Bill said that was the only way. He's gone back to his friend in Hampstead, incidentally. This isn't really his scene.'

They were both silent, and then Hannah, searching for something to say, asked,

'Where's Bran?'

'Staying with the Bolithos. London isn't his scene either. Or mine. But I did hope that you might be interested in seeing what I do.'

'I am. I didn't want to be, but ... how did you know I'd come today?'

'I didn't. I've been here every day since it opened, just in case.'

'Oh.' She felt her cheeks burning.

Stan ploughed on. 'But Bill – well, he thought he could ask. So here I am as you see.'

'Oh, Stan,' said Hannah. 'The only power I have in my life is that of refusal.'

She sat down beside him and felt like crying.

'There's power in the opposite of refusal. More power, I would say, though there are fewer words for it, and they all sound like defeat. To accept, to consent, to yield, to condescend ... none of these are what I am asking for.' He was flushed and awkward, a shy man struggling to overcome his shyness; and she could not help him. 'So tell me instead if you reject rejection. Tell me that you reject it, deny it, disclaim it, as you do what is false and base and wrong.'

'Why should I?'

'Because it's the opposite to love.'

It was the first time either of them had said that word.

Hannah could not ignore it, or the shock it caused her, but she was afraid to acknowledge it.

'You don't know how bad I am or could be.'

'That's not how it seems to me.'

'I could have *killed* you.'

'Only you didn't. I could have left you and Maisy to drown. Only I didn't. What is life without trust? What is love without faith? Would you choose to live in that kind of world?'

Hannah said, 'You mean there are others? Versions in which you and I don't do or say certain things?'

'It's possible.'

'But this is life, not a game. It only goes in one direction.'

He looked into her eyes, smiling faintly. 'How do you know?'

'Because this is real. I know I am *here*. I'm not made of words, or pixels, or computer code. I'm not in a story.'

'Are you sure? Would you like to see my new game?'

'I've never played one before.'

'I can show you.' He opened his laptop – the thinnest, sleekest kind – and its light shone on both their faces. It was like looking into a new world. 'It's not finished, of course.'

'What's it called?'

'*The Golden Rule*.'

'The mathematical kind or the moral kind?'

'Maybe it's both. But yes, "Do as you would be done by."'

'Mum always said that was the only rule. Could you show that in a game people would want to play?'

'Yes, of course you could. Or,' said Stan, with a mixture of diffidence and confidence, 'I can.'

'What do I do?'

'Put these headphones on. Then your finger on this button. There.'

The button quivered under her touch as if alive. She had a sudden, dizzying sensation as if the known world had shifted.

'What do you see?' Stan's voice asked in her ear.

'I can see – I can see someone running. It looks like a tunnel in the Underground.'

'It is. Look around. What now?'

'Oh!' said Hannah, her heart beating faster. 'It's Paddington Station. And here is the train to Cornwall – and here—'

She stopped, for on the screen, she had seen her own face reflected in the window of the carriage.

'So the question is now, Will you catch that train? If you don't you might not meet me,' Stan said. 'Or someone very like me. Will you take that choice? Or would you rather, instead, step out of this place and into the snow – because it is snowing, although it might be pixels – and into a taxi and then—'

Hannah turned to him. 'Then, where?'

'Wherever you choose.'

Afterword

The alert and faithful reader (I hope to have no other) will notice that in writing *The Golden Rule* I have drawn not only on *Strangers on a Train* but on the fairy tale of *Beauty and the Beast* – or rather, its original, the Ancient Greek myth of Eros and Psyche.

What these stories have in common is that both contain an incitement to murder a stranger, perhaps the most terrible of all kinds of crime. In Highsmith's original, two men agree to kill each other's problem relation (a wife in one case, a father in the other) in order to appear innocent. In the myth, Psyche's sisters persuade her to take a knife in order to kill the invisible husband she has never seen but whom she has been told is a monster.

I am always interested in murder, and this novel had its genesis in something that arose from my previous novel, *The Lie of the Land*. I was struck by something that every woman I interviewed about their feelings during divorce said: 'It would be so much easier to be a widow.' I knew at once that I wanted to write about this state of mind, and how it might be manipulated into taking a step further.

A great many women fantasise about killing their partners (possibly why so many women write and read crime fiction) but as far as we know it is rare for them to do so. However, the #MeToo movement continues to rise, and at the time when I began writing *The Golden Rule*, more and more appalling stories concerning abuse and coercive control emerged that cause me to think it may only be a matter of time before some women become as dangerous to men as some men are to women. Perhaps they already are, judging by the BBC's documentary *Abused By My Girlfriend*. I should add that every single act of violence I describe in this novel has happened in real life to women (and men) whom I interviewed, and there are many more that I chose not to include. Novels about divorce rarely seem to show how many real people can not only say but do vile things to each other, and that includes serious physical assault.

This is also a novel about stories – the stories that forge our deepest selves, the stories we tell about ourselves and others, and the stories that we should not believe but do. At the time of writing, not only individuals but the whole country is divided between two opposing narratives of what we are and what we could become; as a story-teller, as well as a citizen, this is of deep concern because in life (unlike computer games) there is no going back once a particular choice has been made.

I do not write autobiographical fiction, but *The Golden Rule* is perhaps the closest I have come to it. Like Hannah, I was a graduate trainee in an advertising agency, a world whose sexism and predatory attitudes to young women appear to have altered very little, if Rachel Cooke's recent article in the

Observer is to be believed. I am grateful to Edith Greaves and Isabel Perry for telling me what a good advertising agency can be like today. My own experiences were sufficiently grim for me, like Hannah, to drop out of a career path and work as a cleaner for over a year during the recession of the early 1980s. Many of my own children's generation are currently working in the gig economy in conditions that are far worse. If Hannah's eventual escape from Generation Rent is due to luck, it is because I can at least give one imagined person that boon.

In Cornwall, I would particularly like to thank Simon and Alice Boyd, and Charles and Charlotte Mitchell, for many years of generous hospitality at Ince, whose Chinese wallpaper and ancient beech tree I have borrowed for Endpoint; Nutty Lim for showing me her spectacular garden (and deerhound) above St Austell, and my brother and sister-in-law Dan and Michelle Heal-Cohen for many walks and conversations at Trenarren, appropriately the former home of Cornwall's own poet and scholar, A. L. Rowse. The fisherman's cottage where Stan will live is inspired by a real place below Trenarren, but both St Piran and Fol and the people in them are imaginary.

I am grateful to my son Will, Naomi Alderman and Cecilia Busby for explaining computer gaming to me, and to John Francis Ward for suggesting Genevieve as a woman's name that can be split into two (particularly as it is a possible variant of Guinevere). Samantha Ellis and Marina Benjamin both helped me create Stan's background as the son of an Iraqi Jew. This novel is set, approximately, in the summer of 2018, and I would also like to thank Sophia Bennett for treating me to the 2019 exhibition of Dior dresses at the V&A, and Elizabeth Meath-Baker for telling me what wearing old-fashioned couture feels like now that a twenty-inch waist has become a fond memory.

The Golden Rule is, like its predecessors, part of an interconnected series addressing the contemporary world in which minor characters become major ones and vice versa. Hannah first appears as a child in *A Private Place*, where Bill Kenward also features. Lord and Lady Evenlode are the uncle and aunt of Andrew Evenlode, who first appears in *Foreign Bodies*, and are also related to Lottie Bredin in *The Lie of the Land*. Lottie's son Xan is, briefly, Hannah's neighbour on the Castle Estate, and both he and his grandmother Marta will be reappearing soon. Hannah's employers, Polly and Katie, feature in *Hearts and Minds*. Ivo Sponge first appears in *A Vicious Circle* and meets his wife Ellen in *Love in Idleness*. I will be returning to Italy in my next novel, in which readers will see what has become of Job and Marta, among others.

As ever, I would like to thank many friends and fellow-writers who have given me information, advice and encouragement, including Kate Saunders, Marcus Berkmann, Jane Thynne, Julia Jones, Louisa Young, Michelle Lovric, Jane Harris, Liz Jensen, Emily Patrick, Michael Perry, Isabel Perry, Su and Euan Bowater, Deb Popplewell, Suzy Robinson, Danuta Kean, Linda Grant, Tanya Gold, Richard Coles, Patrick Gale, Michael Arditti, Marika Cobbold, Elizabeth Buchan, Gillian Stern, Chris Tayler, Meg Wolitzer, Ian Beck and Jane Johnson. I would especially like to thank Kathryn Langrish, whose remarkable writings about fairy tales on her blog *Seven Miles of Steel Thistles* are matched only by those of my Devon neighbour Terri Windling and her blog *Myth and Moor*, both of which provided a stream of scholarly ideas and details. I would especially like to acknowledge Jean Cocteau's exquisitely sinister version of *La Belle et Le Bête*, which remains my favourite film of all time. I hope I am not alone in preferring the Beast to the candy-floss Prince; or rather, in hoping that the best kind of man contains and embodies both.

I would like to thank my agent Ant Harwood, my film agent Rebecca Watson and my editor and publisher Richard Beswick for helping me bring *The Golden Rule* into being. The more I understand how much labour goes into the production of a book, the more grateful I am to be with them, and the wonderful team at Little, Brown that includes Susan de Soissons, Kimberley Nyamhondera, Nithya Rae, Alison Tulett, Antonia Hodgson, Andy Hine and Sophia Schoepfer, not forgetting Nico Taylor for once again designing such a beautiful jacket.

My beloved Rob, Leonora and William, my mother Zelda, my sister Constance and my mother-in-law Jill have all given me love and support but I would also like to thank the other person without whom I would not have time or energy to write: Maria Izabel Rios.

Like Maisy, I entered the sea of stories via Cornwall, and Rosemary Manning's *Green Smoke* (to which, decades later, I wrote an introduction for its republication by Jane Nissen Books). Susan Cooper's *The Dark Is Rising* series, Roger Lancelyn Green's version of *King Arthur* and eventually Daphne du Maurier's novels all informed my ideas as an expatriate child of what England was. Although Devon has my heart, Cornwall has always possessed my imagination, though those who are concerned for the real people who live there all year round would do well to read Catrina Davies's memoir *Homesick* as well.

This novel is dedicated to the late Helen Dunmore, a great poet and novelist, a lover of Cornwall and a champion of other women novelists, myself included. *Ave atque vale.*

2017–19 London and Devon

To buy any of our books and to find out
more about Abacus and Little, Brown, our authors
and titles, as well as events and book clubs,
visit our website

www.littlebrown.co.uk

and follow us on Twitter

**@AbacusBooks
@LittleBrownUK**